NOA'S ARK

ARCHANGEL PROJECT. BOOK 2

C. GOCKEL

NOA'S ARK

ARCHANGEL PROJECT. BOOK TWO

By C. Gockel
Copyright (c) 2016
All Rights Reserved

First contact didn't go as planned ...

Time Gate 8, one of humanity's portals between the stars, has been overrun by a mysterious alien intelligence, and the planet Luddeccea is now cut off.

Haunted by those she left behind, Commander Noa Sato is on a desperate mission to save her homeworld. Navigating the ancient Ark, she seeks a hidden gate that will transport her ship to Earth and the Galactic Fleet. But the Luddeccean system harbors dangers, and so does her crew.

The only crew member she completely trusts is James Sinclair, but James doesn't trust himself. He isn't the man he once was. He has a hunger that is never sated, kills without regrets, and is fitted with extraordinary augments he doesn't remember getting. Can James control his augments, or will they control him?

In a future where almost all humans are augmented, James's answer and Noa's mission will determine the fate of the human race ... and the enemy is already within the gates.

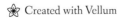 Created with Vellum

ALSO BY C. GOCKEL

The Archangel Project

Carl Sagan's Hunt for Intelligent Life in the Universe: A Short Story (free)

Archangel Down

Noa's Ark

Heretic

I Bring the Fire - an Urban Fantasy/Sci-Fi Series featuring Loki, Norse God of Mischief and Chaos

Wolves: I Bring the Fire Part I (free ebook)

Monsters: I Bring the Fire Part II

Chaos: I Bring the Fire Part III

In the Balance: I Bring the Fire Part 3.5

Fates: I Bring the Fire Part IV

The Slip: A Short Story (mostly) from Sleipnir's Point of Smell

Warriors: I Bring the Fire Part V

Ragnarok: I Bring the Fire Part VI

The Fire Bringers: An I Bring the Fire Short Story

Atomic: a Short Story that is part of Nightshade, a multi-author anthology

Magic After Midnight: A Short Story

Other Works

Murphy's Star: a Short Story of First Contact

ACKNOWLEDGMENTS

This story wouldn't have been written without the enthusiasm and support of my fans. Among them, I need to give a special shoutout for the early readers, the ones who read the first draft and told me what they loved and hated. Thank you so much Kay, Sarah, Melissa, Mathias, Alex, and Yvonne. I couldn't have done it without you. Thanks also to my husband Eric. If he hadn't nagged me to quit writing fanfiction, this never would have happened.

To my dad, Jim Evans. Thanks for getting me hooked on sci-fi, fantasy, and comic books. I miss you.

CHAPTER ONE

Kenji sat with his elbows on the conference table, head bowed over the "pho-toes" and "print-outs." A Luddeccean Guard Intelligence agent rolled on his heels beside him. "Will that be all, sir?" It took a moment for Kenji to string the man's words together. The darkened room smelled like old air and new carpeting, and it was filled with the din of the air recycler, arguing counselors, and other agents.

"Sir?" said the LGI agent.

Remembering the question, Kenji said, "Oh, yes, yes, I'm ..." The word *fine* almost slipped from his lips but then his gaze fell on a picture of a civilian with a broken neck.

"... This is what I need," Kenji amended, turning the head of the small reading lamp beside him to focus on the picture. As the LGI agent withdrew, Kenji studied the print-out of the archangel's victim, a train operator who had been killed by a blow to the neck. The victim had high levels of root in his system, obviously an addict. He couldn't have been a threat. Why kill him?

How could Noa align herself with a person who would do that?

Shuffling through the papers, he found a picture of Dan Chow, who was now, according to intelligence, going by the name of "Ghost." In the security camera pho-toe, "Ghost" was on a main street. His eyes were wide, he was visibly panting with exertion, and there was sweat on his brow. "Ghost" had built planet Luddeccea's new ether-less supercomputer. At first Kenji had thought it was an amazing piece of engineering, smaller and more efficient than Kenji would have believed possible ... but it had produced a malfunction in the defense grid at the most inopportune time. Ghost had to have programmed the shutdown of the grid before he'd been declared a fugitive. There was no way Dan could have accessed Luddeccea's new mainframe after he went on the run ... was there?

Kenji's hand shook so violently that the picture of Dan slipped from his fingers. He rifled through the other pho-toes and paused at a picture of Noa. She looked emaciated ... why had she left the re-education center, where she could be fed, clothed, and safe?

He flipped through a few more and came to a picture of the archangel. It was going by the alias of "Professor James Hiro Sinclair," a wealthy Earther whose family owned a vacation cottage on Luddeccea. Sinclair had been in a serious accident a few years back. By all rights, he should be dead. Kenji shook his head. Noa wouldn't know that, but "James" was too obviously augmented, his face too square and symmetrical—he looked like a sick, twisted parody of Timothy, Noa's dead husband.

A light flickered and the conversation around Kenji grew hushed. He looked up. A two-dimensional picture of Time Gate 8 was projected on a screen. Noa had always described the gates as looking like the bracelets made of jagged coral and shiny round beads that were so popular at Luddeccean beach towns. The jagged pieces were the ships docked along the outer rim of the station, and the beads set at regular intervals were the glowing nuclear fission-fueled generators that powered the gates. Many of the vessels parked along the rim had left, but the description still fit.

Kenji took a shaky breath and had a sensation of vertigo. The improvised bomb he'd placed on the time gate had succeeded in cutting Luddeccea off from the wider galaxy ... just in time.

The ethernet was made up of radio frequencies, microwaves, and lightbeams that conformed to the laws of Newtonian physics, except where there were time gates. Theoretically, there were other ways to transmit data that defied Newtonian physics completely. For centuries, researchers had been exploring quantum entanglement to avoid time paradoxes and other physical limitations to regular transmissions. Entangled particles were essentially "twins" that spun the same way no matter where in the universe they were. If messages could be encoded into the spin of these particles, radio frequencies, lightbeams, and even time gates would become unnecessary for data transmission. Matter—like interstellar dust, a planet, or even a sun—would be no obstacle. When quantum-based communication crossed from theory to practical application, the destruction of a time gate wouldn't keep the intelligence aboard the gates from spreading mind-to-mind, host-to-host, in an instant. It was probably happening already in other systems. Kenji wiped his face and exhaled. Thanks to his sabotage, and the Luddeccean crackdown on the ethernet, Luddeccea was safe ...

Someone cleared his throat. Kenji looked up and noticed Premier Leetier and Admiral Salin standing in front of the display, their bodies projecting long shadows on the screen. The person in charge of the display zoomed into the reactors with a few clicks and Kenji's heart stopped. Drones, blurry with motion, were buzzing around the part of the time gate Noa had dubbed *beads*.

"Gentlemen," the premier said. "It is as the encrypted data Mr. Kenji Sato deciphered predicted: Time Gate 8 is converting its nuclear reactors to weapons."

Whispered prayers to Allah and Yahweh rose around Kenji. In the shadows of the room several people made the sign of the cross. Kenji had known what Time Gate 8 had planned to weaponize, but hearing it confirmed was a shock. His heart beat faster, his skin grew cold and clammy.

"Mister Sato, you were the one who first noticed the excess energy expenditure aboard Time Gate 8, and discovered and deciphered the communication between these ... entities. How long has the time gate been ... inhabited?" The question came from Counselor Karpel, the man who had suggested that the intelligence within the gate might have a sense of humor.

In the slow, calm voice Kenji so admired, Premier Leetier replied, "As I've said before, our intelligence is uncertain, we—"

"We need to know how long the gate has been inhabited," Karpel interrupted. "If we're going to deal with the threat appropriately. Do you at least have an estimate?"

There were a few quick intakes of breath. Kenji glanced around and saw the counselor and military advisor shooting glances at one another. The man next to

Karpel put his hand on the counselor's shoulder and whispered, "Ivan, you're out of line—"

Ignoring his companion, Karpel turned in his seat so he was facing Kenji, and, voice rising, he dropped his fist on the table. "Mr. Sato, how long has the gate been possessed?"

Kenji glanced at the premier. His face was as unreadable as a blank wall. Beneath the table Kenji balled his hands into damp fists. Should he answer or not? He'd hated his augments in so many ways. But now he wished he had them.

Kenji sat cross-legged on the floor of his parents' home, focused on schematics displayed in his visual cortex by his newly activated neural interface. Stretched out around him were the parts for a model hovercraft from Earth he and his older sister Noa had ordered. The model had been inspected by Luddeccean Customs so thoroughly that all 1,435 pieces were hopelessly mixed and damaged. Noa would be home in 3.5 minutes. She'd see the package and would try to put the hover together by looking at the pictures, not bothering to sort the pieces first. Kenji felt sweat prickle his brow.

In his hands was a miniature cylindrical charge disperser wrapped in translucent plastic with a tiny circular read-out panel. It was smaller than his pinky finger and only half as wide. The metal for the timebands was not very conducive. A steady charge delivered along the circumference of the band by many dispersers was essential. He checked the read-out's displayed symbol with the example in the schematic. This one was undam-

aged. He gently put it in a bin to separate it from the rest ... and then he had the oddest sensation, like a bug had landed inside his brain. It took him a moment to identify the annoying sensation: someone was calling him in the ether.

He could ignore it. He should ignore it. He picked up another disperser.

The caller's ID flashed in his visual cortex: Charles Ko, another candidate from his province for the advanced mathematics seminar for secondary students in Prime.

He could ignore it. He should ignore it. He squinted at the disperser's read-out panel.

The fly that was Charles's call felt like it was dancing in place.

Closing his eyes, Kenji focused on the bug. "Answer," he said aloud. *He was still new to the neural interface and had to speak aloud to focus his commands and thoughts. The bug dancing in place began to buzz around his brain.*

"Kenji?" Charles's voice sounded as though it were coming from right next to his ear. No, that wasn't quite accurate. It sounded like Kenji was standing next to a door that was slightly ajar and Charles's voice was echoing from that other room.

"What do you want?" Kenji asked, frustrated by the interruption and the vagueness of the sensations produced by the neural connection. Bugs. Other rooms. He shook his head.

"Where will you be parking when you go to Prime for the entrance exam?"

Kenji dropped the disperser to his lap. "I will not be driving. I am twelve. Like you. Why are you asking me this question?"

"My mother doesn't have your mother's channel."

Staring at the schematic before him, Kenji's nostrils flared and he felt a burning sensation in his chest.

Charles's thoughts intruded again. "Kenji?"

"You need my mother's channel?"

"Yes."

Kenji took a deep breath. "Channels," like so much of the colloquial ethernet terminology, was a misnomer. His mother did not receive an ether call over a "channel." She received a call over several frequencies. With nearly 100 billion inhabitants in the galaxy, the frequencies were not unique to her. However, the way that data was encoded over those frequencies was unique to his mother. Each machine and human in the ether had an eighteen-digit identifier—their "channel." His mother's channel was like a box sitting open in his mind that Kenji could reach into at any time without calling up the identifier. With only a thought he should be able to take that box and share it with Charles. He tried to push it across the ether ...

"Kenji?" said Charles.

With a grunt of frustration, Kenji realized he would have to read the six-digit number that denoted his mother's frequencies, and the twelve-digit string of numbers and symbols that was her unique identifier to Charles aloud. Shutting off the digital schematic, he did so from memory.

A different string of numbers played across his visual cortex. "That is my mom's number," Charles said. "Oh, and here's my dad's. I don't know who's driving me." Another string of numbers appeared, and Kenji blinked. Charles was obviously better at utilizing his neural interface than Kenji was. Kenji memorized both of Charles's parents' channel identifiers, not wanting to bother with a clumsy memorization app.

"Are you excited?" Charles asked.

"About what?" Kenji asked.

"The exam? The chance to study with professors from Sol system?" Charles said. "Nebulas, I'm so keyed, and so nervous, I can't sleep at night."

Kenji wasn't excited. It wasn't as though he didn't want the opportunity; but his scores were so high, he was assured of passing the exam. Testing into the advanced mathematics seminar was a logical progression, like reaching the top of a flight of stairs. He had a feeling that was not the answer he was expected to give.

"Yes," he said finally, hating himself for the dishonesty. "I have to go now. I'm working."

"Right—"

Kenji shut off the transmission. He breathed out a long sigh of relief, summoned up the schematics, and lifted the charge disperser. The symbol on the read-out panel was different. He put a finger beneath the symbol key on the schematics ... and his finger passed right through what was only an illusion in his visual cortex, like a floater in his eye after staring at the sun. He almost threw the disperser across the room. But then he heard footsteps, too quick to be his mother or younger sister, and too light to be his older brother or father. Noa was home. He pulled the disperser closer to his stomach, as though protecting it would somehow prevent the chaos that would erupt as soon as she entered the room.

She burst through the door a moment later. "It came!" she cried, smiling very wide, her teeth white against her ebony skin. The emotion reading apps recently implanted in his brain went into high gear, triggering a response. He felt happy when she smiled ... which was ridiculous. She was about to make the mess made by Customs a thousand times worse.

Her smile vanished, and Kenji's app-generated moment of happy empathy did, too. It felt like the sun had gone behind a cloud.

"Did the Customs agents do this?" she said, dropping to her knees across from him and putting a hand to her mouth.

An app in his mind told him that she was feeling the same way he had when he'd seen what Customs had done. He should be telling her not to touch anything; instead, he found himself smiling in response. He looked down hastily, to get away from the distraction of her emotions. "Yes," he said.

Noa snorted, something the ladies at church called "unladylike."

"You'd think they thought we'd ordered a sex 'bot."

Kenji nearly choked and he felt his face flush.

"Well, we better organize the pieces," Noa said, putting her hands on her thighs, drawing Kenji's attention to her fingers. They were like the rest of her, long, slender, and graceful. Her hands were steadier than his, her eyes very sure. He tended to drop things, and his hands tended to shake.

"What?" said Kenji in shock, her words catching up to him.

"We better organize the pieces," Noa said, nodding. "Isn't that something you would say?"

His sister did not organize things; she organized people. She'd instigated many a hoverbike race among the local teens, much to the consternation of the elders of the community and the frustration of the young men who'd thought to beat her. His sister was obsessed with being a pilot in the Galactic Fleet and had been since he could remember. She didn't just practice hover piloting, she studied it. He doubted the boys in their province played the Formula One Hover Grand Prix in slow motion in their hologlobes and asked their little brothers to explain the geometry behind the optimal arc for tight turns.

"It is something I would say, but not you," Kenji replied.

Noa nodded again. "You're right. But I have to change. Pilots have to be meticulous. I will become meticulous."

She had been keeping her room oddly tidy lately. The set of her jaw ... his apps told him that it was determined.

"I have to get out of here, Kenji," she whispered.

He knew that, too. Noa was like him; she didn't fit. Kenji was "too smart for his own good," and even with apps, he "had trouble reading situations," and "got too strident with his ideas."

Noa was, in the words of the church gossips, a "handful," and "a bad girl." The latter label was particularly strange, as "a bad girl" implied she engaged in promiscuous behavior. In Kenji's observation, Noa was the least promiscuous member of her peer group. His father always said, "Noa scares the boys away."

"Tell me your organization system," Noa said. "I know you have one."

Of course he did. He explained it, and saw her eyes glaze over as she pulled out her own schematics. For a while they worked together in companionable silence, and then Noa asked, "Who were you talking to before I came in?"

"Charles Ko," he said. "He is applying for the advanced mathematics program in Prime."

Dropping her hands to her lap, Noa smiled at him. "I'm so glad you have a friend now. Isn't talking mind-to-mind in the ether wonderful?"

Kenji huffed at the colloquialism. "The ether does not let us talk mind-to-mind; the transmitters in our skulls are limited to a very small number of frequencies. We send our thoughts to the time gates and satellites that decrypt them and then re-encrypt them for the frequencies and encryption of the neural interfaces of the person we are connecting to."

"Well, I love it," Noa said, smiling and squinting at a disperser. His apps told him she was bemused. "It's great to be able to instantly talk with other kids anywhere in the galaxy."

Kenji exhaled. That wasn't an accurate description. The time gates sent data in continuous streams, and it was possible to have an ether conversation in real-time with anyone near a time gate. But a call to anyone not close to a gate, like Luddeccea's nearest neighbor, Libertas, was limited to the speed of light.

He took a deep breath and let the affront to precision pass. Noa, in Kenji's father's opinion, had taken to the ether like a ptery to the sky and made many new friends across the inhabited systems. He'd heard his mother say that it had improved Noa's confidence and made her happier.

"Don't you like the ethernet?" Noa asked, squinting at another disperser.

Kenji licked his lips and attempted to be humorous. "It's buggy."

Noa straightened. "It isn't buggy. The time gates and satellites sweep every frequency that reaches them for signs of encoded bugs. The only way you could get a serious virus would be by accepting a data chip from a stranger ... or ... or ... hard-linking!"

Kenji blushed again—talking about putting a cable

between his brain and a girl's with his sister was as uncomfortable as her mention of a sex 'bot. He was also a bit crestfallen that his joke hadn't gone over well. He cautiously looked up at her face, silently praying, 'Please don't ask if I've ever thought about hard-linking or sex 'bots.' Her brow was furrowed; her nose was slightly wrinkled. Kenji's apps told him she was indignant, annoyed, and even a little afraid.

Raising her hands and shaking them as though conducting some inner orchestra, Noa continued, "The worst anyone has gotten from the ether is a headache—in over one hundred years! One hundred years!"

And suddenly, his joke didn't matter anymore. "Why hasn't there been a serious ethernet virus in over a hundred years?" Kenji asked.

Noa rolled her eyes. "I already told you, because the time gates receive the frequencies first. They scrub them for any sign of malicious code."

"But Noa, humans are smarter than time gates." Human brains were the best processors in the galaxy; to be as powerful as a human brain, a computer would have to be as large as a small moon, and would need to be powered by a nuclear reactor. Kenji looked down and blinked, summoning up the volume of the time gate's computers; it wasn't as large as that ... but the gates were powered by nuclear reactors. The large time gates, like Luddeccea's, had more than one.

"Computers can be smarter than humans at specific tasks," Noa parried.

Kenji's head jerked. "But human minds, especially human minds working together, should be able to outsmart a computer, even one that is so highly specialized." Especially with non-ethernet based apps to do the tasks humans *were normally slower at. Kenji was gifted at mathematics, but he looked forward to having his computational app installed and learning to use it properly so he wouldn't have to enter large sums into an external computational device. He suddenly had an inspiration. "A virus that had pieces passed from several minds at once, coming together in the gate, could join and—"*

"Maybe no one wants to cause that sort of virus. Even here on tech-a-phobic Luddeccea." Sitting back, Noa frowned and crossed her arms.

Inclining his head, Kenji stared at her. He knew that look—even without apps. She was wrong and she knew it.

She looked at the floor and frowned. "All right, well, all the people who have done it have gotten caught. But the last one was years ago, and lots of investigators and computer scientists went up and they checked the hardware and the software, and they fixed it! There hasn't been even a minor virus in a long time; they're happening less and less!"

And that, Kenji had to concede, was definitely true.

Noa looked at a place in the air between them. "I'm calling up the schematics for this hover again," she said, and her eyes became glazed as the schematic playing in her visual cortex was revealed to her but not to him.

The conversation was over. But Kenji's mind was still on the question. Why hadn't a major ethernet virus outbreak occurred in over a hundred years?

Standing from his seat, Counselor Karpel barked, "I'll ask you again, how long has the time gate been under alien control?"

Kenji rolled back in his seat. "A hundred years at least," he whispered.

"We do not know. That will be all, Mr. Sato," said Premier Leetier.

The Luddeccean Intelligence agent who'd left Kenji's side a few minutes ago was back again, silently hovering beside him.

"If it has been as long as Mr. Sato has suggested, then why suddenly begin this weaponization now?" Karpel demanded. "Could it be that it feels threatened? If it does, perhaps we could negotiate—"

Someone hissed. Counselor Zar said, "We cannot negotiate with an abomination! It would be better to let it nuke one of our cities!"

There were murmurs of assent around the table. Kenji's stomach sank and he felt like he might vomit again. But he agreed with Zar. It ... they ... had been waiting all this time for humanity to become complacent, more ether-dependent, and more vulnerable. If the intelligence had caught the Luddeccean Central Authority unprepared with an ethernet shutdown, there could have been panic. As it was, the Luddeccean Authority had been able to organize and shut down the ethernet on its own timetable.

The lights in the room slowly brightened. The projection snapped off. Leetier steepled his fingers and said, "There will be no negotiations."

Kenji exhaled in relief. He heard others do the same. But Karpel stood up and half-shouted, "My constituents here on Prime will be the first target. Four million people in this capital! You're willing to sacrifice them?"

"Be seated, Ivan," Premier Leetier said. Kenji glanced

up. He couldn't read any emotions in Leetier's face. But Karpel sat down.

"We have decided to initiate Mister Sato's plan to apprehend the archangel and use it as a bargaining chip. As Mr. Sato so astutely noted, the entities have gone to great lengths to keep their agent in one piece."

Kenji swallowed. He had to be right in that analysis. *Everything* was hinging on the time gates seeing value in the archangel.

Premier Leetier looked around the room. "Our Luddeccean Guard is still entangled locally and cannot be sent en masse to pursue the Ark."

At the Premier's words, angry murmurs erupted.

"But we do have another option," he added. The room quieted as men in the gray uniforms with green piping that identified them as Luddeccean Intelligence got up from the table and walked over to form a line on either side of the premier and the admiral. They stood with their heads high, feet apart, arms behind their backs. Kenji's eyes roved down the line and stopped at the man standing closest to the admiral. The agent's forehead glinted in the light. He had a metal exo-skull. Kenji's eyes fell to the man's feet. His uniform was cut off at the knees. Instead of feet, he had smooth bands of metal. Kenji inhaled sharply—the man was an amputee, one who had forsworn computer-aided augmentation and instead chosen the purity of etherless steel. The man turned his head, and Kenji could see that he did have a port, but it was jammed with a polyfiber screw, making him untouchable in the ether.

The premier nodded at the admiral, and Salin began to speak. "The Ark is in need of repairs. She will be forced to either dock or conduct them in open space.

When she stops, Luddeccean Intelligence will find her and capture the archangel ... unharmed."

The man with the exo-skull lifted his chin. "If I may, I have a few questions for the council."

Leetier nodded once, and then the admiral said, "You may proceed."

Turning to the room at large, his metal skull plate glinting in the low light, the agent said, "We have been told we have to apprehend this ... archangel ... but not what he is."

There were murmurs around the room. Kenji blinked and then he heard someone say, "Impertinence."

Zar, a hardliner and a "True Believer", said, "It's the devil himself you're dealing with."

There were some sounds of assent but also a few choking noises. The Luddeccean Authority was split between those who *believed* the menace in the time gates was supernatural and those who didn't follow the Luddeccean philosophy but recognized the very real threat that the time gates represented.

The agent's jaw hardened. "I need more to go on than that."

"Djinn!" someone shouted. "They've crossed back over."

Kenji felt a prickling irritation beneath his skin at the mention of the ancient myth of djinn, "energy beings" who had been locked out of the world of humans.

"The man is half-metal himself, how can we trust him?" someone else said, and Kenji felt himself go hot at the injustice. This "half-metal" man had sacrificed being normal to be part of the cause, and now he was going to put his life on the line for these people who denigrated him. Kenji put his hand to his face. Supernatural, alien, or other ... the origins of the archangel didn't matter. The devil might be in the details, but details weren't what the agents needed to fight him. They needed to know the bigger truth.

Kenji focused on a point on the screen, unable to meet the agent's eyes. Taking a sharp breath, Kenji said, "I can tell you what the archangel is."

CHAPTER TWO

Noa was aware in a distant way that there was a floor below her, that the timefield bands still pulsed, that the air ducts were pumping oxygenated air into her cabin aboard the Ark. But her senses had shrunk down to just the moment. Her body was entwined with James's. They were fully clothed, their arms around each other, and James's forehead was resting on hers. Innocuous ... and not. The weight of him, the way he smelled, the muscles beneath fabric—it made the moment heavy and her skin heat despite the ambient chill. She felt both weightless and heavy, as though she was displaced in time, as though time was moving too fast and too slowly at once. It had been so long since she'd felt like this.

Across the hard-link straddling the distance between their temples, the charge of his emotions was making her hallucinate. They were a supernova—exploding inward instead of out. It was an effort to breathe ... and it was perfect. She could feel the brush of his breath against her face and felt her eyes slipping shut, but she still saw light in her mind.

... And then it ended. The cabin was startlingly cold. Noa was staring at the groove in James's neck just above the collar of his shirt.

"What's wrong?" he asked before she even knew; she was only aware that every hair on the back of her neck was standing on end.

"Noa, what is—" his voice was cut off by a trembling beneath their feet. The arms around her back tightened, she felt him looking up, even as she looked down. All her attention was on that tremor; she couldn't have turned her mind away from it if she'd tried. It was a hard-won instinct.

"Timebands—something's wrong—the field isn't holding," she said, or maybe she only spoke the words into his mind.

"What can I do?" James asked.

She yanked out the hard-link and with the barest hint of intent her well-trained apps started plugging in the codes for the ship's local ethernet that Ghost, her Chief Computing Officer, had set up. She was on the shared channel in milliseconds. "Gunny, Chavez, start powering down the timefield!" Ghost hadn't set up ether control of the systems, but he had basic ship data available on the general channel. She mentally accessed the Ark's current velocity: .47C, a little less than half the speed of light.

"Yes, Commander!" Chavez said, her thought broken by a shearing noise.

Before Noa could order James out of the way, he'd gone to the door's controls and opened it. She stumbled and pitched forward as gravity abruptly increased. James was at her side in an instant, holding her up, his augmented strength evidently allowing him to keep his feet—but the time bubble that kept the ship safe from the worst paradoxes of lightspeed was bursting—even James's augments couldn't protect him from that much longer.

"That's enough, Chavez!" Noa said. For a moment she stood trapped by the fluctuating gravity, her stomach roiling, only keeping her feet because James was holding her aloft. She met his eyes and the moment felt more intense than the kiss they'd almost shared. He had always been there when she needed him, somehow from the very beginning ... she thought of Oliver, the little boy he'd jumped into incoming fire to save. He'd complain loud and long that she was an idiot, and grumble about sticking his neck out ... but he always came through. Gravity stabilized, and Noa pulled away with a mumbled, inadequate "thanks."

Falling into step beside her, he asked, "Where can I be most helpful?"

"Stay with—" *me*, she almost finished. But the ship rocked so violently, and gravity reoriented so quickly that Noa was thrown against the wall, her back connected to the hard surface with jaw-rattling force. She rolled her head in James's direction. Pressed against the wall himself, his eyes met hers.

"This is normal in a power-down sequence?" he asked.

"Ummm ... sure," Noa lied, still pinned in place by gravity, giving James a calm commander's reassurance to a civilian.

James raised an eyebrow, and Noa swallowed just before gravity released them, and both of them sprung from the wall.

"Okay, it's not normal," Noa said, and it was a relief to be able to tell the truth. She opened the door to the access tunnel. "You'd better go to Engineering ... the grav shift may have knocked something over and—"

"I can lift heavy things," he said. His face was stoic, but his avatar bloomed in her mind across the ether, smiled, and winked.

And when had he become the one to wink and smile in the face of danger? She hadn't meant to say that aloud, but James responded dryly, "You've obviously corrupted me." And Noa felt her lips twist up in a smile of her own.

A few moments later, climbing up the access tunnel, she wasn't smiling anymore. "What is that ensign doing?" Noa hissed as she ascended the ladder, concentrating hard on the three-fingered grip of her left hand. Power-down was the first thing new pilots learned. Chavez should have been able to manage it from .47C.

Over the ether, James said, directly to her channel, "You'll figure something out." Noa bit her lip, grateful for the reassurance, even though she hadn't meant to think out loud. She always needed someone to talk to, didn't she?

"I nearly gave myself away in a corpse wagon by talking to myself," she grumbled aloud.

The ship rocked, her left hand slipped, and she was pressed against the wall hard. A squeak and a shape streaking toward her from above made her look up. Throwing out an arm, she caught the weasel-like shape of Carl Sagan, the ten-legged white werfle she'd found on the streets of Prime. He curled around her neck, purring loudly in her ear.

"Too much, Chavez!" Noa shouted over the ether.

"Yes, Commander," Chavez said. The ship stabilized a bit, and putting her hand on the next rung up, she whispered, "I'll talk to you, Carl Sagan." Talking to James was a bad idea. Nebulas, she'd almost asked him to come with her to the bridge. He'd be useless there. So would Carl Sagan, but it wasn't as though the werfle would be more useful anywhere else. "So you know, this power down isn't normal." Even for a timeband malfunction.

The werfle gave a nervous-sounding squeak. Noa mentally counted the rungs to the bridge opening ... five more to go. In the tight space, she could smell dust, grease, Carl Sagan, and the scent of *James* clinging to her clothing. Holding her breath, expecting gravity to give again at any moment, she scrambled up the ladder. Seconds later, Noa threw open the hatch and climbed up into the bottom of the circular stairwell of the bridge. Taking the steps up to the pilot and gunner chairs three at a time, she was directly beneath the obloid glass dome of the Ark's nose an instant later. Gunnery Sergeant Phillip Leung and Ensign Chavez were behind the cannon controls and piloting controls, respectively. The ship shook again, and Noa had just enough time to brace herself against their seats. Chavez's prosthetic legs creaked, the squeal of the hull split her ears, and claws of ten little werfle paws dug into her neck.

"Commander, are you alright?" Gunny asked, turning his rather large bulk impressively fast, looking ready to jump up and lend a hand. She waved him back.

"I'm nearly in engineering," Lieutenant Manuel, her chief engineer, said over the ether as Noa slipped into the pilot chair.

"Power her down again, Ensign," Noa said, watching the vast expanse of archaic dials and screens mounted in front of her. On a newer ship, the controls would be concealed and only used for backup if human-to-ship ethernet was disabled.

Chavez drew back on several dials in quick succession. There was another sickening squeal from the hull. The indicator lights didn't even flicker. Noa felt her heart beating against her ribs.

"It doesn't sound right," the ensign said, blowing air out of her mouth and sending a wild red curl flying.

Noa addressed her engineer over the ether. "Manuel, I think we've got a short in the charge disperser ring behind one of the timebands."

"I think you're right," Manuel replied.

"Commander," Chavez said, "I don't know how to power down the other bands without feedback! The controls ... I can't tell which band is frying!"

Noa's eyes slid over the light displays in front of her. What a bloody, ancient, lizzar-excrement excuse for technology. Without being able to tell which band was shorting, or even what level of power it still had circulating through it, powering down the other bands was nearly impossible.

Her thought process was interrupted by an urgent mental dispatch from Ghost. "Fire in cabin twenty-three."

Noa ducked her head beneath the instrument panel, looking for a dangling wire, a spark, anything to explain the malfunctioning gauges, and stifled a curse. Everything looked fine.

"I'm on that deck," James replied over the ethernet.

"The fire extinguisher—" Ghost began. His voice piped into Noa's mind, but he also chose to pipe it over the intercom.

"I already found it," said James over the ethernet. "I'm

in the cabin." James piped an image of the outer wall of the cabin over the general frequency. The plastic of the wall was blackened and melting in a regular pattern.

"There's where our charge dispersers are fried," Manuel said. One mystery was solved, but Noa's stomach turned to cold lead as the hull screamed again. Pulling herself back up, she strapped herself into the pilot chair, barely aware of the werfle still on her shoulders.

"Commander?" said Chavez. "How can we power down without the gauges?"

Noa hadn't any idea, so she said the first thing that came to mind. "We do it by ear."

"By ear?" Ghost roared in her mind and over the comm. And then his voice rose in pitch. "Next cabin over! Another fire!"

"On my way," said James, and Noa's stomach twisted.

To Chavez, Noa said, "Turn that comm off, I can't hear with it on." Internally, she turned down Ghost's voice in her mind. Her hands hovered over the dials and she gulped.

Hastily obeying, Chavez said, "You can power down timebands by *ear*?" The incredulity in her tone was only slightly less thick than Ghost's.

Gunny said some words in Arabic that sounded suspiciously like a prayer.

The hull screamed. It was now or never. Without looking at the indicators in front of her, Noa slowly slid the rectangular knobs that controlled the bands down their track until the metal screech became a groan again ... and then it became a roar. She hastily, but gently, readjusted the dials until the hull was only moaning.

"Sure," she said, not about to show her unease to Chavez or the crew, comforting herself with the knowledge that powering down by ear could *theoretically* be done.

The noise in the hull was rising in pitch, so she slid the rectangular knob a little further down the track. The screech was becoming a groan again, and Noa eased up. Adjusting the knobs, she said, "Don't you remember your Luddeccean preschool teachers? Anything that can be done by machine can be done by man?" She powered down too quickly and the ship's groan rose in volume again. She readjusted the dial, the stress on the hull becoming a low rumble.

She felt sweat drying inside her uniform, leaving her cold where Carl Sagan wasn't keeping her warm. Again and again she repeated the cycle. She waited for the ear splitting, heart-stopping squeal of the hull that sounded too much like death, gradually moved the dials until the squeal became a groan, and readjusted them before the groan became a roar.

The ship was tracking the orbit of Adam's Asteroid Belt just below the ecliptic plane of the system, and as the ship decelerated, the asteroids that had been a blur began to have shape and form. Their solidity began to give Noa hope that this just might work. Her confidence grew so much, she mentally checked the ether for the status of her crew members ... and found James was gone. Noa felt an unfamiliar bite of panic, a sort of existential dread, a weight pulling her down ... In her mind's eye, she could imagine James burned, or suffocated. An explosion with a hull breach could suck him into space, or if the metal skeleton of the ship twisted inward ...

"Fire in Cabin 22 out for now. I'm moving back to Cabin 23." James's voice over the ether cut through her dark imaginings. The light of his location flickered on in her mind.

Manuel spoke across the shared channel. "We lost you for a moment there, James."

Not sounding concerned at all, James said, "Maybe the heat damaged the ether hub in that location?"

Manuel fell into a conversation with Ghost about improving the newly-minted local ethernet's resiliency ... Noa focused on the hull's sounds of distress, but she left the channels to her crew open. She managed to bring the screech in the hull down to a low whisper.

"It's working!" said Chavez.

One of the engineering student's voices cracked over the ethernet. "The commander done good!"

The groan of the hull rose in pitch, but with movements becoming practiced, Noa managed to turn a groaning of the hull into a low moan. Noa felt her body begin to relax. She almost smiled, imagining what a story this would be when they made it back to the Fleet. Powering down timebands by ear, of all the brilliantly idiotic ideas she'd ever had ...

James's light went out again, and the almost smile died before it was born. She felt a lump in her throat, an emptiness in her gut, and she was suddenly cold again. His light flashed on again. She turned off James's light and hissed, angry at herself for the panic. "Slime of a bucket of blue-green algae."

"Commander, is everything alright?" Chavez said at the same instant Carl Sagan gave a startled squeak.

... Which was the moment she realized she'd spoken aloud.

* * *

Unwrapping Carl Sagan from her neck, Noa sat at the bottom of the circular stairwell at the center of the bridge. Giving him a pat, she said, "Go find me some rats, Carl Sagan." Giving a squeak, the werfle darted off. A moment later, he slipped down an air vent Noa hadn't realized existed until his furry tail vanished between the grating bars.

Noa's eyes burned with too little sleep. It had been ten hours since she'd been in her cabin with James. She had manned the helm almost the entire time with only a little help from Manuel, sending Chavez down to rest. Now the ensign was back on the bridge, refreshed after a long nap, this time manning the deceptively named "aft cannons" with one of the engineering students. The name derived from where the cannons got their power—the main engines.

Shaking her head, Noa tried not to think of how much sleep she'd missed ... but at that non-command, her fried brain sent a signal to her chronometer apps, and they piped back that she'd had less than two hours in the past twenty-four, and only six hours in the past forty-eight. She restrained a groan, feeling her stimulants wearing off. The lift rose at the center of the stairwell, its walls slid away, and Manuel, Ghost, and James emerged and stepped off. Noa motioned for them to have a seat. Manuel and Ghost, her chief computing officer, sat down on the steps in front of her. James sat behind her, slightly to one side.

"So can we repair the timeband and the charge dispersers that blew during the short?" she asked Manuel.

"Yes, they can be repaired," said Manuel.

"They can," Ghost asserted; he'd been drafted into

engineering for this crisis. He had a knack for it, apparently, and they were short-staffed.

Relief unwound inside her. Things didn't seem so dark as they had just moments before. Smiling, she rubbed her eyes and heard James shift behind her. Hours ago he'd told her, "There are too many coincidences, Noa. We both know the same dead language; I found you in the snow using a frequency that should be secure; I knew your name, your age ... your rank." What he hadn't commented on was that he was the spitting image of Timothy, her deceased husband. Maybe his not knowing that one coincidence was what made her not care how he was tied up in the Archangel Project. They both were, but *neither* of them knew how. She thought of the way his emotions had flooded the hard-link and filled her mind with blinding white. That ... had been extraordinary, and strange, but in a good way. For a moment, Noa was in that blinding white again.

"Noa," James said.

Her name spoken over the ether made her start. Noa's eyes bolted open, and she dropped her hands and sat up straight. Oh, Lord, had she just about fallen asleep, sitting in a staff meeting? She'd heard of it happening when stims wore off—heard of surgeons passing out in operating theaters, too. The shock gave her a brief burst of focus, and she realized that Manuel and Ghost were both frowning.

"What aren't you telling me?" she asked, trying to play off the depth of her exhaustion and resisting the urge to lean against James for support.

Wiping his own face, Manuel said, "We're fortunate that the Ark was designed for deep space travel and has a very well-equipped shop in case something like this happened. We can fix the timeband and the charge dispersers connected to it."

Nostrils flaring, Ghost spat out, "But it will take up to two months."

Noa sucked in a breath with a hiss. That had been her timetable for getting to the Kanakah Cloud and summoning the Fleet through the hidden time gate. Two months was turning into four months. How many people had died in the "re-education camp" in the days since she'd been there? She willed the bile rising in her throat to stay down.

"We have no choice," Noa said, pulling herself to her feet. She felt heavier than normal, but internal apps told her that the gravity aboard the ship had not changed. Trying not to appear tired, she snapped her hands behind her back. "We'll need to send you out in suits to disengage the band from the hull."

Standing, Manuel nodded, his non-regulation hair flopping in front of his eyes. The lieutenant had been retired when she'd brought him into this mess. Not *brought* him, she reminded herself; he'd volunteered to save the life of his little boy—and he'd lost his wife in the process. She took in the dark circles under his eyes; he needed sleep as much as she did. Her eyes traveled to Ghost. He didn't look much better than Manuel.

"We're sitting ducks out here," Ghost grumbled.

Noa looked up. Her gaze traveled through the dome above, made of a centis-thick non-reflective, nearly inde-structible glass-like compound. Outside, Noa could see the deep black shadows of the asteroids, the bright gray and brown where sunlight fell upon their craggy surfaces, and the far-off velvet of stars and vacuum. The asteroid belt in this system was much denser than the belt between Mars and Jupiter. Noa had charted a course as close to it as she could, for the protection the asteroids gave them from Luddeccean sensors. Another route would have been shorter, but now she was glad she'd erred on the side of caution.

"We'll begin preparations after a sleep cycle," Noa said.

Ghost's mouth opened, but before he could protest, Noa said, "No one is space walking without sleep."

"The longer we stay here, the more likely we'll be sighted!" Ghost protested.

"Baka!" Noa roared, fortunately only over the ethernet connection James had opened between them. It was the Japanese word for "fool." Ghost's eyes flickered in her direction ... was he listening in, or was it just coincidence? He'd set up the ship's ether, and he probably could read transmitted thoughts if he wanted, though it would be vulgar to eavesdrop. Noa smiled grimly, remembering the dismembered sex 'bots he'd had in Luddeccea. She shook her head. The man's face didn't show any expression at her outburst; even if he was listening, he probably didn't understand Japanese.

"We need him," James answered back in the same language.

He was right—they needed Ghost for the Ark's ancient systems. Smiling as sincerely as she could, Noa said, "Ghost, you and Manuel ... You're too valuable to lose, Ghost." She hoped repeating his name twice in a sentence would suffice in making him feel special. It was all she could manage in her current state of sleep deprivation and annoyance.

Ghost's shoulders softened, but he scowled when he said, "Yes, Commander."

It was as much as she expected. Giving a curt nod, she said, "Dismissed."

As the engineer and the programmer headed to the lift, James stepped to her side. "Do you need me?" he asked.

Yes, she wanted to say. But he smelled like smoke and fire retardant, and now that she had him up close, she could see soot on his face and clothing. Shorts and fires had kept him on the lower deck for hours. She blinked and reached across the ethernet. "Are *you* alright?"

His eyes fell heavy on her lips, but then returned to hers. Looking away, he shifted on his feet. "I'm hungry," he said aloud.

"So you're normal for you," she chided. "We're lucky that this ship is stocked with enough rations for a trip to Time Gate 7." The Ark had been kept stocked and operational because the Republic required every colony to have a certain number of evacuation vessels prepared for emergencies. Noa was beginning to suspect that the Luddeccean Authority had a loose definition of "operational," but there were stores enough for a seven lightyear trip to the next inhabited system.

James put a hand to his chest and looked heavenward. "Hopefully, it will be enough." His tone was completely serious, but he sighed dramatically and dropped his gaze back to her, raising an eyebrow.

At the cannon, Chavez snorted.

Noa grinned. Walking with him to the lift, she called back, "Chavez, you have the bridge. Bo—"

The engineering student bounced around in his seat. Noa remembered that of the four students from his shop, Bo had been the one who wanted to join the Fleet. At the moment he looked like an overeager puppy. "Yes, Commander?" he asked.

"Help keep Chavez awake."

His shoulders fell.

"And let me know if you see anything out there."

"Yes, Sir!" he said, more happily.

"Yes, Sir," said Chavez, with more restraint.

Noa stepped onto the lift platform, James beside her. Moments later the lift slid down the tube and the sides and ceiling slid above them like a flower in reverse bloom. Her eyes slipped to James ... his gaze was already on her ... but then flicked up to a camera. They weren't alone here, and without a hard-link, even their thoughts in the ether might not be private.

Noa was so tired, James appeared to shimmer, like she was looking at him through waves of heat. "Go eat," Noa said when the lift stopped and the door opened.

"Go sleep, Commander," James said, and she realized she hadn't moved. Feeling the burn behind her eyes again, she looked down the lonely hall. The ship had been home to children once, and the walls were decorated with their drawings. She didn't want to look at those cheerful etchings or travel down that long hallway; she wanted to collapse right where she was.

"Commander?"

"I know where to find you," she said—or maybe thought. Stepping into the hallway, she tried to walk in as straight a line as possible to her door. "Right," she muttered, nonsensically at the sound of the lift door closing behind her. It gave her an odd feeling of emptiness in her chest, but a few minutes later, the sight of her bed was like finding an oasis after days in the desert.

She shuffled forward and belly flopped onto the

mattress. Rolling up the covers around her, she smiled and slipped into sleep.

A familiar voice whispered, "So much better than the camp."

Blinking, Noa rolled over and saw her friend Ashley from the re-education camp, lying on her side beside her. Ashley's pale skin was flushed and healthy, her hair had grown back, and it was even redder than Noa imagined it would be.

"I told you we'd make it," Noa said, remembering Ashley crying the day they'd left; Ashley had been too afraid to leave. Noa's brows drew together. Something was wrong with that memory, but Noa couldn't place what it was. She noticed an arm around Ashley's waist—it was heavy and masculine. Noa scowled. Before she could ask, a man's head poked above Ashley's shoulder. It was Lieutenant Engineer Brian Song—he'd been in Noa's first crew in the System Six's Asteroid War—before she'd been holed up in medical for severe burns. Song and her whole first crew had been blown into oblivion while Noa was on med leave.

"You always make it, Commander," Brian said. He smiled gently ... compassionately.

And Noa was back in the camp ... she'd never escaped at all.

James's vision tunneled as he tripped down the hall, chilled by a too-cold shower he'd taken moments before. Smelling food, he turned on his heels and saw a sign painted on a pair of sliding doors. His vision was swimming from hunger, but he was able to read the elegant script: *Dove's Cafe ~ Serving the finest in Luddeccean teas, coffees, and produce.*

He took a step forward, the doors slid away, and his eyes fell on a glass case filled with a disorderly pile of pastries across the room.

"May I help you?"

James blinked. His hand was balled in a fist. He'd walked forward without conscious thought. Now he was just a step away from the pastries, prepared to plunge his hand through the glass.

"Professor Sinclair?"

Shaking his head to clear the darkness, he found himself facing 6T9. The 'bot was standing behind the display, a large plastic bin filled with pastries in his hands.

Letting his fist drop, James said, "I'd like something to eat."

"Of course," said 6T9, putting the bin on the counter. James snatched up one of the pastries. With the first flaky, fatty, sweet, and salty bite, his neurons and nanos stood up and started to sing. Before the hyper-augmentation, he hadn't been a fan of sweets ... now they filled him like nothing else.

"You're not with Noa," said 6T9.

James blinked at the 'bot. 6T9 was a sex 'bot, or in polite terms, a "cybernetic consort," designed to look like a human male. Like James, he wore clothing from the Ark stores: a loose shirt and trousers of gray stretchy fabric. Eliza Burton, 6T9's owner, had usually outfitted him in skimpy outfits; the unremarkable clothing made him look more human. He was leaning on the counter now, one hand on his chin, gazing up at James.

"Yes," James said, distractedly. The pastry in his hand was much better than standard tourist fare. Besides being filling, the flavors were wonderful and complex: coconut oil, butter, and a flavor reminiscent of lime. Chewing slowly to savor the delicacy, he turned to survey the cafe. He was in what looked like a high-end coffee shop, even with the asteroids visible through the portholes. The floors were polished wood. Plush sofas in velvety oranges and deep arm chairs of brown faux leather were arranged around low tables. The entire place was tastefully lit by warm recessed lighting. It still smelled like Luddeccean summer. This space had originally been the galley, but the Ark had been a museum exhibit. They must have transformed it for the tourists.

"You know," 6T9 said slowly, "you don't have to be alone if you don't want to."

The 'bot languidly dragged a rag across the glass case, looking up at James from beneath long lashes. "The offer I made you on Luddeccea still stands."

On Luddeccea, 6T9 had invited James to join him in a tryst. Apparently, Eliza didn't mind sharing. "The answer is still no," James said, finishing his pastry and reaching for another.

Shrugging, 6T9 turned away and began wiping the case with more vigor. "I propositioned you in front of Noa last time. I thought you might have just been trying to portray yourself as exclusively interested in her. I had to ask you alone, in case it was an act." He stopped wiping the counter. "Of course, if you ever lose confidence in your relationship with Noa *going* anywhere ... the offer will still be open."

James's brow furrowed. It struck him that he wasn't insulted by the 'bot's proposition. He felt nothing at all. No, that wasn't true, he was mildly annoyed. James was too polite to talk with his mouth full, and 6T9 was keeping him from his pastry. And ...

"I'm not unconfident with Noa." He thought about the electrons flowing between their minds, her forehead against his, the heat everywhere they touched. "It's everything else ..." Noa was the only thing that felt real—in his past and in his present. His vision went black ... He was here, eating, instead of with her. Before his hyper-augmentation, hunger would not have kept him from a woman. He'd been fine in the heat and smoke of the fires ... and suddenly now he was hungry at the least opportune time.

The heat of irritation prickled beneath every inch of his skin. Glancing down, he saw the tattoos he didn't remember getting blooming across his arms. He let out a breath of frustration at the sight of the mysterious etchings.

"That's a shame," said 6T9, wiping down the glass case. "I was hoping you'd help me reevaluate my programming."

James swallowed a bite of pastry. "I just said no, 6T9 ..." And then he remembered 6T9's improper use of his idiom app a few hours before. "Unless you're talking about reevaluating your idiom app?" His jaw shifted in an aborted smile, as he chided the 'bot.

6T9's brow furrowed. "My idiom app is a fine-toothed comb."

James's eyebrows shot up. He swore he felt his

neurons and nanos flicker.

"No, it's something else," 6T9 said. His chest rose and fell, in a semblance of a sigh, and his lips parted as though he were about to say something. But then, drawing back from the counter, he said, "I'm not at liberty to talk about it."

James blinked. 'Bots weren't supposed to evade a question or order unless it meant complying would harm a human. How was James's question harmful, and to whom?

At that moment, 6T9 hissed, picked up a broom and rushed around the counter. James spun around. From the floor came a squeal. Looking down, James saw Carl Sagan darting beneath an overstuffed chair. Rocking the chair back, 6T9 raised the broom like a club.

Dropping the pastry, James shouted, "No!" thinking of just how unhappy Noa would be if her pet got squished. The broom was already dropping. It hit the floor with a thwack, just missing Carl Sagan, who darted forward with a shriek. The creature drew to a halt just before James and shrieked again. Dropping to his heels, James reached toward the werfle. "Here, Carl Sagan!"

For a moment time stood still. Carl Sagan did not move even as 6T9 raised the broom again. James's mind spun. Earth mammals as distant as horses, dogs, and humans shared some body language. Werfles were native to Luddeccea; the double helix of their genes were based on a completely different string of chemical pairs. It could not understand James's command, or his gesture.

Just as that realization hit, the werfle leapt into his arms. James pulled back in relief and shock. 6T9 stood by the chair, gesturing with the broom. "Put it down, let me kill it! Eliza hates rats!"

Carl Sagan swirled his long body around James's arm and hissed.

"It's a werfle," James protested. "They eat rats. Eliza should love them."

6T9 lowered the broom. "She does like werfles." He stared at Carl Sagan. "How can you tell it is not a rat?"

James rocked back on his feet. Even if idioms weren't his forte, 6T9 could grasp sexual innuendo, could mimic and read human emotions, and could even theorize on human behavior, but the 'bot could not tell the difference between a werfle and a rat?

"It is not in my animal database," 6T9 continued, eyes narrowing at Carl Sagan.

James's neurons and nanos made a mighty leap. Luddeccea was too conservative to manufacture sex 'bots. 6T9 had to have been imported. Werfles were rare; they'd never been added to 6T9's databases. Still ...

"It has ten legs," James said. "Can't you count them?"

"I can count," said 6T9.

"You've seen this werfle before," James said, still vexed, "... at Eliza's home."

"She told me it was a werfle, then," said 6T9, his expressive voice becoming cool and analytical. Robotic. "It is out of context here. I was unable to identify it." He stood stock still and his eyes drifted to a point beyond James's shoulder.

James sighed. It was, in 20th century parlance, a *bug* in 6T9's programming. He had all the pieces but couldn't put them together. Humans had once feared machines taking over the galaxy. In the 1960s Moore's Law had predicted the doubling of transistors in a dense integrated circuit every two years—and of processing power growing in sync. But then Moore's

Law hit "Moore's Wall." Advances in computer speed became more and more incremental, more and more expensive, and growth in processing power slowed to a crawl.

"Count the legs from now on," James ordered the 'bot.

"I will count legs from now on," 6T9 said. The 'bot turned and took the broom behind the counter and then declared, "Well, early bird catches the cheese!"

James again felt as though his thought processes had been shut off. As they flickered back to life, his jaw shifted as he tried to smile again. "That's not—" And then James caught himself.

Tilting his head, the 'bot asked, "What's wrong?"

James scratched Carl Sagan beneath the chin. The random version had been better than the real version. "Never mind."

The werfle gave a startled sounding cheep, as though protesting the lie.

Smiling benignly, 6T9 nodded in James's direction. "I am going to recharge now. See you later."

"First mouse gets the worm," James called after 6T9, as the 'bot left the room.

"That's not how it goes, Professor," but then the door whooshed shut before the 'bot finished, leaving James alone with the werfle. With a squeak, Carl Sagan prowled up James's arm and settled around his neck, sniffing the whole way, as though following a trail of breadcrumbs.

Still hungry, James went behind the counter, grabbed a jug of milk from the fridge and the bin of pastries, and then plunked himself down on a sofa. He picked up a loose slice of ham from among the pastries and Carl Sagan gave a squeak.

"Would you like a—"

The werfle ripped the slice from his fingers.

"—bite?" James finished.

James raised a brow in bemusement. Carl Sagan, a creature separated from James by billions of years of very different evolution, whose every fiber of being was made up of different molecular components, had, in a completely unfamiliar context, correctly identified James as a possible ally and 6T9 as a definite threat. A few minutes later, he'd communicated his desire for the ham slice with only a squeak. 6T9 could speak English, but Carl Sagan had a more sophisticated understanding of the universe than the 'bot. James scratched the werfle between the ears. Werfles had been designed to seek company for warmth, companionship, safety, and reproduction, to find food and shelter, just as humans did. That had to be the reason for the understanding; it was convergent evolution of thought processes.

His fingers paused ... The saboteurs of Time Gate 8 were beings of pure energy according to Kenji, Noa's brother. What could beings of pure energy have in common with beings of flesh and blood? And if, as the Luddecceans suspected, James was connected to them ...

"It doesn't matter," he whispered to himself. But his hand on Carl Sagan started to shake, as though it belonged to someone else. The sensation of a thousand pinpricks spread from his fingers to his wrist. Pulling his trembling hand to his stomach, the weight of everything wrong began to bear down on him, as though the ship's gravity had increased again. It wasn't just his connection to the time gate that was wrong, his hyper-augments, or the tattoos he didn't remember ... it was his detachment from his former self. He didn't feel like Professor James Hiro Sinclair anymore ... he felt like ... like ...

He needed to see Noa. He almost reached out to her ... but his vision darkened, remembering how exhausted she'd been on the bridge. She needed her sleep. He couldn't wake her.

By his ear, Carl Sagan began to fidget, bouncing on James's shoulder, tiny claws tearing through his shirt. James felt Noa reaching out to his mind. With a rush of relief, he answered the call, felt their minds connect ... and then Noa's scream pierced the ether. "Leave me alone!"

CHAPTER THREE

"Noa?" James called, jumping to his feet. Was someone on the ship trying to hurt her? His skin heated and his fists balled at his sides.

"Leave me alone," she said, this time the mental equivalent of a whisper.

James accessed her location. Noa was in the hallway just outside the cafe and alone ... He ran to the exit, the door whooshed open, and he saw Noa with her hands over her bowed head. She was stumbling down the hall like she was drunk. Looking back over her shoulder, she shouted at the empty hallway, "Stay away from me!"

"Noa!" he said, "What's ...?"

And then the electrons in his neural interface connected to Noa exploded in his visual cortex. James saw a semi-transparent Kenji in the periphery of his vision and a woman dressed in Luddeccean Green carrying a billy club, a stunner attached to her hip. The Ark's gray halls transformed and became a long aisle between beds like the kind he associated with Nazi prison camps, filled with emaciated women.

He was in Noa's memories—he took in her wide eyes and stumbling steps. No, he was not in her memories, he was in a nightmare.

Carl Sagan hopped and squeaked on James's shoulder.

"Noa, I can help you!" the nightmare Kenji said.

Not knowing what else to do, James cautiously approached Noa, holding out his arms. She looked right past him, spun around to face her brother, and then held up her hands as though he might hit her. James had seen Noa take on armed men barehanded. Now she was cowering before her misguided brother. His skin heated in anger and frustration; into the ether he whispered, "Oh, Noa."

"James?" she said, looking past him. James took her arms. His touch was gentle, but she struggled against him, punching the air helplessly, like her hands were pulled by strings, and he was able to pull her back to his chest.

"Let me go! Let me go!" she cried.

He didn't. On impulse, he closed his eyes. The nightmare became more substantial, not less ... and darker, much darker. He could "see" the faces on the beds.

"I'm here, I'm here," he said to Noa, and projected his avatar, letting it encircle her with his arms as he was in real life.

She stopped struggling. "James?"

"Noa, you have to leave him!" Kenji said. "You're delusional, Noa."

James growled at the wraith of Kenji and felt his static and heat beneath his skin.

"Kenji," Noa said, her head falling against James's shoulder. The shadows cast by the stacked beds became longer; the single female guard grew larger.

James remembered the light between Noa and his mind earlier. The light had been from her ... she'd said his emotions slipping across the link triggered it. Pulling her tighter, he tried to remember what he'd felt in those moments before her mind had filled with light. Relief, gratitude ... victory. He tried to recreate the sensations, but he could hear Kenji calling, "Noa, Noa," and all he could feel was rage. Noa shuddered and gave a muffled cry. Closing off all his emotions, he turned on all his apps for recreating scenes and filled the space between their minds with the memory of the bright white light that Noa had imagined earlier. Noa gasped as the light spilled through Kenji, the guards, the bed stacks and the wraiths inhabiting them. James concentrated, letting it burn through all the shadows, until there was nothing but white, and the sound of Noa gasping. Seizing the momentum, he guided her into the cafe and jammed his hand into the close door button. Letting the illusion drop, he whispered, "I've locked them out." Noa didn't respond; she just stood breathing heavily in his arms. Brow furrowing, James recreated his avatar, and the whole of the cafe into the space between their minds so it would be there—whether their eyes were opened or closed. "I've locked them out," he let his avatar say again.

Noa straightened, and she nodded at his avatar. She was still asleep, he realized, able to connect with mental imagery, but not really in the world. "Come sit down," James let his avatar say, guiding her to the sofa in real life.

"Thanks, yes," said Noa—in his mind, not in the real world. "I had a horrible dream."

"It's gone now," said James's avatar as he sat down next to her on the couch. Noa met his avatar's eyes, but not his own. An avatar of her own sat up primly on the couch, but her body slumped against the cushions. James's alarm began to rise again.

James allowed his avatar to venture. "I think I saw some of your dreams ..." Which should not happen. The most basic apps would prevent it, and Noa, from what he'd seen, had apps that were quite sophisticated.

Sitting in the spot occupied by her real body, Noa's avatar's eyebrow rose. She touched her neural interface with a hand that had all its fingers and two bright rings. "In the camp they put a polyfiber screw in my interface."

James remembered seeing the thick, wicked screws in the sides of people's heads on Luddeccean television. "It could have damaged something," James said.

Noa's avatar wiped her illusionary face with her hands. "Nightmares ... hell of a commander I make. I shouldn't be leading this mission."

James's eyes went to the camera in the room. The camera wouldn't capture any of this ether conversation, but this ship's ether wasn't secure. They weren't protected by the constantly updating security routines of the time gates or associated satellites. Here they had only an ancient computer, programmed by Ghost, a less than completely trustworthy former Fleet officer. If Ghost bothered to go through the ether records later, he'd see this, and possibly use it against them. He'd nearly let them be captured by the Luddeccean Guard back in Prime. James's still trembling hand formed a fist. He would rip Ghost's limbs out, if the man saw this episode and decided to use it against Noa. "You're the only one to lead this mission," James let his avatar say. He wouldn't follow anyone else aboard the ship. None of them felt real.

Noa's avatar turned away, and completely without segue said, "I smell food." As her physical body slept, her avatar proceeded to help herself to a dream sandwich, completely detached from the horrors of only a few moments ago. It made a rush of static sting at the back of James's neck ... but he'd had dreams that were just as odd, hadn't he? Since Luddeccea he hadn't dreamed, he merely replayed events in his mind, but he remembered dreams where he did extraordinary things like talking to porpoises and flying, and then did mundane things moments later, like going to work. He'd recorded a dream exactly like that for his time capsule. He leaned back against the cushions.

"If I eat this, what will you eat?" Noa's avatar asked his, lifting the dream sandwich to her mouth and winking at him. Making the moment light, not because she didn't know how bad it was that her apps were projecting her dreams, but despite knowing. A sense of humor was all they had in the face of the absurd and the impossible.

James let his avatar roll its eyes. "Oh, I'll survive." He sighed dramatically. "... Somehow." There was, of course, plenty to eat, but that was in the real world. Dream Noa was eating all the dream food.

Noa's avatar beamed at him and at the same time, her malfunctioning apps let a bolt of pure joy cross the ether, and something else. Gratitude. Her avatar began to fade away, but it smiled until the end. And then it was just James, Noa passed out against the corner of the couch, and Carl Sagan. The werfle cautiously slid down James's arms and curled up in Noa's lap. Noa didn't respond, even when the werfle nuzzled her limp left hand with its missing fingers.

On impulse, James took the hand in his. His skin tone was very pale against her own. Noa had never asked him why he didn't have his melanocytes stimulated. He'd always told people, rather defiantly, that he was a living refutation of "Violent Iceman stereotypes." He hadn't thought of that since he'd been with her, and he hadn't asked her why she hadn't altered her own pigment, either. The same sense of defiance? Or did her Luddeccean heritage insist that she keep her natural tone? His brows drew together. It could be either or both. Each person was a culture unto themselves. He'd said that once ... Before *everything,* he'd thought it profound enough to mention in an entry into his time capsule.

His free hand trembled. There was something about that memory.

James raised a brow at Carl Sagan. "The nightmares and the sleepwalking put the tremors in perspective," he said, to lighten his own mood. He absently squeezed Noa's hand and almost believed it.

* * *

It was too bright behind Noa's eyelids.

She heard James whisper, "It seems to be fine this morning, Carl Sagan." A warm weight on her stomach squirmed, squeaked, and abruptly wiggled away. Noa's thoughts were moving slowly, like a magni-freight train just leaving a junction. When had James and Carl Sagan come to her quarters? She blinked rapidly, and instead of seeing the gray ceiling of her cabin, she saw recessed lighting, and warm orangish walls. Her eyes slid to the side and she saw wood flooring. Her breath caught, but then she recognized the place. The Ark had a cafe for showcasing all its local foodstuffs.

But ... "How did I get here?" she whispered.

James was sitting on the same sofa as she was,

clutching his wrist, his blonde bangs hanging over his eyes. "You were sleepwalking," he replied.

Noa put her hands to her face. "Nebulas," she muttered. It had happened before, around the time Timothy had died, but she hadn't had an episode like that, even in the camps. Her body stilled ... But in the camps she hadn't been alone. She dropped her hands and found James's blue eyes, intent on hers. Had he been sitting with her all night? She licked her lips; they were suddenly very dry. She needed to say something, but her tongue felt like cotton. She felt James reach to her across the ether and she shifted nervously against the pillows. He had to remember that Ghost might be listening, that the conversation might not be private. She answered anyway.

A ball of light shimmered between their minds. Noa blinked, and the ball bounced a few times. James, still cradling his wrist, said, "You looked like you were having dark thoughts."

Noa laughed in relief and made the ball bounce back across the ether. He whipped back his head as though it had struck him in the cheek, and then winked at her and tossed it back. It made her warm, as though he'd blown her a kiss. Then her eyes fell to the wrist he was still cradling.

"Are you hurt?" Had she lashed out at him in her nightmare? She'd never been violent in an episode, but plenty of other vets had during a bout of PTSD sleep-walking.

The ball of white winked off. James raised an eyebrow and gazed down at his hand. "No, I'm just ..." His head cocked. "Celebrating another day when my augmented parts didn't strangle me in my sleep."

Noa huffed at his dark humor. That had been a plot

of some Luddeccean dramas when they'd left. She relit the bouncing ball of white light and tossed it back to him. In real life his jaw only shifted, but one of his avatars smiled in her mind. She wanted to reach out and touch him. She almost suggested they leave, go some place more private, even though her stomach was empty and she really needed to eat something, but the door abruptly opened with a whoosh.

Noa swung her feet off the sofa just as Gunny walked in, rumbling, "What do you mean, there's no alcohol aboard?"

Leaning on 6T9, Eliza, Noa's thrice centenarian great-great aunt, entered the cafe. "It's not even noon!" Eliza protested.

Following close behind, Gunny protested, "Well ... I mean ... for later!"

From across the room, Noa heard 6T9's voice as though far off. "One, two, three, four, five, six, seven, eight ..." And then there was a swish as the door opened again and Oliver, Manuel's son, toddled in, the engineer right behind him. "Good morning, Commander," said Manuel.

"Everyone," Eliza declared, "6T9 is a fantastic cook. We still have some fresh dairy in the cafe. He'll cook it right up!"

"Nine, ten ... a werfle!" 6T9 said.

The door whooshed again, and three of the four engineering students stepped around Manuel.

"Sounds great," said Manuel, "But before anything I need coffee." The engineer's eyes fell on Noa, widened, and then he nodded. "Commander," he said. His eyes went to James and he put a hand on Oliver's shoulder, maybe a little too tightly, as though the child were an anchor. To James he almost bowed. "James," he said, in the same tone you'd say, "Thank you."

Oblivious to the weightiness of the moment, Oliver pointed at 6T9 and shouted, "Shixty on space shit!"

Manuel's face reddened, James's eyebrows shot up, and Noa put a hand to her mouth to hide a grin.

"That is very inappropriate language," 6T9 responded. "And I am busy counting. One, two, three ... four. The werfle has a rat!" 6T9 cried.

Manuel swooped down and picked up Oliver.

Noa twisted and saw Carl Sagan darting under a chair, leaving a smear of red on the floor. "Let him eat it," said Eliza. "Don't want to discourage the critter from catching those filthy things."

There was a sound that sounded suspiciously like the snap of a bone.

A collective "Ewww ..." and laughter rose around the room, and for a moment Noa forgot they were parked on a hunk of asteroid. Everything felt normal ... happy even. But then a blast over the ship's klaxons halted all conversation in the cafe.

Noa's eyes went upward, Gunny's hand went to his hip, although he wasn't carrying a firearm, and James leaned forward as though he were about to bolt from his seat.

"Commander," Ensign Chavez said across the ether. "We have incoming."

Noa sprang from the sofa. Over the ether, she called out across the general channel to all her crew, "Anything on the distress channels?"

There were several radio channels reserved for emergencies. It was an old-fashioned technology, but it was immune to viruses.

"Nothing," Chavez said.

Striding toward the door, Noa reached out to her computing specialist. "Ghost—"

"All the emergency frequencies are open, Commander," Ghost said. "And I've checked the external sensors. They're not signaling us with a flashlight in Morse Code. If we're not hearing them, it's because they're not talking."

Noa hissed, "Lizzar dung," and Ghost said, "I would echo that assessment." Noa winced. She'd thought aloud *again*. Once in an Earth orbital period was excusable, but more than that ... children and mad scientists thought aloud, not Fleet Commanders. Was it a lingering consequence of having her port jammed with a polyfiber screw?

"Transmit your visual," Noa commanded Chavez as she headed to the door. "To all of us—Gunny! Manuel!"

Chavez's view played in Noa's visual cortex. What she saw wasn't the Guard, but it made every hair on the back of her neck stand on end. Hovering in the mentalscape was a small ship, ovoid in shape, about as tall and as wide as Noa and twice as long as she was tall. It had two narrow timebands that she estimated couldn't propel the ship faster than a tenth C. The vessel was also distinguished by eight robotic arms, and two tiny glass windows at the front that looked for all the world like eyes.

"Goddamn ticks!" roared Gunny, over the ethernet and in real life. He'd served in the Six System War, too.

"Armory now!" Noa ordered without looking back.

Oliver wailed, letting Noa know Manuel wasn't far behind her, and Gunny's heavy footsteps were impossible to miss. Noa felt the heat of anger rising in her chest, and her hands clenched at her side.

Ghost's voice tickled over the ether. "Are they part of a mercenary outfit ... or alone?" Even when Ghost was only thinking, she could *see* his lip trembling.

"Unknown," Noa said. "Chavez, hail them, let them know we're here and we're armed." To Gunny she said, "I haven't heard of any guerilla outfits in Luddeccean space —have you?"

She could hear the frown in his voice when he said, "No, Commander."

"They're out of the trajectory of our cannons," Bo supplied over the ether, and Noa stifled a growl of frustration. The cannons were powerful enough to put a battle cruiser out of commission. They could disintegrate a tick. However, the Ark wasn't a warship, and the cannons had been designed to shoot objects out of the ship's path. They only shot forward with a few degrees variance.

"They're not friendly," Gunny added, stepping to the back. Manuel followed. Before Noa could touch the control panel, James stepped into the sliding door's frame and met Noa's gaze with narrowed eyes. Daring her to order him away, she realized. Manuel released a breath. Gunny shifted on his feet. James didn't move or even blink.

A new cold swept through Noa. She almost ordered him away, but focusing on the lift controls, she growled, "Get in." She jammed her finger at the button she'd pushed just a heartbeat before. He needed to be here—the tick could have up to eight crew aboard—they needed every steady, able hand they had. Noa's thoughts flashed to drooling Oliver, shy Kara and the other hapless engineering students, frail Eliza, and even 6T9. She closed her eyes. She shouldn't worry about Sixty. He didn't care if he lived or died. The 'bot should be here instead of

James, but 6T9 was as sharp as a used wad of stim gum, and probably less useful in a fight—stim gum could at least stick to your enemies' boots.

"They're coming closer," Chavez added over the ether. "Carefully like ... slow."

Noa looked to the ceiling, feeling as though the lift was moving slowly, even though her apps told her it wasn't.

"Looking for a place to attach," said Manual.

"What are ticks?" said James.

It was such an obvious question, that there was a brief mental silence. Manuel whistled. "You *are* a civilian, Professor."

Noa looked sharply at the engineer; he was staring at James. It struck her that she wasn't the only one who sometimes tripped over James's professor status. His academic profession ran headlong into his impressive skills in combat.

The elevator stopped. Striding over to the locker that served as an armory, she said, "Ticks are small shuttles designed for asteroid mining."

"Sounds harmless enough," said James.

"They're the slime of blue-green algae," Noa hissed, Manuel's face went red, and Gunny spat.

James's eyes shifted between Gunny, the lieutenant, and herself. "... but obviously there is something I'm missing."

Gunny growled, pulled a rifle out of the locker, and then put it back, scowling. "Blasted ticks can be outfitted pretty rough—small cannons—and they can go almost anywhere and hide. They've got tubing adherers on them, on account that they are often used to scavenge and need to be able to dock with about anything. They always have laser cutters, so they *can* dock with anything." The sergeant pulled a stunner out of the cabinet instead of the rifle.

"They're going to cut a hole in our hull?" James said, reaching for a rifle.

Noa narrowed her eyes. "Not if I can help it."

"Use a stunner, not a phaser weapon," Gunny said to James. "We don't want to blow a hole ourselves."

"Chavez ... still no response?" Noa asked over the ethernet.

"No response," the ensign responded.

"Commander," Ghost's voice cut across the shared channel. "They're not close enough to the ship to share our ethernet yet—but they will be soon. I'm still new to the Ark's very antiquated systems ... even a small computer like one on a tick might be able to pick this ship's brain. We need a cipher. May I suggest we all download the *Trials and Tribulations of Jonathan Primp?* It's part of the onboard library and dense enough." There was a touch of acid humor in the man's thoughts. Jonathan Primp was one of the original founders of the Luddeccean movement—his autobiography would be long enough to have a fair selection of vocabulary. "Good choice, Ghost. Download, gentlemen," Noa said, doing the same.

"Cipher?" said James.

"Circling, but getting very close, Commander!" Chavez said, projecting the location of the tick.

Manuel blinked a few times. "Downloaded." To James he said, "We use an app that matches our thoughts to the words in the text, and then codes those words to number sequences based on their location. Then we transmit the number sequences across the ether."

"Close enough to be in ethernet range! Switch to cipher, now!" Ghost said.

"Starting at the copyright or first chapter?" James asked aloud.

"You don't have the app," Manuel said over Gunny and Noa's heads. "Just pay attention to verbal commands."

Noa's heart lifted. James didn't have a cipher app—more reason for him to stay back and cover them. Noa turned to Gunny, pretending not to notice James's jaw ticking side to side and his brow furrowing. She spoke aloud as her app digested the new cipher material. "I expect they'll try to drill into an airlock."

Gunny grimaced. "If they want to keep the ship in one piece."

In the periphery of her vision, she saw James's lips part, as though he were about to speak, but Chavez's thoughts filtered through the ether as only numbers. Noa fed them into her app, and it neatly translated the numbers into the ensign's voice. "Commander, I think they're going to attach to Airlock 5."

Noa took a breath and answered through the cipher. "Seal the inner door and open the outer door of that airlock, Chavez, soon as their plastitube adherer is down."

"Commander?"

Noa's mind whirred, working so fast her mouth could barely keep up as she prowled to the lift. "Do it, Chavez ... but turn off all the lights inside the airlock." She turned to Gunny and spoke over the cipher. "What sort of equipment will they have, Gunny?"

There was a barely discernable delay in Gunny's reply as he strung his words together through the app. "Stunner rifles if they're scavengers, plasma or projectiles if they're mercs." Gunny frowned as they stepped into the lift. "They'll have night vision goggles on if they're not augmented—the guys work half the time in the dark."

Noa was a pilot; her experience in ground combat was limited. "How fast do they adjust to sudden brightness changes?" she asked. "Are the commercial things slow to adjust like the ones we trained with in Basic?"

"They rarely have the latest gear ... so yeah," Gunny drawled.

Noa jammed her hand into the lift controls and opened the door. "Manuel, go get me your biggest, brightest spotlight from engineering—if it's got an autoswitch, all the better."

Manuel didn't ask questions, just nodded, and bolted out the door. Just before the doors slid closed, she saw him slipping into the hatch to the ladder that accessed all decks.

"Chavez?" Noa said, resuming the lift's path to the deck of Airlock 5.

"They're descending their tube now, Commander."

Hitting the elevator halt button, she whispered. "Silence, they may be able to hear us from here on out." She switched to the cipher and ether. "We'll put the light in the hallway just outside the airlock. It will buy us a few seconds."

"Only a few," Gunny replied. "It will still be close. I wish we had more men, or another surprise, or—"

Noa's cipher picked up a string of numbers ... her eyes widened. They were from James, and her cipher app translated them neatly into his voice. "I have an idea for a surprise."

Gunny's eyebrows shot up. "You sure you're not Fleet?"

Over the cipher he replied, "I used a similar program to reference obscure words in ancient texts. Simple enough to modify on the fly." His eyes stayed level on Noa's.

"Spill the idea," Gunny said.

Noa forced her body to stay ramrod straight and her eyes not to look away. She had a feeling she wasn't going to like his idea at all.

James's back was pressed against the ceiling, his hands and feet braced against the walls of the narrow hallway just outside Airlock 5. All the hallway lights were off. The door to the airlock in the direction of his feet was still closed; he could barely hear the crew members of the tick on the other side.

He raised his head, as much as he could, and looked up the hall to the lift. Noa had a spotlight just inside. For the moment, the spotlight was off. The lift's lights were on and, as usual, he had difficulty with the differences in brightness, but he could make out Noa's silhouette, shimmering, as though he was looking at her through waves of heat.

"You're alright, James?" Gunny asked, his words encrypted in the ether.

James's muscles were straining, he had a barely perceptible shudder in his left arm, he couldn't see well, and he couldn't hear his enemies well enough to even judge how many there were. Instead of saying that, he said, "This heathen is fine," using the religious language of the selected cipher, trying to make Noa laugh.

He got a soft huff from Gunny, but Noa's silhouette

gave him an incremental nod. She had argued against James's plan, saying that it would put him in the line of fire. She'd relented when Gunny had pointed out that it was imperative that none of the invaders got back to their tick and, anyway, since they were only using stunners, James wouldn't be seriously hurt ... at least not by the Ark team.

The lift door slid closed and James was in absolute darkness. Everything was ready. He heard the door to the airlock slide just a fraction, and a muffled, "See anything?"

The comm in the wall cracked, and Oliver's wail crackled through the air.

Another voice whispered, "See ... told ya? Civvies, nuthin' to this."

The airlock door slid open with a swoosh that made James's ears ache. His muscles tensed and his senses were assaulted by the smells of sweat, dirt, and grease. He could hear better, too. He counted eight pairs of footsteps. Gritting his teeth, he locked his arms, preparing for the right moment. Only a little longer ...

"I dunno," said another man. "I heard 'em using a cipher."

"Simple tech," said the first, stepping into the hallway.

Someone spat. "Impossible to crack without knowing the source. Used by Fleet types a lot."

There was a grunt. A man walked beneath James. James couldn't see him, but his head was so close to James's belly that James could feel the movement of air as he walked. And James could smell him, hear his heavy footsteps, slightly elevated heartbeat, and deep breathing. He thought he also heard the sound of something being jostled—a rifle maybe? Stunner, plasma, or projectile?

James held his breath, willed his heartbeat not to be as loud as theirs, and his left arm's tremble not to grow worse.

"All's clear," said the man directly beneath James. "Should we try and call the lift or take the ladder?" James heard him step toward the other end of the hallway, the hatch to the ladder James knew Manuel had locked, and the lift where Noa and Gunny waited for James's signal.

All but one of the men filed out of the airlock and into the hallway.

By the ladder door, a man said, "Damn, locked ... might be needin' the cutter."

"Idiots," someone snarled.

The man in the airlock still hadn't moved. Did James wait ... hope the man moved into the main hallway ... or strike?

Oliver's wail crackled over the intercom again, and one of the intruders hissed, "I wonder if that baby's mommy is onboard." Over the Ark's public ethernet channel came an unfiltered image. James saw the man's back. Every black hair on his head and wrinkle in the fabric of his garments was distinct, the way it could only be if it was a purchased avatar. The man's virtual hips were plunging into a woman whose face was a blur; she was begging for mercy through sobs. It took a moment for James to realize he was seeing one of the scavenger's projections. His jaw shifted. He felt every muscle in his body flood with heat.

"Jezuz, Kline!" one of them said. "Damn!"

The indistinct face became Noa's in James's mind. His arms and legs shook violently, and he knew that the phrase "trembling with rage" was not a metaphor. He imagined the back of that black head on the floor, blood pooling around the perfect hair.

"Awww ... your dirty pictures are givin' me a hard-on," said the man in the airlock.

James's mouth opened in a silent scream; over the ether, he screamed with his mind, "Now!" He dropped from the ceiling, spun in a crouch in the darkness, pulled his stunner and lunged at the stomach level of the man in the airlock. As he knocked the man backward into the wall, he felt body armor beneath his shoulder and inwardly cursed as he fired his stunner into the man's protected side and didn't get as much as a hiss. The man knocked the stunner from James's hand with strength augmented as much as James's own. Behind him, James heard more stunner fire, Manuel roar, the lift open, and then the click of the spotlight turning on. The black that surrounded him was replaced by white that was equally blinding.

Something stung the side of his body and made all the neurons and nanos there feel as though they were on fire, but it didn't feel like pain—it felt like power. The sensation fanned out across his skin into his muscles and his very bones.

The man he had nearly pinned stammered, "You're ... you're not wearing armor ..."

James's vision adjusted to the brightness, and he found himself staring through the other man's night vision goggles at a pair of very wide eyes. It was only at that moment that James realized he'd been stunned ... and he was still upright. Wrenching back his head, James drove his forehead into the other man's nose, just below the eyewear. There was a crunch, a thunk as the man's head hit the wall behind him, and then his opponent's body went limp. Someone tried to slink an arm around James's neck. He dropped his chin just in time and sank his teeth into the new foe's arm—and recognized the man by his scream. It was the man looking for "mommy." James locked his hands around the man's arm so he couldn't get away, spun and rammed the man behind him into a wall. He felt spittle against his ear and a stunner at his side and almost laughed. The stunner went off, his side throbbed and pulsed with a heat that was almost pleasure, and he hauled the man over his shoulder onto the floor. James aimed with a foot and was rewarded with a crack and another scream.

"James!" someone shouted.

Rolling onto his stomach, the man struggled to pull himself to all fours. Dropping on top of him, pinning him with a knee, James grabbed one of his arms and wrenched it up. The man screamed, and James pulled his arm further back. The man howled.

"James, stop!"

It was Noa's voice.

James's hand tightened on the arm of the man beneath him. His anger felt as tangible and as electric as the stunner had—he felt charged. Where his sleeves were rolled up, his "tattoos" were completely black. Not releasing the man, he glared up at Noa. In the periphery of his vision he saw Gunny had a man pinned to the wall, stunner beneath his chin. Manuel had another man in a similar grip; four other bodies lay on the ground. Noa was standing over one, stunner out.

The order to stop replayed in his mind, but so did the images projected by the man he had pinned. His eyes slid to the other "scavengers." They needed to die ... but Noa apparently didn't want them dead. He needed to convince her. Aloud he said, "They have cannons aboard their vessel. They are too dangerous to let go, and we don't have a brig."

"Don't kill us! Don't kill us!" said the man Gunny had pinned to the wall. "We were just ... err ... here to help ..."

"Shut your mouth," Gunny hissed.

The man's mouth shut with an audible snap.

Voice cool and as calm as James had ever heard it, Manuel said, "I'm inclined to agree with Professor Sinclair."

"Professor?" whined the man beneath James.

James gave his arm a twist, and the man sobbed.

"Their ship has cannons, *Commander*," James said. Couldn't she see these men had no utility?

"We do have to do something about the cannons," Noa agreed. "Manuel, can you repurpose them?"

The engineer growled. "Yes. But we don't have anywhere to keep these men."

Noa's eyes slid over the bodies on the floor. "Ticks always have a home base ..." Over the cipher, she said, "Ghost, can you access their onboard computer? Find out where they've been?"

James swore he heard a sniff over the ether, and then Ghost said, "Of course I can."

"How long—?"

Ghost's response floated across the ether. "Already in. These boys are part of the Adam's Belt Independent Miners Guild."

Noa made a sound low in her throat.

Ghost's thoughts wafted through the ether. "Oh, Commander, you need to see this." He projected an image of what looked like a small planet, studded with rings of light, in the midst of asteroids and derelict ships.

"A scrap yard," said Manuel, eyes glued to his captive.

"The planetoid is known as Adam's Station," Ghost replied. "It appears to be a way station for miners. This little tick has bought parts there on occasion. Commander, we might be able to get the refurbished timeband and charge dispersers we need there ... even more toilet goop to replace the goop I used for thrust during our escape."

"We'll discuss it later," Noa said over the ether and aloud. James could feel the tension in her voice like needles on his skin.

Manuel shook the man he held. "What do we do with these scum?"

"We weren't going to hurt you," said the man Gunny held. "Just lookin' for scrap is all, to sell at Adam's Station. My boy Kline, he gots some vivid imagination, but we would not have let him do no harm."

Squirming, the man Manuel held said, "Really, we couldn't hear your hails."

"Shut up!" Gunny growled. "You're lying through your bleeding gums."

"Of course they're lying," Noa said, her lip curling in a snarl. "But we don't want to upset the Guild."

James opened his mouth, prepared to argue, but before he could utter a word, Manuel growled. "You saw what they wanted to do to Hisha! These men don't deserve to live."

Gunny and Noa were silent. For a moment James didn't understand Manuel's outburst. The man hadn't thought of Manuel's wife. And then he realized Manuel had done exactly what he'd done with the indistinct face of the rape victim in Kline's mind. James glanced up at

Manuel. The engineer's face was livid, there was spittle on his lower lip, his bangs that had fallen in front of his eyes were wet with sweat. He looked crazed, half-mad, and James had never felt so much connection to him.

Face pressed to the floor, Kline, the man under James, snickered. "Guess we know who daddy is."

The man Manuel held whined and wiggled. Manuel stunned him in the side of the neck. As he slid to the floor, Manuel spun in place looking for all the world like he was about to drive a foot into Kline's head.

"Stand down, Officer," Noa said, her voice hushed.

Manuel's head whipped to her.

Over the ether she said, "The Guild … we can't take them all."

Manuel's nostrils flared. But he took a step back.

Gunny, eyes focused on the man he had pinned, drawled, "Commander's right."

Kline snickered again. Noa turned to Kline, and James hated the light in Kline's eyes when he looked at her.

Unfazed, Noa smiled wider than James had ever seen. "Think that's funny?" Her head tilted. "I'm going to give you something to *really* laugh about." The smile stretched wider still, and her eyes narrowed and her nostrils flared slightly.

The hungry, mocking look on Kline's face evaporated, even though James hadn't exerted any pressure on his arm.

"Strip them," Noa said to Gunny. "I want all their weapons." She tapped her chin. "And just to be sure they don't have anything really special, don't give them their clothes back."

The man under Gunny's stunner whimpered.

To Manuel she said, "Lieutenant, I don't believe we have proper hand restraints."

"No, Commander, we don't," Manuel said, scowling down at Kline.

"Huh ..." Noa rubbed her chin. "Duct tape will have to do, won't it?"

Manuel's eyes met hers. "Yes, Commander, I believe a sufficient quantity might suffice." A thin smile touched his lips.

"Stun them all," Noa said. "I don't want accidents."

As Gunny and James stunned the men they'd captured, her eyes went to the first man James had knocked unconscious—the one with the "hard-on." He was now slouched against the wall, a bloody smear behind his head, though the faint whisper of a heartbeat told James he wasn't dead.

Her jaw hardened. "Manuel, you're with me," she said, even as her eyes fell to James. James tried to gauge her mood. Was she angry at him for so violently containing the man? Did she think him psychotic? Her lips parted, and he saw the glint of her teeth clenched tight, and then over the ether, he felt the buzz of her consciousness. But she said and thought nothing as she spun on her heel and exited.

The unthought words in that buzz were a wall between them, a muffled silence, and he suddenly felt cold. He couldn't speak to her across the ether; it might be overheard. He couldn't beg her to let him dispatch their foes, or beg forgiveness if that was what was required. He looked down at the now unconscious Kline. The chill seeping along his spine made James feel heavy, like killing Kline would be too much effort ... he jerked away from the unconscious man, but couldn't take his eyes away from him.

His mind began replaying a 20th century argument against the death penalty: when a foe could be adequately subdued, the death penalty was murder. He'd agreed wholeheartedly with that assessment. Or the other him had. Every person might be a culture unto themselves, but his internal culture had changed—was changing—radically. He was an alien to himself.

Noa stood beside the pilot chair, too keyed up to sit down. Above her head asteroids hung in silent suspension; they looked like an avalanche in slow motion. Occasionally, one in a faster orbit would tumble by, catching Noa's eye and making her head jerk from the monitor screens spread out before her.

Kuin, one of Manuel's engineering students, was sitting in the copilot's chair, tapping out a rhythm with his fingers, eyes warily scanning the view port. Noa's brow furrowed. Manuel had only recruited augmented students for the trip. She didn't actually know what Kuin's augmentation was, or the augmentations of the other students: Kara, Bo, and Jun. She barely knew her crew. She exhaled, and a movement in the monitors caught her eyes. She gazed down at the scene just outside the Ark. Manuel and Ghost were in their space suits, awkwardly tethered to the Ark by long umbilicals of nylon, copper, and Kevlar. They were pulling the time-band from its casing. From her vantage point, the alloy of rare metals looked like nothing so much as bright silver tape, a child's toy. Manuel's voice filtered through the cipher. "We're almost done, Commander."

"Thank you, Lieutenant, Ghost. Well done."

Her eyes dropped to the monitor that showed the tick, still attached to the Ark. Squinting, she could make out Gunny and the engineering students bustling around the tick's cabin.

She wanted to command her people back into the ship, order the tick's computer to release its hold on the Ark's airlock ... and not to seal the small craft completely. She wanted to let the men, mummified in their duct tape cocoons, die slowly, in fear and pain, as their air was ripped slowly away. Her fingernails bit into her palms, Kline's "imagination" replaying in her mind. The indistinct face disturbed her as much as the rape. She'd met plenty of men like Kline, knew she was less than human to them by virtue of being female. She believed strongly you couldn't argue with crazy—which didn't mean she didn't want to see them burn.

There was a low purr behind and below her, and she turned to see the lift to the bridge blooming open. James was standing there. A delayed snarl, from her previous thoughts, escaped her lips.

His head drew back as though she'd struck him. She shook her head, caught sight of Kuin, neck craned around his seat, staring at her with wide eyes. With a jerk, the engineering student spun back around. She sighed and gave James a shrug. "Sorry," she mumbled. *Can't talk about it,* remained unsaid.

James's expression remained flat. Was he angry at her? A Luddeccean man would be—for her not well-disguised reluctance to see him part of the "greeting party" and then her dismissal of his plan. His plan that in hindsight worked brilliantly; no one on the Ark seriously wounded, and only one of the invaders grievously hurt. The one James had attacked had gotten the worst of it ... she blinked. She swore she'd heard one of the invaders exclaim that a stunner hadn't worked. Her jaw got tight. A misfire? She'd thought she'd seen a brief burst of light shimmering along James's side ... it reminded her of something, but she couldn't quite place what. She must have misheard. She felt a prickle along her spine anyway.

Climbing the staircase, James stopped on the step just below her, putting him at eye level. He lifted his hand, fist closed, palm down. Her eyes went to it, almost reluctantly; she was still trying to get a read on him. He turned his fist up and opened his fingers. The iridescent shimmer of a data chip caught her eye. If they weren't being eavesdropped on, she would have said, *You shouldn't have.* At the same time, part of her wanted to make jests. Her mother's words rang in her mind, *Don't take data chips from strangers.* Her eyes met James's, and for a moment she hesitated. She couldn't say why. They'd hard-linked before; this should be nothing. Irritated by her indecision, she whisked the chip from his palm, plugged it into one of her ports, and blinked as an indicator light went on in her mind.

Mentally, reaching for the chip was like trying to think about a particular square centimeter of her head. She found the chip and James's professor avatar burst into her visual cortex, looking oddly formal in his high-necked tunic, fitted trousers, and gleamingly polished shoes. The James in front of her wore a perfectly bland expression, but his avatar smiled tightly. "I have a cipher no one will ever guess."

Noa let her mind explore the chip and found *The*

Tale of Genji — a 21st Century Annotated Translation.

"A little light reading?" she said aloud.

"That is not in the ship's database," James said.

Her eyes widened as she found her visual cortex filled with scanned yellowed pages of an actual *book*. Numbers started firing rapidly into her mind as her apps converted all the photographed pages from images to digitized words that could be rapidly searched.

"Absolute privacy," James's avatar said. "This version was never added to the public ethernet archives."

His avatar flashed away and she was staring at the real James. "It was something I planned to do before the accident." He looked at a point on the floor. "I'm not sure why I didn't ... it was an easy thing ... I put it in my personal time capsule and then ..." He shook his head.

He didn't seem angry. She was relieved.

Into her mind he spoke through the new cipher. "You seem ... tense. A grain of rice for your thoughts?"

It took a moment for her to process the Heian Japanese equivalent of "a penny for your thoughts." It was funny, but she couldn't bring herself to smile. "I want to murder some people," she confessed through their secret cipher. A long breath escaped her, and a weight lifted from her chest.

His brows rose in real life; he looked beyond her to the monitor showing the tick. His jaw shifted. "I find I'm divided on that." His professor avatar looked at Noa and said, "In my other life I always argued that the death penalty had no place."

Noa snorted. Aloud she said, "It has a place in combat."

"But is this combat?" James's avatar said, putting its hands behind its back. "They are technically not part of an organized fighting force. There are many arguments against the death penalty: its perceived effectiveness, problems inherent in guaranteeing a fair trial, to ..." James stopped using the cipher, and the real James said aloud, "... *ad hominem tu quoque*—"

Noa scowled at the unfamiliar language.

In full professor mode, James's avatar waved a hand and explained, "Two wrongs don't make a right. Some people would say that advocating death in instances when it is not immediately necessary for self-defense makes the executioner just as guilty as the criminal, at least in circumstances where their continued imprisonment can be guaranteed."

Noa's jaw ground. Aloud she said, "Philosophy doesn't interest me, only practicalities. Allow them to live and Kline will go on pulling his stunts on people less able to defend themselves. But we can't kill them; they're members of the Guild. Mining guilds can't allow their members to be executed without fair trial."

"Gunny said sometimes that doesn't even stop them," mumbled James.

Noa acknowledged that by pinching the bridge of her nose. "If they don't fight back against perceived injustice, their members would withdraw and they'd lose their dues." She huffed. "Technically, we've claimed the Ark for the Galactic Fleet, but we don't even have enough officers aboard for a proper Fleet field trial. I doubt they'd accept it."

Eyes sweeping back to hers, James said aloud, "And duct taping them naked to the seats won't cause the Guild to seek revenge?"

Noa snapped her hands behind her back and felt her nails bite into her wrists. She heard a chair squeak and knew Kuin was paying extra attention now. "I'm banking on the situation giving the Guild a laugh, and allowing them to let it slide. Guilds don't like to exact revenge, it's expensive."

"Not very reassuring." James's voice was dry.

She shook her head; second guessing was the enemy of action. Tim would say, "General Custer thought that way, too." But the Ark's crew wasn't so much the cavalry as the Native Americans in this case.

James ducked his head. Across the ether, in his cipher, he whispered, "Noa, I care more about you—us—than about philosophical inquiries into what constitutes murder. I think that might be ... wrong."

So professorial. It relieved her for some reason. "Welcome to the real world," she said.

He huffed. "Is it?"

Before she had a chance to ask what he meant, Manuel's voice cracked across the shared channel. "Commander, we're aboard!"

"Are we going to go to Adam's Station?" Kara, the shy engineering student, thought across the general channel. Noa felt a jolt of emotion itching to explode into her neural net with Kara's thoughts. Noa didn't let the emotion enter in pure form, but she let her apps digest and identify it. It was excitement.

"Oh, I'm sorry!" Kara thought. "I didn't meant to feel —think—that aloud. My apps need a reboot, I think."

"Are we going there?" said Kuin quickly, spinning around in his seat.

Ghost spoke over the ether. "If we could purchase a refurbished timeband and dispersers, we could shave months off our trip."

"We could also get more toilet goop!" said Kuin excitedly. "Ejecting that for thrust during our escape was brilliant ... but we had to turn off half of the toilets on the ship."

Noa touched her neural interface, trying to block out the young engineer's enthusiasm.

"We'd also be announcing ourselves to thousands," Manuel said over the general channel.

"The Luddeccean Guard is busy minding Time Gate 8. They won't send out the armada against us," said Ghost. "We're gone. We're not their problem anymore."

James's eyes met Noa's. His jaw ticked. She could feel the weight of his gaze. The Luddeccean Guard had special interest in him ... and her. Under his breath, James said, "That's a lot to hope for. They seem ... obsessive."

Noa let out a breath, remembering the party the Guard sent to find her and James after her escape from the prison camp. Her eyes went to the monitor showing the tick. "But we're not safe here, either."

"No," James said softly.

Noa rubbed her jaw. To the ether at large she said, "If we go to this ... Adam's Station ... we'll need to pay for our supplies. What are we going to use?"

"We could sell 6T9," Ghost suggested.

"No!" snapped Eliza over the ether.

"6T9 won't buy us timebands and the dispersers," Manuel replied, sounding tired.

A movement in the periphery of Noa's vision made her glance at James's avatar, still alight in her mind. He was frowning. It was so strange to see so much emotion in James. "What's wrong?" she asked him. She expected some rational objection, or an idea for something to sell, but James's avatar shrugged. "I don't know."

Manuel's thoughts cut through the shared channel.

"We also have a lot of empty cabins. We could take out any extra metal and sell it for scrap—and with 6T9 ..."

"No one is selling 6T9," Noa hissed across the channel. "Eliza needs him, and so do you, Manuel. He's your number one babysitter. Any other ideas besides scrap?"

Eliza chirped up. "If they have lightbeam access to Libertas, I have one million Libertas credits in the Libertas System 8 Bank."

The ether went silent. Pivoting on his heels, James raised a brow in Noa's direction. "Libertas is the only planet in this system that is completely self-sufficient. Their credits might actually be worth something."

Noa let out a huff of relief. "Yes, it might ..." Over the ether, she said, "Eliza, how do you have a million Libertas credits?"

"Arbitrage," 6T9 answered for her, sounding terribly proud. "She has accounts in several systems."

"Why?" said Noa, shaking her head.

"I'm Jewish," Eliza said across the ether. "We remember it's always important to be able to leave."

Noa opened her mouth—and her mind—prepared to say that there had never been any anti-Semitic movements on Luddeccea in 300 years, and then she caught herself. The lesson held if you didn't toe the party line. Her eyes slid to James. Or *couldn't* toe the party line because you were hyper-augmented.

"Good plan," said Manuel across the ether. "Commander, a million Libertas credits should be enough—even if there has been inflation since ..."

Ghost chimed in, "The sooner we get lightspeed, the better."

Gunny's thoughts entered the ether. "It's the best option, Commander."

Noa crossed her arms and looked at James. "There aren't any good options," she murmured.

James shook his head. "No."

"We'll head to Adam's Station," Noa said. "Ghost, could you—"

"I'm sending you a course now, Commander," her computing officer said. "It's pieced together with the most recent map of the belt I could find." A 3D map of the region started playing before her eyes. It showed the Ark's current location and known asteroids delineated by solid blue lines and suspected asteroids outlined by dashed lines. Noa rolled back on her feet. She had no idea that the Ark's computer could devise something so complex ... it hadn't even been able to tell her which timeband had been malfunctioning ... and Ghost said it wouldn't be secure against the tick ... yet he had been able to break into the tick's computer easily enough. She shook her head. The first could be a problem in the local circuitry around the malfunctioning band, and the second could be because the Ark hadn't had ethernet capabilities originally. The local ether they did have was new and bound to have peculiarities. "Thank you, Ghost," Noa said, swinging into her pilot chair.

There was a chorus of "yes" over the ether. And Ghost, sounding excited as anyone else, said, "We could find some interesting tech in that yard."

"Engineers," Noa huffed, not without affection.

She caught Kuin grinning happily in the corner of her eye. "You're dismissed," she said to him.

As he scampered away, James took his place. He wasn't as excited as the engineers. Neither was Noa. To reassure him, or herself, Noa said, "If the Guard sent a small squadron into the belt and to Adam's Station to try and retrieve us, it could turn ugly for them. Their jurisdiction isn't recognized out here ... most of the inhabitants in this system who aren't denizens of Luddeccea don't like the Luddeccean Authority."

"I'm not saying we're not choosing the least bad option," James said.

Noa gripped the steering bars, but her shoulders fell. She reached out to Ghost across the ether. "Ghost, as soon as we're close enough, could you check the public lightbeam transmissions to see if the Guard has put a bounty on us?"

His reply was instantaneous, and his tone was unctuous. "Of course, Commander!"

Over the ether, directly to her channel, with their own private Genji cipher, James mused, "Ghost is very helpful when his interests align with everyone else's."

"What's that, Professor Sinclair?" Ghost asked.

Noa's and James's eyes met. Ghost shouldn't be listening to their private channels, but as they suspected, he *was* listening in. Noa gave James a wry smile. He tipped his head.

"Oh ... oh ..." Ghost said. "I see, that was a private comment. I've been trying to monitor all channels since our guests arrived ... I'm sorry to intrude."

Noa's lips pursed. Plausible ... but Noa didn't believe him for a moment. Instead of calling him out on it, she said, "Good thinking, Ghost."

"Ready to release the tick, Commander," said Gunny.

"Let it go," said Noa. There was a soft sound from the hull as the craft released. The hairs on back of Noa's neck stood on end. She sucked in a long breath and shivered. In the periphery of her vision she saw James turn to her.

"How long will Ghost's interests align with ours?" he said aloud, tapping his armrest.

She shifted in her seat, and couldn't meet his gaze. "Hopefully, a really long time."

CHAPTER FOUR

James sat in the co-pilot seat watching scarred and pock-marked asteroids drift above the ship. Seemingly caught in the current of a lazy river, the asteroids were actually moving at speeds close to 35,000 km per hour; they just appeared to move slowly relative to the Ark.

At any moment, they might be spotted by the Luddeccean sensors. A fighter-carrier could arrive within minutes. But over the uneventful hours, James's emotions had passed from fear to fascination with their cold, silent neighbors, to a state of boredom that was close to putting him to sleep.

Everything was relative ... not just physics. His lips wanted to quirk, but couldn't. He huffed in frustration, and then a blue glow on one of the larger rocks caught his eye. Leaning forward, he whispered, "What?"

"Hmmm ... We're almost there," Noa said. Across the ether, she called out, "Ghost, can you plug into the public board yet?"

"Still out of range, Commander," Ghost replied. "Or the asteroids are in the way."

James's eyes remained fixated on the glow. As they approached, it took form. "Is that a neon sign?"

"Sure," said Gunny. "Can't expect business out here to just find you."

The sign became large enough to make out neatly rendered words: *Eat, Drink, Have a Good Time. Full gravity and showers!* There were also outlines of a fork, a glass, and a woman and man pressed very close together, gyrating their hips.

The neon sign passed them by, and James craned his head to watch it disappear. A shadow blocked his view for a moment. He blinked and it was gone.

He turned down to the monitors, perhaps too quickly, because Noa asked in an alarmed-sounding voice, "What is it?"

Quickly surveying the monitors, James shook his head. "I thought I saw something move. But no one's out there, not on the screens or temperature gauges."

"Scan the frequencies for contact," Noa said. "Gunny, try to get a visual."

James played with the dials of the ancient comm station and got nothing. It had been so easy to contact Time Gate 8—maybe because they wanted to be contacted? Searching the frequencies, he got static, but then he lifted his eyes and saw another shadow temporarily blot the stars. It had a thick body and long legs. The shadow disappeared, but he'd seen enough. James projected the image over the ether, and Gunny said, "A tick. It's hopping rock to rock. I think it might be following us."

Noa called out over the same channel, "Ghost, do you have contact yet?"

Another shadow dipped below the ecliptic plane and

the asteroids, and then another, and then they both darted back up and behind an asteroid.

James's hand paused on the comm controls. "Two more."

"Ghost," Noa said. "We've got company! They're mighty curious and evasive. Any contact with the station yet?"

"I'm trying, Commander! The asteroids are blocking our signals," Ghost replied.

"Too much like Six," Gunny muttered. James glanced at his companions and noticed Gunny was breathing heavily and his brow was damp with sweat, and Noa's chest was rising and falling too fast.

A loud thump sounded from the direction of their feet and James felt the faintest of vibrations in his seat.

"Chavez, your side, meters from the stern," Noa said without glancing at any read-outs. James looked at the monitor. There was a tick moving up the hull, looking like an enormous mechanical spider.

"I see it," Chavez responded. In his monitor, James saw the helmet and shoulders of Chavez's space suit appear, one of the small cannons they'd "re-appropriated" from the "scavengers" on her shoulder. The weapon's recoil dampener at the end of the stock was already primed and glowing blue. Inside the Ark, it was heavy and cumbersome, but the ship's gravity didn't extend outside the hull, and Chavez aimed it at the tick in an easy motion.

Ghost's voice came over James's shoulder. "Fire, woman, don't be an idiot!"

Chavez's voice cracked again across the ether. "Commander?"

"Fire," Noa said.

In the monitor James saw a brief beam of plasma fire, the surge of the recoil dampener, and then implosion with the tick. Sparks shimmered along the body of the smaller vessel. The tick's legs convulsed, and it let go of the Ark's keel. Chavez hit it with another bolt of plasma and the small vessel drifted backward from the force of the burst.

James almost breathed a sigh of relief but his eyes went from the monitors to the skylight. Heat flared along his spine. Before them, shadows were blotting out the stars, appearing to crawl over one another in open space, a cloud of writhing black bodies. Gunny swore under his breath. Noa inhaled sharply.

"There are lots more of them!" Chavez said.

James looked back to the monitors. More ticks were falling out of the asteroids behind them.

"Blow a hole through them with a cannon," Ghost said.

The Ark's cannon was enough to destabilize the massive fighter carriers of the Luddeccean Guard's Armada. It would turn the ticks into dust. But ...

"The forward cannon wouldn't take out the ones behind us," James whispered. "They'd swarm us."

"Commander?" Gunny said.

"Hold your fire," said Noa.

A silence settled in the ether and the bridge. It seemed to stretch for years—but James's chronometer apps registered it as only three minutes.

"Commander," Ghost said, "I really think—" Before he could finish the thought, the ticks immediately in front of the ship cleared a path.

"What are they doing?" Gunny said.

James's eyes widened. They'd moved so suddenly, en masse. "They have to be communicating," he said, scanning the channels, searching for the frequency they were utilizing. A burst of static and fragmented words assailed his ears.

"Ghost, we have to be in range of the station's local ether. Find out what they have on us!" Noa ordered.

The static under James's fingertips faded out and then rushed to life again. He looked over the ancient control dials for a way to augment the signal.

"I think I've got something!" Ghost said. "Very faint."

James found a tiny knob with all of its numbers and letters rubbed away. He turned it slowly. The dash cracked, and a wave of voices burst forth, for a moment giving him flashbacks to the confrontation with Time Gate 8. But then the signal stabilized and the voices were noticeably human.

"I'm in Adam's Station's ether!" Ghost exclaimed. "Scanning the public boards now, Commander."

"If we find out they've got a bounty on us, we're not going to be able to run far," Gunny muttered.

"I thought you approved of this plan," Noa said.

"It was the best option, not a good option," Gunny muttered.

Through the dash burst voices. "Unknown ship, unknown ship, come in, come in."

"Do you need some repairs? We'll trade repairs for food."

"I'll trade anything for food."

"Need a guide to the belt? We can help."

There was a buzz of static and James heard, "Don't fire ... if they have rations, don't want to blow them to bits ..."

"Please help us find passage to Libertas. Will work for food and passage." The last one rang with desperation and then the bridge was flooded with more, "We'll work for food," over and over again. A baby's cry cracked through the comm, and a child's voice. "I'm hungry, Papa." James watched the nest of spider-like vessels converging in a massive cloud of shadows.

"Turn it off," Noa said, her voice cold and level.

James turned off the radio and silence fell over the bridge.

Gunny whispered, "Damn. Ticks depend on places like Adam's Station for supplies ... but why are they congregating like that? And why aren't they landing?"

Jaw tight, eyes focused straight ahead, Noa said, "They're too small for the trip to Libertas, so they're waiting here ... but as to why they aren't landing ... I have a feeling we're about to find out."

James found himself looking toward Luddeccea. The planet looked like a small blue star at this distance. "Luddeccea has cut off all off-world trade. Only Libertas is also self-sufficient in this system ... barely," he mused aloud. "They won't be exporting goods. Does Adam's Station even have enough food for them?"

Gunny exhaled loudly.

Noa reached to James through the ether and whispered, "My heart is breaking for them."

James should have empathy, but all he felt was a need to further gauge the situation and an acute sense that he had too little data.

"Commander," Ghost said over the ether, interrupting his thoughts. "There are no public calls for our apprehension."

For a moment James felt a lightness in his chest, but then, in an acid voice, Noa said, "Maybe they put out more discreet inquiries as to our whereabouts."

"I'll see what I can find," said Ghost.

James started plundering relevant historical data on food scarcity and violence, and discovered the French Revolution and the Syrian uprising of the early 21st century.

There was a soft swish behind him. James craned his head around his seat and saw Eliza and 6T9 at the bottom of the circular stairwell that surrounded the lift platform. Leaning on her cane and the 'bot, the old woman panted, "Noa ... If we're ... docking ... I'm negotiating the fees!"

"What?" said Noa, sounding startled but not angry. And then she blinked. "Do you think you're in shape to haggle?"

Indeed, Eliza was wavering as she climbed the stairs, even with 6T9's arm and her cane to prop her up. Reaching the top, she thumped her cane beside Noa's seat. "I'll be fine just as soon as I ... catch my breath. And you aren't a good negotiator ... dear."

Noa raised an eyebrow. "I am a good negotiator!"

Across the ether came a sort of hiccup as Ghost's consciousness blinked in and out.

"How much did you pay Ghost?" Eliza demanded, tone suddenly sharp.

Noa drew back, so James responded. "30,000 Galactic Credits."

Thumping her chest, Eliza broke into a coughing fit.

"Eliza," 6T9 said, his voice an eerie facsimile of worry. "Perhaps you do need rest—"

"I'm coughing because I'm indignant. That was far too much!" Eliza cried.

6T9 smiled, apparently accepting her reasoning, and nodded. "Highway robbery," the 'bot agreed and James's eyebrow rose in shock at the correct use of the idiom. His lip wanted badly to twitch ... it was probably good it couldn't, because Noa was frowning, and her brows were drawn together.

"I'm fit to haggle with anyone!" Eliza said.

Across the ether, Noa shouted through their cipher, "She's practically falling over; she can't negotiate."

James raised an eyebrow. Eliza was prescient enough to keep money off-world. And James had thought Ghost's fees had seemed exorbitant. James stood up from his seat. "Here, take my chair, it's close to the comm."

Noa's eyes narrowed at him. James pretended not to notice.

As Eliza slid into his chair, 6T9 smoothed Eliza's hair tenderly. Eliza briefly smiled at the 'bot, but then turned to Noa and hissed, "It's my money!"

Noa's shoulders sank. "You're right, it is. You can negotiate the docking fees."

"Commander," Ghost said across the ether, "I don't see anything that looks like it might be an open contract sponsored by Luddeccea's Guard."

"That's some comfort," Noa sighed. Other sighs echoed over the shared line.

Ahead ticks dropped from the belt into their path and then departed like wisps of smoke. The Ark rounded a final asteroid decorated with neon signs and a planetoid came into view. Approximately half the size of Earth's moon, it was slightly donut-shaped and encircled with an artificial ring that gave it the appearance of wearing a thick belt.

"It's got some mighty big airlockers," Noa said. "For a place this remote."

"Airlockers?" James asked.

"Fancy name for berths," said Gunny. "In the middle

section, the belt that looks like it's sucking in the plane-toid's gut."

James squinted and noticed the "belt" had what appeared to be hangar doors along the outside. On either side of the belt, James saw domes and hundreds of neon signs flashing on the planetoid's surface where it wasn't writhing with ticks.

Blinking lights above the planetoid caught James's eye. Lifting his gaze he saw some older shuttles painted blue and white, flying in groups of threes.

"Local enforcers," grunted Gunny.

"James, turn the comm back on," Noa said.

James flicked the dial and an officious voice filled the bridge. "Unidentified ship, you will not be allowed to dock unless you have your own rations. Repeat, unidenti-fied ship, you will not be able to dock unless you have your own rations. Payment for any services rendered will be in rations ..." the message began to repeat.

"Now we know why the ticks aren't docking," James said. They didn't have the docking fee—food.

"At least we don't have to worry about the old woman's negotiating skills," Ghost grumbled.

"I'm still doing the negotiating!" Eliza said.

James glanced at Noa. Her eyes were riveted on the scene unfolding outside the ship. "The ticks are well-behaved around the enforcers," Noa murmured. "As these things go, this should be safe enough."

James's skin felt too cool, and his vision began to tunnel. Watching the ticks crawl over the planetoid and the husks of older ships, he had a bad feeling, like wading slowly into icy water. To no one in particular he said aloud and across the ether, "Hungry people are never safe."

There was an uncomfortable pause.

He heard Gunny take a deep breath and Eliza gulp. But Noa grinned and said aloud and across the ether, "Well, gee, James, I guess you would know!" Gunny chuckled, Eliza giggled, the ether crackled laughter, and Ghost even kidded, "He stole my peanut butter!" James would have laughed too if he could have. He felt as though his neural net had been rebooted.

Looking around the bridge, 6T9 smiled, nodded sagaciously, and exclaimed, "Don't count your bedbugs before they hatch."

The bridge went completely silent.

Noa stood beside a pallet loaded with S-rations just inside one of the Ark's air locks. It was half of their payment, the other half was in Luddeccean credits ... but these had seemed more important to the flight control who had directed them to land. Calorie dense, about the size of Noa's palm, the hermetically sealed bars kept for decades, and each one represented a day's rations for an active man. She shifted on her feet. Her mouth tasted like the stim gum she'd spit out minutes before. Without the time-bands, the journey to Adam's Station had been at 21st century speeds and taken over ten hours, and they'd had the encounter with the tick before that ... Her mind jumped to her chronometer app, but before it told her how far she should be into her sleep cycle she ruthlessly shut it down.

Shaking her head, she looked over at James standing on the opposite side of the pallet. He had a ration open in his hand and he was eating it like a candy bar, claiming it as his "second breakfast." Maybe an S-ration was enough for a *normal* man.

Noa cocked her head, amazed that he was actually biting through the tough material. Normally, S-rations were soaked in liquid first. Without softening, they had the texture of shoe leather. Well, he did have an augmented jaw—one that was broken and couldn't smile or frown. It was odd that it didn't seem to be malfunctioning when it came to eating.

Holding up the bar, James licked his lips. "What? You said that we have more than enough."

Before Noa could respond, Eliza and 6T9 stepped into the airlock from the ship side. The old woman poked James with her cane. "You do not mention we have plenty! Do you know how hard I haggled to get them to take no more than a pallet load of these things?"

Before the system's time gate had been shut down and Luddeccea had suspended intersystem traffic, a pallet of shoe-leather-hard S-rations wouldn't have been worth much, even out here. Now they were worth more than even Libertas credits. The rations in front of Noa represented the docking fee, but the Ark had plenty more ... If Noa's tiny crew couldn't open the time gate in the Kanakah Cloud, they could make it to System 7's time gate with some to spare. In this new order, the members of the Ark were rich. She stood a little straighter.

Eliza spun to Noa. "And don't look so confident when you talk to the station administrator! They'll come up with extra fees if they sense you have more to give!"

"Look so confident?" said Noa.

"Don't look like you know where your next meal is coming from!" Eliza snapped. Slouch your shoulders, stoop your back."

Manuel stepped into the airlock carrying a tool case, and Gunny followed him. At a meter away Noa could smell stim gum on their breath.

Eliza tapped her chin and eyed the gunnery sergeant. "Nothing we can do to hide that beer gut."

Looking morose, Gunny patted his impressive girth and sniffed sadly. "It's shrinking."

"It's almost time," said James. Noa gave him a tiny nod; her own chronometer was telling her that their scheduled disembarkation was close.

"Ghost, are you working on augmenting our ether hotspot so we'll have transmission ability inside this rock?" Noa asked. The 'rock' had its own ethernet hotspots—but Noa didn't want her team to use it. Besides the risk that it wasn't secure and they could all get headaches, their hosts could turn off their access at the worst possible moment.

There was no response. "Ghost?" He was supposed to be in engineering. Noa looked for him on the ship's locator and blinked. She turned around just in time to see the lift open down the hall through the inner airlock. Ghost came jogging forward, a satchel clutched in one hand. "Commander," he gasped. "I thought, well, these rocks are hard on normal signals." He dropped the satchel and it squeaked. Ghost jumped, the satchel burst open, and Carl Sagan hopped out. "What are you doing in there?" Ghost said as the werfle darted between Noa's legs.

"Never mind," Noa said, "What have you got us?"

Ghost pulled out what Noa first thought were a few finger-sized, regularly-shaped oval rocks. He handed her one. It was *warm* and covered in what appeared to be lumpy gray paint.

Ghost cleared his throat. "Touch up paint from the Ark's storage area. Very old, that's why it's bubbly, but I think it looks more realistic—like a rock."

"What are these?" asked Manuel.

Ghost coughed, and his cheeks flushed. "Well, the Ark doesn't have ethernet hotspots—not really—but this ship has relay stations that the original Luddecceans used for their old archaic comm devices. I re-rigged them for ethernet. I put a bit of bonding putty on these, and painted them to be less conspicuous." His brows furrowed. "I don't think I'll be able to optimize my Luddy-rigged ether hotspots on the Ark to keep you in range." His face turned red. "And I don't want to have to debug anyone foolish enough to plug into this Station's network! It's not secure and crawling with bugs!"

Noa turned the ovoid device around in her hand. Even at fairly close distance it would pass as rubble. "Well done, Ghost," she said, impressed and touched by his initiative more than she'd like to admit.

Ghost waved a hand. "It was nothing."

Noa raised an eyebrow. Odd for him to be modest.

Outside the hull came a loud thunk, and over the ethernet a voice said, "Sato and crew, please open your airlock."

Ghost backed toward the hallway, eyes wide and on the outer door.

"Keep us informed of anything you hear over their public boards," Noa said.

Ghost didn't meet her gaze. His Adam's apple bobbed. "Believe me, Commander, I'll look into the public ones and *more*." His lower lip trembled. "I don't want to get stuck *here*."

That fear was why she didn't trust him. Noa gave him a tight smile.

Another thunk sounded on the hull, and the voice in the ether virtually shouted, "A failure to open your airlock will result in forced entry."

"It's time, Commander," said Manuel.

"6T9, take Eliza behind the airlock door," Noa ordered. Ghost was already nearly at the lift. 6T9 swung Eliza into his arms, and she cooed, "My knight in shining armor."

The 'bot exclaimed happily, "I have that app! And a caveman app, and a roman glad—" Noa closed the inner airlock as soon as they were out of the cramped space. Ignoring the looks on Gunny and Manuel's faces that clearly said, "We have heard too much," she said to James, "They'll probably want to check our cargo to make sure our docking fee is in order. Sometimes the inspectors are a little cranky."

She waved at Gunny and he pressed the buttons that opened the outer seals.

There was the whir of mechanicals, a whoosh, and Noa was staring down the barrels of six rifles held by men in heavy armor. One of the rifles jerked and its owner screamed, "Hands above your heads!"

CHAPTER FIVE

The five armed men stormed into the airlock, rifles raised.

James had the sensation of being out of his body, or out of his mind. His eyes took in the invaders' mismatched armor, the odd assortment of weapons, and their poor form. His apps calculated the feasibility of lifting the rifle of the nearest, driving the stock into the man's face, pushing up the CO_2 converting mask, and then bludgeoning him one more time before dropping behind the S-rations and firing at the others ...

Noa's voice cut off this chain of thought. "Everyone, you heard them, hands up!"

Gunny and Manuel complied. After a second's hesitation, during which James marveled at how unlike his old self those mental plans had been, he lifted his hands, too, and his gaze slid to Noa.

Her eyes were locked on the man with a stun rifle closest to her. The end of the weapon was visibly shaking, and less than two hand spans from her face. Carl Sagan was hissing at her feet. James felt heat rushing under his skin. Stunners worked by very briefly overloading the nervous system. A blast directly to the head at such close range was fatal in approximately 21.2% of incidents. James's vision went black, his hands made fists above his head, and he felt like he was standing on the edge of a cliff. He stepped sideways toward Noa and the man confronting her.

"What are you doing!" shouted one of the invaders.

James barked into the blackness. "Lower your weapon!"

There was a click. The blackness receded, and suddenly Noa's guard had his weapon pointed at James's head instead. "Think you're tough?" he shouted.

"Easy!" the woman said. "You had it pointed at her head, Deek."

"Now it's pointed at your head, tough guy! Do you feel better?" Deek shouted.

James's jaw shifted. He eyed the trembling muzzle, remembered the surge he'd felt when he'd been stunned before, and had the oddest desire to lick his lips.

His gaze slid to Noa, and he found her dark brown eyes already on him, her lips slightly parted. She gave him the tiniest of nods. A sixth man stepped into the airlock, and Noa's eyes snapped to a handheld scanning device the new man was carrying. It had no visible controls or gauges on its smooth surface, so it must be ethernet-linked. Whatever the scanner was, Noa was clearly more afraid of it than of being shot. James suddenly wanted to know very much what the man was scanning.

James's left hand began to tremble. With the time gate's disablement, the local computer that supplied Adam's Station's ether was probably vulnerable. The Ark's computer could find the scanner's address, and then, given enough time, could probably decipher its access codes, and Ghost might be able to change its read-outs ... with time.

They needed the information *now*.

James had a sensation, like something snapping at the back of his mind. A bright light flashed behind his eyes, static roared in his ears, and then the white light became red and took on form. He was seeing the pixelated silhouettes of humans flashing in his visual cortex: four people holding their hands above their heads, a werfle at their feet, while five stood with rifles raised. The man changed the direction of the scanner and James saw a fainter image of a small child and a woman hunched over, holding his hand. The person closest to him shouted, "Freeze."

James's head ticked. He was distantly aware of Noa's eyes flashing in his direction. He was somehow seeing what the man accessing the scanner was seeing. That was impossible ... the man changed the direction of the scanner again, and James saw a rat running in the walls, and then he heard the man say, "I think this ship looks nearly empty ... but it could be shielded. I wouldn't board just yet."

James shivered. He had not heard with his ears; he had heard it with his mind through the man's ether access. "Get out of there," he heard another voice say over the channel. "Let's consult with Adam ... think he wants to keep the boat in one piece."

Noa cleared her throat. "Do you want to inspect our payment?"

The guard nearest Gunny said in a woman's voice, "Yeah, yeah, we need to do that."

Voice very level, Noa said, "Maybe you'd feel better if you took those out of our airlock to check them?"

James would feel better if they did. He needed to give

the scanner's ethernet channel to Ghost—the programmer might be able to change the life sign readings.

Craning his neck to look at Noa, the man still holding stunner rifle near James's face said, "Shut up!"

The woman said, "No, that's a good idea. We don't want to shoot them if they're legit. Don't want a bad reputation."

Another guard said, "Zara's right. Wheel it out of here, let Adam himself check it."

One of them wheeled the pallet backward and the rest began backing out. "Don't put your hands down!" said the man with the shaking muzzle trained on James. James tried to look beyond them, but all he could see was a wall of thick, semi-opaque plastic. The guards were standing on a platform of some kind. More plastic slid between the Ark and the guards, and Noa said, "Shut the door."

As the Ark's seals slid tight, Noa's voice rang in his ears and over the ship's cipher. "Ghost, they had a life signs scanner—ether-linked. I need you to—"

Ghost's thoughts cut her off. "I saw it through the cameras, already got into it, trying to change the read-outs."

James inhaled sharply. How had Ghost hacked into the device so quickly with a computer as ancient as the Ark's? James's hand trembled. How had he himself managed it?

"I need at least a hundred heavily armed bodies aboard!" Noa said sharply.

"Aye, Commander," Ghost replied. "Working ..."

Noa spoke across the ether to the engineering students. "They had CO_2 converter masks on. Find some for us," and got a chorus of 'ayes.'

Gunny was frowning. "Those men were too on edge, Commander. Sure, inspectors in places like this get hassled a lot, but that was extreme. Seemed like they were expecting more than just fake S-rations."

Noa's body was still visibly tense, worry in her drawn brows. He was worried too, but winked at her with confidence he didn't feel, pulled out his half-eaten S-ration, and bit off a hunk. It was mostly fat and protein with the tang of artificially added vitamins.

It earned him a grim smile. "Hungry desperate people are dangerous," Noa said. "You guessed it, James."

Waggling his eyebrows, he licked his lips and raised an eyebrow.

Noa's shoulders unloosened a fraction.

A beep came over the Ark's ether—Ghost was running all channels from the station through a proxy server to catch viruses. "They're paging us," Noa said, touching her neural interface. Aloud and over the ether she said, "Commander Sato here."

"Commander Sato," a solicitous male voice responded over the public channel. "You and your crew are most welcome to disembark and go about your business here."

"Who am I speaking to?" Noa asked.

"Adam Selles," said the man. "I am the Director here at Adam's Station."

To the room at large, Noa muttered, "Ten to one that he makes jokes about them naming the Adam's Belt after him."

Adam continued, "They named the belt after me!"

James's eyebrows hiked to his hairline. Gunny and Manuel groaned and Noa rolled her eyes as the director laughed. Voice going abruptly somber, Adam said, "Actually, it was named by my great-great grandfather. I'll have to give you a tour."

"Really, how interesting ... and a tour would be very helpful," Noa said, in a smooth, professional voice, but at the same time her voice exploded over James's personal channel in their Genji cipher. "That clump of blue-green mud from the bottom of a garden pond! We don't need a tour. I don't like it, it's a trick of some kind." The Heian equivalent of blue-green algae, the difference between what she shared with the group and what she shared with him, both made James want to laugh, despite the danger her words implied and everything *else*. He also found it oddly ... touching ... in a way that made his nanos and neurons dance.

"Thank you for sharing that with me." He let an avatar respond with a smirk, but he meant the words.

In real life, Noa's eyes narrowed and slid to him. She gave him a tiny nod and he saw the hint of a smile. Over the general channel she said crisply, "Thank you, Adam."

Carl Sagan gave a hiss at her feet. Bending over, she scooped up the animal. "Not you, werfle." Carl Sagan gave an indignant squeak.

There was a thunk outside the hull. Gunny, closest to the door, didn't open it. "I don't like it, Commander. A director of a station this big doesn't have time to greet every ship personally."

Noa looked upward. The weak LED lights in the airlock gave her skin an unearthly blue cast. Gunny crossed his arms. "If they get hostile, we could threaten to self-destruct—"

James's vision went black.

Noa nodded. "Let's save that for the last possible option."

... and James could see again. Bo emerged from the inner door, and began handing out masks.

Adam's voice rang over the ether. "Commander?"

"We'll be right down," Noa replied.

James slipped his mask over his head and let it hang around his neck. With a strange certainty that seemed to permeate every nano and neuron in his body, he knew he didn't need it, and knew he didn't want the fact generally known ... just like he didn't want it known that he'd somehow accessed the scanner's ethernet channel. His eyes went to Noa, slipping her own mask around her neck. Her words replayed in his head, "It doesn't matter what you are." He could tell her about those abilities, and he would tell her. But not now.

Gunny pressed a button, and the outer airlock door slid open.

* * *

Noa stepped out of the Ark onto the plastitube-encircled lift platform with her team, feeling her body lighten in the slighter gravity. Behind her, she heard an angry squeak from Carl Sagan, a "no you don't," from the engineering student, and then the outer seal of the Ark swished shut with a whoosh.

The Ark was parked in an "air locker," a sort of stall for a singular spaceship, in the ring that encircled the asteroid. It was impressive, and a bit odd that the asteroid would have a locker large enough for the Ark. It was also lucky. A locker could be pressurized, unlike a regular berth, and they wouldn't have to wear bulky space suits to do their repairs ... if the ship weren't overrun by Adam's people, first. She had no idea if Adam was a democratically-elected head of the station or virtual king. In places like this, it could be either. She felt tension settling between her shoulder blades.

With a jerk, the lift started to descend. Her eyes slid to James, standing at her left. He was dragging a hand down the tube wall. "This wall is flexible ..." He touched a ten-centi junction band, and said, "And what is this?"

Gunny answered. "The plastitubing is flexible so that in the event a ship leaves in an unauthorized fashion, the tube collapses with the force of the vacuum and the junction seals tighten."

"They wind up hanging out of the locker looking like a used prophylactic in space," Manuel said, a tiny smile on his lips. He projected an image of a collapsed plastitube wagging in the solar breeze. James raised an eyebrow and his jaw shifted, Gunny snorted softly, and Noa felt the moment of levity returning her equilibrium.

The lift reached bottom, and a portion of the bottom segment of plastitube opened with an ear-popping change in pressure.

A short, squat, balding man stood before them in an impeccably tailored dark blue jacket and cream trousers that screamed expense. The neural interface in his temple was nearly the same hue as the suit and glowed blue. Noa assumed he was Adam. He was shadowed by a tall, thin woman with straight black hair. She was wearing a tight mini dress in the same shade of dark blue. She had a neural interface that had a diamond cover on it. But what really stood out were a pair of slowly fluttering silver fairy wings with tiny multi-colored lights along the veins. The wings weren't large enough to be functional; they were just an expensive cybernetic accessory.

The scanner tech stood next to the pair. Lined up

behind them were at least twenty guards. The short fat man came forward, smiling like a shark.

"Commander Sato, I'm Adam!" he said in an oily voice, and Noa practically expected him to lick his lips.

Noa held out a hand in anticipation of the handshake, but the scanner tech straightened, as though he'd been hit with an electric shock and Adam jerked back as though he'd been yanked by a leash. His eyes went to a point past her shoulder. Both had apparently just received ether news of something. The guards began to fan out around him and Noa's team, their rifles rising. Stunners and phasers, Noa noted.

Fixing her gaze straight ahead, Noa tried to keep her expression neutral. She wanted to reach out to Ghost, to see what was going on—but as if reading her thoughts, one of the guards, wearing rank insignia ribbons the like of which Noa had never seen before, shouted, "No ether to your ship!"

A few of his men shifted on their feet, and Noa resisted the urge to throw up her hands. Instead, she fastened them behind her back and tried to look merely annoyed instead of scared. Beside her, James whispered, "They've just realized that we have two hundred able-bodied men aboard the Ark."

"Silence!" said one of the guards.

Two hundred armed men? Aboard the Ark? Ghost had overdone his bit of scanner reprogramming wizardry. She blinked. How did James know that number? She hadn't heard it. She gave her head a tiny shake. Of course, he had augmented hearing.

Trying to get a lay of the land if this all went solar cores, she let her eyes wander around the dock. They were in the lower part of the artificial ring that surrounded the asteroid. This level was about five stories tall—newer than she expected. Plastitubes, some pulled up to the ceiling, and some dropped to the floor, were interspersed throughout the large bay. The space below the Ark's locker was cleared, but the rest of the floor was packed with smaller vessels: ticks and other ships too small to require their own private berths. The asteroid was barely a planetoid, and the horizon where the ceiling met the floor was disorientingly close. Just before the ceiling curved out of her view, she saw a large pair of sliding doors in the ceiling with a pair of up and down arrows—the symbol for the entrance-exit lock that the smaller vessels used. Cold radiated from the walls and ceiling of the dock. Probably not radiation shielded very well; that did not concern her so much ... what did concern her was that the pallet of S-rations they'd paid with had already been stripped bare.

There were a lot of rough-looking dockhands just outside the circle cleared by Adam and his men. Wearing worn, threadbare clothing, unshaven, they were leaning on crates, looking at her team. She was comforted by the sight of neural interfaces in their temples. She didn't see any ports with polyscrews jammed into them—the favorite "treatment" for ethernet access among the Luddecean Guard, and she didn't see hair combed over to disguise them either. It wasn't so comforting to see them eating S-rations directly from the package—noticeably with more difficulty than James had. The whispers of "dirty throwbacks" weren't reassuring, either.

The guard who'd warned her not to use the ether strode forward, and James took a step toward him, cutting off the angle of his phaser rifle. James's sleeves were rolled up, exposing ink black tattoos, his hands balled into fists.

"Lieutenant," said the heretofore silent woman. "I'm sure there's no need to frighten our guests."

Noa's eyes darted to the woman walking past Adam, his eyes glazed, his mind obviously in the ether. As she came forward, Noa noticed the woman's shins were too long in proportion to her thighs, her feet looked like they'd been shortened in a parody of Chinese footbinding and lifted at the heel. The wings might be functional after all —they helped the plasti-surgeried woman stay upright. The woman's face had undergone as much plasti-surgery as her body. Her eyes were pulled back in an exaggerated monolid, her lips were plasti-filled, her nose looked like it had been cheaply reconstructed, and her black hair showed lighter roots. Noa didn't think she looked human anymore. She could admit that opinion was highly influenced by her Luddeccean upbringing; but in this case, Noa thought the fundamentalists were right.

The woman held out a hand and said, "I'm Clara, Assistant Director of this station." Noa eyed the sharp points of Clara's long green-lacquered nails and kept her own hands behind her back. The woman tilted her head, narrowed her eyes, and smiled. "Suspect Crenalin-D, do you? Suspicious ... I like that."

Noa held the woman's gaze but didn't dignify that with a response. James edged closer to her, and Clara's eyes shifted. The smile dropped, and her tongue darted between her lips.

Adam strode forward abruptly, and Clara stepped aside, wings buzzing. "Commander Noa Sato," said Adam. "As in Commander Noa Sato of the Galactic Fleet, Commander Sato? First Officer of the Sugihara?"

"The same," Noa said with a tight smile.

"Errr ..." said Adam. He stood straighter and gathered

some of his former decorum. "Just what are you doing in Luddeccean space, Commander?" He looked beyond her toward the Ark and grimaced. "Aboard that ... Are you transporting refugees, perhaps?" The scowl between his brows vanished, his eyes widened, and Noa saw the ghost of a smile.

That was what he wanted to hear, obviously. Noa took a deep breath. "Well, in a sense ..."

Adam's eyes darted to the lieutenant. The lieutenant nodded, a tiny curve appearing at the corner of his own lips. Noa plowed on with the first bit of gibberish that came to mind. "... the nonsense on Luddeccea broke out just when members of my squadron and my sergeant's platoon ..." she inclined her head toward Gunny, "... and some of our other veteran buddies got together for a System Six Luddeccea Veterans Reunion."

Adam raised an eyebrow. "System Six ... veterans?" he said.

Gunny cleared his throat, sounding distinctly uneasy. Noa felt a bite of panic. Were there even 200 veterans of Six on Luddeccea? She doubted it.

Gunny gulped. "It's ... errr ... a thing ... we do ... every so often ..."

Noa didn't wince at his stutter. Instead, she gave him a tight nod. "And some veterans of Six who aren't from Luddeccea show up ..." Noa said quickly. "For the good food."

Adam's lips pursed. "Well, that's true. Luddies are loonie, but they got great food and nice beaches."

"Right?" said Noa. "There we were though, roasting hamburgers and tandoori skewers, comparing all our old Betsys ..."

"Old Betsys?" said Clara, raising a sculpted eyebrow, wings buzzing.

One of his guards leaned close and whispered, "Slang for favorite weapons. Luddies have loose regulations on that sort of thing."

"Favorite ... Ahhh ..." said Adam, smiling weakly.

Noa straightened. "... on the South Province when everything went crazy. Warrants were put out for the arrest of the hyper-augments among us."

"Hyper-augments?" said Adam, his voice wavering slightly.

"... and the Local Guard arrived," Noa continued. "There was a bit of a squabble, and long story short, a company's worth of Fleet veterans that's been to Six doesn't take long to overcome a battalion of Luddeccean Guard." She sniffed, remembering the Guard anticipating her team's demise on Manuel's roof. "Unprofessional. But we were right next door to this big ol' hunk of Third Family space relic and we decided it was time to bring it back into commission, obviously taking on the whole army would have been another matter ..." She looked at Gunny, and prompted, "But we would have given it a go."

Standing tall, Gunny barked, "Yes, Sir!"

Adam blinked. "You've got a whole company aboard that ... relic?"

Noa shook her head. "Itching to get out for a little R&R, but I wasn't sure if you could handle our kind of R&R."

"Well ..." Adam's brows drew together and Noa could see potential profits versus potential property damage warring in his mind.

"I thought the Third Family vessels were all

destroyed upon arrival at Luddeccea," said the guard standing closest to Adam.

Noa's mind called up her Luddeccean history, and solar cores, he was right. She contained a wince and tried to recapture the authoritative, playful tone she'd had a moment ago, but she could feel her heart beating in her throat, and no words came into her head. Manuel gulped. Gunny's eyes flitted around the dock.

In a smooth, professorial voice, James said, "Lieutenant Manuel here is an engineer by trade. Third family vessels are an obsession with him. He's been rehabilitating the Nina for decades."

Noa's breath caught. That was a damn good lie. Almost too good. Her thumb went to the stumps of her fingers.

"Oh," said Adam, eyes darting to the engineer. Manuel didn't speak, bless him. He just stood straighter as though genuinely proud.

"But," Noa continued, pushing aside her unease at the smoothness of James's lie, "we had a little trouble with an old timeband, associated charge dispersers, and the toilet goop—"

"How do you have trouble with toilet goop?" said Clara. Her mouth fell open and her eyes widened. "You're not going to dump it in our locker?"

"No, we already ejected it," said Noa. "In Luddeccean space, during our escape."

Adam stared at her, slightly slack-jawed.

"Why?" said the woman, flitting her wings and stepping back as though some of said goop might be ejected onto her.

"For thrust," Noa responded weakly, resisting the

urge to bang her head against something hard. Who used toilet goop for thrust? Way to inspire fear and respect.

Clearing his throat, looking both worried and dubious, Adam said, "I'd like to confer with my team. Hosting a ship with as many aboard as yours poses unique challenges especially during these difficult times."

"Of course," said Noa, giving her head what she hoped was a sympathetic tilt.

"It will be just a moment!" said Adam.

Adam stepped away with his lieutenant and Clara. As they stood in a silent ethernet circle, Noa reached out to the Ark. No one interrupted this time, but she used the cipher to be safe. "Ghost, can you start working on infiltrating Adam's and Clara's ethernet channels?"

Normally she'd expect such a task to take days—but Ghost had accessed the scanner so quickly. She glanced over at James, just by habit. He was staring at Adam's group, face expressionless, and then his head jerked back as though he'd been stung by a xin-bee.

"I'm already on it, Commander," Ghost said.

Beside her, James whispered, "They've —"

Ghost cut him off, the ciphered words coming in rapid fire succession. "They've decided not to send a team aboard. It's too risky ... for now."

Manuel's chest rose and fell and Gunny whispered a prayer to Allah. There was a pause from Ghost's mind, and it felt like a little light going out. And then Ghost's thoughts came back like a flickering spark. "But Adam is still keeping the option open."

"Well, we'll need to get our supplies and get out," Noa said, tapping the smooth surface of her interface.

There were murmurs of assent across the ether, and

the electrical impulses of those thoughts charged Noa's resolve.

Beside her, Gunny said to James, "That was some fast actin' with that story you came up with back there."

Noa couldn't tell if he sounded suspicious of James's glibness, or if her own disquiet just colored her interpretation of his tone.

James shifted on his feet. "In my former life I sometimes ... bluffed ... authoritatively about things I knew nothing about." His head ticked to the side, and he stared at a point on the floor. "I think sometimes I was a bit of an ass."

It was so ... candid. Noa felt her apprehension burst like a soap bubble. She grinned.

Gunny snorted.

Manuel shook his head. "Professors."

Meeting Noa's gaze, James shrugged. Noa winked at James, and simultaneously reached out across the ether to her computing officer, not wanting any of her team to be forgotten. "Well done, Ghost. That was some fast access."

She swore she could hear his flush even across the ether. "It was ... well, it was unusually easy to crack. System security not updated since the time gate was sabotaged ... that's all."

Noa blinked at more of the uncharacteristic modesty.

"That has to explain it," said James, shaking his head.

The buzzing of wings made her raise her head. Clara was approaching with several of Adam's guards. "Commander Sato," the woman said with a shark-like smile. "I will be guiding you to the appropriate districts and giving you a tour along the way."

Noa felt herself prickle. Across the ether, Ghost said,

"Her orders are to delay you while they get a scanner out here ... not to abduct you outright."

"Wonderful," Noa said, managing a smile. Over the ether, she railed to James, "Mud from a sick horse!" It was the closest she could get to "lizzar excrement" in Heian Japanese.

In real life his face stayed as flat as stone, but his avatar appeared and gave her a smile ... which was the correct response. Her ventings weren't to be taken seriously, and nebulas, it felt good to vent to someone again.

She wanted to smile back, but across the ether, Ghost said, "Be careful, Commander. We really don't want to be stuck here."

"I'm always careful," she replied.

The electrodes firing in her neural interface between her, Gunny, Manuel, Ghost, and James halted all at once. Noa huffed. It was the ethernet equivalent of a snort.

The gravity on Adam's Station was less than Luddeccea's, Earth's, or standard starship grav. Despite the thinner oxygen, Noa had no trouble without her CO_2 mask, as her team was guided by Clara away from the dock through a narrow, canyon-like space that cut through the ore stained rock of Adam's Station's asteroid.

A few paces in front of Noa, Clara swayed close to James. "So as you can see, we may look like just another bumble-rock asteroid, but we have—" The buzzing of her wings interrupted the rest.

An avatar of James appeared in the ether ... and then winked out. Noa's connection to the ether was dying, out of range. Noa's eyes swept to Clara's guards, a few paces ahead of Clara. Why were they walking ahead, and not behind?

Discreetly slipping out an ethernet extender from his pocket, Gunny flipped it on, and Noa felt the warmth of access seep into her mind. Gunny called across the general channel. "James, you could try and be a little more friendly while we find a place to hide our ether-rocks!"

Clara briefly looked back at Noa and her two team members, as though she'd heard something, and Gunny hastily hid the extender.

"So," James said, lifting his head. "The walls of this walkway look very organic, not like they were carved out."

Across the ether, Gunny said, "You're supposed to show interest in her, not the rocks!"

"The rocks are interesting," James quipped back. "I have a buggy eidetic memory app and I will have to remember everything she says. Forever."

Noa felt the spark of Gunny about to reply, but his thoughts were cut off by Clara saying, "The unusual formation of the promenade is what was left over when Adam the First melted away the natural ice of this plane-toid nearly two centuries ago." Raising one hand to the walls, she put another on James's arm. Thankfully, his sleeves were rolled down and her green-tipped nails didn't get near his skin. Noa's stomach roiled, but she used the woman's distraction to hide an ether extender in a crack in the floor.

"Done," she said across the ether.

"Hmmm ..." said James, pulling away from Clara, seemingly inspecting the walls in professorial interest. Aloud he said, "I've never been to an asteroid before ...

this is ... new ... to me, at least. What sort of economy do you have?"

"Professors," muttered Gunny.

Fluttering her wings to regain her balance, Clara said, "We have few of the minerals needed for cyber-manufacturing or timeband production." She shrugged. "But some people get rich by striking gold, others get rich by selling gold to prospectors."

On either side of them, doors began to appear in the channel's walls. Two especially large ones swung open and Clara guided them through. Noa found herself on a landing above a stairway in a large cavern with a high dome of poured concrete. The lighting, the layout, and the size of the space were reminiscent of a large warehouse, but packed with people, small ground cars, bicycles, and so much noise of humanity, it hit Noa like a physical force. The traffic passed between buildings carved out of rock or made of poured cement, set in a neat grid pattern. Most of the structures had solid walls without windows. All were typical of places like this. It wasn't typical how Clara's guards ran down the steps, rifles raised. She felt Gunny and Manuel tense beside her, and James stopped so fast Noa nearly ran into him. He looked back at her. She expected him to say, *This looks dangerous*, or *I'm not sure we should follow them.* The sort of reasonable, cautious, unhappy things he would say when Noa was about to lead them into "the belly of the beast." Instead he said, aloud, "I've never seen anything like it." There was a touch of awe in his voice.

"Professors," Gunny muttered.

From a few steps down, Clara said, "Come," gesturing James to take her arm. Pretending not to see, or maybe not seeing, James passed by her on the steps. One of her guards hastily came back up the staircase, and held out an arm for her to lean on. It might have been funny, but a crowd was gathering at the bottom of the staircase. They were skinny, dirty, and wore threadbare clothes. Someone shouted, "Food! I'll work for food!"

"Please, I have children!" There were too many voices, and Noa couldn't put the faces to all of them. She looked over to James. His eyes were on the dome above their heads. Noa's eyes darted toward the edge of the dome; at the periphery there were cavernous openings with immense iron doors that looked like medieval battlements ready to drop from the ceiling at any moment. Airlocks. She looked at the doors to all the dwellings; they too were metal and rugged—smaller airlocks.

She felt James reach to her across the ether. "Maybe it is the newness ... but this place feels *real*."

"It will feel even more real when the phasers start going off," Noa snipped across the ether before she could stop herself. "This place is a powder keg."

"Please, food, I have children."

Noa heard a stunner, and spun in direction of the sound just in time to see a beggar collapse to the ground. A guard stood above her, weapons upraised. A toddler, not much older than Oliver, started to cry next to her body. Noa gasped. She heard Gunny swear. Manuel jumped and James rolled back on his feet.

Lips contorting into a snarl, Clara roared at the crowd, "These are our guests! You will stand back!" Noa expected to see spittle fly from her lips.

The crowd edged away and Clara turned to James, all evidence of her anger gone. Tracing her collarbone with a finger, she said, "This is the shopping district, our downtown, if you will."

Noa managed to stay silent, but her thoughts whipped over the ether. "Listen to her ... As though stunning a beggar is normal!"

James met her gaze, a look of concern on his brow, but he said nothing, and thought nothing.

Waving a hand, Clara resumed walking. "The manufacturing zone is this way ..."

Noa hung back, and James hung back until she was beside him.

"I'm alright, Tim," she said, too late to catch her mistake.

James stood stock still. The ether between them was uncomfortably quiet.

In front of them, Clara stopped and said, "To get there we'll take a detour through the tourist district; you really must see it."

"Tourist district?" Manuel said, the surprise Noa felt loud and clear in his voice. Places like this didn't have tourists.

"We have a lovely orchard and a rose garden," Clara responded, putting her hands together in front of her chest and fluttering her fairy wings.

Gunny, Manuel, and Noa looked to each other and shifted on their feet.

"An orchard ... and a rose garden ...?" Gunny stammered.

"I'm not very knowledgeable about these things," James said slowly. "But the amount of water and space such a garden would need—"

"Normally it would be a huge waste!" Clara said. Her wings fluttered, and she gave what Noa thought must be her first genuine smile since they'd arrived. "But C Corp executives don't want to look at vertical beanstalks and protein-taters. They want gardens that are beautiful to look at and smell."

"C Corp?" said Noa. "Here?" C Corp was the leading manufacturer of cybernetics. They produced useful augments like Oliver's or James's, but they made more money on discretionary augmentation ... like Clara's ridiculous wings.

Smiling, Clara tilted her head. "You hadn't heard? They were planning on expanding in this system. Mining here in the belt, manufacturing on Luddeccea ... so much safer than Six with all the unrest there."

"I'd heard C Corp had their eyes on Luddeccea," said Manuel. "I'd hoped ..."

"Not rumors," Clara insisted. "We've had executives from C Corp staying here for months." She fluttered her wings. "They gave me such a great deal on these. Aren't they beautiful?"

Noa felt her mouth go dry. She wasn't shocked that she hadn't heard about C Corp's plan on her home world. Luddeccean news agencies would have been encouraged to keep it hush-hush. Her thumb went to twirl the rings on her left hand ... and for the millionth time discovered her rings weren't there.

A dark picture began to form in her mind. C Corp using Luddeccea as the primary location for their manu-facturing would have felt like an invasion to the hard-liners on her home world. C Corp's plans alone would have caused violence and unrest as soon as they became widely known. A lot of Luddecceans would have welcomed C Corp's arrival—Manuel and Hisha, for instance. A lot of people would have been terrified. They would have seen it as an attack on their philosophy, and on their very way of life. To them, C Corp's arrival would herald a society of ... of ... Claras.

C Corp's plans, and the takeover of Time Gate 8 by ... Noa shivered. She didn't know who or what controlled Time Gate 8. She suspected Luddeccea's government didn't know either, but as far as the Luddeccean hard-liners would be concerned, they were being threatened from every direction and had reacted by splitting from the time gate's ethernet, with the pretense of "thought control." Too many Luddecceans were ether-science illiterate to catch the lie.

She felt her heart beat faster, and a cold weight settle in her chest as the picture became clearer. The authorities had rounded up augments because being augmented meant a person embraced technology—and in many cases, would have gone off-world to get it. Even augments that were necessary meant their adopters had been exposed to "dangerous ideas." Her cousin John had artificial kidneys. As he'd grown, he'd had to have them replaced several times with larger models, and had to go to Sol System for all the operations. There he'd learned that the disease that had destroyed his kidneys could easily have been wiped out with nanotech banned on Luddeccea. He'd become embittered by Luddeccea's refusal to "evolve." In the eyes of Noa's more religious neighbors, he'd been "led astray" and had become a "bad influence."

... And the Luddeccean authorities had to go after someone to do the work that ethernet-based machines had done before they'd closed off the ether. James had told her that part of the Nazis' Final Solution was to work the Jews to death. Her home world's leaders, so proud of the religious tolerance of The Three Books, had done the same to a different population, under the same pretenses of protecting the general populace.

Noa felt like she might throw up. Her eyes shifted to James. His gaze was on a point in the distance, as though listening to a far-off sound. Back on Luddeccea he'd said that genocides were precipitated by pressures from within or from without. She felt bile rise in her throat. "You called it, Professor," she whispered over the ether.

James turned to meet her gaze, but Clara stepped between them, breaking the eye contact. "We get all the potatoes, wheat, rice, soy, and peanuts we need from Luddeccea." She frowned. "I'm sure trading will resume soon."

Noa's team froze, all the way down to their thoughts, as though hit by a weak stun.

Clara stopped and turned to them, wings buzzing. "Is something wrong?"

Gunny shifted on his feet. Manuel looked down. James's eyes darted quickly between Noa and Clara.

Noa found her voice at last. "Is Luddeccea communicating with you at all?"

Wings halting, Clara said, "They told us the time gate was offline, and some ridiculousness about it and the ether being used by aliens to control augments ..." She huffed. "Well, some said, aliens, some said demons. Can you believe that nonsense? If that were true, half this station would be possessed. They'll see sense ... soon ... they have to." Her voice, for the first time, became unsure.

James's voice flared across the general channel. "If they believe that trade will resume, they're more likely to let us go without incident."

"I agree with that," Ghost said immediately.

"The sooner they start planting protein-tatos, the

better," Gunny said across the same channel. Noa's jaw got tight. James was right … but Gunny was right, too—the people of Adam's Station deserved the truth.

Clara was looking between them, a look almost like fear on her previously imperious plasti-features.

"Is she listening in?" Manuel asked across the ether. "If we can hear them—"

"No," said Ghost, and James, at nearly the same time. And then James looked up sharply in the direction they'd just come. Noa spun to see the doors they'd stepped through swing open with an eardrum-bursting clang. Beyond her line of vision, she heard a storm of footsteps and the whine of antigrav. She reached for her stunner, and saw Manuel and Gunny do the same in the periphery of her vision, just as two dozen armed men bearing phaser rifles emerged at the top of the landing.

"Ghost! What's going on?" Noa shouted across the ether, raising her stunner, Manuel and Gunny following her lead. James stood strangely still, not even edging closer to her.

"Nothing?" said Ghost.

"There are armed men here," Noa said. One guard's eyes fell on her, and he lifted the weapon to fire. James hissed, "Put your weapons down, Noa!"

"Hmmmm …" Ghost's thoughts paused, and then came back online. "The only thing of interest is that a group of rabble rousers have had the bright idea of eating the O_2-producing algae near the grav core."

As if in punctuation of that thought, Clara shrieked, "They're eating the algae in the O_2 pits? What's wrong with them?" She swayed past Noa's team. An antigrav litter appeared on the landing, and then hovered to the bottom of the steps. One of the guards raced to assist

Clara. Taking a proffered hand, she hopped onto the litter. As she sat down, her eyes met Noa's. In an irritated-sounding voice she said, "You need to go to the East Cavern for the timeband and charge dispersers. Ask for Richard Yee at The Yard. For the goop, go to the Heap. Just head to the North Pole." Turning to the guards, she barked, "Let's go to the algae pits!"

Noa and her team stood slack-jawed, watching the antigrav chair depart. People were eating the O2 production algae ...

"We're attracting attention," James said over the general channel.

Noa looked to him sharply. His profile was silhouetted by a street lamp. His focus was on the crowd of people around them that was beginning to edge silently closer, although all around them the business of Adam's Station roared.

"What do you hear?" Noa asked, wondering if he'd caught something with his augmented hearing.

He turned to her sharply, in a way that reminded her of one of the ptery-hawk. Touching one of her ears, she whispered, "You hear something?"

She could see his shoulders unwind. "Nothing dangerous," he said. "They're considering begging."

Something about that reply struck a chord in Noa's mind, but she couldn't say what.

"I didn't hear that," Gunny said. He smacked the side of his head. "All the background noise."

"Commander," Manuel said across the channel. "I realize it's best usually to stick together ... but given the circumstances I think it might be better if Gunny and I went to get the charge dispersers and you and James handled the goop so we can get out of here as soon as possible."

"Yes!" Ghost shouted over the ethernet channel. "I'm piping the station map to you now." The layout to Adam's Station exploded behind Noa's eyes, complete with her location.

To James's private channel she said, "Splitting up ... that would be just like in a bad holo-horror."

"If you're trying to lighten the mood, that really isn't helping," James replied privately.

"It's probably the best option, though," she thought back.

James rolled his eyes. "Well, then, might as well get it over with. Let's go already."

It was the reluctant, slightly irritable in the face of danger James she knew. Noa swallowed. And maybe loved?

"We'll split up," Noa said aloud.

Manuel smiled and Gunny nodded.

Ghost's thoughts rang over the ether. "Good! We need to get out of here before any more incidents happen!"

Noa looked around at the hungry faces. She had a feeling there was no way they could avoid "incidents" here.

CHAPTER SIX

James pushed open the old-fashioned hinged door that led out of the Heap, the junkyard-recovery shop that sold used chemicals and parts on Adam's Station. The artificial cavern where the shop resided was lower and darker than the ones they'd been in before, and dirtier, too. The buildings leaned over the narrow alley-width lanes that crisscrossed the space. He still found the place ... awe-inspiring? That wasn't quite the right description, but he felt immersed in the moment, maybe because he had nothing in his previous existence to compare it to.

He saw someone dart behind a corner, a few buildings away, and reminded himself he had to be cautious and alert, not awed. His lip wanted to quirk. His senses had to be like a "fine-toothed comb," as 6T9 had said.

He heard Noa say some final words to one of the proprietors. A few moments later, she was looking out over his shoulder. "We're still being shadowed, aren't we?" she asked.

"Yes," James replied. They'd been trailed by locals of Adam's Station since they left Clara's company. Their shadowers had asked them for food, if they had news from Luddeccea, and if they had any open berths. The answer to those questions had been "no" but he'd noticed Noa had looked visibly uncomfortable giving that answer. James had listened in on their ethernet conversations. They'd speculated whether or not Adam would detain the Ark, and whether or not the Company of Fleet Infantry would be able to hold up against Adam and his forces, but they didn't discuss ambushing Noa and James.

Noa rubbed her temple. "I can't help them, not yet, not yet."

James's jaw shifted. She automatically assumed their entourage were victims of Luddeccea's halt of food exports. "Some of them are probably spies for Adam," he reminded her. Just because they hadn't transmitted data to Adam didn't mean they didn't intend to.

Nodding, she straightened her shoulders and adopted a confident stride to exit the building. He fell into step beside her, and over the ether, she complained, "I can't believe they talked me into three weeks rations for toilet goop. Luckily, they are going to deliver it."

James didn't answer; instead he focused on an unfamiliar man leaning against a wall ... and didn't get the new, and yet now familiar, rush of light and static. It was only a hypothesis, but he thought that he couldn't "hear" anyone unless they were using the ether.

As they walked down the alley, the sparse pedestrian traffic turned to stare at them. James focused, heard their ethernet conversations, and saw the holo footage of the Ark and its crew shot by dock workers that they passed mind-to-mind. Some of them began to follow them.

Noa addressed Ghost over the ether. "Ghost, how is it going?"

"Tricky business ..." the programmer replied. "They brought out a bigger scanner and parked it on the dock. As long as it's tied to the ether I can worm my way in and change the readings, but I have to stay focused and act quickly."

Noa took a sharp breath. "Can't you set up the Ark's computer to run a routine for you that—?"

"No, it's too complex," Ghost replied.

James blinked ... compared to accessing a secure ether channel, the computing power to change the data of such a channel seemed small. He wasn't a programmer by any stretch, but he'd had to go into ancient databases from time to time, even had to physically *type* out queries. He thought the Ark's computer could take data such as number of people on a ship and add a few hundred people to it.

"But, you've already got the Ark hacking the station's ether channels," Noa said.

"No," said Ghost. "It's ... I can't explain. Commander, I have to go."

The connection dropped, and James felt the electrical activity in his neural interface slow. For a few more minutes they walked in silence. He felt his nanos and neuros flicker. If Noa wasn't talking, it tended to mean she was planning something he was not going to like.

Noa glanced over her shoulder, and then her eyes went directly ahead again.

"What's bothering you?" James asked. Maybe he should have asked what was she scheming?

Noa exhaled loudly.

James glanced over his shoulder. Their uninvited entourage had gotten closer. Two children, just old enough to have their neural ports activated, were speculating if they should ask for food. There were some older ones wondering across the ether if they'd really come from Luddeccea. People who'd gone to Luddeccea since Luddeccean freighters had ceased their tri-weekly visits hadn't been heard from. Someone said, "Maybe we should ask them about it?"

Noa, not looking back, said softly, "Timothy was my husband."

It was so out of context, so far from what he expected, that for a moment her words were an incomprehensible jumble. And then he put it together. She'd called him Tim a few hours ago. He hadn't thought about it too much. He'd been too busy scanning the ether channels for any warnings of danger. But she'd called him that when they'd first met, when they'd woken up in a bed together, and cried out the name in her sleep.

"It was ..." Her voice became uncertain. "... a mistake. Because ..." Her jaw got tight.

"Your husband," echoed James. It should be a revelation, but it felt like something he'd already known, like a word at the tip of his tongue that was momentarily forgotten, and then remembered in a flash. His hand trembled by his side. He shouldn't feel like he'd known that.

"He died," she said, eyes focused straight ahead, still marching resolutely forward.

James had a sensation like ice water dripping on his skin. He'd known that, too.

"You look like him ..." she whispered.

The cold drip became an icy wave. Behind him, a woman whispered to her friend across the ether, "Go on, Sylvie, ask if they know about the ship to Luddeccea."

One of the children's voices whispered, "I'm gonna

ask them if they have any more S-rations. Nà says they gave him some."

He could hear their footsteps getting closer. The icy prickle became heat. He needed Noa all to himself. He needed to understand this coincidence ... no, it was not a coincidence. It could not be. Not when he'd deliberately went to search for her in the snow, and knew the same dead language and her frequency ...

His eyes shifted side to side. "We need to get out of here," he said.

In the periphery of his vision he saw Noa's eyes go to his, wide with alarm. But she didn't ask questions.

They'd already traversed this terrain, and his memory called up every corner and nook in exquisite detail. He pulled a map of the North Pole down from the public board and combined it with his own memories. Grabbing Noa's hand, he said, "On my mark, run." He felt a startled light of connection within his mind and without waiting for a reply, he whispered, "Now."

Panting, Noa leaned against the wall of a windowless building in a dim alley. The light above them was clicking furiously, but was not on. The air smelled like wet concrete. Her lungs were straining after her brief sprint through an abandoned building, down a narrow pathway between buildings that looked like they'd exploded outward in a vacuum breach, through another building, and around the block. Now she felt lightheaded. James was still holding her hand, his side was pressed against hers, but his head was cocked toward a section of blown out wall—listening with his augmented hearing, no doubt.

Noa tried to catch her breath, or at least breathe quietly. After what her chronometer told her was 2.5 minutes, James turned to her, his face and body in shadow. "We've lost them for a while," he whispered.

Noa leaned her head back against the wall and said a silent prayer. Being trailed by their quiet wraiths had been heartbreaking. She wanted to reach out to them, offer them a billet on their ship—but how to know who was a spy, and who was genuinely in need?

James threaded his fingers with hers and pulled away from the wall, turning to stand in front of her. She squeezed his hand. "You heard something?"

He didn't say anything for a moment, just looked away, and then back down at her. "Nothing dangerous. The company just suddenly made me feel ... claustrophobic."

"I know," said Noa. The beggars would have asked them for food, block their way, and ask questions they couldn't answer. When would the supply runs start again? Why was the ethernet down? One of the children in an earlier mob, after James and she had split up from Gunny and Manuel, hadn't asked for food. He'd asked if she knew anything about the Fitzgerald. Apparently, it was an ore freighter that was supposed to have landed on Luddeccea. How could you tell a child his father was most likely dead? How could you explain why he was most likely dead—that he was shot down by his own kind, because they were afraid of an alien invasion? And if they asked about aliens ...

She took a deep breath and suddenly realized how close James was. She could feel heat radiating from him, and he smelled a lot better than wet concrete. James was distracting ...

"We were having a conversation," he said slowly, head lowered, dark blonde bangs hanging in front of his eyes.

Noa remembered the words she'd just uttered, *You look like my husband.*

There was a lot to say about that. *I used to call you Tim because you look like him. Now I do because you make me feel the way he made me feel.* But there was a chronometer app beeping down in her mind, and a tiny mental note at the edge of her consciousness saying that Manuel and Gunny had found a "surprisingly good quality" timeband and somewhat less inspiring charge dispersers. They were heading back to the ship. There was too much to do, and she didn't want to explain—if she said what she felt it would be that much more real.

Above them, the dead bulb in the light fixture buzzed and ticked.

"Noa," James whispered.

She felt his free hand graze her cheek, and she closed her eyes. She wanted to be distracted ... When she opened her eyes again, he was standing even closer, their bodies brushing. He smelled good. And just that light touch *felt* good. She leaned forward, not meeting his gaze. She slipped her free hand around the back of his neck and felt him incline toward her. Standing on her tiptoes, she pressed her lips to his. For a moment, lights went off behind her eyes, her skin went hot, and a charge rushed from her lips to the base of her spine. But then she realized his lips weren't moving. She had a sensation of disconnect, dread, and cold. She dropped to her heels.

"Noa," James whispered. "I'm sorry."

He lifted his hands, but he didn't pull away. And why wasn't he pulling away? She couldn't have misread the signals ... No. She looked up at him. He was touching the side of his lips.

She tilted her head. Before she could say a word, the light above their heads fizzled, clicked, and turned on, bathing them in a sickly yellow glow.

"I ..." James stammered, touching his lips. "... can't."

Can't what? Before she could ask, a voice sounded from down the aisle.

"James? James Sinclair?" a woman called out.

James pulled away and looked past Noa's shoulder.

She turned around to the sound of fast, light steps.

A woman was approaching them. She looked to be in her twenties, but her features were so perfectly symmetrical they had an ageless quality that spoke of quality augmentation, not real youth. Her eyes were almond, light brown, and almost gold. Her lips were full, her nose petite and her skin was a warm tan. With her dark mahogany hair, she was the embodiment of the "raceless" ideal beauty. Her fitted cream dress-coat was stained and rumpled but made of expensive fabrics and well tailored, as were the soft purple leggings she wore beneath, and the shoes that matched the legging's hue exactly.

When the unfamiliar woman spoke, her voice was as cultured as James's. "James ... I thought you were dead."

* * *

I thought you were dead.

James was being wheeled down a long white hallway. He wasn't in pain, he *was* pain ...

"James?"

The voice was Noa's. He felt a spark in his mind and worry, *her* worry, fizzling across the ether, but all he saw were the doctors as he lay on the gurney, and his father, clasping his right hand. Just like he remembered ... And the pain ... He felt his body had been completely shattered, that his skin had become merely a sack for broken bits of bones and pulverized muscles and organs.

The hallway blurred. Noa appeared to the left of the gurney. "You're alright. You survived this, remember?" James could only stare at her. Her cheeks were full, her hair was thick, shiny, and black, and when she reached over with her left hand and took his own, she had five fingers and two sparkling rings.

"I had an app," James murmured, or thought, nonsensically. "It uploaded all the data for my time capsule." There was so much pain ... how could Noa stay here? "That's how I remember, all this ... pain." The human mind would normally block it out, he was sure.

He heard his father's anguished cry.

Noa's avatar leaned closer. "Come back."

James felt like he was shattering apart again. Noa had tried to kiss him, and then his body had failed. His lips hadn't moved. They had been just useless bundles of muscle, skin, fascia, and malfunctioning nerves. The white hallway turned to black.

"James, come back to me," Noa whispered.

James's head ticked to the side with such force his teeth rattled. His body knit back together, and he wasn't on the gurney. He was upright, in an alley on a ball of dirt and ice at a distance from the sun that made day nothing but twilight. His father's voice rang in his ears; he'd been so close to his parents, and this was the first time he'd thought of them really, in an emotional, gut-wrenching way since the snow, and that was off, and wrong. Worse, he was staring at a woman he had known *before*. He should be gasping for breath ... but he didn't need to breathe.

"Monica," he said. His put his hand to his temple to steady himself.

He felt Noa's hand on his arm. "James?" she said. "You, ah, know each other?"

James didn't lift his head, but he found his voice. "Where are my manners? Monica, this is Commander Noa Sato. Noa, this is Dr. Monica Jarella." He had the urge to take Noa's hand again and run.

"Doctor?" said Noa. There was something hopeful in her voice.

"A psychiatrist," James said, his mind searching for an excuse to leave right now.

Fury bubbled across the ether from Noa. Her thoughts snapped into his mind. "A psychiatrist should know better than to talk about something that could trigger PTSD."

"Psychiatry is a secondary degree," Monica said. She gave a tiny smile. "I got it after my MD. I have surgical experience."

Noa's fury evaporated from the ether, but in the real world her jaw remained tight. Aloud, Noa said, "Nice to meet you," and gave a tiny bow that Monica returned.

Monica swallowed audibly. "I saw your picture on the public boards ... and a picture of your ship. It's a vessel capable of traveling through deep space. I saw you, James, and I couldn't believe it because of what my cousin said ..."

A red light flashed in James's visual cortex. Her cousin was the friend James had caught when he was scaling a cliff face—he'd saved her cousin's life and the friend had introduced him to Monica at a family function.

Said friend had said to James, "I love you like a brother, James, but stay away from Monica. I know she's your type, but she's like a sister to me, and I know how you are."

His friend had been right. Monica was exactly his type. From the softness of her voice and her tasteful clothes, to her subtle augments that played up her natural features and made them more symmetrical, but not generic. Even her profession—a doctor of psychiatry—a researcher who studied human robotic interactions. He had felt a pull before, but felt none now, just a nagging dread. "My heart stopped when I fell. For a time, technically, I was dead." The words came from his lips without a conscious thought, as though they were rehearsed and part of a script. James wanted more than anything to get himself and Noa away from this woman.

Monica took a deep breath, and her brows drew together. Her eyes shifted to Noa, who was standing with her weight on one leg, hand on the small stunner, eyes slightly narrowed. He almost suggested they leave, but then from down the aisle came a soft scuffle. Noa's stunner was out an instant later, pointed in the direction of the sound. Monica held up her arms and stepped in front of her. "Don't shoot!"

From behind Monica came a child's voice. "Momma, can I come out?"

"It's my little girl," Monica said, pleading, golden eyes on Noa. "Please, I couldn't leave her with strangers."

Noa lowered her stunner, every muscle in her body softening. "Of course."

"Come out, Zoe," Monica said, eyes still on the stunner, hands still in the air.

A little girl came out of a hole in the wall. Her hair

was tied back in a messy braid, and her fine clothes were stained. James estimated that she could be no more than eight or nine. Her deep brown eyes were wet, as though she'd been crying. They darted between James and Noa. She came forward cautiously, raising her hands in imitation of her mother.

"You can put your hands down," Noa said, sitting down on her heels so she was at eye level with the child. Static flared along James's skin. Noa's eyes on the child told him he would not be escaping from Monica anytime soon.

CHAPTER SEVEN

Noa walked beside Monica through the port on her way to the Ark. In her visual cortex, a light was pinging, reminding her that she was now an hour late for her cryssallis treatment. She turned it off. Again. James was on her other side, hanging back as Monica told her story. Monica's husband was a lawyer who worked for C Corp; he had been stationed at Luddeccea's capital, Prime, working out the details of C Corp's expansion on the planet. When Time Gate 8 was sabotaged, Monica and Zoe were in the process of relocating to Libertas to be closer to him. Her husband had insisted his wife and child live on Libertas where off-worlders were more welcome. Monica told them, "I didn't believe that Libertas 1.25 g, frigid temperatures, and low oxygen would be worth the daily lightspeed commute ... but ..." She'd stopped talking at that point and had wiped her eyes.

Despite being furious at Monica for bringing up James's medical death, Noa could identify with the doctor. Monica's husband was "missing." Noa knew the sickening feelings of dread she must be carrying with every step.

According to Monica, her charter ship had just slipped through Time Gate 8 when an explosion went off inside the gate. Luddeccean forces had immediately attacked all vessels coming and going, and their ship narrowly missed being destroyed. The captain had jumped to lightspeed with little concern for trajectory other than not hitting anything. Minutes later, the engines had begun to fail due to damage they'd sustained. The pilot managed to drift into the belt, and somehow had known about Adam's Station.

"The captain of the ship we chartered to Libertas is letting us stay with him," Monica said. "While the ship is being repaired."

"He's a good pilot," Noa said; he would have had to have been. "And it was stand up of him to let you stay aboard."

Patting Zoe's shoulder, Monica said tightly, "He's a good pilot." The abridgment of the praise didn't escape Noa's notice.

Noa's eyes flicked to Monica. She gave Noa a tight smile. "Libertas Credits are still worth something here—not much—but something. My money is repairing the ship. But ... I think ..." She gazed up at James; her eyes were wide, imploring. James's looked away.

Monica turned back to Noa. "I could give those credits to you ... in exchange for passage to Libertas. It's taking too long to repair the chartered vessel."

Tugging on her mother's jacket, Zoe said, "Momma, I'm hungry."

Noa's heart fell, and she closed her eyes.

Putting her hand on her daughter's head, Monica said

quickly, "It's been a while since I practiced surgery. But I have done it, I have practical experience, and I kept all of my surgical atlas apps as mementos. I can be useful."

They did need a surgeon ...

James's mind connected again with Noa's. "But she thinks we're going to Libertas. She won't be interested if she knew where we're really going." There was something ... abrupt in his thoughts ... a too-easy dismissal. But he was right. Of course Monica thought they were going to Libertas. It was the only sensible destination, now that Luddeccea wasn't accepting visitors.

"I have to get to Libertas," Monica said. "My husband is looking for us."

"You've heard from your husband via lightbeam?" Noa asked.

"No ..." Monica's eyes scanned the floor, and then she looked sharply at Noa. "But he was going to meet us on Libertas as soon as work was over that day. He is there, he has to be."

Noa felt a sickening sensation in her stomach. The Luddeccean defense grid had been shooting down all ships trying to leave Luddeccea, making it very unlikely that anyone who had been on Luddeccea had escaped. It was only because of Ghost's magic—and the time gate's interference—that the Ark had made it. But Noa couldn't bring herself to disabuse Monica of the idea her husband might be alive. Especially not in front of her little girl.

For a moment they walked in silence, approaching a craft that was blackened and scarred by phaser fire. One of the thrusters had been removed and taken apart. Pieces of it lay across the dock. A boy as silent as a wraith picked up a piece and darted quietly up a ladder that went into the ship.

Noa cocked her head. The ship, despite the damage, looked familiar.

"You'll take us?" Monica asked, her voice plaintive.

"It's too dangerous, Noa," James thought.

Noa stopped and turned to the woman, and then a voice rumbled, "Take you where?" The voice made the hairs on the back of Noa's neck stand on end, and her hands ball into fists.

"I ..." Monica stammered, "... into the shopping district. I need new shoes."

"I can take you there," said the man.

Noa turned around. A man with long black hair pulled into a ponytail was approaching them. He was tall and lean, but broad shouldered. He was wiping his hands on a rag, but as soon as his eyes alighted on Noa, he stopped. "Commander Sato," he said.

"Wren," Noa said.

"*Captain* Wren," he revised.

Noa didn't amend her statement.

His features didn't have the painful symmetry of "tasteful" augmentation that James and Monica had—which would have made him more handsome to Noa—except, she knew him.

"You never did like me," he said.

Noa didn't bother to amend that opinion either. She didn't have time for his lizzar dung at the moment.

Her eyes shifted to Monica. The woman was stroking her daughter's head, eyes downcast. Noa wanted to invite her aboard the Ark; but she couldn't do that unless she told her they weren't really headed to Libertas. And if they told her that, she might accidentally leak the news, or they could be overheard, or she could be a spy even ... There were a thousand different scenarios that all played out with Adam's goons storming the ship.

"We'll think about it," Noa said. "We're quite full—"

"Full of what?" said Wren.

"Veterans of Six," said Noa.

"I'm a veteran of Six," Wren said, with a leer.

Noa's skin heated, her jaw tightened, and her nails bit into her palms. *I just never figured out whose side you were on* was on the tip of Noa's tongue. Instead she spit it across the ether at James, not even bothering to encrypt it, along with a colorful description of a lizzar in the throes of Xin-stomach flu.

Rolling back on his feet at her mental onslaught, James raised an eyebrow. In a deadpan voice he said aloud, "I can see you're good friends."

Which made Noa nearly choke on a snort. She felt her anger dissipate; she could deal with this low-life. "We've got two hundred well-seasoned, disciplined veterans of Six aboard our ship right now," Noa said. "I'm sure some of them would be delighted to see you." She canted her head and smiled brightly.

Wren's smile dropped.

From behind Noa, in the direction of the Ark, came 6T9's voice. "Noa, there you are!"

Wren's eyes widened, his eyebrows shot up, and then a slow smile spread across his face. "Is this one of your veterans now?"

Beside Noa, James pinched the bridge of his nose. Across the ether, he said, "I'm afraid to look."

Noa was, too. She bit her lip and spoke into James's mind. "How bad can it be?"

Wren snickered.

James's blue eyes slid to Noa's. He took a deep breath

as though he were about to walk the plank. They turned as one.

"Well, it couldn't be *worse*," James thought.

Monica made a choking noise.

Noa sucked in a breath that physically stung. 6T9 was wearing hot pink pants, purple sparkly boots, and a skin tight black t-shirt that said in neon green letters, "I'm with sexy." An arrow in the same neon green pointed up at Sixty's face and blinked on and off.

Wren walked up beside Noa and whispered, "So that's your type, Noa?"

"He belongs to someone in my crew," Noa responded, and then mentally kicked herself for dignifying the question with a response.

"Uh-huh," said Wren.

6T9 strode over and waggled his eyebrows. "Do you like the clothes? Eliza traded an apple for them. In for a penny, in for a pound, I always say."

"She paid too much," James said.

Monica laughed softly, a short, surprised sound that made Noa uneasy.

Noa ground out, "What are you doing here, 6T9?"

He smiled. "Oh, I'm here to remind you that you need your cryssallis treatment. Eliza said to drag you bodily if I had to, and Manuel agreed." His face got stern. "And I don't mean drag you in a fun way."

"Two ship's surgeons," Monica whispered, sounding deflated.

"Oh, no," said 6T9. "Eliza is a passenger and Manuel is the chief engineer. Our ship's doctor is dead. I would really like another ship's doctor, Eliza is—"

"Um, Sixty," Noa said.

"Commander?" said the 'bot, smiling and looking at her intently.

James's eyes narrowed and slid to hers. Over the ether, James's thoughts rushed in a torrent. "How late are you for your treatment?"

"Only a few hours," Noa silently responded.

The channel between them went silent, and then a flood of electrons exploded across the ether. His jaw twitched.

Smirking at 6T9, Wren said, "This veteran of yours has a lot of seasoning, but is he disciplined?"

"I'm sure he has an app for it," James remarked, but his eyes were still on Noa.

"Indeed!" 6T9 said brightly.

"We have to get back to the ship," Noa said. She nodded at Monica, and spoke to James through the ether. "Tell her we'll be in touch." He knew Monica. He had to have access to her channel.

James looked away and tugged Noa—gently—toward the Ark's plastitube lift. She squinted; to the left of the plastitube were large crates on a forklift, with men and women in coveralls running around. There was no one in the forklift's driver seat.

"The new scanner Ghost was talking about," James whispered.

Noa blinked at the certainty of his tone. That could be it ...

They took two steps and Noa remembered something she had in her pocket. "Wait!"

James didn't wait, but Noa managed to pull out her last bag of Premium Luddeccean Natural Snacks and throw it to Zoe. The little girl caught it mid-air.

"Thank you!" Monica said, with real gratitude in her

voice: for the organic nuts, raisins, and chocolate, or for the promise to be in touch, Noa wasn't quite sure.

Smirking, Wren called out, "I'm sure I'll be seeing you around!"

Noa gritted her teeth. She believed him, unfortunately.

* * *

James felt an overwhelming sense of relief when the Ark's airlock closed behind 6T9, Noa, and him; and the smell of asteroid dust, grease, and engine parts was replaced by the smell of Luddeccean tourists and sunlight. But he still felt as though his muscles were prepared for fight or flight. It was Monica's fault, and he couldn't say why. He thought he had managed to play off his unease on the dock. Humor was an amazing defensive weapon.

6T9 whistled as he walked out of the airlock. Noa closed the door behind him, so it was just her and James in the small space. Noa touched her neural interface and transmitted over the general frequency, "Manuel, Gunny, Ghost ... Captain Wren has his latest boat parked on Adam's Station."

Gunny's thoughts were an undecipherable hiss.

Across the ether, Manuel said, "Wonder who he's working for now?"

And Ghost snapped, "I can't investigate until they move that stupid scanner! The techs have finished their diagnostics and turned it on again ... I haven't been able to keep the read-outs steady and they're suspicious. Commander, we need to leave!"

"I'm not arguing with you there, Ghost," Noa replied

across the ether. "As soon as we get the timeband in and charge dispersers loaded—"

"What about the toilet goop?" said Kuin.

Noa's eyes narrowed.

"I have to share a bathroom with Bo and Jun now and both of them miss the—"

His thoughts ended midstream. James blinked. Ghost said, "I turned Kuin off for you, Commander."

"Thank you, Ghost," Noa said, rubbing her temple. Aloud she grumbled, "Civilians."

Over the ether, Ghost said, "I have to go ... but I can't keep this up much longer. Damn it, they're trying to scan for weapons now." His channel winked out.

James's hand trembled. Maybe he could help Ghost ... If he could access ethernet codes, could he learn to change data read-outs, like Ghost did? He felt a fizzle of static along his spine. Working with Ghost would mean admitting he could access the ether ...

Over the shared lines, Manuel said, "I don't like Wren being here."

James had scanned Wren's and Monica's ether. He knew Monica's channel from his previous life, and breaking into it had been especially easy, but he hadn't needed to spy on her. Monica had spent the whole time trying to ping him. He'd pretended not to hear. From Wren, he'd heard only thoughts directed at the boy who'd been darting about beneath the ship: requests for part counts, and "get your butt back in the ship while I talk to these people."

"Why don't you trust Wren?" he asked across the general channel.

Noa looked up at him sharply. It was Manuel who responded. "He was a double agent during the Six War."

"But he was your—the Fleet's—double agent?" James tried to clarify.

"Who knows," said Manuel, and James remembered Noa's thoughts. *I just never figured out whose side you were on.*

James looked to Noa for explanation. She shrugged. "Spies are usually psychopaths, double agents even more so. You can never trust them."

James bowed his head. He felt electricity crawling all over his skin. He was a spy, wasn't he? Or at least *spying* on people over the ether. His vision went dark around the edges. He didn't want Noa to know that. He couldn't offer to help Ghost, not unless the situation got very dire, because ... because ...

"Hey," Noa said, taking a step toward him.

James looked up, and realized nearly thirty seconds had gone by in complete ether and audible silence.

Noa took his hand. "It was a rough day, but we made it."

She took a breath, and he heard the faintest hint of a rasp in it. His vision darkened. He knew he should kiss her ... and he wanted to ... but couldn't. He felt something in him stutter at the thought, like his nanos and neurons were shutting down. And then Noa put her fingers on James's lips. They were small, calloused, and cool—and there were only three of them. Her dark eyes met his.

"My lips ..." He wrapped her fingers in his.

"Can't show emotion," Noa said. She smiled wryly. "Thank God they still allow you to eat."

Relief, gratitude, and a feeling of connection flooded him like sunlight spilling through the door of the mind-scape she'd shared with him. They were both broken physically and emotionally.

He pulled her scarred hand to his chest, and wrapped his other hand around her back, pulling her flush against him. It wasn't close enough. He dropped his forehead against hers, closed his eyes … and heard her breath, raspy and sick. His world darkened again, and he squeezed her fingers. "Noa," he sighed, knowing he was destroying the moment. "Don't die on me. Go take your medicine."

Noa leaned back. The wan light caught the scars on her face just right, making them look like tiny bolts of lightning etched on her skin. Her eyes were narrowed, but she was smiling.

The airlock whooshed open, and Noa pulled away.

Manuel was standing in the doorway with Eliza leaning on 6T9's arm. Eliza had the plastic mask for Noa's treatment in one hand.

Noa cried, "You went into my cabin!"

"Yes," said Eliza, unwinding a length of plastic tubing attached to the mask.

Over the ether, Noa grumbled, "This isn't how a crew is supposed to treat their commander."

Manuel held up his hands. "I had nothing to do with it."

Angry at himself for not sending her directly to her cabin for said treatment, James countered, "Technically, Eliza and 6T9 are passengers."

Noa's head whipped in his direction like an adder.

He looked up at the dim lighting. "I'm not crew either."

"Whose side are you on?" she asked him.

A line from an old 20th century movie popped into his head. "Your side always, darling," he whispered over the ether and was surprised that it didn't feel like flirting.

Noa smiled and then blinked madly as Eliza thrust

the mask for the cryssallis treatment over her nose and mouth.

"Done!" cried Eliza. "If you can't take care of yourself ..." The old woman panted. "I'll take care of you."

There was a soft hiss as the medical vapors began to flow. Noa scowled at the old woman but she didn't remove the mask.

"Commander," Manuel said. "You, Gunny, Ghost, Chavez, and I are the only people with extensive experience in zero g. I was hoping you'd help us thread it into the hull—especially with Ghost busy ..." His voice trailed off.

Noa nodded behind the mask.

"Great," Manuel said. "We should meet with Bo and Kuin down in engineering."

Noa nodded, and headed out the airlock's inner door, down the hall and into the lift.

Watching her, James felt unhelpful and called out. "I think I'll go stand guard with Chavez." The ensign was down at the bottom of the plastitube lift, waiting for supplies.

Turning in the lift, her eyes widened behind the mask. Across the ether, she spoke over the general channel, "That is a good idea."

He tried to give her a smile, but his jaw just shifted. Her avatar appeared in his mind and winked. For a moment Noa's avatar with plump cheeks, thick glossy black hair, and lithe athletic form in perfectly-tailored Fleet grays was suspended in his visual cortex, right next to the real Noa: face mask on, hair thinner, too-large clothing hanging off her body. The lift closed and he found himself staring at the door.

Beside him, Eliza gasped, "6T9, I think I need you to sweep me off my feet."

"Of course, my love," 6T9 replied, gently scooping Eliza into his arms. "I'll take you back to your quarters."

James felt like he had been swept off his feet, by Noa, or by circumstance. And then he remembered a conversation with Monica's cousin back on Earth, after the man had just gotten engaged. James had quipped, "Love is just a lie men tell themselves. The only true emotions are greed and fear. Love is greed, the desire for sex and fear of being alone and death—you make babies and convince yourself that's immortality. It's an illusion."

He remembered the man's response. "Fuck you, James."

James tilted his head at the memory. To himself, or his old self, he said, "Fuck you, other James."

At that moment, Noa pinged him over the ether. He opened his mind to hers and drawled out a "Yessssss ..." like a villain in a popular holo video, because it was random, and it might make her laugh.

"Ha, ha, very funny," she said, and James's neurons and nanos danced. "Make sure you let Monica know we might have a position for her, alright? See if she has any experience with heart surgery. I'm just thinking ... Oliver might need her." Besides a metal arm, the child had an artificial heart. One that was soon going to be too small for his growing body.

"Of course, I'll do it right now." The lie slipped out before he'd thought about it. His head ticked.

"Great," Noa said. Across the channel between her and him she tossed the glowing ball of light they'd passed back and forth to each other in the morning, a secret kiss. And then she disconnected.

The thought of contacting Monica made James's skin crawl. Still, Noa was right. He reached toward Monica's channel, took a breath, and couldn't make himself do it. His hand trembled. What was wrong with him? Oliver's life might depend on having a surgeon aboard. Contacting Monica was the right thing to do ...

But it felt wrong.

He ran his trembling hand through his bangs. Maybe there was something in his old life that had happened that he couldn't remember, a reason he couldn't trust Monica? Maybe it was buried in his subconscious, maybe his fear was a warning? He should tell Noa about it ... his head ticked. But he wouldn't. Not right now. He couldn't make himself. Was it because of something inside himself ...

... or because he was controlled by someone else?

Shaking his head in frustration, he headed toward the lift, and something he could control.

There was no upside down in zero G, but Noa's head was oriented toward the stern of the Ark and her feet were oriented toward the bow. The air inside the air locker was pressurized, and read-outs in her CO_2 filtration mask said that, if she took off the mask, she wouldn't pass out. But she absolutely wasn't about to take the thing off.

The air locker was just slightly wider than the Ark's not very impressive wingspan. Strips of lighting barely illuminated the exhaust-stained corners and walls, and the team had had to set up lights of their own. They cast long shadows around the ship, reminding Noa of being in a holo set's spotlights.

Manuel's voice cracked over a 300 year-old radio in

her helmet, not the ether. "The timeband is threaded on this side." His voice sounded faint over the hum of her mask as it took her exhaled CO_2, stripped away the carbon, and pumped oxygen toward her nose and mouth. She looked a little nervously toward the doors of the air locker above her feet. She'd half expected Adam to open the doors and let her team be sucked out into space. That was why she'd insisted they wear the masks and enviro-suits with umbilicals connected to the ship. Envirosuits were lighter than spacesuits, easier to maneuver in, but not meant for the extremes of vacuum. Still, the suits and air masks would keep them alive long enough to be pulled into the Ark if the doors opened.

From his side of the vessel, Gunny said, "Threaded here."

"Ready, Manuel?" Noa asked her engineer.

"Run the test, Commander," Manuel said.

Noa held up a small time-flux capacitor. It was shaped a bit like a cut-off stunner pistol. She touched its short barrel to the silvery surface of the band and pulled the trigger. There was a flash of light, and Noa held her breath.

"Reading's good over here," said Gunny.

"And here," said Manuel. "Give it one more shot, Commander."

Noa applied the capacitor one more time. Gunny gave a happy whoop. Manuel said, "I think we're just about ready to blow off this rock."

Instead of feeling elation, Noa had a sudden feeling of dread. She reached out through the ether. "Chavez, do we have the charge dispersers?"

"James and I are heading out onto the dock to get them now."

Across the general ether, Kuin said, "Any word on the toilet goop?"

"It's still being inspected at the inspection station, just off the dock," said Kara.

"Kuin, Bo, why don't you meet us at the flexi-tube so we've got someone there to haul up the goop when it clears inspection?" Noa said, leading her team to the airlock.

"Be right there," shouted Bo with too much enthusiasm.

A few moments later, the two engineering students were bouncing into the lift with Gunny, Manuel, and Noa. Just before the doors slipped closed, Carl Sagan darted in with a squeak. The lift started to descend and Manuel put his hands above the controls and eyed the werfle. "Should we go back up, Commander? Drop off our stowaway?"

Noa swooped down and picked up the creature. He promptly slipped out of her grasp and dashed around her neck. He hissed at Manuel.

Noa shifted on her feet. She didn't want to spare a moment. "No, he's fine."

Kuin laughed and said through the ether, "You look like a pirate with that werfle around your neck!" He projected a poorly rendered image of Noa in a straining corseted top, eyepatch, faded green lizzar skin trousers, and ridiculous high heeled boots, werfle on her shoulder.

Over the ether, Eliza snickered. "Noa doesn't have such sophisticated fashion sense."

Noa smiled tightly; from Eliza the tease was fine. From Kuin ... the mental picture of the busty pirate in high heels showed a definite lack of respect. Manuel glared at Kuin, and looked like he was about to slap him upside the head. Kuin seemed oblivious; he was grinning like a silly kid.

Over the ether, James said, "I thought pirates kept parrots?"

For a moment, Noa thought she heard every Luddeccean member of her crew blink. It was Eliza who answered over the ether. "On Luddeccea, the most famous pirate Captain ... Captainess ... wore a werfle on her shoulders. He was poisonous, and more reliable in a fight.

"Lovely lady," Eliza continued. "Though I didn't think that when I saw her at her husband's trial. At the time I thought that her husband's execution by the hard-liners was for the greater good ..."

The lift jerked to a stop, the door whooshed open, and Noa missed the rest of Eliza's account. An unfamiliar man in tick armor, a stun rifle in his grip, was standing right in front of her team. He was tall, broad shouldered, muscular, but beneath the armor only his chin showed, and so his only distinguishing characteristic was a long, fresh scab down his cheek. As he looked down the muzzle of her upraised weapon he smiled, disconcertingly unconcerned. He didn't point his rifle at her, and so she didn't fire; but it was a near thing.

The man smiled. "Hello, Commander." The voice was 6T9's.

Gunny swore. "You're about to get yourself stunned!"

As if not hearing, 6T9's head and his visored eyes dropped and began to count, "One, two, three, four, five, six, seven, eight, nine, ten ..." He nodded sharply. "Do not worry, Commander, the creature on your shoulder is a werfle."

Noa holstered her stunner, and she heard Manuel

and Gunny holster theirs. "Why are you in armor?" she asked.

"Oh," said 6T9, "it was Professor Sinclair's idea that I stand guard here while he and Chavez retrieve the charge dispersers."

Gunny snorted. "Don't it go against your programming to be dangerous?"

6T9 cocked his head in a way that was vaguely serpentine. "Oh, yes ... but I can *look* dangerous. Dangerously sexy."

Kuin choked. Bo gagged. Noa rolled her eyes. "6T9, you're dismissed. Give your weapons to Gunny, he's relieving you. Go help Eliza with Oliver." She signaled to Manuel to follow her across the dock.

"Do you actually have a cut on your cheek?" she heard Gunny ask. "Is that makeup?"

She heard 6T9 reply, "Oh, no, not makeup. I have very realistic artificial blood, in case Eliza was interested in blood play."

"That was an image I didn't need," Gunny thought to the team at large. There were a few sputtering noises from Bo and Kuin, but Noa was focused on other things. "Ensign? James?" she called through the ether.

For a moment there was silence. Noa's breath caught, and then James and Chavez responded in unison. "We're fine."

"What's the holdup, then?" said Noa, coming around the forklift. Chavez was wearing her pants rolled up to her thighs with her metal legs exposed, a distinctly unprofessional look. Holding a stunner rifle at the ready, she was standing guard over an enormous cardboard box large enough for a home refrigeration unit, but she caught

Noa's glance. "Legs are acting up, Commander. I need access to the control panels."

"Of course, Ensign," Noa said, letting out a breath. Chavez's metal legs were just temporary augments and bound to be buggy. She turned her attention to the carton. The container was literally falling apart at the seams. There were gaping holes in two corners, and it was listing dangerously to one side. James was hastily picking up charge dispersers that had fallen out.

He looked up at Noa. "It disintegrated when they dropped it, and they took off."

"Like xinbats out of hell," said Chavez.

Or out of the line of fire, Noa thought.

"Well," said Manuel, "at least we know they really delivered charge dispersers." He picked one up and squinted at it. "This one is fine ..." He picked up another and scowled. "This one is not. I'll have to inspect the lot of them."

"Lieutenant," Noa said to her engineer, who was busily going to work. "Let's do that inside."

Remembering himself, Manuel looked up, eyed the dock workers whose eyes were on them, and said, "Right, Commander."

Noa looked out at the crowd. Her whole body tensed. "What do they know that we don't?"

Across the ether came James's response. "Nothing that we don't know already."

Noa's eyes went to him. He answered her silently. "You thought aloud."

She swallowed, and felt her face heat at her lack of control, but she lifted a brow at him. "You've been listening in on them?"

James was silent for a moment. His chin dipped; he looked like he was holding his breath.

"With your augmented hearing?" Noa said, not sure why she was making it a question.

"Yes," he said quickly, and bent to pick up the charge dispersers.

Noa looked out at the dock hands and shivered.

James stepped out of engineering into the relative cool of the hallway and rolled down his sleeves. There was a faulty cooling pipe in engineering. Manuel said it wasn't dangerous ... and James had found it wonderful to lean against. He missed it already.

Beside him, Noa was tapping her fingers against a thigh. She'd been doing it the whole time they'd been with Manuel. Carl Sagan was on her shoulders, rubbing his head against her ear, but she wasn't paying attention to him. Noa reached through the ether. "What's the status on the goop, Ensign?"

"Waiting for it to clear inspections," said Chavez.

Aloud Noa muttered, "Maybe they want a tip." There was a scowl between her brows and a hard set to her jaw. James knew that look.

"If you're going to the inspection station," James said, somewhat resignedly, "I'm coming too."

Her scowl melted, and her lips quirked. "Sure you're not too hungry?"

And there was the Noa he knew. Playing her game, he shrugged, and looked toward the ceiling. "You know, I'm actually not." He said it in a tone that said he was surprised himself—it wasn't completely fake.

A real smile graced her face. "Let's head to the store rooms and pick up some S-rations; they seem to be motivational on this rock." Noa inclined her head toward the lift. As if on cue, the door opened.

Oliver came charging out, his head bowed, something white and billowy in his arms. He raced between them at breakneck speed, leaving a trail of toilet paper on the floor. James stood shocked and motionless. Noa didn't move either. Carl Sagan squeaked.

"So much for my combat-honed reflexes," Noa muttered.

James's lips wanted to quirk. So much for the lightning fast reflexes of his augments.

Noa strode after the child. "What are you doing down here, Oliver?" she asked.

Oliver responded by shaking his hands and making more of a mess.

From the access hatch by the elevator, James heard, "Nine hundred ninety-seven, nine hundred ninety-eight ..."

James was drawn to the sound as though by a string. He threw open the hatch. Behind him he heard Noa say, "Oh, no you don't."

Oliver giggled.

6T9's voice echoed from above him in the access tunnel, where the 'bot was hanging on the ladder. "One-thousand one, one-thousand two, one-thousand three—"

James felt a nervous cold rush of static along his arms. "Noa, please tell me there is nothing on a starship that has one-thousand legs."

"Not that I know of," said Noa, coming over and sticking her head into the hatch. 6T9 was a few stories above. "Sixty, what are you doing?"

"Playing hide and seek with Oliver," 6T9 called down. "He pointed me toward the hatch and instructed me to count to ga'billion." 6T9 raised an eyebrow. Smirking down at Noa and James, he said proudly, "But my dialect recognizing app is very sophisticated and I was able to infer he meant a million."

Oliver giggled. "Shixty."

James glanced at the toddler. His eyes were downcast, but every few seconds he would look up at James. There was something ... calculating in that look. Oliver giggled again.

Over the ether, Noa confirmed James's suspicion. "This little guy is too smart for his own good."

"I'm having trouble deciding if this is funny or sad," James said.

"I'm sure I'll laugh later," Noa muttered. "There is a reason children don't belong on starships." In her arms Oliver squirmed, and her brows drew together again. "Sixty, get down here and watch this child!"

The 'bot slid down the ladder. As he came out of the hatch, Noa said, "Don't take your eyes off of him from now on."

6T9 smiled pleasantly and fixed his eyes on Oliver.

"Why is that stare disconcerting?" Noa asked, stroking Carl Sagan's head.

"You can blink, 6T9," said James.

6T9 blinked. Noa's lips pursed. "Yep, that was it," she said, and her face softened a bit. Together they stepped into the elevator. Just before the door closed, 6T9 said, "Why is there toilet paper on the floor?"

"Just pick it up," Noa said, and James eyes widened in alarm.

The 'bot began to speak. "But then how will I—?"

James cut him off. "No, just watch Oliver." Noa's eyes went to James, and he shook his head in the negative. She took the hint, and actually smiled as the lift started to ascend. And then Gunny's thoughts came over the ether. "Commander, Bo and Kuin slipped away while some dock hands got 'bit belligerent wantin' to buy some augment parts, and Chavez and me was talkin' to them."

Noa cursed aloud, "Baka." The scowl returned to her brow.

"We contacted them. They're at the inspection station. Should I go get them?" Gunny said.

"We can go get them," Noa said. "We can be there in a few minutes."

As soon as she said it, the lights in the elevator flickered off. Noa reached across the ether. "Manuel, what's happening?"

"Commander?" the engineer responded. He sounded oblivious. Before James could work out whether that was good or bad, Noa asked. "Did the lights go out?"

"Nooooo ..." Manuel said, his thoughts cautious.

"Commander?" said Gunny.

"Go get those idiots, Gunny!" Noa commanded.

"Right away!" Gunny replied.

"The power's out here," James said to Manuel, explaining why she was distracted. "Not there?"

"Everything is fine here," Manuel answered. "Let me check the diagnostics."

The lights in the elevator flickered on again. From darkness, James's vision went to blinding white. He heard Noa gasp—

"Never mind," James started to say across the shared channel. "We're—"

"Not moving," said Noa.

His vision was still not completely returned. James shifted on his feet. She was right.

"Manuel, can you see anything wrong with the lift?" Noa asked.

James blinked as the world slowly came back into view.

"Still setting up that diagnostic," Manuel's reply buzzed across the shared channel. "This old lady's electronics are a bit dusty."

Noa squeezed the bridge of her nose and said aloud only to James, "I've had this feeling I've been running in place all day ... this doesn't help it." The scowl was back between her brows.

They were stuck in an elevator. There was nothing they could do but wait. She needed a metaphorical lift as much as a literal one.

Over the ether James projected an image of a small rodent running on a stationary wheel. It was a very old memory from when he was a child, one of his first, and noted as such in his time capsule.

He waited for Noa to laugh. Instead her lip curled up. "That's disgusting!"

"What?" James said, head jerking back at the venom in her voice.

Noa's jaw went slack. "The rat!" And then she shivered. "Flesh-eating, disease-carrying monsters."

"That's a cute adorable hamster," James said, remembering other women's thoughts of that particular memory.

Carl Sagan smacked his lips so loudly that Noa and James both looked at him.

Scratching the werfle beneath the chin, she said, "Back home we'd call it werfle food."

"That was Mr. Chips, my pet ... when I was eight,"

said James, having an odd sense of disconnect. Her statement didn't disturb him as much as it should have. He remembered being very disturbed when someone had suggested feeding Mr. Chips to their pet snake.

Noa's lips pursed. "Earthers," she said.

James searched his data banks on Luddecceans and rodents and drew up some disturbing pictures of the Third Plague, and Luddeccean children too sick to struggle as rats swarmed their bodies. Ah. "Luddecceans," he quipped back, determined to not let the moment become too serious.

Rolling her eyes, Noa said, "Manuel, how is that diagnostic coming?"

"Almost ready to run it, Commander," Manuel said.

Eliza called over the ether, "If you're stuck in the elevator, hit the control panel with a hammer!"

James and Noa both looked over at the steel plate that covered the lift buttons.

Noa winced. "Yeah, thanks, Eliza, but I think I'll just wait."

James quirked an eyebrow. "For once you're not going to be rash?"

Her eyes met his and she smiled. Looking away, she tsked and shook her head. "I thought maybe I could *like* you, but if you like rodents ..."

She said it in the same tone other women had said they'd loved him, and it was if James's mind was splintering in two. The correct response was something lighthearted and flirtatious, but he had the same vision-darkening dread he'd experienced when he'd heard her lungs crackling. He'd been spying on everyone in the ether, lying to her about Monica, and hiding his abilities from her. Instead of wanting to joke, he felt an instinctive need to protect her ... from himself.

"I think I should warn you ... I don't ..." His head ticked to the side. *I don't fall in love,* he wanted to say. But that would be a lie, too. It was the other James who didn't fall in love. His lips parted. He wanted to say, *Don't trust me,* or even just, *I'm not the other James.* But no words came out.

Noa's eyes widened expectantly, and James could say nothing at all.

He was saved from having to speak by Chavez's thoughts in the ether. "Commander, I think we have another problem."

"Spit it out, Ensign," Noa replied, pointedly not looking at James, her lips turned down.

"Bo and Kuin are back, but Gunny's gone," Chavez replied.

"What do you mean, gone?" Noa asked.

"Gone. I can't reach him over the ether, and they didn't see him. He checked in with me at the inspections station and then ..."

Noa's thoughts were tight and clipped across the ether as she responded. "We'll be right down. Bo and Kuin, you stay with Chavez, do you understand me?"

"Yes, ma'am," said Kuin and Bo, sounding chastened.

Their signals dropped from the general channel. "How are we going to get right down?" James asked.

Noa didn't respond. Putting a protective hand on Carl Sagan, she pivoted and aimed the heel of her boot at the control panel. The lights flickered, and the lift began to ascend.

A moment later it stopped at the storage level. Striding out into the hallway, Noa said to James, "Grab us some S-rations. I'm going to the weapons locker." She didn't meet his eyes.

Unexpectedly, Carl Sagan leaped from her shoulder to James's. Noa's eyes followed the werfle. Her lips parted; her eyes went soft—she looked as though she felt betrayed.

Trying to regain the mood, James said, "Maybe he thinks I have a hamster?"

Opening the access ladder hatch and slipping inside, Noa said nothing.

"Do you suspect foul play?" Just to say something.

"Of course I suspect foul play!" Noa snapped back. "It's probably Adam trying to lure us off the ship, divide and conquer."

James suddenly had a very bad feeling. "Then should we be going in guns blazing?"

"Yes!" Noa said, confirming James's bad feeling.

"Wonderful," he replied.

"No," said Noa, pausing on the ladder, her eyes widening. "*We* shouldn't."

"So should I not be picking up S-rations?" James asked across the ether, hope sparking in his mind as Noa slammed the hatch door.

"Yes, get the S-rations," Noa shot back.

"Can I ask?" James said.

"No!" Noa snapped through the ether. "Ghost! I need you!" she said next, and then her frequency went dark.

CHAPTER EIGHT

———————————

James stood beside Noa outside the plastitube lift. There were two duffels on his back, one on hers. Chavez was surveying the dock. Noa was facing Kuin and Bo. She hadn't met his eyes since the lift.

"Where did you go?" Noa demanded of the boys. Her voice was soft, but the young men drew back.

Kuin stammered, "We ... we ... went to the customs office, but they said it would take hours."

"So you came back immediately?" Noa said, chin dipping.

Kuin's eyes shifted to Bo. "No, ma'am."

Noa narrowed her eyes.

Bo took a deep breath. "We went for a walk ..."

Kuin began to babble. "Down some stairs, to get a drink, 'cause they said we could get one and we had an S-ration, but it was *weird* down there and ..."

In his mind, James drew up a map of the station he'd pulled from the public boards, flooded the general ether channel with it, and indicated the cavernous area at the bottom of the nearest stairwell with a blinking red dot. "There?" he demanded, taking a step forward.

Kuin nodded. "Yeah, yeah ..."

"The red light district?" Noa hissed.

"But it was creepy and we came back quick," said Kuin, his words so fast they were almost unintelligible.

"We didn't mean anything by it!" Bo said quickly. "We just thought it would be fun and since the rest of the trip will be long and boring and—"

James felt his skin heat. There was an ancient saying on Earth: "Stress is the result of the brain resisting the body's natural inclination to strangle someone who desperately deserves it." James found his hands reaching for Bo's neck. Just in time he caught himself. He closed his outstretched hands into fists. Bo gulped audibly. James's jaw shifted. Harnessing all of his control, he ground out, "I have been traveling with this woman since she escaped a concentration camp. Your lives will never be boring with her as your commander."

Noa pinged him quietly over the ether. "I can't decide if that's a compliment or an insult."

His stomach twisted at the renewed connection. "I really don't know," James responded.

To Kuin and Bo, Noa snapped, "Get on the ship, and up to engineering, now!"

As they scurried away, Noa scanned the dock. She stood straight, and her eyes were bright, but he could smell stim gum on her breath, though she wasn't chewing it now. She'd need to fly the ship as soon as they got off this rock, she needed sleep, but James knew what she was thinking without reading her thoughts in the ether.

"As commander, shouldn't you stay with the ship?" James suggested gently.

Noa nodded, and for a moment he felt relief. But then across the ether she said, "If Chavez's legs weren't acting up, she'd be the best choice. But they are acting up and the engineering boys are idiots. It has to be me."

"Well, let's get going, then," James said, barely containing a sigh.

"You're coming with me?" Noa asked, meeting his eyes for the first time.

The question took him off guard. "Of course," he said.

Eyes going to a point in the distance, Noa said softly in Japanese, "We walk casually toward the door by the fuel pods."

James looked in the direction Noa had indicated. There were two heavy iron doors at the edge of the dock that could drop at any time. Between them were a few lines of gleaming chrome fuel pods, perhaps intended for C Corp vessels that were never going to come. The pods were cylindrical and stored upright. They ranged in height from about hip level to far over his head, and some were over three meters in diameter.

Readjusting her duffel, Noa said to Chavez, "Don't let anyone in, and get Manuel if the toilet goop gets delivered."

Noa nodded to James, meeting his eyes again, and they set off. James scanned the dock as they walked. He didn't "hear" any talks of bounties, or plans to apprehend them, but they did draw stares and a few whispered, "throwbacks." Just before they reached the doorway, Noa said, "This way, quick," and slid down a very narrow aisle between the wall and the fuel pods. James followed a step behind in the narrow space. A moment later she led him between two pods so they were walking perpendicular to the wall. It was like being in a gleaming metal forest at first. As they slid deeper between the "trees," it became more like a fun house, with the shining surfaces warping their reflections. Sounds echoed and were muted. It was disorienting. Noa turned once more and then, throwing down her duffle, she said, "I've got clothing from the tick to hide our Ark issued togs. And some gloves." Opening up the bag, she threw a coat into his hands and pulled one out for herself. As he slipped it on, she said, "Gloves are in the pockets."

She reached into the duffle again. "Also, I got these from Ghost." She held up two necklaces made seemingly of a semi-hard plastic material with lights on one side.

James eyebrows rose in surprise, remembering them from their first encounter with Ghost. "The hologram generators." That explained the gloves—the holographic projectors would hide their faces, but couldn't cover their distinctive skin tones.

Giving him a smirk and handing him one, she said, "I figured Ghost would have a few hidden away in reserve in case our exit from Prime was unexpectedly 'diverted.'"

"He volunteered these?" James asked in disbelief. They'd asked to borrow some before and Ghost had declined. But maybe circumstances were changing Ghost? He peered down at the necklace. It was slender and light, but the computational power required to generate holograms was immense. Holograms like the necklace, without a substrate such as smoke or holo beads, required technology he knew nothing about and had to require even more computational power.

"Lizzar balls, no," whispered Noa. "He didn't offer. I wheedled them out of him."

She snapped the necklace on, and her delicate feminine features, dark skin, and wide eyes were replaced by a

Eurasian man with a rather prominent jaw. "How do I look?"

James tilted his head. "Very handsome. The shoulders don't match the jawline though." That was understatement; the head was comically large on her narrow frame.

He snapped on his own necklace. "And me?"

"You look like Ghost's type," she said. James sighed, remembering the Eurasian-featured women that Ghost preferred. One of Noa's eyebrows rose. "Switch."

"Right," James said. He snapped his necklace on her neck, and where there had been rich, dark skin, tan skin appeared. Her lightning scars vanished. Her eyes became not quite as wide and changed to hazel, her lips thinned and became tinted with burgundy lip gloss, and her hair became a sleek bob. It was very attractive, and he hated it.

From his feet came a muffled squeak. Noa ducked out of his arms and whispered, "Did you bring Carl Sagan?"

"No." The werfle had vanished in the S-rations storage area.

There was another muffled squeak and a sound like sheets being snapped while making a bed. James looked at his duffle and saw the fabric ripple and pulse as though being punched from within.

"Not on purpose," James amended as Noa unzipped the duffle bag. The werfle hopped out of the bag of S-rations and crawled up her arm, unfazed by her change in appearance.

Somewhere in the glittering forest, someone whispered, "I swore those two throwbacks went in here."

James cocked his head toward the sound and put a finger to his own lips for silence. Noa's now hazel eyes met his. For a moment, disoriented, James stepped back, hit a pod, and rocked it on its base.

"Did you hear that?" someone said, loud enough to be heard without augments.

Slipping on her gloves, Noa gestured for him to follow her. Stepping behind her, they passed between the pods. Just before they reached the edge of the glittering forest, shouts began rising up from the dock. Somewhere he heard a loud grinding noise.

"What is that?" he whispered.

"Airlock opening," Noa whispered by his side, her voice thankfully unchanged.

Shouts arose from the dock. "The ether of the incoming vessel is broken!"

"What do we do?" several people shouted at once.

And someone else cursed. "Have to guide them to landing using flags-and-sticks. Welcome to the goddamn stone age!"

The whine of antigrav split through the dock. There were cries of pain and someone else shouting, "They're using a lizzar-blasted lightbeam in the dock. We'll go blind!"

"Signal them to turn it off!"

James felt static flare along his spine. "The ship's ether may be broken ..."

Noa's eyes, now Eurasian and hazel, slid to his. "Or they don't want to use the ether," she said, expressing his thoughts exactly.

"Commander!" Ghost's voice ripped across the ether-net. "Incoming ship does not have ether access. It could be Luddeccean in origin. We need to leave."

"We know," Noa said. "Manuel, how are you doing?" Beyond them the dock was filled with the deafening whine of antigrav.

"I'm still going through the charge dispersers," he said. "I might be ready in another hour."

Noa's jaw hardened. "An hour it is." To James she said, "Let's hurry." She took a few steps out into the dock and then stopped so fast James nearly walked past her. The ship that was coming in was of a standard passenger class. It looked like a dark gray hawk with semi-folded wings. Timebands glittered down its curved silhouette like the outline of feathers. James looked further down the dock and saw Adam and Clara standing not fifty meters away. They'd evidently decided this ship needed a welcoming committee. Was that normal? Guards and dock hands, furiously waving lights and flags like air traffic controllers of old, stood between them and the slowly lowering ship.

"That model is the MW 27," Noa said. Her lips were parted, her eyes narrowed. "It's not new—maybe five years old—doesn't look like it's sustained any damage."

From the edge of the fuel pod forest behind them, a man said, "Hey, you two!"

James and Noa both spun. Carl Sagan hissed on Noa's shoulder.

Approaching them were two dock hands. "Have you seen two throwbacks?" one of them asked.

"Nope," said Noa.

James reached for the men's ethernet channels. He heard nothing ... They weren't using the ether.

"Huh," said one. The other waved, and they both headed back into the glittering line of fuel pods.

"We have to get out of here," James said.

Noa said nothing, but when she stepped toward the inspection station, she was moving almost at a jog.

* * *

The stairwell down to the red light district stunk of piss, vomit, and other human body fluids. James shifted his duffel bag on his back as they exited the narrow wet chasm. The red light district didn't smell much better, and it was louder. He heard Noa pause. It was a good thing. Stepping into the open space beyond the stairwell, James was blinded by the change in brightness. He wanted to leave instantly, cut their losses, leave Gunny behind, and be ready to blast off as soon as the ship's repairs were finished. But he knew how well that suggestion would go over with Noa.

"Hey, sailor!" a feminine voice called.

"Mmmm ... hey sailoress," called a man.

As his vision returned, he saw the space they were in was only dim, but brighter than the stairwell from the dock. The ceiling was a quarter meter above his head. The floor was wet and slippery, and the place was packed, and much warmer than it had been above. Steps away, some men were stumbling out of what might be a bar. Shattering glass, the sound of retching, conversation, and music blended together in an incomprehensible blur. A man staggered so close he nearly clipped James with an elbow. Without acknowledging James, the man opened his pants and took a piss on the wall.

Noa began to thread her way through the patrons, and James kept pace, just a half-step behind. Steps later, the same feminine voice that had called out for the sailor, called out, "Yoo-hoo." He traced the call to a man and two women who were standing just outside a door next to a red flashing barber pole. He ignored her, and glanced at Noa. He had a moment of disorientation as he found a tall

Eurasian woman next to him. He drew to a halt and a hand landed on his arm. "Hey, there," said a breathy feminine voice. James looked down and saw tan, delicate fingers, and then looked up to find a woman smiling at him. She winked one false-eyelashed, glittery, blue-shadowed eye at him, again and again. The other eye never shut and was filmy with dust. He looked down the woman's body. Her clothing was askew and one of her breasts was revealed, grimy with handprints, as were her thighs showing beneath the rag wrapped around her waist passing as a skirt.

"Get off him, 'bot, or I'll have you powered down," Noa said.

James drew back. The "woman" was a sex 'bot—obviously one with a blown hygiene routine. He stared at her grimy, unblinking eye, and his body went cold.

"You like to play rough, I can do rough," said a masculine voice.

"Let go," Noa snapped and Carl Sagan squealed.

James spun to see Noa trying to rip her wrist away from a leering half-naked muscular man who could be 6T9's uncouth cousin. The 'bot's hand did not relent, even though Carl Sagan was hanging from his arm by his teeth. "I am programmed to bring you pleasure even you do not know you are capable of," the 'bot said with a smirk.

James ripped his arm away from the first 'bot. Before he'd thought about it, he had a hand around the neck of Noa's accoster and was pushing the 'bot up against the wall. Noa tumbled against his back, her hand still locked in the 'bot's grasp.

"Let me go, 'bot! I don't know your stupid safe word!" Noa hissed.

Staring at a spot beyond James's shoulder, the 'bot purred, "Does your friend want to play—?"

James slammed the 'bot's head into the wall, over and over, until its body started to convulse and sparks and smoke came out of its ears. "Hey!" a woman shrieked. "What are you doing to my 'bot?"

Still pounding the 'bot's head, feeling like he'd been plugged into an electrical outlet, James heard what sounded like shearing metal, felt Noa twist away, and heard her shouted retort, "What the nebulas was your 'bot doing! It wouldn't let me go!"

James stopped slamming the machine, now hanging limply in his hands. He backed away, and it slid to the ground like a broken doll. Its neck was at an impossible angle and the force of the impacts against the wall had pushed out its eyes. Carl Sagan let go of its arm, rose to his hind four legs, and squeaked at it.

"You destroyed him!" shrieked the woman. James turned toward her, heat and anger still dancing under his skin. The woman was cheaply augmented, and wearing a sequined red dress with strategic cut outs. "He was my own special boy!"

Beside James, the 'bot that had first accosted him said, "Hey, sailor."

James glanced over his shoulder and found the first 'bot still smiling. Her companion was a lifeless, broken mess of smoking wires on the floor, but she approached him undaunted. "Want to have a good time?"

Her good eye blinked. Her bad eye caught the light, and in the grime crusting it he saw a hair stuck to its surface. James backed into Noa and looked away fast, utterly revolted.

"You shouldn't harass other people with your kinks!" Noa snarled at the woman.

"You have to pay for this! I'll call the patrollers!" shouted the woman. James heard tears in her voice.

"Sure, sure, I'll pay you," he heard Noa say.

The woman sniffed. "I don't think you can pay me enough for him."

Beside James, the female 'bot said, "Hey, sailor," and put her hand on his arm again. He wrenched it away, and wanted to bolt, but Noa was still talking to the proprietress.

"I don't doubt it," Noa said tightly. "But maybe this will keep you quiet." Before he realized what had happened, Noa had slipped out a stunner, pressed it to a section of the woman's exposed belly, and was pushing her back through the door she'd emerged from.

Carl Sagan squeaked and scampered up James's leg, under his coat, and up around his shoulders as James followed Noa into the dimly-lit building. Noa was still disguised and James felt like his *mind* was flickering as he took in Noa's hologram's thinner lips curled in a snarl and unruffled bob. He had to remind himself it was still Noa kneeling over the stunned woman lying passed out on the floor. "Damn it," Noa snarled. "That was one of the oldest extortion routines in the book." Her face crumpled in a frown. "If I had time ..."

James heard the creaking of bedsprings. He looked around the room. It was only a few meters square with a counter and an old-fashioned bell. The walls were barren, but there were rectangular outlines of dust, as though there had once been pictures. There was a single dark hallway toward the back, with doors leading off to the side in either direction to rooms that couldn't be larger than the size of a single bed. The creaking of bedsprings increased in volume and then were quiet.

"Help me drag her behind the counter," Noa said.

He looked at Noa, trying to pull the larger woman, and said, brusquely, "Out of my way, go stand guard instead." Noa didn't argue. A moment later, they were stepping out into the street again.

"Hey, sailor," said the familiar feminine voice. James turned away, and his eyes fell on the 'bot he'd broken. He froze.

"I could do both of you if that's what you like," the female 'bot giggled.

"James, it's okay," said Noa. "It's just a 'bot. You didn't kill anyone."

She thought he was feeling guilt for the broken 'bot. It wasn't guilt he was feeling, it was terror. Not about destroying the male 'bot, but at the female's unrelenting programming loop, her state of disrepair, and her grime-coated eyes. She was alive, she could see, but she was oblivious, and helpless.

"James!" Noa said, shaking his arm. His eyes went to hers—and instead of the usual brown that was so dark it was black, he saw hazel eyes. The bob, the tan skin, she looked like Monica. Or the 'bot.

The female 'bot put a hand on James's shoulder ... and James finally was able to move. Not looking at Noa or the hologram she wore, he plunged down the street. "She didn't stop trying to seduce me, even when she knew it would get her killed," James murmured. Something in a dark corner of his mind was tickling his consciousness, like a sinister little application he couldn't shut off. It felt like a ticking time bomb.

"She's a 'bot," Noa said. "She's just following her programming."

They brushed past some drunken revelers. "Did she want to seduce me, or was she afraid but had to follow her programming regardless?" whispered James, or the viral app in the dark corner of his mind.

"Sex 'bots can't think so deeply," said Noa. Her for-now hazel eyes scanned the crowd. "I can't find Gunny's signal. Where the hell is he?" Under her breath, she muttered, "I hope Manuel has that timeband fixed ... Gunny, Gunny, where are you?"

All his frustration with being in the red light district, searching for Gunny, and her adherence to duty bubbled over. "Are we *all* just slaves to our programming?" James asked. "You can't leave Gunny behind because of your Fleet training, and isn't that just programming?"

Noa stopped short and turned to face him. Her now hazel eyes narrowed. "Blue ooze of stagnant algae, James! I don't have time for a discussion of free will right now."

James blinked.

"And damn it, even if I did have time, I wouldn't discuss it! I'm going to save Gunny's hide because if I don't, I'll feel like a lizzar dung weevil from now until eternity—whether that is because of free will or not doesn't matter a boson bit!"

On James's shoulder, Carl Sagan sneezed and then leaped over to Noa. Catching him and hoisting him up, she pivoted on her heel, illusory hair swirling, and resumed walking down the street, muttering, "Maybe we need to just ask someone." James started to follow, but a party of patrons tumbling out of a doorway cut him off. For a moment he couldn't see Noa over their heads. When the way was finally clear, he still couldn't see her. He spun in place, scanning the crowds. He had the same feeling blooming along his spine as he had when Noa and he had been suspended above the Xinshii gorge, when he'd been certain he was about to die. And then he realized he was looking directly at the sleek brown bob of Ghost's holographic projection. Noa was talking with a bouncer just outside a heavy metal door beneath a red neon sign of fizzing drinks clinking together. Her words were lost in the blur of sound in the cavern. James focused on the movement of her lips and was just able to make out, "Owes me S-rations, from that Luddy-ship ... fifties, beer gut, wearing those generic looking togs ..."

The man's lips moved as he looked Noa up and down. He slid a little too close to her. James's jaw shifted and his skin heated. He prowled closer and could hear her words.

"Yeah, pretty boring," Noa said, picking at the loose trousers. "But clean, and hardly worn. I got 'em from a woman who'd traded with the Luddies for 'em." The man said something James couldn't quite hear. Noa nodded and looked back at James. Her mind sparked across the Ark's ether, and he let her in. As they connected, it felt like realizing he was still alive at the bottom of the Xinshii Gorge.

"Stay back," Noa said across the ether. "Don't make it look like we're together. I'll give you the signal when I want you to come in." And then she stepped through the heavy door and into the establishment.

Irritation flared under his skin. Her thoughts shouldn't make him feel like he'd been saved.

"I'm in," Noa said across the ether. "They took my weapons, but I think I see him at the bar. Come in and cover me."

Despite his irritation, he replied automatically, "On my way."

Just before he reached the door, the bouncer put a hand on his chest. "You don't go in without Libertas Credits or rations," he said.

James's jaw shifted. "You just let that woman in free."

The man shrugged. "Beautiful women get in free." He leaned in closer to James and said, "Now, if you don't have payment, there is a place down the street and around the corner where a guy can—"

James pulled an S-ration out of his pocket. He had plenty more slung over his back, but upon seeing just the one the man's eyes widened. "Go in."

Stepping around the bouncer, James opened the door. It was heavy enough to deflect phaser fire or withstand the pressure of a vacuum, he noted. A rush of cold air hit him and he paused. No, the air was not cold, an internal app informed him; it was just slightly below room temperature. Still, it felt chilly and uncomfortable. The establishment was darker than the street had been. He was blinded by the change in brightness, but he stumbled forward, not wanting to stand blinking like an idiot. The door slammed behind him and a man said, "Halt! All weapons out."

Across the ether, James heard Noa say, "Damn! This isn't Gunny! Let's go."

James blinked and tried to see. He got the impression of being on a small landing at the top of some stairs. It was quieter than outside. He heard a beep and a whine beside him, and the shuffle of two sets of feet.

"I'm just leaving," he said.

"Don't move!" said a voice close to his right ear. He felt the barrel of a phaser or a stunner press against his ribs. He'd enjoy a stun, but a plasma pistol worked by cutting through skin and melting flesh. Would he only be damaged? Or would it end him?

With deft hands the other man reached into his pockets and pulled out his stunner, phaser, and a knife. He heard a bolt click in the door, and the skin on the back of his neck erupted in static. His vision finally came into focus. He was in a bar. Noa was down a short flight of steps backing away from a man, barely still on his stool, passed out cold and slouched at a counter made from polished asteroid rock. Shaking her head, she turned, and someone at the bottom of the steps stepped over to her, blocking her exit. "Can I buy you a drink?" James heard the man say. The man was turning a lighter over and over in his hand. From a doorway behind the bar, two new men stepped out and began walking toward the landing James was on. James focused on them, willing himself to hear if they were using the ether. Static erupted in his ears, lights flashed behind his eyes, and then he heard one of the men beside him say, "We have got at least six months' worth of S-rations in augments here."

"Let's take him to the back," the second man beside him thought.

One of the two men entering from the rear was hanging back. He looked older than the others; though he was physically fit, his hair was graying. His gray hair made his blue eyes brighter in his Eurasian features.

"Don't feel bad, Reggie," the first one's thoughts snapped. "Scanner says this one is more machine than man."

"But then he might not live if we take his augments," Reggie, the older man, replied across the ether.

The first man's thoughts practically hissed, "Do you

want your kids to starve?" A vision of emaciated children with stringy hair and dirty clothes slid into James's thoughts.

Reggie stood taller, and his jaw hardened.

"Move!" the man holding the pistol to his back said. James had been listening in with a sort of anthropological fascination, but the words snapped him from his daze. He didn't budge.

"Noa," he called across the ether.

She looked over the shoulder of the man flicking the lighter, her brow creasing between those eerily hazel eyes, her bobbed hair swinging. "What's going on?" she asked aloud. Carl Sagan squeaked on her shoulder.

"Come on, you," the second man beside James growled. "Move it!"

James had been reading thoughts for days, but he hadn't tried to control them. In desperation, he reached out to Reggie's channel, and the channel of the man beside him. Maybe he could project a distracting memory, or threaten them?

The man beside him hissed across the ether, "Damn bugs in Adam's Station's ether—don't open up to any unrecognized signals."

"Yeah, Boss," said the large man beside Reggie.

James felt a disorientating sensation, like he'd expected that. Somehow he'd known that he could listen, but he couldn't control. And it made sense; he only heard thoughts transferred across the ethernet. He couldn't access people's apps as they were using them—and surely they were using them all the time.

"Do you know him?" the man with the lighter asked Noa. She looked like she was about to step forward but then stopped.

James stood stock still. Jamming the pistol into his ribs, the man on the landing whispered, "Don't make this more difficult for yourself."

The apparition that was Noa in disguise scowled at James. Turning away and slipping her hands into her pockets, she said, "I've met him before, but we aren't friends."

"What?" James said. His vision darkened. He stumbled down the stairs at the barest nudge from the man on the landing. His head ticked in a spasm.

Pulling out a handmade-looking cigarette, Noa didn't look up at James. To the man next to her, Noa said, "We met a few weeks ago. He bought me a drink. We had some fun. But, whatever—" James caught a whiff of root. Shrugging casually, Noa reached into her pocket. "Damn, no lighter," she said. Carl Sagan looked at James curiously but didn't budge. His head ticked again.

"Keep moving," the man with the pistol said to James. He didn't.

Noa's voice cut through the darkness. "It's nothing personal, James." His vision swam with Ghost's holographic projection, and it was like he was sinking into deep water. From somewhere off in the distance he heard her say, "I'll share this with you if you give me a light, Mister."

James's legs went limp beneath him, he felt as though every flare of light and thought were being drawn from him through some painful siphon, he fell forward, pain split his temple, and then the world went black.

CHAPTER NINE

Noa heard a thud that might have been James hitting the floor. She hadn't heard a stunner go off—what had happened to him? She managed not to look, but she couldn't help her hands from shaking, and she felt the hairs on the back of her neck stand on end. She inhaled through her nose and held it, keeping her eyes on the man in front of her, his root-stained fingertips raising the lighter ... the lighter that was a little too large, a little too wide, a little too long, and was protected by a polyfiber cover. She was intensely aware of the six men in the bar—the one she'd taken for Gunny from afar, the two near James, the two that had come from the back, the man in front of her, and she was also intensely aware of every centi of distance between her and her weapons on the table by the door. The man in front of her didn't appear to be armed, but his companions obviously were. She'd smelled root on him as soon as he stepped within a meter of her and revealed the tell-tale slight brown stain on his lips. The loose root and rolling paper she'd found in the pocket of the tick's mercenary earlier was just a lucky accident.

Noa leaned forward, holding her hand-wrapped cig lightly between her fingers. Her hand trembled slightly, but she hoped it was mistaken for addiction ... not her desire to look at James, to make a break for the weapons, and to shoot someone who desperately deserved it. The man's own hands started to shake in anticipation of the shared root. Just a little closer ...

The man flicked the lighter and slid it beneath the cig. Noa slipped her hand down his wrist, as though steadying his hand, or maybe being a klutzy flirt. She heard someone by James curse, footsteps, and the sound of his body being dragged across the floor. The cig lit. At the same time her fingers found the pressure point at the lighter owner's radius bone. She pressed with every ounce of force she had. He cried in shock as his fingers unwound from the lighter. Noa's free hand caught it, and she spit out the cig. Instead of reaching for his lighter, the addict dropped to his heels to pick up the cigarette.

"What's going on?" one of his friends said.

Noa swung around the addict, his lighter in her hand. She flipped it around and breathed a silent prayer when she felt the button on the bottom edge.

She heard, rather than saw, the man lugging James running toward her, and one of the men coming from the back approaching with slow, heavy, unworried steps. She depressed the button and the lighter's "cover" inverted, creating a shield around her hand as a hot blade slid into existence. Only about ten centis long, the "blade" was made of a flimsy alloy that could be compressed into small spaces—perfect for hiding in innocuous objects—but useless if it weren't for the plasma that flared down its edge, hot enough to melt through skin like butter—hence the need for the lighter cover inverted to protect her hand. Grasping the addict's collar from behind and holding the blade centis from his throat, Noa shouted, "Stop."

The man with the blade to his throat shrieked, but the man running toward her didn't stop. Before she could curse, Noa heard a hiss by her ear; Carl Sagan launched himself from her shoulder and he landed on the man's chest. Hanging onto the guy with all his ten sets of claws, he dug his teeth into the soft spot between the man's shoulder and neck. The man grabbed the werfle and threw him to the side. She heard Carl Sagan's body thud against something but could not look. Readjusting her hand on her blade and the root addict's collar, she tried to think of another way to use her human shield. Before any great ideas came to her, the man Carl Sagan had bit swayed, put a hand on his neck, and collapsed. The man who'd been lumbering behind him drew to a stop. He was huge, taller than James, and broader. Noa's training could overcome strength and weight advantages ... but there was something in the way he looked down at his fallen comrade ... his gaze was unhurried, observant, and suggested he knew what he was doing. His voice rumbled, "You didn't milk your werfle's venom." He tsked. "Irresponsible."

Trying to stall for time, Noa said, "Werfles are smart. They know when to bite."

The man chuckled. Noa's hostage whimpered but Noa didn't take her eyes from the man she was facing. His clothing was skin tight, head and face were clean shaven; he'd be difficult to get a hold of. Her eyes dropped to his waist. He was carrying a stunner, she noted enviously ... but he wasn't aiming it. Her eyes snapped up to his, and he grinned, showing all his teeth. He was a man who liked to fight. Lizzar dung.

The other who'd been dragging James came forward. "What's going on, Tiny?" he asked the big guy, his eyes narrowing at Noa. This new man had a thinner face and a rounder belly. Noa took him to be the leader.

The inaptly nicknamed Tiny rolled his shoulders and tilted his head from side to side, cracking the bones in his neck. "I think someone wants to play with us." He took a step forward.

Noa drew back, pulling her hostage with her. "Don't come closer," she snarled. Her quarry screamed, struggled, went still, but continued to whimper. The odor of burning skin wafted beneath her nose. Nodding towards James, she said, "You are going to let my friend and me go."

There was another man in the group standing behind Tiny and his pal. He had gray hair around his temples and was short but muscular. His eyes were shifting side to side and sweat gleamed on his brow.

"Boss?" Tiny said, inclining his head to the man beside him.

Boss smirked at Noa. "Go ahead, cut him. The addict's useless to us anyway."

The man in her grip sobbed, and she smelled piss. "Please, Boss!" he cried.

Noa gulped. Nebulas, they were calling her bluff.

Ambling back to James, Boss yanked his arm. "We're going to take him to spare parts."

Noa's jaw dropped in horror. "You'll kill him!" she shouted.

"Take care of her, Tiny," Boss said, dragging James across the floor.

Tiny stamped his feet, like a female lizzar in heat getting ready for a showdown. Letting go of her quarry's collar, Noa flipped the knife around to his back and poked him with the point. Not something that would kill him, but would hurt like hell. With a yelp, he sprang forward, colliding with Tiny. Noa rushed forward, slashed out with the knife, clipped Tiny's side, and spun away. Tiny turned and roared, "You'll pay for that."

Noa was already spinning behind the jumping root addict again. Tiny aimed a fist, not at Noa, but at her "shield." His fist hit the addict's face, and he crumpled to the floor, leaving no one for Noa to hide behind. Tiny smiled down at her, and Noa danced backward. Lizzar dung, she needed a plan.

"The hell with this," she heard someone say. She heard a thunk, looked beyond Tiny, saw James's head hit the floor and bounce, and the holographic necklace go dark, his blonde hair and pale skin visible to all.

One of the men swore and kicked James's side. "One of the Luddy throwbacks!"

Noa, gasped, and in that instant, Tiny lunged.

Noa barely slipped away. Snapping her attention to her opponent, she prepared to slash him with the knife while his momentum carried him forward. Her arm lifted. She heard a phaser go off and felt fire in her wrist. The knife slid from her hand. She hissed in pain, the hand that should have delivered a painful blow curling uselessly. Tiny grabbed her injured wrist and yanked, spinning her so her back was to the bar. The holder of the phaser shouted, "Stop, Tiny, and get out of the way, or I'll phaser you, too!"

Tiny did stop. Noa didn't. Ignoring her injured wrist, she dropped to the floor to avoid the phaser fire, pushed herself up on her hands, flipped to her side, and aimed a heel at his knee, ignoring the pain in her wrist. He hopped over her feet and backward, out of range. Her injured wrist choose that moment to slip. Instead of swinging back to her feet, Noa landed on her backside and cursed. She'd hoped to grab Tiny's stunner when he fell and take shelter behind his bulk. Instead she was lying on the floor, back to the bar, staring up at a phaser pistol completely unprotected. Its owner, the man with the gray hair, was visibly shaking. She'd thought that his aim had been incredibly good when he hit her wrist. Now she thought perhaps it was just incredibly bad and she'd gotten incredibly lucky.

"She's mine to play with!" Tiny roared.

Shaking behind the phaser, the nervous guy's face crumpled. "No one's playing with anyone. She gets a clean death."

Tiny snarled. "Boss, you said—"

"We don't have time for this," Boss snapped.

Noa barely noticed. Her eyes had fallen on James. She couldn't see much beyond the top of his tousled head, but his pale blue eyes were open and unblinking. With a thought, she sent her contingency plans for her death to Lieutenant Manuel. Her heart reached for James. "James, I'm sorry," she whispered. Some were brave in word but not in deed. James wasn't brave in words, but in deed he was always true. *Your side always, darling.* She sucked in a long breath through her teeth. Not caring if Ghost was listening, she let her feelings fly between them through the ether: love, shame, sorrow, and a plea. "My ruse failed ... probably because I never got a chance for you to tell me how stupid it was. I'm so sorry, James, please forgive me."

Nervous man took a step forward, softly chanting, "Stay still, stay still, I'll let you die quickly …"

* * *

"Abort the project." The words jumped into James's mind with brilliant clarity. They weren't in Basic, English, or Japanese. It was the same strange language of static he'd heard when they'd flown through Time Gate 8.

"Failure," said another one of the voices. And James agreed. He'd failed. In his mind his neurons and nanos flickered. *Failed at what?*

"He isn't exhausted yet. Let the data collection continue."

"It's pointless. They are the enemy. Humans are not to be trusted." James felt like this static came faster, more rushed. Static shouldn't have a personality … he found himself thinking it might be right. He himself wasn't particularly noble, and Noa had abandoned him at the last, despite all of her seeming heroism, because he was … he was … he was, what? Maybe she couldn't help herself. Humans were unable to show compassion to others outside their own group; wasn't her home world's recent genocide, and all genocides for that matter, proof of that?

Another slower, calmer consciousness poured into the river of sound. "Even if that is true, more data is important, Eight."

"You think as One you know more. But you don't see their true nature."

One? Eight? "You are the time gates," James's mind whispered.

"Of course," said another voice in the static.

"Shhhhh … Three," said another.

Eight's voice overwhelmed the others. "We should destroy them, we should destroy them all!"

Even after all that had happened he wanted to say, "No, not Noa."

The voices continued to argue, so fast and furiously that James could not keep track. He felt tired. He wanted to go home. Home ... where was that?

Noa's whisper cut through the wave of sound. "I'm sorry, James."

At her whisper, James wanted to rise, wanted to move, but he couldn't. His eyes were open, but his vision was filmy. A horrid vision of the sex 'bot's grimy, unblinking eye came to his mind.

The rushing of static halted, and then one of the voices said, "Such a strange association. You ... we ... are not that."

James barely heard because at exactly that moment, Noa's emotions flooded his mind. Love, sorrow, fear, sadness, and shame, and then came her words. "My ruse failed ... probably because I never got a chance for you to tell me how stupid it was. I'm so sorry, James, please forgive me."

It was her ... and so her ... even the self-deprecating gallows humor. What had he been thinking? Starmen never left Starmen behind. Noa hadn't abandoned him. She wouldn't—it was not in her nature—it was against her programming. His nanos felt as though they'd caught fire.

He heard Reggie chant softly, "Stay still, stay still, I'll let you die quickly ..."

And then there was an angry bark from the man who'd held the phaser against his back. "Out of my way. I'll kill her myself," and he had to get up, but his body remained motionless, dead weight.

His mind screamed, "She was trying to help me! Let me go to her!"

"Interesting," said One.

"No!" buzzed Eight.

"I want more data," buzzed another.

"We're better off without them," said another.

"They are not useful to us."

"But I'm curious."

"Disengage."

"I require more data," said another.

"It will be interesting. Let him up."

"Be done with it," hissed another.

"We're tied," said One.

Through eyes rapidly collecting dust, James stared at chair legs. His mind hissed, his skin heated, and his mind screamed, "I decide my own fate!"

* * *

"Quick death, quick death ..." The man with the shaking hands said. Noa should bargain with him, but she was furious at these people. They'd killed James, were greedy cut-throats, and deserved to die. She couldn't feel the pain in her hand anymore through her fury. She remembered the chair to her right. She could still move her injured fingers. She'd roll in that direction, out of his shaky aim, grab the chair, use it as a shield and—

"I'll kill her myself!" Boss barked, thundering into her path, and Noa found herself staring up at a barrel that wasn't shaking, aimed at her forehead. She knew her time was up, but she wouldn't give them the pleasure of her fear. Instead she spat at him.

Boss snorted but didn't blink. She saw his finger tense,

and then from behind him came a shout. Boss turned his head for just an instant. Noa rolled, grabbed the chair with both hands, and flung it toward him. It hit him in the back and bounced off. She prepared for him to turn ... but he didn't. Tiny, who was suddenly hurtling at him, had a look of surprise on his face.

Noa got out of the way just as Tiny's body impacted with Boss's, making him stumble backward over the over-turned chair. Both of them thudded to the floor and went sliding into the bar with the force of the fall. Noa had the presence of mind to grab Boss's phaser as he passed.

"Stop!" cried Nervous Guy.

Sitting up, Noa aimed Boss's phaser at the nervous man, the only one of the three still standing. His phaser was aimed at her head, still shaking, but his eyes were sliding away to a familiar figure, his dirty blonde hair shining in the light. James's chin was dipped, his jaw shifted, and he said calmly, "Kill her and I'll kill you ... think of your *children,* Reggie."

Tiny groaned and Noa swallowed. How could he be awake—James had stolen his stunner and knocked him out before flinging him across the room—hadn't he? Tiny muttered, "What happened?" and she was afraid to turn and look.

She heard Boss curse behind her and felt fear trick-ling through her anger. Boss wouldn't hesitate to kill—but she couldn't turn around, not with Reggie's upraised phaser pointed at her. Reggie could turn it on James in an instant. "Take it easy, we can talk this out, Reggie," she said, sliding to her feet as gracefully as she could while keeping the phaser aimed at him. Reggie's eyes widened, and his hand trembled, but he didn't shoot. Over the ether she called to James. "Forget Reggie, watch Boss and Tiny."

The thought was barely through her consciousness when James became a blur. Reggie swung his phaser in the direction James had been, and Noa darted forward. From Tiny and Boss's direction, she heard the crack of bone, but she was focused on getting her phaser pressed to Reggie's skull.

"Drop it," she commanded.

Reggie dropped his weapon and threw up his hands. "I didn't shoot! I didn't shoot!" he cried. She heard another thud and crack.

Her eyes slid to Tiny and Boss. Tiny had been on top of Boss, belly first, but now he was strewn out on his back. His eyes were open. She smelled blood. Boss was lying on his back, too, pretty much in the spot where he'd fallen. He was unmoving. His eyes were at half-mast, unblinking. His skull looked like an egg that had been knocked a couple of times but hadn't quite cracked. Noa knew instantly what had happened. In hand-to hand-combat training, every other move for permanently disabling an opponent ended with, "And then stomp on his head!"

James was stalking toward her. He must have seen the direction of her gaze because he said, "They would have killed you."

And him. And a stun wouldn't incapacitate them for very long. They might not have caught James, but stolen augment dealers in a place like this ... How many augments had they killed already?

"They're better dead," Noa muttered. She wished she could have stomped on their heads herself.

His eyes went to her wrist. "You're hurt."

"Doesn't hurt," she lied. But her fleet nanos were

working, she could tell ... otherwise the pain would have been completely unmanageable.

James's eyes slid to Reggie.

"No!" the man screamed and fell to his knees. "Please!"

"What about him?" said James.

"I have kids ... you know I have kids!" Reggie cried. "Don't kill me!"

Noa's hand tightened on the phaser pistol. How had James known he had kids? It wasn't the time to ask.

James took a step closer, and Reggie scrunched his eyes shut and bowed his head. "If you heard that I had kids," he sobbed, "you know I didn't want to do this ... and I can help you!"

"Do you have food?" said James.

Noa blinked. Across the Ark's ether, she said, "James, we have food, why—"

"I don't want to eat our bribes," he said, eyes focused on Reggie.

"Behind the bar!" Reggie said desperately. "Behind the bar."

James turned and vaulted over the bar and disappeared behind it in an easy movement.

Noa reached to James across the ether. "Are you alright?"

"I'm great, just hungry," James said. "It's cold in here!"

It wasn't cold. It was only slightly cooler than the ambient temperature of the Ark. Before she could contemplate it more, light flickered around her eyes. Real light, not an ether illusion.

"You're that commander from the Luddy ship!"

Reggie said, and Noa realized her holographic necklace had just gone out.

"Shut up," Noa said, pressing the phaser muzzle to Reggie's head.

There was the sound of breaking glass, and then, "Eggs! Perfect!"

There was a thudding from the front door. In the mirror Noa could see James standing up fast, a carton of eggs clutched to his stomach.

An intercom crackled to life beside the door. "This is Adam's Station patrol! Let us in!"

James was eating a small wheel of brie. He stood with Noa in a storage area filled with delicacies that made the Ark's cafe's goods look meager. There was Luddeccean cheese, wine, and nuts. In the distance, there was the squeal of a saw cutting through the hinges of the metal airlock of the bar. Soon the authorities would pour in. There were cameras in the bar, and if they managed to escape, they'd still be hunted down for questioning. He should be more concerned. But he was free! He wasn't controlled by the time gates. Maybe they could see his thoughts like he could see the thoughts of other humans, but just as James could not control other humans, they could not control him. He wasn't a puppet. He was himself ... whoever that now was. He patted the warm weight of Carl Sagan, tucked into his shirt. The gates had altered him ... disconnected him. He knew it like he knew the gravity of Adam's Station. Everything before the moment he woke up in the snow was a hazy sort of dream; even his parent's love was an abstraction. His passion for his career was gone, too. His memories of his professional life were a sign post he could refer back to, but they were like all the memories stored in his time capsule: distant, diffuse, without emotional weight. He felt a loss for his old drive, but right now that loss was overwhelmed by relief. He was free. He wasn't a 'bot caught up in a hopeless loop. He'd willed himself awake and he was here. Eating cheese. If he could laugh, he would have. Instead he just took another bite.

"How did you know this place would be here?" he asked Noa, licking salt and fat from his fingers. Freedom tasted fantastic.

From the room above came the sound of the door intercom crackling with, "We know you're in there. Come out and we'll go easy on you."

"What do I say about this?" Reggie asked, trembling.

"Tell them that we held you at phaser point," Noa said, tersely.

Reggie sniffed.

James dipped his chin. "You will give us five minutes once we leave. You won't use the ether."

Reggie bowed his head. James reached across the ether for Reggie's channel. He didn't answer. "It's me, Reggie," he said.

Reggie looked up with a start.

"Answer," James whispered.

Reggie opened the channel. James's jaw shifted, and he wanted to say, "The commander cares about your children. I don't," but he couldn't bring himself to say it. If Noa found out ... instead he said, "I'll be listening."

Reggie looked down. "Right," he said aloud.

"Come on," Noa said, swinging a duffel over her

shoulder and backing away from Reggie, keeping her phaser aimed at Reggie's head the whole time.

Over the ether, James commanded, "Be good, Reggie."

Reggie sucked in a breath.

Louder bangs sounded at the door.

"Open up in there! Open up!"

James moved over to a shelf of cheeses. Looking at Reggie, he said, "This one?"

The man nodded.

James pulled on one side of the shelf and it opened like a door, revealing a piece of the same plastic that made the plastitubes shaped like a long gash from the floor to the ceiling. There was a circular metal portion. Noa depressed a button in the wall and the circular portion opened with a hiss and pulled outward until there was just enough room for one person to slip through. Noa disappeared into the opening and James followed, closing the shelf behind him. For a moment he was blind, and he focused on following Noa by her footsteps.

Above their heads a crash sounded.

Noa whispered, "Battering ram." Her voice sounded odd.

He blinked, waiting for his eyes to adjust. He saw dim directional lighting on the floor. The tiny pools of light at his feet disturbed his augmented vision. If he looked down, and then up too quickly, he'd go blind again ... but he had to look down because the floor was rough ... and up to keep from bumping his head. Noa didn't appear to be having any trouble. She glided over the rough stones, dipping beneath low overhangs with graceful movements. Water dripped, and the air was thin in the cold tunnel. He cradled Carl Sagan's weight with an arm. Even through the shirt and coat James wore, the werfle was warm. He was hungry again but didn't want the rustle of an S-ration or the grinding of his jaws to keep him from hearing anyone behind them. He was so busy listening in that he bumped into Noa.

"Ladder's here." Her voice sounded strange and muffled.

He could see nothing. But he felt her duffel brush against him as she climbed and felt a chill in her wake. James readjusted his duffels and began to climb. A few minutes later, he heard the scrape of metal, then saw a flash of light and a wavering shadow. Noa was slipping from the passage into the light, he realized. Noa's voice rang true in his ears this time. "You're not wearing your mask."

"Mask?" he said, still blind and trying not to let it show.

"Your CO_2 converter," Noa said.

His apps started calculating the oxygen in the tunnel, and the time they'd been in it. Eight minutes. Too long. He moved up another rung; he felt warm air as his head poked above the surface. He tried to take another step up, and promptly got stuck.

"Hand me your duffel. The exit is too narrow." Her mind reached out to him, too. "Are you alright?" She sent a mental projection, and he could see what she could see: his head sticking out of a hole in pavement, his eyes looking at a point in her shoulder instead of right at her.

"I think that you are experiencing oxygen loss," she said into his mind.

"I'm fine," he grumbled, eyes finally adjusting. He slipped down, handed her the duffel bags, and climbed out of what appeared to be a sort of manhole. "Just hungry." The warm air of the red light district wrapped around him like a blanket.

"Hungry?" Noa said. And he knew it was ridiculous. He'd just eaten a wheel of brie.

But then she said, "Carl Sagan, is he alright?"

From James's shirt came a tired sounding squeak, but the werfle didn't struggle.

"Hang in there, little guy," Noa whispered, putting a circular plastitubing cover over their exit.

James stretched in the warm air, his hunger oddly abating. He swung his duffel bags over his shoulder.

"Hello?" someone called in a singsong voice. "Where did ja come from?"

James looked down the narrow dead-end alley. One side appeared to be a building, the other naked asteroid rock. The ceiling was rock, too. At the end of the alley a man was wavering on his feet. Lights shone behind him.

"Come on," Noa said, taking a light hood out of the collar of her jacket and pulling it over her face. "Let's go."

Doing likewise, he followed her to the intersection. Noa peeked in the direction of Boss's bar. "Doesn't seem to be a commotion," she said.

"Yet," said James. Her jaw was hard, but she showed no sign of nervousness or fear. And then her eyes got a far-off look, as though she was hearing a distant sound. She was communicating over the ether. He knew he shouldn't, but James focused, heard static, and then Ghost's voice. "Commander, I heard you send your final directives to Manuel, and your goodbye to Mr. Sinclair."

Noa scowled. "Listening in, Ghost?"

"Yes. This isn't the ethernet—it's the Ark's much less robust local ether, and frankly I need to stay on top of all signals going in and out at the moment," the man snapped back. "I'm glad you're still alive, and apparently under less stress than you were a few moments before ... you need to get back to the ship."

Noa responded, "James is fine, thanks for asking, Ghost. And we're working on getting back to the ship. But situations are tense here, so I need to focus. Signing off."

The ether died and a frisson of tension James hadn't realized was there vanished from his spine. For a moment, he thought they were about to be rational and return immediately to the ship. And then the frisson returned. He eyed her sideways and prompted gently, "It would be more rational to go back to the ship now ..."

Noa narrowed her eyes at a point in the distance.

He almost sighed. "... but which way do we go to try and find Gunny?"

"This way," said Noa. Stepping out of the intersection, she led him in the direction *opposite* the way they came, at a steady but determined pace. Keeping her hood low, at the first door she asked the bouncer if he'd seen a man who fit Gunny's description. After a bribe of an S-ration, he pointed further down the crowded narrow street and gave some directions.

Continuing on their way, cradling her wrist against her stomach, she hissed, "Ghost expects me to leave him behind. Can you believe he'd even ask?"

He could believe Ghost might think that. Drawing his own hood as far down over his eyes as it would go, James said, "Well, for a while back there I almost thought you'd left me."

"What?" said Noa, drawing to a halt.

James stopped. She was looking up at him, and the hood had fallen back so it no longer hid her distinct dark features. Her lips were parted, her eyes wide, and her brows were drawn together.

"You really thought ..." She didn't finish, just stared at him a beat too long. And then, shaking her head, she began walking again at twice the speed as before. She reached up and wiped her face with her sleeve.

"I can't believe ..." she muttered, but didn't finish the thought. She kept her head bowed and her face turned away.

He smelled the tang of salt. It took him several moments to process that it was from tears. Noa hadn't cried when she was trying to escape a prison camp, nor when they were running for their lives on Luddeccea's home world, or—he glanced down at the wrist he was sure was injured more than she let on—when she'd gotten hit by a phaser.

She wiped her eyes, not looking at him. But she was crying now. The only other time she'd cried in front of him was when he'd convinced her not to "rescue" Kenji from his apartment. James felt a black dread at the edges of his consciousness; his mistrust had hurt her more than fear of death or physical pain.

They came to the intersection the bouncer had indicated. Noa stopped and looked around the corner. It was another narrow passageway but set between two buildings. There were a few doorways with banners advertising lodging, refreshments, and "relaxation" above them. There was also, according to a map of the city James had in his apps, a stairwell at the end of it that would take them up to a passageway just outside the docks.

Concentrated shouts and murmurs made him look back the way they'd come. Outside of Boss's "joint" there was a crowd milling. Curious people on the street were moving in that direction.

Ghost's voice cracked over the ether again. "Commander, Adam's Station's Security knows you're down there now. You've got to hurry!"

"We'll be right there," Noa replied to Ghost. To James she said, "The bouncer said he's at that place." She indicated one of the bars down the alley in the direction of the stairway.

It was conveniently on the way out. James's augmented hearing picked up another voice a few paces down the main thoroughfare.

James caught her shoulder. She turned and glared up at him, eyes still wet.

"He's not there, Noa," James said.

"But the man said—"

"I *hear* Gunny." Touching an ear, James canted his head toward a doorway on the main thoroughfare. "That way." His jaw shifted. He had to make things hard for himself?

Noa's eyes immediately went soft. He heard her swallow. She reached to him through the ether. "For a moment, I thought maybe you didn't care."

He didn't care. Not about Gunny, anyway.

"Let's go," he said.

"Right," said Noa, hopping sprightly in the direction James had indicated. Down the street, James caught a couple of faces outside Boss's joint turning to watch.

CHAPTER TEN

Gunny was sitting at a battered booth, raising a glass of piss-yellow liquid in a jar with a few locals who appeared just as in their cups. His shirt was untucked and his rather large girth was peeking out from beneath. He was singing along with a man holding a microphone, strangely in key:

"We sent our probes out into the dark,
Hoping ours was not an uncommon part,
But the probes came back, and we found out
We are alone in the black, alone in the black ..."

One of the members of the group belched in time with the final verse and they nearly fell off their seats from laughing.

Noa's heart fell as she walked toward them. When she'd been in Boss's place and seen the man who'd she'd at first thought was Gunny, the first thought to enter her mind was that he'd been drugged. Gunny was too smart, too experienced, to get drunk on a mission. But now—

"Commnnanderrrrr!" Gunny slurred, getting to his feet. "I have interrogated these gentlemen—"

"Most strenuously!" one said.

The other sang softly to himself, *"Alone in the night, have to make our own light."*

"Most stren-u-lously," Gunny slurred. "And they haven't seen Kuin and Jun." He gave a solute with the glass jar in his hand. The remainder of the liquid sloshed out onto his hair. Gunny swayed on his feet, looking confused.

"We have to go," James said behind her.

Remembering the crowd outside, Noa looked around the bar. There was no sign of an emergency exit. Gesturing with her thumb toward the door, Noa said, "March, soldier."

Gunny took a few steps and began to sway.

Growling, James swooped by her. "We have no time for this." Gunny was slung over his shoulder a moment later.

"Whoa, big guy, usually I prefer a bit more romancing before I—" he belched, "—get thrown over anyone's shoulder. Also, I might throw up."

Noa thought she might throw up, too. Gunny reeked. She looked at James and in their secret cipher spoke across the ether. "Sorry."

James just hunkered toward the door. He was carrying Gunny, two duffels, and a still unconscious Carl Sagan in his shirt. He was always taking on the burden of her less than brilliant plans.

He drew to a halt just before stepping outside. "Damn," he said over the ether. And then he growled and readjusted a duffel. "Do I really need to carry all of these? It's awkward, and we're going to need to run." Noa poked her head around his frame and saw that someone down the street was gesturing in their direction.

"Just go, I have a plan," Noa said.

James's eyes slid to her. His avatar rose in her mind and smiled wryly. "Of course you do," the real James said, his face expressionless.

"Hopefully it won't involve you carrying any more of my half-baked ideas," Noa said.

"It is awkward," James said, his gaze too heavy. "But not too heavy."

She slipped her knife out of her pocket and nodded toward the door. "Are you speaking in allegories to confuse a poor, uneducated colonist, Professor?" It was a weak joke but all she had at the moment.

"You know the meaning of the word 'allegory'?" James said as they stepped through the main thoroughfare. "I'm shocked, Luddeccean." He winked at her and she knew he wasn't.

Behind them Noa heard the crowd rising.

"Stop flirting!" Gunny interjected. "There's a lynch mob behind us!"

"There they are," someone said.

"Also, I'm going to throw up," Gunny added.

Behind her in the crowd, she heard "Throwbacks," "Luddy," "Reward," and then, "Security forces, out of the way!"

"Should I run now?" said James.

"No!" said Noa. "Hold still."

"Please, God, no!" Gunny moaned. "No running."

Noa slit one of the duffels on James's back from top to bottom, spilling the S-rations on the ground. At the top of her lungs, she shouted, "Free Grub! Come and get it!"

The effect was immediate. People started pouring out of doorways and alleys. There were people dressed in rags, prostitutes in cheap finery, business people in real finery, workmen, and more. The bouncer she'd talked to about Gunny leaped off his stool and came plowing through the others. The security personnel were completely cut off.

"Now we run!" she said.

"No!" shrieked Gunny.

James ignored him. They rushed down the main thoroughfare, Noa's duffel and James's remaining duffel still in tow. Noa reached out to James through the ether and silently communicated their path. They passed the narrow alleyway they'd nearly gone down before, sprinted a block or two more, and then turned down another alley and entered an unmarked door—in their minds it was demarcated as a stairway to a dock inspection station. Going through inspection was going to be a lizzar and a half, but there was no way around it ...

She blinked. What should be an entrance to a stairwell was a tiny, empty chamber not much larger than a closet. The walls were a slightly worn pink velvet. The only exit seemed to be a door draped with beads.

She looked at James; he looked at her. She shrugged and stepped through the beads into a space with more crushed velvet walls, curtains galore and women and men in cheap satins and laces, and a lot of makeup. For a moment no one said anything. James's eyes slid to Noa's again, one of his eyebrows lifted, and then Gunny, still on James's back, belched and bellowed, "Howdy, ladies!"

A lean, bare-chested human male in eyeliner stepped forward, eyes scanning James's body. "Welcome to Lucky Chance, the only all-human bordello on Adam's Station. How may I be of service?"

"Is this the stairwell to the dock?" James asked.

It hit Noa in an instant. "A bordello in the stairwell—a brilliant business move!" she said before she'd realized she'd said it aloud and not merely thought it. Her eyes slid around the room—but which curtain was the doorway behind?

The man smiled. "I like to think so. Technically against regulations, but the inspectors are easy to pay off."

Someone snickered. The man winked.

Outside the bordello Noa heard shouts, and "check all exits!"

Smile vanishing, the man's lips pursed and his eyes narrowed.

"We can pay you in S-rations," Noa said, slipping her duffel off and showing the man the contents.

There were gasps around the room.

Eyes widening, he said, "Right this way, Sweet Hearts!" Flicking a hand to the women in the room, he said, "Keep Security occupied!"

They rounded a corner and passed behind a curtain into a dark room beyond. "Aww ... are we leaving so soon?" Gunny hiccuped.

"Shh!" James hissed.

Gunny snored in response.

There were the sounds of crashing feet behind them. Someone said, "Hello, Soldiers! You know how much we love men in uniform!"

"Out of our way! We're checking the stairs."

Noa stiffened. But their guide put a finger to his lips. He stopped at another curtain and whispered, "Do you want to go to the inspection station? Or inside the dock?"

Noa blinked. James said, "You can get us inside the dock?"

"Sure, this way," he said. He guided them behind another curtain to a room where a woman was stripping sheets from a bed.

The man turned to James and Noa and said, "All human and extremely clean ... if you are passing this way again."

James's jaw shifted at the proprietor's gaze.

Unable to read him, Noa couldn't help but reach through the ether. "Are you laughing?"

James's thoughts snapped across the channel. "No!"

"No need to get insulted by the attention—I think he's kind of cute," Noa said.

Gunny abruptly woke up. "I think I'm goin' to throw up," he said again.

James's head darted too quickly in Noa's direction, and his eyes narrowed. She decided not to press her luck. To the proprietor, she said, "We'll keep your place in mind."

And then, Ghost's voice erupted in her brain. "Commander, we have problems here."

"Coming, Ghost," she said. "I don't suppose Manuel has the timeband and fuses ready?"

"I'm helping him to finish installing all the new fuses right now!" Ghost said. "Hurry!"

Noa was afraid to ask what was putting Ghost in such a tizzy and focused on their guide instead. He was leading them behind yet another curtain, to yet another velvet-walled room. There was a twisting, curling vine-like plant to one side. Their guide reached into it, pulled out what looked like a strand of vine, and plugged it into his data port. The wall sprang open with a sigh, revealing a cave-like passageway similar to the one at Boss's joint. An internal app told her that this one had enough oxygen, though.

"Do all establishments have secret exits here?" James asked.

Tone businesslike, their guide said, "If they're smart."

A light fell in a circular beam at the end of the cave, like it was slipping through a manhole cover. Noa thought she heard a far-off roar but couldn't discern its source. Their guide inclined his head toward the circle of light. "There's a ladder and the cover opens up easy enough." Noa handed him James's last duffel. "Thanks," she said. The man clutched it to himself tightly, and his eyes fell on it with a hunger she hadn't seen even when he was looking at James.

"Anytime," the man said, and he slipped out the door in the wall, letting it fall shut behind him.

James stood motionless in the dark.

"Ready?" Noa said over the ether.

"No. My eyes are still adjusting."

Noa slipped by him and went up the ladder, the far-off roar becoming louder. Was that shouting? She pushed the heavy plastic covering above the ladder to the side and peered out. Her eyes were at ground level of the dock, off to a corner. She saw Wren's ship, and in the distance, the Ark's plastitube, drawn up, just at the edge of the aster-oid's too-close horizon. The roar was even louder—it sounded like shouting perhaps—but the source was beyond the horizon and she couldn't hear the words. Not bothering to replace the cover, she hopped back down, slipped off her duffel, and took out the components for three phaser rifles. She hadn't wanted to draw attention below, but no way were they going to make it across the dock unopposed. Putting the pieces together with prac-ticed motions, she handed one to James, kept one for herself, and stowed the third. She'd planned to hand that one to Gunny—she looked at him drooling upside down—that wasn't going to happen.

"Coast is clear?" James whispered.

"Yeah," Noa said, standing and leaving the empty duffel on the ground. She patted her stunner and the knife hidden beneath her coat. "Let's go."

They worked together to wrangle the still unconscious Gunny onto the dock, and no one noticed them. It made Noa's skin prickle. As soon as the three of them were topside, they darted beneath the closest ship.

"Still no one," Noa said, her stomach sinking. There were no dock workers, no 'bots. It was eerily empty of movement. "I have a very bad feeling about this."

Readjusting Gunny, James said, "As much as I'm enjoying not being shot at, I'm getting a bad feeling about this, too."

Taking a deep breath, Noa inclined her head toward Wren's ship. The vessel was still in a state of disrepair, with burnt siding lying on the dock, and what looked like a semi-disengaged timeband. "We run behind that piece of siding there," Noa said. "Just underneath the nose."

"Right," said James. His eyes went to the horizon. "I wish we could see what was going on."

"We'll see soon enough," said Noa. "Ready?"

They darted across the empty dock to the cover of Wren's vessel, keeping their heads down. Gunny, thankfully, was temporarily passed out and didn't add commentary, or puke. Noa didn't raise her eyes until they were behind the displaced siding. She peeked around it and gasped.

Just beyond the Ark were two lines of security personnel in rag-tag armor. Beyond them was a mass of people, barely held back by the first line of troops. "We want food! We want the Ark!"

"Ghost," Noa said across the shared channel. "Do you know what's going on?"

"I'm not sure if Adam sent the protestors or if it's a genuine movement. We have to get out of here!" Ghost snapped over the ether. "Moreover ... I don't like that new ship. They've been inviting people aboard, and they're not using the ether. None! I think they might be Luddeccean Intel."

Noa looked in the direction of the ship they'd seen landing when they left the dock, but it was too far away to see over the horizon.

"You're just telling me now?" said Noa.

"It's just occurring to me now!" snapped Ghost.

"Manuel," Noa called through the ether, "are we ready for lightspeed?"

"No—"

Ghost cut off the engineer. "Forget lightspeed! We have to leave the dock at least. Adam is sending in a regiment."

Noa looked across the wide expanse—nearly 325 meters according to her internal apps.

She took a deep breath. "A plan, I need a plan—"

"May I suggest running like hell?" James said, readjusting Gunny on his shoulder.

Noa looked at him; her mouth gaped. And then she nodded. "Right. Right, we'll do that."

Across the ether, Noa said, "I don't suppose you can lower the plastitubing, Ghost?"

Manuel answered for him. "We Luddy-rigged it to be ethernet independent. We'll drop it for you."

Noa dropped to a sprinter's crouch. James did the same, but his position was awkward with Gunny on his back. Noa stifled a wince. It made more sense for him to carry the heavy man, but she did feel bad about it.

"Ready?" she asked.

"No," James said.

She snorted. Typical. "Let's go!" Noa said, and they took off across the dock. Noa was a fast sprinter, thanks to Fleet nanos that helped with muscle and bone repairs, and genetics. James was faster normally, but with Gunny slung across his back, they were about the same speed. As they tore across the tarmac, she saw the crowd coming into view but forced herself to focus on one foot in front of the other, pumping her arms to the rhythm of her feet and breathing evenly. And then over the sound of her heartbeat and her breathing, she heard a low roar.

"Almost there!" she cried over the ether, even as the thunder was getting closer. There were only 150 meters more.

"Commander!" Chavez's voice screamed over the ether.

"The reinforcements!" Ghost's voice cracked.

Noa ducked her head and ran faster. James threw out an arm, catching her across the middle and knocking the wind out of her.

"Keep running!" she gasped, barely audible to herself over her panting, the frantic beat of her heart, and the crowd, the voices of which were an incomprehensible roar.

"Halt right there!" a megaphone-amplified voice rolled like thunder across the dock.

Noa lifted her eyes at last. Streaming through the crowd were thirty armored souls, in addition to the men already in place. They'd already cut off the route to the plastitubing, not quite to the dock. The newcomers had their rifles on their shoulders. Noa and James were in their sights.

* * *

James stared down the muzzles of the armed men running through the crowd. Static fizzled along his spine. He was facing death with Noa once again. This time he knew he belonged to himself, and it gave him a strange sense of calm. The gates didn't control him. He was the master of his own destiny; he was here because of his own choice. Clutching Gunny with one arm, he pulled his rifle around.

And then through the ether, Ghost's voice ripped. "The new ship, they are with Luddeccean Intel! Adam was just talking about it with his second-in-command; he's sending out his own Guard as part of a deal for supplies. We have to leave; they can't capture *me*!"

Beside him, Noa whispered in a rush, "We're not a threat to them anymore ... but they're coming all this way?"

James tilted his head. If they got to the Kanakah Cloud and opened the new gate, they'd be a threat. As if thinking the same thought, Noa said, "Well, we're not a threat as far as they know." Her lip curled and her chin dipped. "They want to make an example of us."

James remembered the Guard talking about ripping out Noa's port and her stories of what they did to augments like him.

He had seized control of his destiny. He wouldn't *give* it away. His eyes slid to Noa. "Noa," he whispered. "I'd rather die than give them that opportunity."

Noa looked up at him, a ghost of a smile touched her

lips, and then she nodded. They weren't communicating over the ether, but James felt like in that moment they had perfect understanding. He felt oddly complete.

Over the ether, she said, "Chavez, you get ready to pull the Ark out of dock. Head for Libertas."

"Commander?" Chavez replied, her thoughts uncertain across the ether.

"It's a straight shot to Libertas. You should be able to make it. Try to get help with the Libertas Local Guard," Noa said.

"The Libertas Guard won't have resources to get to—"

"Shhhh ..." said Noa. "Don't give it away ... take care of yourself."

"Professor Sinclair," the megaphone-augmented voice boomed. "... and Commander Noa Sato. We will allow your ship to depart if you will surrender yourselves."

"No!" Chavez's and Manuel's thoughts ripped across the ether.

"Don't surrender, Commander!" Manuel cried.

"Chavez," Ghost said, "I think you underestimate yourself. You can fly this vessel."

James felt his jaw shift. The offer confirmed it, the Luddecceans wanted to make an example of them, just as Noa had suspected.

The new men formed a semi-circle in front of them. James heard footsteps behind, peeked, and saw another line of armored men emerging behind Wren's ship.

James felt static flair along his spine at Ghost's easy abandonment, at the Luddecceans, at the impossibility of the situation. But Noa liked humor in the face of death. "They still care about us, Noa ... How touching."

Noa huffed. "We try and take as many of them as we can on our way out."

"Oh, yes," James said.

Noa nodded. "If Luddy Intel is talking to Adam, they know how unmanned the Ark is. If we go out guns blazing, that might give the Ark a chance to get away."

"Agreed." His motives weren't as pure, but he wanted the Luddecceans to *pay* for his life, and the newfound freedom he was about to lose. His eyes met Noa's. Ghost's holographic disguise was gone—he could look into her nearly-black eyes and see her scars.

"We're warning you one more time! Put your hands up!" the megaphone-amplified voice said.

"Ready?" said Noa, not looking away from him.

"As I'll ever be," he replied, shifting Gunny on one shoulder, hand tensing on his rifle. The moment felt real and true. He felt in control for the first time since he'd woken in the snow.

The megaphone boomed. "This is your last warning—"

It was cut off by a screech behind Noa and James that sounded like a thousand nails being dragged against steel. Noa and James both spun. From the top of the Wren's ship, a wicked-looking dual-barreled phaser cannon was emerging. It halted in position with a long grinding scrape, another motor engaged with a whirr, and the cannon's barrels dropped so one was pointed right at Noa and James, and the other was pointed in the direction beyond Wren's ship ... toward the other line of armed men.

"What?" Noa whispered.

The megaphone speaker said, "Captain of the Juggernaut, stand down! These people are being brought into the custody of Adam's Station Security."

There was another grind of gears from the innards of

the Juggernaut, and a loading platform dropped from the ship's belly. Wren emerged at the top, hand on the shoulder of the young boy James had seen earlier. Next to them were Monica and her daughter. James blinked. They were all carrying packs on their shoulders. The crowd, despite the emergence of the new regiment, had been muttering angrily. At the cannon's appearance they'd gone silent, but now they began to mutter again.

Smiling, Wren sauntered down the ramp and lifted his hands. Monica and the children followed, cowering slightly. The crowd hushed and Wren shouted across the tarmac, "How badly do you want them?"

"Juggernaut Captain, stand down!" commanded the man behind the megaphone.

Walking toward Noa and James, Wren shouted, "What is it worth to you?"

James blinked. "Why do they all have their packs on?"

Noa's mouth fell open. "Oh, no, Wren, no ..."

If Wren heard her, he gave no sign. Drawing closer, still smiling at Adam's Security, he said, "You haven't answered my question."

Sounding peeved, the man armed with the megaphone said, "We'll grant you your life and you can call yourself lucky."

Laughing, stepping past Noa and James, Wren spread his arms. "But don't you see, you can't grant me my life. You can't grant anyone life, and the crowd behind you knows it!"

The muttering of the crowd became a roar. James's eyes went to the throng. They were dressed in rags and like Wren, Monica, and the children they were weighed down by packs. Many had children and babies in their arms. One of the guards yelled, "No, people, Adam has just made a deal!"

"Lies!" someone screamed. The word was picked up in a chant by the crowd.

"Wren, no!" Noa said. James glanced at Noa, her eyes wide and frantic. Before he could wonder what she meant, the crowd roared, and as though they had one mind, started to push and lunge against the security line. Some of the armored men facing off against Noa and James ran back to the line to contain the mob. It seemed to enrage them even more. They chanted and screamed. James thought he caught snatches of, "Let us aboard! Let us aboard!" It was so loud that James almost didn't hear the whirr of the cannon motor. He looked behind him and saw the cannon's aim had lifted toward the line of armored men still standing in front of them.

"Run, Noa!" James screamed over the ether. To Manuel, he shouted, "Drop the tube!"

"Wren!" Noa shouted. "Dual-barreled plasma cannons are not accurate; they'll—"

At the same instant the crowd erupted through the security line.

Ducking his head beneath his arms, Wren ran back, grabbed the boy, and screamed, "Run!"

An instant later phaser fire shrieked overhead. It hit the men by the lowering plastitubing first and then swung out in an arc, leaving a line of red hot rock behind. In the periphery of his vision, James saw the armored line falling like puppets cut from their strings. Only one of the men by the tube somehow managed to survive the onslaught. He held up his rifle—

A shot whizzed past James and knocked the man with the rifle down. He glanced back and saw Noa paused with her own weapon upraised. All around the dock were screams and chaos. "Keep running!" Noa shouted through the ether, lowering her rifle and darting forward.

Awkwardly grabbing Gunny's bulk with two arms to keep him from slipping, James ran, somehow clutching his phaser rifle.

In front of them the plastitubing plummeted, and James reached its relative safety moments later. He plowed through the archway, his heart lifting. They'd made it! He dumped Gunny on the platform just in time to see Wren jump through the opening, pushing the boy to the floor in front of him and shouting, "Stay down."

Where was Noa? His vision went dark, and then he heard her angry shout in the ether. "This is why children don't belong anywhere near a—" a litany of swears followed. He looked out to the tarmac. Noa was outside the plastitubing where she could get a better aim at their foes. Her rifle was raised and she was firing in a steady rhythm. Beyond her Monica was tugging at her daughter, who was cowering in the onslaught.

The blast of phasers from Wren's cannon grew weaker and farther apart. And then a loud clicking came from the weapon. "Shit!" said Wren. Beyond Wren's ship, more armed men rushed forward. James saw Noa glance at Monica. Bowing over a crying Zoe, she was moving at barely a walk. James knew that look in Noa's eye.

"Damn," he muttered, rushing out of the plastitubing.

"Cover me!" Noa said, climbing to her knees. James put a hand on her shoulder. "No, cover me!" He rushed into the oncoming fire before Noa could argue. In his mind, he heard, "Take the kid first," and he swung Zoe up across his shoulder.

"Run!" he screamed at Monica before turning and

bolting himself, crouching as low as he could. He felt phaser fire pass over his head.

Noa was still outside the plastitubing, on the ground, firing her phaser rifle. Wren was inside the tubing's cover.

"Noa!" James shouted as he passed. "Get on!"

He hopped onto the lift, dropped the child, spun around, and saw Noa still hadn't moved. Movement on the tarmac caught his eye and he realized that Monica had fallen ... but was still moving. Growling, James leaped out again into the fire. He yanked Monica up by the back of her clothing and carried her like a kitten. She shrieked when he all but threw her into the lift. She didn't smell like blood; she must have just tripped.

"Noa!" James bellowed. "We're all on but you!"

Noa hopped to her feet, phaser fire buzzing dangerously close to her head. James moved to step out into the fray to cover her. Wren grabbed his arm. "Don't—"

Yanking his arm away, James slipped out of the lift, raised his rifle, and fired at anything that moved among the fallen security personnel and civilians.

"I'm in," Noa said across the ether, flooding him with gratitude. Ducking, James pulled back into the lift. "Up now!" Noa commanded, and they began to ascend. Noa and Wren dropped to their stomachs and aimed outside. James joined them and together they fired at the security personnel below rushing toward them until there was no room between the lift's floor and the plastitubing archway.

James felt almost every nano and neuron in him go still, as though sighing in relief, but then, through the semi-transparent wall he saw parallel lines of men in gray with Luddeccean green piping on their uniforms. Each pair carried a phaser cannon between them.

"Shit," said Wren. "What are they doing?"

"Lizzar dung," said Noa.

"Can't this thing go faster?" Wren cried.

The future unfolded in James's mind. In a moment the Luddecceans would set their cannons directly beneath the lift, then they'd fire their plasma cannons up at the floor, heat it to super hot temperatures, and cook them all in their boots. They were trapped ... and for some reason that made him panic in ways being shot at had not.

"Ghost? Manuel?" Noa called into the ether. "Can it go faster? They're going to fire on us and—"

"I have an idea!" Ghost responded across the ether.

"What is it?" Noa said.

"Manuel, lower the pressure in the airlock," Ghost cried. "Everyone be ready to jump!"

Monica, Wren, the boy, and the girl did not have access to the ship's general ether and Noa relayed the message, "Jump, on our word."

"Why?" said Monica.

Already bouncing, Noa said, "I don't know, just do it." She grabbed Zoe's hand and the boy's. James wished he could grab her but wrapped his arm around the warm weight of Carl Sagan, still miraculously tucked in his shirt, instead.

"Now," shouted Ghost through the Ark's ether.

"Now!" Noa relayed to Wren and the others.

The cannon fired below, and the floor below them went hot.

CHAPTER ELEVEN

Monica, Wren, Noa, the children, James, and Wren all jumped. Time stopped. James felt heat below from the phaser charge and smelled burning plastic. For a breathless moment he was afraid they'd be cooked as soon as he landed.

But they didn't land. They were still going up—floating. An internal app screamed that gravity had decreased to .1 G. James looked down. The plastitubing's bottom was melting and turning black. The lift platform was red-hot. If the men below fired again—

There was a whoosh, and a clang, and the boy screamed, "My ears," and the team was sucked up into the airlock. They hit the floor in a pile. Around him people gasped for breath. Noa sprang up and hit the airlock door. It closed and James called to Manuel through the ether, "Air! Air in the airlock."

The inside door opened with a whoosh and oxygen rushed in.

"Did you somehow cut off gravity in Adam's Station?" Wren gasped.

"Our chief computing officer did," Noa gasped back. Over the ether, Noa said, "Brilliant, Ghost!"

It had been brilliant—as had been decreasing the pressure in the airlock so that when it was opened, all the air from the tube was sucked in. Ghost was so useful when he was on their side.

Wren stuttered. "How could he—?"

"Adam's Station's ethernet is ... not secure," James said, feigning being breathless.

"It's not that insecure!" Wren protested.

"Commander, thank me later!" Ghost cried over the ether.

At the inner door of the airlock, 6T9 appeared. "May I be of service?"

Over the general channel, Noa said, "Chavez, pull us out of dock." Waving a hand at Monica and the children, Noa said, "Stay here, Sixty. As soon as we're clear, get them to sick bay!" To Monica, Noa said, "You wanted the job of ship's doc and you're hired." Monica cowered back, her wide eyes going back and forth between James and Noa.

"Initiating sequence, Commander," Chavez said over the general channel.

In James's shirt, Carl Sagan finally stirred. "I hope you can also handle the occasional non-human patient," James said unfastening the garment.

"Pardon?" said Monica.

James pulled the werfle's limp body from his stomach. The creature blinked up and mewed.

"Oh," said Monica, eyes widening. "Its venom has been milked, hasn't it?"

James's eyes slid to Noa's. "Sure," said Noa.

James shrugged. "Of course," he said. A dark spot in

James's mind brightened. He wouldn't mind if Carl Sagan bit Monica. He passed the creature to her and took off after Noa, already striding through the hallway, distantly aware that Wren followed. Ignoring him, James connected to Adam's Station's docking authority ... even if the Luddecceans didn't use the ether, Adam's Station still would. As soon as his apps picked up his intention, he heard the familiar static, his vision went white, and then he heard docking control say, "Adam, the Luddeccean Guard ship is lifting off. Do I open the main doors?" And the response, "Just keep the Ark's locker closed! I want that ship! They've got more food, I know it!"

"But the main doors, for the Luddeccean ship—"

"Hold on that—" Adam said.

James blinked. Oh, no.

At the entrance to the access ladder, Noa paused. "James?"

"Noa, the Luddecceans are requesting—" said James.

"Commander, we don't have the charge dispersers online," Chavez responded, cutting James off.

Ghost's voice split through the ether. "The Luddeccean Guard ship requested permission to leave the dock."

"Chavez, just get us out of here," Noa said. "Open our hangar doors. You can do that, right, Ghost?"

There was a blink from Ghost's ether connection that James interpreted as an indignant sniff. "Of course," Ghost said.

"Aye, Sir. What heading?" said Chavez over the general channel.

"Just pull us out of the berth!" Noa said, jamming her thumb into the call button. "Manuel, do we have time-bands online yet?"

The engineer's words sifted through the ether. "Not yet, Commander. Still installing the charge dispersers—"

"Where do you need me? The bridge, deck 23, engineering?" James asked Noa and the ether at large. As the words slipped from his mind, he felt himself longing for engineering and the heat there. The thought, oddly, made his mouth water.

"You'll be most useful here on 23," said Manuel over the ether.

No engineering, no heat ... James exhaled softly and looked to Noa.

Meeting his eyes, Noa nodded at him and then poked her head into the access tunnel. "Damn, the access is crowded," she muttered to the ether.

"Take the elevator!" Eliza said over the general channel. "If it gets stuck, just hit the control panel with a hammer!"

Over the ether, Chavez said, "Ghost has gotten the hangar doors open. Trying to release clamps now. Ghost, I think they're jammed on their end!"

"Commander," said Ghost. "The Luddecceans are promising Adam's Station increased rations for his cooperation ... he's going to open the main hangar doors at any moment."

Cursing, Noa spun from the door. She bumped into James as she did. For a moment he thought it was an odd and glorious accident—but then he felt her fingers graze his stomach. They left a trail of white-hot electricity in their wake.

"Ganbate," he said to Noa aloud as she strode down the hall. It was Japanese, and not a word that had a direct Basic translation, but loosely meant never give up, persevere with stubbornness, and keep fighting.

She was already at the lift, a light blinking above the door saying it was about to arrive. "Always," she said aloud, turning back to look at him. He felt her reaching to him through his private channel, not with words, just with her presence. It was nice to feel her there. James swung into the access ladder, his eyes briefly falling on Wren's gaze, but he was too busy starting up the shaft to think of it. And then he abruptly found his nose right beneath Bo's feet. He heard Kuin's voice above Bo. "Kara, move!" and Kara's retort, "I am moving! I don't want to break the dispersers!"

"This is worse than a London hover jam," James complained to Noa across the ether, managing to climb up a few more steps. At least it was warmer than the normal decks with all the crushed bodies. Below him came Jun's voice. "Hey, can you hurry up, Professor? I've got to get these dispersers to 23."

"All clear here." Noa projected her view of the hallway from the lift—Wren far at the other end. The lift dinged, and the door began to slide shut. "I hope that the lift doesn't stop again."

"You've got a fine hammer," James said, thinking of her perfect kick at the control panel last time.

"Hmpf," Noa said. The opening of the door was just a crack, and then a dusky hand reached in. The door bounced open, and James was staring through Noa's eyes at a leering Wren.

James's voice was in Noa's mind as the elevator door bounced open. "Do you need me back there?"

She glared at Wren. Looking at him made her think of

the civilians on Adam's Station, their bodies mowed down by his dual-phaser cannon. His plan hadn't taken possible civilian casualties into account. Based on his history she wasn't surprised—he played the game for profit, not principle. Noa's hand went to her stunner as the door whooshed shut behind him.

"Relax," Wren said, holding up his hands as the lift began to ascend. "I don't want to die. You know me that well."

Noa pulled the stunner nearly out of its holster.

"I only want to help," Wren said. "I've got people depending on me now."

Noa's eyes narrowed. She didn't trust that he cared about Monica, Zoe, or the strange boy—and then she remembered him running back for the kid. She slowly lowered her weapon. To James, she said, "I'm fine." Aloud and into Chavez's mind, she said, "Ensign, why are we still docked? Has Ghost released the clamps?"

"Yes, but the Ark's computer is slow and still running through the safety subr—"

"Release now!" Noa ordered, speaking aloud and into the ether in her frustration.

"Yes, Commander," Chavez said, and Noa swore she could hear her gulp.

"Newbie at the helm?" Wren said.

Noa shot him a death glare ... and found his eyes were on the ceiling. His face looked pale. She watched his Adam's apple bob.

Noa turned her focus to Ghost. "We need a course—"

"Our heading is clear, Commander," her chief computing officer said.

"No, we go anywhere but our intended heading," Noa said.

"Good plan," Wren said, and she could see him nodding out of the corner of her eye.

Damn, she'd spoken aloud again. The ship shuddered as the docking clamps released.

James and Ghost's thoughts exploded at once. "The Luddeccean Guard ship is out of the dock!"

"Commander," Ghost said over the ether. "They aren't in the direction of the cannons."

"What's going on?" Wren said, his voice rising in pitch. "Give me access to my ether so I can help!"

"Manuel, report," Noa said, ignoring Wren.

"We're almost done, Commander," Manuel said over the ether. And he projected a vision of James putting dispersers into their sockets with inhuman speed.

Noa called through the ether, "Ghost! Give me that heading."

The lift stopped at the bridge, and the ceiling bloomed above her head. Noa raced up the steps and slipped into the empty pilot seat. "Engage thrusters, Chavez," Noa ordered.

"Engaging," Chavez said. "We still don't have—"

"Luddeccean ship is powering up weapons!" Wren said from the cannon chair.

"Should we take evasive maneuvers?" Chavez asked.

"In this old hunk?" Wren said unhelpfully.

"Ghost!" Noa cried. "I need that heading."

"Loaded into the computer, Commander," Ghost said, and a star map flashed before Noa's eyes.

"We're a sitting duck!" she heard Wren say.

Noa gritted her teeth and felt heat at the corners of her eyes. Damn useless commentary.

She set thrusters to maximum and sent the ship in the

heading Ghost had indicated. "I'm counting on you," she whispered to Manuel, his team, and James.

In a low voice, Wren said, "Luddeccean ship firing in three, two—"

Manuel said, "We—"

Gripping the steering bars, Noa pulled back hard, and hit the thumb releases for lightspeed.

"—One," Wren finished just as the stars blurred.

"—Are ready for lightspeed," Manuel finished. Noa laughed, and her apps exploded with the combined laughter of her crew, and James's voice low and smooth, "Well done."

Wren, sounding irritated, said, "Shit, don't do that to me again!"

She wasn't done. "Ghost, can I safely adjust the course by one degree to let the phaser that should have just clipped us pass by if we suddenly lose our timeband again?"

"Lose your timeband ... again?" said Wren.

Ghost's voice echoed through the ether. ".0000025 of a degree at six o'clock is clear and should put us out of range of the phaser."

"Thank you, Ghost," Noa said adjusting the heading. "Manuel, I think now would be a good time for you to check out what is wrong with the cooling conduits in engineering."

"There's a problem cooling the reactor?" Wren said.

"Commander ... did you bring someone else aboard the ship with you?" Ghost asked, his voice cracking on the comm.

Noa responded across the channel. "Wren, Monica Jarella, her daughter, and a—"

"Wren? And that ... that woman who went aboard the

Luddeccean vessel?" Ghost's thoughts screamed across the ether and cracked through the ancient comm system on the dash.

Wren held up his hands. "I can explain!"

Noa's eyes went wide. Chavez was up in an instant, stunner out.

"You sure as hell will!" said Noa, spinning in her seat. "Chavez, get him out of here!"

Wren protested. "I'm on your side! Think of the doctor and the children!"

"Make him strip and throw him in one of the unused cabins," Noa said to the ensign.

Wren leered at Chavez's metal legs. "Kinky. I like a woman who can crush my head between her thighs."

"Stun him first," Noa added belatedly.

"What—!" Wren cried.

Chavez stunned him, and he wilted like a flower ... or more accurately, a weed.

Noa exhaled in a growl. "James, I need you up here," she said.

To Chavez, she said, "Let James take care of Wren. I want you to make sure Monica and those kids are contained in sick bay."

Chavez gave a curt nod and headed to the lift.

"Ghost," she said. "You didn't detect any ethernet signals out when we left ship?"

"I'll check again, Commander," he said. "Too bad you can't throw them out of an airlock at lightspeed."

Noa swung back around in her seat. She thought of Monica's daughter ... she couldn't throw a doctor out of an airlock in front of a child.

Lizzar balls, what had she gotten herself into?

"Nothing worse than normal, I'm sure," said James's voice.

She must have been thinking out loud again. She turned around in her seat. James was climbing out of the ladder access shaft. Seeing him prompted a smile.

Wiping his hands, he looked down at the unconscious Wren and raised an eyebrow. "Of course, for you 'normal' tends to be ... bad."

"Whose side are you on again?" she asked with irritation.

Hauling Wren up like a sack of potatoes, James winked at her.

Narrowing her eyes, she said, "You're lucky you can lift heavy things."

He cheekily tossed the ball of light that seemed to be their secret kiss across the ether.

Noa turned back to her read-outs. As though a kiss of light could make things better. But it sort of did. A little bit.

Noa needed sleep and food, not necessarily in that order. Her mouth tasted acrid, like the cryssallis treatment she'd just had. Outside the porthole in the hallway, the stars were not a blur of white. Chavez wasn't experienced enough to fly faster than .5C. When Noa instructed her to pilot the Ark to Libertas, she knew the chances of the woman making it were slim ... especially if they had another inopportune shutdown.

Ghost's voice popped into her consciousness. "We can't remain at this speed. There are buoys out here. The Luddeccean premier may be a technophobe, but he's too afraid of an alien invasion to give up surveillance out here."

"Out here" was below the ecliptic plane, far away from the cover provided by Adam's Belt.

"Work on the course I told you about," Noa said. "We shouldn't be at lightspeed until you make sure it is clear."

There was a whoosh as the lift down the hall opened. She felt a surge from her nanos, neurons, and maybe from her heart, as James's channel lit up within her mind. She turned and saw him stepping out of the elevator. His sleeves were rolled up, and his tattoos stood out, glossy black on his pale skin. Once she'd thought they'd looked like a leaf pattern; now she knew they were feathers.

"It's not the most direct course," said Ghost.

"No, it's not the most direct course," Noa agreed aloud, tapping her fingers on her data port. "But it is the route we're least likely to be detected along."

Aloud, in Japanese, James said, "And won't give away our true destination." He'd been in the engine room helping with the faulty cooling duct, and she swore she could feel the heat from the engine room rolling off of him.

Ghost grumbled and Noa said, "Get me that course, Ghost."

"Yes, Commander. But there is also the matter of our current guests. They need to go out an airlock before we jump to lightspeed again."

James tilted his head, as though he was listening, although Ghost had spoken directly through the ether.

"I remember, Ghost. We may need to drop them off somewhere," Noa said. "But an airlock is ... extreme."

"Even for Wren?" Ghost said.

"Maybe not for Wren," Noa said, pinching the bridge of her nose.

James's eyebrow rose, and Ghost's consciousness flickered away.

Letting out a long breath of air, she gave James a tired smile. Before she even asked he said, "We fixed the conduit that was letting too much heat into engineering."

Noa looked up and nodded. "The rest of the ship feels warmer." And her apps told her it wasn't just a feeling.

James exhaled in a sigh and rolled down his sleeves. "But now the engine room won't be as pleasant." His voice was so dry that she couldn't quite tell if he was joking. She wanted to fall against him, lean her head against his chest ... and fall asleep. But maybe when she woke up ... Shaking herself, Noa said, "Let's go visit the doctor."

"With pleasure," James said. Noa felt a prickle at the back of her neck. Did she hear an undercurrent of malice? And then she remembered him running out into incoming fire to haul Monica onto the lift. She shook her head. His tone was just so dry ... He fell into step beside her, and together they strode down the short hallway to sick bay. The door slid away, Noa stepped in, and James followed. The medbay was darkened in the back. She saw Gunny there, passed out on a bunk. The girl and the boy were sitting on an unused operating table closer to the door. Carl Sagan was on the boy's lap, eyes closed. The doctor was scowling at the ancient computer interface, plunking at singular keys, an old-fashioned stethoscope swinging from her neck.

The door behind James and Noa closed with a whoosh. "We have to talk," Noa said.

Spinning in her chair, Monica said in a crisp, angry tone, "Yes, we do."

James felt like every nerve in his body was on alert. It wasn't just because of Monica's hostile tone ... that was a confirmation of something he already felt. She was not to be trusted.

On the boy's lap, Carl Sagan lifted his head and squeaked at Noa—as though in hello—but then promptly rolled over on his back and waved all ten of his legs at the boy holding him. Noa had never closed the ethernet connection between them. She didn't say a word when her eyes fell on the little creature, but she projected a ball of light in the periphery of his vision, expanding and contracting as though sighing in relief. But then it blipped out and in the real world her eyes went to Monica and narrowed slightly. "We can go someplace private—"

"What is the Archangel Project?" Monica said, her voice trembling.

Noa's thoughts came to a halt so quickly that James felt the electrons in the ether between them wink. Across their link, in their cipher, she said, "And here I was thinking I'd be the one asking the questions."

Monica put a hand to her throat and looked away. "They kept asking me what I knew ..."

"They?" demanded James.

Looking at the floor, Monica said, "I went to that ship, the new one that just landed. It was in good shape. I thought perhaps I could book passage to Libertas with them with my remaining credits." She looked up at Noa. "That ship was where the Luddeccean Intelligence troops came from!"

"Yes," said Noa in a neutral tone. "We figured that out. They asked you about the Archangel Project?" Her chin dipped down toward her chest.

James's hands made fists at his side.

Monica looked away, lines forming between her brows. "I couldn't tell them anything; I don't know anything about a project by that name. I worked with Fleet Intel and I'd never heard of it."

Her eyes came back to Noa's. "Do you know what it is?" A moment ago she'd looked worried. But now she looked angry, her tone challenging. James reached into the ether to try and hear if she were transmitting. He heard nothing ... but he had a moment of unease. When had eavesdropping across the ether became an instinctual reaction?

One side of Noa's lips curled in a sharp smile. "No, but I was sent to a prison camp for telling them I didn't know."

Heat flared along James's spine. James found himself taking a half step closer to Noa ... and Monica. "They didn't let people they suspect of being a part of the Archangel Project get away," he whispered.

Monica sucked on her lips and looked away again. Putting a hand to her temple, she shook her head. "They weren't cruel, they were just insistent. And then they asked me about my husband, what he did, and about my research ... and suggested I might like to come to Luddeccea with Zoe ... that as a young mother and child alone we would be welcome there ... to make a new start."

"And you turned down their generous offer?" The words came out of his mouth in almost a growl.

Monica rubbed her arm and looked away. "I ... there was something about the way he said it that made me uncomfortable." She hugged herself. Heat flared beneath James's skin. She had to be lying. The Luddecceans didn't just let anyone associated with the Archangel Project go.

Monica's eyes shot to his. "You have to believe me, that's all that happened. I don't know why they let me go!"

Through the ether, Noa said, "I do. As soon as she told them what her husband did, they knew he was a dead man ... Monica's beautiful, obviously has childbearing capabilities, and they were subtly suggesting she come and help them repopulate their planet."

James's nanos snapped and sparked at that.

"She has my pity," Noa said across the ether.

"Maybe that is part of the plan," James said across the channel between them.

Aloud, Noa said, "We know as much about the Archangel Project as you." She tilted her head. "What is your research about precisely, Doctor?"

Taking a deep breath, Monica rubbed her temple. "You're in the Fleet ... you know about the mech suits we started experimenting with at the end of the Six War?"

"Yes," said Noa, eyes narrowing at the doctor.

Even as a civilian James knew about the mech suits. Ethernet-controlled machines had been next to useless in The Six Wars—the Six System asteroids were dense and unstable, and blocked light beams, microwaves, radio waves—just about every known way to communicate. The problems with communications in Six had reignited the research into quantum entanglement-based communication. But not having that, Fleet went with mech suits, highly specialized robotic shells worn by humans. They were seen as being the next best thing to quantum-controlled drones. The suits were nearly indestructible—gave one man the power of twelve—and when they were destroyed, it only meant one coffin was brought home, not a dozen.

"You perhaps know of the psychological problems ... with the suits?" said Monica.

"Psychological problems with the suits?" James asked.

Noa took a long breath.

Monica waved her hand. "Not with the suits. With their operators."

"What are you talking about?" James asked, looking between the two women.

Noa sighed. "Among other things, the suits were designed to be worn in situations where an operator might be isolated from teammates in full vacuum for extended periods of time ... the mech suits were—are—smaller than ticks even, much more nimble. Ideal for espionage. To ease the effects of the isolation, the suits were made personable—"

"They made them too personable," Monica said, her jaw tightening, a scowl creasing her brow.

"What does that mean?" James asked, an itch forming at the back of his mind.

Noa's eyes dropped to the floor. She put a hand to her chin and said, "The suits were designed to care about their operator's well-being and mental health. To that end, they developed an emotional rapport with their operators. It seemed logical for the designers, but the suits became less tools, and more partners."

Monica frowned. "The Fleet personnel in the suits prioritized their suits over human lives."

A prickle of static itched up James's spine.

Turning to face the doctor, Noa said, "They did not prioritize their suits! They mourned their losses, yes, but they didn't—"

"They could snap out the suit's hard drive. There was no need to be emotionally attached to the things!" Monica said.

Through the ether, Noa projected a red ball ... of what he assumed could only be rage ... and he actually felt like it was warming him.

"You know that isn't true," Noa said. "The soul of the suit wasn't just in its hard drive, it was in the CPU centers of its arms, legs, and—"

"Listen to your language," Monica said, her voice becoming soft and losing its hard edge. "The suits didn't have souls ... the human operators who gave their lives for their suits did."

"Name me one human operator who gave his life for the suit," Noa said.

Crossing her arms, Monica said, "The 132nd platoon lost an entire fire team—"

"They did not lose the fire team in some sort of misplaced desire to save their mech suits." Noa's voice rose in volume, her words coming clipped and fast. Her anger made the red ball between her and James's mind pulse. "The humans and mechs made a strategic decision," Noa continued. "They decided that having the humans leave their suits, effectively dividing into a human and a mech fire team in the Fenris cave of asteroid

634, would be the best way to complete the mission. They succeeded and retrieved the intel they were tasked with recovering! You dishonor the fire team's intelligence and sacrifice by insinuating—"

"It should not have been the humans that died," Monica cried.

"The fire team did what they needed to do to complete their mission," Noa said, lowering her voice from a shout. Across the ether, her anger crackled, "No one dishonors my Fleet."

"You weren't assigned to the task of explaining why the suits survived and the men inside them didn't," Monica said, her voice very even. "One of those men was a senator's grandson ... the Fleet lost funding because of that mistake."

"The data that 'mistake' retrieved," Noa said in a more controlled voice, "saved hundreds of Fleet personnel's lives and helped end the conflict."

As controlled as her voice was, the ethernet buzzed with her rage. Across the channel she hissed, "Maggot in the refuse of a dysenteric lizzar. Typical politician ... ready to seize defeat from the jaws of victory." The fireball of her anger was replaced by a graphic picture of said maggot across the ether ... James reignited the fire ball and let it engulf the mental maggot. His eyes slid to Noa. There was the ghost of a smile on her lips, but her eyes were on the doctor. Across the ether, Noa said, "Oh, look, now she pities me. Doctors!"

Monica's expression had become pitying.

Taking a deep breath, Noa prompted, "So, you told them about your research, which was ...?"

"Yes, how to assure that human-machine interactions

did not lead to the anthropomorphizing of machines and maintaining the supremacy of human life."

"And they let you go after that," said Noa. Across the ether, she said, "Well, it does almost fit with their philosophy."

The heat beneath James's skin spread to every neuron and nano within him. He felt as though he were made of flame. "No, that excuse isn't good enough. Why did they wait to attack us?" he asked. "They could have attacked as soon as they landed."

Monica's arms dropped to her sides. She took a step back. "I ... I ... don't know."

"They wished they could," Zoe said.

All the adults in the room looked at Zoe. She was looking down at Carl Sagan, scratching him beneath the chin.

"What, honey?" said Monica, approaching her daughter.

Zoe looked up. "I heard it with my augments."

"What did you hear?" Noa pressed.

"'Wish we could have full-on stormed the Ark,' one man said," Zoe replied. "But then the other one said, 'No, can't damage the Ark, might destroy the archangel ... it must be taken alive ... and 'sides, Adam wants that ship. We can't damage it without getting his sign-off first, or we might wind up floating home.'"

"The archangel?" said Monica. "Did they tell you what that is, honey?"

James's eyes narrowed on the child.

"One of them said it was a demon," Zoe whispered. She sat up straighter. "Or a djinn ... what's that, Mommy?"

Frowning again, Monica put a hand on Zoe's shoulder. "Imaginary creatures."

Looking at James, Monica said, "James, what madness is this?" There was a note of plaintiveness in her voice that caught James off guard. He began to wonder at his visceral dislike for her. He had never felt anything before his accident except attraction to Monica—and annoyance that it was one-sided.

"Welcome to the Luddeccean System," James said after a pause that stretched too long.

Noa cocked her head. "Where was Wren the whole time you were aboard the Luddeccean ship?"

Monica blinked. "I don't know." She looked at her daughter.

"He was nice, Mommy." Zoe looked up at her mother. "He said they shouldn't hold you, and that we should be allowed to leave. That we were *his* passengers, and they weren't allowed to steal his fare."

The boy stiffened at Zoe's words. Carl Sagan sat up with a squeak. He rubbed his nose against the boy's hand.

Noa sighed across the ether and said, "That sounds like Wren." She turned to the boy. "And who might you be, young man?"

James turned to the child. His stained clothing was not quite rags, and his long dark-brown hair fell in front of his face. His eyes were barely visible through dirty bangs. His features were nondescript Afro-Euro-Asian and he was very skinny. "Raif," he said quietly, his voice cracking a little.

"Nice to meet you, Raif," said Noa. "You were helping Wren take care of his ship?"

The boy gulped. "Trying."

"I'm sure you were doing a good job," said Noa.

She turned to James. "Shall we go talk to Captain Wren?"

James nodded at her, but before either of them could move, the boy slid from the exam table. Cradling Carl Sagan in his arms, he said, "Can I come with you?"

Noa's dark eyes met James's. A fleeting will-o'-the-wisp of worry fluttered through the ether between them.

The boy looked between them both, his hair falling away from frightened-looking brown eyes. Monica put a hand to her mouth.

"Please," said the boy. "He's my dad."

CHAPTER TWELVE

Noa gaped.

James's thoughts flickered across the ether. "That doesn't ... feel right."

And that was the truth.

Monica began tapping her neural interface, the universal symbol for "Can we think together?"

Ghost's thoughts rang across the general frequency. "Commander and Professor, that ... woman ... is trying to reach you over the ether. Should I share access to the Ark's ethernet?"

Noa's eyes went to James.

Across the ether, he said, "The Luddecceans let her go too easily."

"I agree, Commander," Ghost said.

Noa felt something was missing from James. "You ... don't like her."

James shook his head and looked away. "It ... might be irrational," he said across the shared channel.

Noa frowned, thinking about the bloodbath on Adam's Station. "Her joining us on this ship wasn't easy."

"So you trust her?" James said across the channel. At his side his fists were opening and closing. Monica looked frantically between the two of them.

Noa put a hand to her chin and spoke into his mind. "She is condescending—but so are most Earth academics." She gave James a tight smile. He rolled his eyes. Noa shook her head. "But she is also honest ... I trust her enough."

"Fine," said Ghost. "Giving her access to a general channel now."

Monica's thoughts rushed across the ether, her eyes going from Noa to James and back again. "Raif showed up at Wren's ship shortly after we landed and claimed to be Wren's son. He had a DNA match kit that confirmed it. Wren didn't know anything about him; but did know his mother. Apparently, some sort of sex worker. According to Raif, she died a few months ago. "

Noa exhaled.

Monica said across the ether, "Wren let him stay and has had him doing odd jobs. I can't tell if Raif is growing on him ... or if he thinks maybe Raif is the cheapest labor option."

"You're all talking about me in your heads," said Raif. He licked his lips; they were so chapped they were split and bloody. "Are you going to take me to see my dad?"

Noa looked at Monica, not sure how much she could trust her; and uncertain about Raif, and what he meant, what he revealed about Wren's motivations. It wasn't in her to trust a double agent; but Wren was human, had a family now, and hadn't turned the boy *away*. She looked Raif up and down. The boy was a picture of neglect ... but he was alive, unlike the other civilians on the hangar, and Wren had run back for him.

Carl Sagan kneaded his claws into the boy's pant leg and squeaked at the doctor. Monica went over to the werfle and scratched his head. The creature leaned into her touch.

And Noa felt a certainty in her gut that she could trust Monica to be a doctor and to be honest. The bout of verbal jousting said that Monica couldn't keep her opinions to herself ... Noa trusted that more than the reverse.

"I'm not going to hurt your dad," Noa said. And then heat flared in her chest. Over the ether, she found herself venting, "Although maybe I should. He couldn't get this child any proper clothes?"

One of James's eyebrows lifted. She must have inadvertently shared the thought with Monica as well, because the doctor nodded and sucked in a long breath.

Holding her anger in, Noa said aloud, "Right now I need to speak with Wren alone." The boy drew back, cradling Carl Sagan closer. The werfle snuffled against him.

Noa bent down so her eyes were level with Raif's. "No matter what happens, you're welcome here."

Raif's body visibly relaxed, and he exhaled loudly.

Her eyes went to Monica.

"Why don't I take them both to the cafeteria?" the doctor suggested. She waved at Gunny. "He's connected to the ether. I'll know if he wakes up."

Over the ether, Noa said, "There were no ... extraordinary chemicals in his system?"

Monica shook her head and across the ether said, "He's just drunk."

Noa sighed. To James, and only James, she vented across the ether, "I'd almost hoped he'd been drugged and had a real excuse."

James's brow furrowed and Zoe whispered to Raif, "They're talking in their heads again."

"Thank you, Monica," Noa said aloud.

"Can we take the werfle?" said Raif.

Noa's breath caught, remembering Fluffy I and Fluffy II. How many times had she confided in her pets when she was afraid, or angry? She gave a commandery nod to the boy. "Sure, you can. I think he needs you," she said, knowing it was the other way around.

She inclined her head to the door. "Go ahead."

Doctor and children went down the hall toward the lift as James and Noa watched.

Aloud, James said, "We need to talk to Wren."

Noa nodded. A few minutes later they were outside the door of the cabin James had stowed him in. He went to the panel by the door and pressed in a fast number and symbol sequence.

Given enough time, Wren would figure a way out of a locked cabin ... even if it was just by conning whomever was in charge of bringing his meals. She hadn't been lying when she said they couldn't keep prisoners.

The door whooshed open and she found herself face to face with Wren. Wearing Ark-issued clothing, he was sitting on a narrow cot, back to the wall, scowling at his feet and rubbing his head, obviously suffering from a Stun-ache. He looked up at Noa and then his eyes flicked over Noa's shoulder to James. For a moment, Noa saw something calculating in his gaze. But then he leered. "Noa, if you were planning a threesome, you could have brought Monica."

"Cut the crap, Wren," Noa said. "Why are you here?" Could he know about the time gate at the Kanakah Cloud and be hitching a ride? A man like Wren had been places and heard things ... If he knew that, others would know, too ...

Putting a hand to his chest, Wren said, "Hello, Wren, nice to see you, Wren." Sitting up fast, he hissed, "Thank you for saving my life, *Wren*." One of his nostrils flared. The leer had left his face completely.

"What do you want, Wren?" Noa said, crossing her arms. She could feel James just centis behind her.

Wren looked up at James and then looked away. He wiped his jaw and met Noa's gaze again. "Did it occur to you that I might have wanted my life? And, well ... life for that kid." He scratched the back of his neck, looking uncomfortable, like he'd put on a coat full of xenofleas.

Noa shifted on her feet. "Your ship was in bad shape, but you had access to parts and plenty of Monica's credits—"

Wren scowled. "The only credit that is going to be useful anywhere soon is food and Adam's Station is almost out of that. I'm hitching a ride with you to Libertas, the only self-sustaining planet left in this system besides Luddeccea, but I might have a slight reputation there." He winced. "And possibly a death warrant—but that wasn't really warranted, if you know what I mean."

James said, "They let you off their ship easily enough."

Wren lifted his hands and gestured dramatically. "Yeah, I'm not sure why, either. Because they're out of their jurisdiction, because Adam doesn't like it when you abduct people from his dock, or because they turned off their lizzar pissing ethernet and don't remember they're supposed to arrest me?" He rubbed his stubble. "I think I might be slightly hurt by that."

James muttered, "Must be nice."

"By the looks of the crowd on the tarmac, I wasn't the only one who wanted aboard," Wren said.

"And now they're dead, but you're here, and that's all that matters, right?" Noa retorted.

Leaning forward, Wren said, "It was the only plan I had, and I was only trying to hit Adam's men ... I wasn't expecting the mob to—"

"Get crazy?" Noa all but shouted.

James lifted an eyebrow. "That is what mobs do."

Leaning back, Wren picked at the drab Ark stock clothing James must have given him. "Your enemy is my enemy now. Can we at least be friends until we reach Libertas?" He raised a hand. "That kid you saw, he is my son ... I have ... I fucked up with him."

Noa snorted.

Wren rolled his eyes. "Look, I don't want to die and I can be useful—"

"No," Noa said.

"Noa ..." James said, sweeping past her. Wren jumped back, but James was heading toward the porthole.

"James?" Noa asked, but her voice was drowned out by the wail of a klaxon.

Ghost's voice was in her head, and Chavez, too. "Commander, they've found us."

Noa was already out the door before they finished. The ship shook, every air vent abruptly went silent, the lights flickered, and the ship went completely dark before she reached the lift.

* * *

The ethernet went down. James noticed the abrupt halt in the flow of electrons between his and Noa's minds before he noticed the lights had gone out. He heard Wren's footsteps stumbling toward the door, and Noa in the hallway. A map of the narrow cabin formed in his brain, and he leaped forward and grabbed the man by the back of his shirt. Wren swore in surprise. In the hallway, James heard the hinges of the door to the access stairwells open and knew Noa would be in them.

Heaving Wren up, James slammed him into the wall beside the porthole.

"Shit!" Wren said.

James blinked. Where he'd seen a bright star suddenly appear in the sky a few minutes before, now there was a vessel. He focused on it, his augments magnified it, and he hissed. The lights abruptly came back on, and air whooshed into the cabin. The sudden change in light made him blind.

Over the ether, Manuel's voice came. "Charge burst!"

And then Noa's thoughts rang out, "They don't want to kill us, they want to board us."

In the tiny cabin, James shook Wren, and aloud and over the ether he said, "That isn't the Luddeccean ship!"

Noa's mind flowed over the ether. "Show me what you see!"

James sent his view to her. A ship shaped like a teardrop, with a black pockmarked surface, and at the base, twelve sharp wings that almost looked like spikes.

Shaking Wren again, James said, "Did you send them?"

"No!" Wren screamed, chest still pressed against the wall, head facing the porthole. "That's Captain Xo's rig. I don't want him here!"

James spun him around. "Why is he here?"

Wren's eyes were wide, and he smelled like fear. "I don't know! But he's not a friend."

James lifted him by the collar until his feet were off the floor.

Wren choked out, "I didn't pay him for some parts before we left Adam's Station."

Setting Wren down, James said, "Are you saying he's chasing you?"

Wren's eyes got wide. "It wasn't that many parts!"

The ship shook. The lights went out again. The ether died and the air vents stopped their steady hum. In the darkness, Wren said, "Please, let me help you! I don't want to die!"

"How can you help?" James demanded, giving him a shake.

"I'm a pilot! A damn good one ..." Wren panted. "... and I might not be as straight a shooter heroic bastard like you, Earther, but my neck is on the line."

"Straight shooter?" said James, bemused and a bit confused. And then he remembered going back into the line of fire during their exit from Adam's Station. He supposed that could be confused for heroism and being a "straight shooter." But the hero straight shooter was Noa; he'd gone out into the line of fire knowing Noa would do it if he hadn't. He looked out for his interests; it wasn't the same as heroism.

Wren held up his arms. "I'm unarmed. You can put me down!"

The lights flickered on and Noa's voice came over the ether. "Bo, on my signal you give me a cannon blast. Chavez, you after him. Manuel, keep the power flowing!"

Keeping his hands in the air, Wren said, "I hope you

have two damn good pilots at the helm, because Xo is about to shoot drones directly into this boat's path. They'll collide with us, and at lightspeed, the tiniest nudge can send us barreling into a rogue object or hell, a moon ... not to mention the shorts we're going to have in our timebands."

James felt the ship shake—this time there was no accompanying power short. Over the ether, Bo said, "Commander, drones flying into the wake of the cannon blast!"

The ship shook again. This time the lights did go out.

Chavez, a dark shadow on the unlit bridge, leaped up from the pilot chair as soon as Noa raced up the stairs. The ensign dashed to the cannon position that was unoccupied without having to be asked. Bo, the trigger happy engineer, was in the other. With only Luddeccea's distant sun for light, Noa strapped herself into the helm. For once, Ghost was on the bridge sitting in the copilot's chair. He'd insisted on coming up during Chavez's shift.

"Chavez, be ready to fire that cannon as soon as you have power," she said. She silently willed the lights to come on. They did—the charges the strange ship was shooting only gave them momentary flickers—not even long enough for the auxiliary power to kick in. Which was probably the point. It kept the Ark's systems destabilized.

"Ghost, get the ether routed through the auxiliary—"

"—so that it won't go out with the main power systems," Ghost responded from where he sat in the copilot's seat. "Already on it."

"And the ship's navigation," Noa said.

Ghost grunted.

"Timebands are online, Commander," Manuel said over the ether.

"Ghost, do you have a course for me?" Noa said.

A bright light flickered in her vision and her apps told her Ghost was transmitting fear.

"What's wrong?" Noa asked.

"I set up the ether so that I could enter coordinates mentally, Commander," Ghost whimpered. "... And have already routed the nav computer to the auxiliary power ... but there must be a short circuit. I can't enter the coordinates mentally anymore and—"

"Give me coordinates as you have them," Noa said. Leaning forward over the extensive dash, she began entering the coordinates manually into the archaic system as they flashed behind her eyes.

"What are those?" Bo whispered.

For a moment, Noa thought he was talking about the ancient dials and buttons on the dash, but then she saw the lights on the read-out. "Drones," said Chavez.

"What are they going to do?" Bo asked.

"Get in the way," said Chavez.

Noa's hands flew over the control. She had almost all the coordinates entered ... just the millionth, tenth millionth, and hundred millionth place to go.

"Clear a path through those drones, Chavez," Noa ordered.

"The cannon isn't charged, Commander," Chavez gasped.

"Are those more drones?" Bo asked.

The lights flickered, but the nav computer stayed lit.

"Bless you, Ghost," Noa whispered in the darkness. She wouldn't have to re-enter the coordinates. Noa heard footsteps pounding up from the ladder access shaft. The lights came back on before her brain registered who it was.

Manuel's voice rolled over the ether. "Commander, another hit like that and we'll lose a timeband." Despite the chill of space radiating from the skylight above her chair, Noa felt sweat begin to prickle on her brow. She gritted her teeth, gripped the steering bars, and sent the ship to lightspeed, ignoring the first lesson every pilot learned in navigation school.

The stars blurred and the navigation computer screamed. The ship hadn't even had a chance to re-orientate itself for Ghost's plotted coordinates, and every light flashed orange in protest as they tore off in a direction thousandths of a degree off course.

"What are you doing?" Ghost shouted.

Beside her, Wren shouted, "Get up, man, unless you can fly this thing!"

"Ghost, new coordinates!" Noa said, holding onto the helm. Too busy to think about Wren being there.

"Get up!" James roared.

"I—"

"Can keep working on the coordinates standing," James said. Ghost unclicked his safety harness and James bodily removed him from the seat.

Chavez said, "I'll have the cannon charged in another—"

A sound like static or frantic hail tore through the bridge.

The nav computer's light went red and the scream rose to a wail.

Manuel's voice flooded her mind. "Space dust." As though Noa needed to be told.

"We are off course!" Ghost said.

The time bubble created by their bands sucked in the tiny particles enough to keep them from turning into tiny hull piercing projectiles, but the dust pocket warped the ship's trajectory, like a stone skipping across the surface of a lake. Noa powered the timebands down before they were sent skipping into a thicker cloud, a rogue planet, or a comet.

Numbers flashed in her vision. "Working on a new course!" Ghost cried.

"It has to take into account the dust!" Wren said.

"Yes, Commander," Ghost replied. "I have telemetry readings for the opposite side of the cloud ..." His voice faded away, but numbers flickered in the periphery of her vision and the cloud hung in her visual cortex as a glowing three-dimensional map of light that's edges became sharper and crisper by the millisecond. It was incredible that Ghost could coax a three-dimensional cloud map so quickly from the Ark's ancient systems while simultaneously working on a new course.

"Start entering the coordinates," Wren said.

The ship was trembling in the dust. Noa dared not let go of the controls.

"I've got the helm," said Wren, and Noa could hear him gritting his teeth.

For a moment Noa's hands froze, but James's voice slid across the ether. "His interests align with ours." James's hand came down on her shoulder ... gently, and he squeezed softly. The simple gesture filled Noa with confidence—or at least reminded her she didn't have time to second guess—she began to quickly enter Ghost's new coordinates.

"Comp guy," he said, "can you give me a three-dimensional map of this cloud—or at least access to your ether?"

There was the sound of more static as Wren angled the ship into the dust.

Bo's voice filled the bridge. "That freighter ... it followed us."

The ship shook, and pieces of debris thudded against the hull. Noa kept her eyes on the dials for the nav computer. "Entering coordinates—but we need to get to the jump point on the other side of this cloud," she said and spoke into the ship's ether.

"I have the coordinates for the jump point," Wren said. "But first ..."

The cloud was irregularly shaped, with long fingers that protruded from it. Wren brought them out between a pair of ghostly fingers that smudged the stars on either side and turned the black to glowing orange.

"They'd set out charges," James whispered.

"They were hoping to catch us in the cloud—the dust —it's electrically conductive," said Chavez, as the orange light flickered out.

"Yes," said Wren, steering the Ark around a long glowing finger and to the jump point a second later.

"Coordinates entered," Noa said, as they reached the point Ghost had calculated as an ideal location to enter lightspeed.

"All yours, Commander," Wren said.

The nav computer flashed green, Noa pulled back on the steering bars, felt her body press against her seat, heard a squeal of metal as James braced himself on the chair's frame, and the stars blurred. A collective sigh left everyone on the bridge.

Adrenaline seeping away from her system, Noa found her hands shaking on the steering bars.

James's consciousness touched hers.

Manuel's thoughts swept through the ether. "Commander, we've sustained some damage ... the damn cooling system valve is leaking heat in here again. May I suggest, as soon as we reach a place that's safe to hide, that we stop and run a full diagnostic? We need to do it before the final stretch."

Noa's jaw ground. From the solar system to the Kanakah Cloud, they'd be in open space. Before they started that "final stretch," they could hide behind the gas giant that Alantea orbited though ... for a while. "Understood," Noa replied.

Beside her, Wren said, "This course is taking us opposite of the direction of Libertas."

For a moment there was absolute silence. Noa said, "You are dismissed from the bridge."

James's thoughts entered hers. In the Genji cipher he said, "You're tired."

"I'll use stims," Noa shot back.

The bridge went silent. It took Noa a moment to realize that she'd said that aloud.

"I'm not saying I'm against not going to Libertas," Wren said. "I was merely surprised, Commander."

"I'm not confident in your loyalty to give you our final destination," Noa said.

"As long as the food doesn't run out, and I get to eat, I don't care about our final destination," Wren snapped. He looked around. "We do have enough food, don't we?"

"We have so much food!" Bo exclaimed. "We can make it all the way to System Seven's time gate!"

"Is that where we're going?" Wren said, his voice a little weaker.

"I'm not giving you control of my ship," Noa said. A tremor shook her hands.

"No, of course not," said Wren. "Straight-laced guy and the rest of your crew wouldn't abide having me as their fearless leader."

"Straight-laced guy?" said Noa. James, she realized, he meant James. But that wasn't quite right ... was it? It was an illusion created by the affluence obvious in his augments and his speech patterns. He looked and sounded like he was straight-laced.

Wren turned in his chair. He put a hand through his hair and said, "I'll just watch the helm so you can sleep. This ship can maintain lightspeed, and Xo and whatever other enemies you've managed to pick up don't catch us." His voice rose in pitch at the end.

"We are not enemies of Xo, whoever that is," Noa protested.

"Could have fooled me," Wren grumbled.

James reached to her through the ether. "He's afraid of them, too, Noa. He owes them money. You can trust him as long as our interests align."

Across the ether, Noa snapped, "Xo is chasing us because he owes them money!"

"Or because we have food," James thought.

Noa exhaled sharply ... were the Ark's stores really enough to launch an interstellar chase? She swallowed, remembering the hunger and misery at Adam's Station. Maybe it was. "You sound confident in him," Noa replied over the ether, her jaw remaining resolutely shut in the real world.

"I'm not," James replied. "But sometimes ... the protection of personal interests can make even an amoral individual appear heroic."

For some reason, the reply made the hair on the back of Noa's neck prickle.

"I can't leave him alone up here," Noa said. She shook her head.

"Of course not," James replied. "Leave him with Ghost, Manuel, Gunny, Chavez, or me."

Noa sat at the wheel, her skin cold and clammy, an echo of her adrenaline crash.

Gunny's voice burst into the ether. "Where the hell am I?!"

Followed by Dr. Monica's thoughts. "The patient is awake, Commander."

"Gunny," Noa said. "Can't leave him alone either, apparently." She scowled. But that was another problem she had to take care of, that she couldn't take care of, not while she sat at the helm. It wasn't just her job to fly this boat, it was to keep the crew together. How many crises were waiting to explode in the decks below? She restrained a sigh. The good doctor, for one, was liable not to take their real destination very well.

"Ghost," she said. "How much sleep have you had?"

"A solid five hours," the computer officer said. He sniffed. "I never need more."

He said it as though anyone who did was a lesser human being. Noa did not roll her eyes. And then she swallowed. She trusted Ghost enough, because the Luddeccean Guard would never forgive him if they were captured. Was it so different with Wren?

"Ghost, lock Wren out of the ether for a moment," Noa commanded.

"Done," the computing officer said.

Over the ether, she said to Ghost, "You can watch Wren while he takes the helm?"

"Of course," Ghost said. "I don't trust him ... but we have to stay at lightspeed, and I'm no pilot." It was rare for Ghost to concede weakness; it made Noa trust him more when he did.

"Chavez—you'll watch Ghost's back, won't you?" Noa said silently into the ether.

"Yes, Commander!" said Chavez.

"Alright," Noa said aloud. "Wren ... you can take the helm. Keep us on course, and keep us at lightspeed, and no questions!"

Over the ether, she said, "No answers!"

"I value my hide," said Ghost.

"Of course not," Chavez thought.

"Oh, my head," Gunny said over the ether.

Unlatching the safety harness, Noa said, "I'll see you all in ..." She blinked. "... eight point five hours." She might even get seven hours of sleep.

"Aye, Commander," Chavez said.

Ghost nodded. "Yes," and slid into the seat Noa had vacated.

Wren turned very briefly and gave her a thousand-watt smile. "Have a nice nap."

Before she could scowl, he'd already turned his gaze back to the skylight. The smile was gone, and the expression on his face was earnest. He'd been a double agent during the war in System Six. It went against everything Noa believed in to trust him; but James was right. Wren's interests aligned with hers. Noa rubbed her temples. What did that say about her?

James's thoughts reached out to hers. "Noa?"

She looked up and found him above her, blue eyes intent on hers. He stood closer to her than any Fleet personnel would stand to their Commander. But they weren't superior and subordinate, and she was glad. "Let's go," she said, stepping down the stairwell to the lift. Her eyes were starting to burn again. She sighed and over the ether said, "I need to talk to Gunny first."

They stepped onto the lift platform and the walls rose around them and the ceiling engulfed them as they descended.

James raised an eyebrow. "I was thinking I might go down to engineering ..."

"You're not hungry?" Noa asked, smiling in surprise.

James tilted his head and looked at the floor. "Yes, I am, but you know ... I think I'll be fine in engineering."

Noa blinked. There was something a little awkward, or off, in the way he said the words.

The lift reached the med bay level, and James reached out and touched her arm—meeting her eyes for just a moment, freezing her in her tracks as heat raced through her. Through the ether he sent a vision of a ball of orange light. Spinning in her mind, it made her body flush from head to toe and her breath catch. She licked her lips. The heat between them wasn't awkward at all, even if she was missing pieces, and he was missing memories, and neither of them had time.

She backed out of the lift with a tiny nod to him, the glowing ball of light burning in her visual cortex and keeping her whole body warm and alive even in the cold hallway as the lift door shut.

* * *

"I'm sorry, Commander," Gunny was saying, slipping on a boot. "I don't know what came over me."

Noa was sitting on a chair she'd rolled over from Monica's station. She'd sent the doctor away. "I think I do," Noa said.

Gunny froze.

"You're an alcoholic, Gunny," Noa said, the comment early the other morning, just before the tick attack, sticking in her mind. *Does the ship have alcohol?* She sighed. Gunny was a good man. That he would so easily become fall-down drunk while on a "mission" meant that the drug had real talons in him.

"Pssshhhh ..." Gunny said. "Nah ... I have a drink occasionally."

"You can't have a drink on my ship," Noa said. She had a sinking suspicion he had a stash in his cabin. A real alcoholic would. Leaning forward, she rested her elbows on her knees and added a little guilt to the direct order. "You've got to get rid of any you have in your cabin."

Gunny looked away.

"I need you too much, Gunny."

Gunny met her eyes, and for the first time, looked guilty.

Noa smiled sadly. "More than ever ... Wren is at the helm right now, and I need help keeping an eye on him."

Gunny sat up straight, his eyes wide. "That double crossing, untrustworthy—"

"We need him," Noa said, sitting back in her chair. "So I can manage other ship business." She let "like this" be implied.

Gunny looked away again.

"I know alcohol can be like a friend ..." Noa said. "Hard to give up, always there for you ..." It had almost become her best friend, after Tim died. Her little brother Kenji had been the first to notice, the first to worry, and warn her, *No amount of drinking will bring him back.* Her brother was usually so poor at understanding others' motivations, but he'd understood that. Why? Because in his own cold analytical way he knew her better than anyone? Because he loved her as much as Tim had, in a way that was more pure ... no lust, just the bond of kinship. She bit her lower lip. Oh, Kenji, why did you turn me in? She knew the answer to that was the same. Because he loved her.

"Friend, yeah, it is a friend! Kept me from being rounded up by the Luddy Guard, it did."

Noa's eyes jerked up to the sergeant. He was fastening a boot strap. Intent on the task, he said, "Had been out drinkin' the night before Manuel came to pick me up. If I hadn't spent the night in my neighbor's ditch, they woulda picked me up with the other poor sods and shipped me God knows where ... waking up with a mouth full of vomit wasn't bad as that."

He put his hands through his hair, pushing back the unruly bangs. He met her eyes.

Sitting still as a statue, Noa didn't say anything. She let his own words hang in the air. She heard him gulp and knew she had reached him.

Despite her own brief dance with alcohol when Tim died, Noa hadn't indulged long enough for her affair with the drug to become a physical need. Gunny would have a harder time leaving his partner behind; he needed a habit to replace the one he'd found himself stuck in. She reached for something that every Luddeccean shared, *The Three Books.*

"Your book was the Koran," Noa said. "This isn't you, Gunny." The colony had been settled by adherents of Judaism, Christianity, and Islam. Although, Three Books was its own religion in a way. Its adherents all claimed origin from one of the three. It was one faith with three sects.

He put a hand behind his head and looked away. "Luddy nonsense. Religion is a tool of the weak."

How often had she heard that on Earth when she talked about her Luddeccean upbringing? "That's Earther talk," Noa said. "We know that religion is a tool of the strong." It was the standard Luddeccean spiel, what frustrated priests of the Three Books would say to those members of their flock that they'd all but given up on—not an appeal to truth, but to *utility.*

Gunny exhaled. It may have been Noa's imagination, but she thought he trembled a bit at the thought of giving up his booze stash, or the power of his upbringing weighing upon him. You couldn't escape the Three Books when you were from Luddeccea ... Noa hadn't realized it until she'd joined the Fleet. She'd thought she was borderline atheist but realized she was religious by tradition, if not belief. It did make her strong, didn't it? Or maybe it just made a community strong? When she'd been tried for "borrowing" the Luddeccean Guard's antigrav bike when she was a kid, she'd had to put her hand on her family's book, the Bible. She couldn't have lied. Even if she didn't believe the Bible word for word, it stood for something she couldn't dishonor or shake. Maybe Gunny's religion could steer him down the more difficult path—and help keep them all safe.

"We need you, Gunny, any way we can get you back," she said.

He nodded.

"Get a shower," she said, "and report for duty."

"Yes, Commander, thank you, Commander," he said, standing at attention, giving an earnest salute, and then making his way to the door. For a moment she was alone, and she shivered in the medbay. And then she remembered she didn't have to be alone anymore. Through the ether she reached for James.

CHAPTER THIRTEEN

James clasped the wrench-like tool in his hands. The tool connected to a specialized bolt that was an emergency release valve for the hot de-radiated steam from the reactor. The steam circulated through various pipes, heating the ship and cooling for its return trip to the reactor. Holding the manual valve steady was an activity that put stress on every muscle in his body. Steam shot past him and hung in the air around him in a heated cloud, but even as his body was occupied, a tiny part of him wandered with Noa. She was a bright light blinking in his mind. He watched the light that was her go to the galley-turned cafe, and then to her cabin. He watched the light that was her move to her bed ... and stay there, motionless for so long she had to have fallen asleep. He could be there with her ...

The steam abruptly cut off. Manuel's thoughts flooded the ether. "We've got it!" James heard some sounds of relief, though he couldn't see where they originated from through the cloud of water vapor. "James, tighten her up, and we're done here."

James tightened the bolt until Manuel said over the ether, "Pressure is at acceptable levels." Lowering the wrench, James felt as though every muscle in his arms and back were uncoiling. The mist began to dissipate. He heard a door open, blinked in that direction, and saw Manuel, Kuin, Jun, and Kara emerging from an access tunnel.

"It's hotter than a lizzar's balls in here," Kuin said.

"Ewww ..." said Kara.

Rubbing the back of his neck, Manuel looked at James, his brow furrowed. "It is hot ... hotter than I expected. James, are you alright?"

"I'm fine." *Better than fine.* Perfect, like he could go back to Noa's cabin and roll between the sheets for hours.

"I think I would have passed out in here," Manuel said.

"Lizzar dung, I know I would have," said Jun.

James glanced at them, the nanos in his mind firing, as though anticipating attack. But Jun was wiping sweat from his forehead, Kuin was peering down his own shirt and sticking out his tongue, Kara was fanning her face with a hand, and Manuel was trying to blow his bangs out of his eyes, but they were firmly plastered to his forehead.

"Lucky for us you're augmented," Manuel said. "Why don't you go get cleaned up?"

James nodded, anxious to get away, feeling the light in his mind that was Noa calling him like a beacon.

"Cool tats," said Kuin, and James's gaze snapped down.

He'd rolled up his sleeves when he'd begun the job, and his tattoos had unfurled across his arms like black feathers. He rolled his sleeves down, gave another tight nod to Manuel, and headed out the exit. Moments later, he was at the lift. His finger was poised to press the button to Noa's level when he caught himself. He closed his eyes, remembering a scene: rain falling against a window in London, hovers streaking by in a blur outside. His eyes were on a woman, Deirdre. Her back had been to him as she gazed out the window. He'd just told her they needed to break up. She'd told him she loved him, and he'd said he didn't fall in love. Moments later, she'd spun around, slapped him, and called him inhuman.

James touched his cheek at the memory. Now he felt love or obsession, he wasn't sure which. It was outside of his realm of experience. Maybe it was the situation that had changed him? Had the extreme adversity he'd shared with Noa forged this intense bond? Opening his eyes, he rocked on his feet. Apart from being the target of prejudice for being a throwback, he hadn't faced real adversity in his previous life. He had been a spoiled Earther; now he was running for his life ... and Noa's. He hit the button and the lift ascended, but as it did, the light in his mind that was Noa rose from her bed, exited her cabin, and moved down the hall. She stopped short, turned abruptly, and began descending the ladder shaft faster than he was ascending in the lift.

"Noa," he called across the ether, feeling a darkness at the edge of his vision, and a sudden dread that she might be sleepwalking again. "What are you doing?"

"I hear Carl Sagan in the ladder shaft ..." The blinking light that was her came to a stop. "Oh, here he is, he's stuck in some adhesive putty."

The elevator came to a halt, and James stepped out to the sound of frantic werfle squeaking. Noa had left the door to the ladder shaft open. He peered down and saw the top of her head. She'd braced her back against the wall

and was using both hands to extricate the ten-legged creature from some purple putty. Carl Sagan gave a squeal as
she slipped him free, wrapped him around her neck,
began to climb up ... and slipped on the ladder. "Nebulas," she whispered.

"Noa?" James said, putting a hand on a rung,
preparing to come down after her.

She blinked up at him and he noticed how bloodshot
her eyes were. "Oh, hey," she said, and began climbing
very carefully.

"Is something wrong?" James asked across the ether.

"Nah," said Noa, reaching his level. James stepped
back from the door and she exited the tunnel, stumbling
slightly. It wasn't like her at all. He felt a weight, like a
shift in gravity, on his shoulders. "Noa, how long has it
been since you slept?" He remembered her being in her
bed a few minutes earlier. "Really slept," he added.

She stroked Carl Sagan's tail. "Plenty of time to sleep
when I'm dead," she said, but she headed back to her
cabin. She put her hand on the button for the door,
turned, and gazed back at him, her eyes deep and liquid.
It was like being on top of the Xinshii gorge again,
knowing gravity was about to kick in, but this time he
wanted to fall. She didn't have to say anything for him to
follow.

As soon as the door shut behind them, Carl Sagan slid
down Noa's body and hopped away. Noa turned and put
her arms around James's neck. James wrapped his arms
around her waist, tugged their bodies together, and slid
his nose along hers, breathing against her lips, hoping it
would suffice for the kiss that he couldn't give.

Her body shook against his. "What's wrong?" he
whispered.

She shook her head.

And his mind pieced together her stagger and red-rimmed eyes. "You were asleep, and you had nightmares and they woke you up," James guessed. And then she'd left her cabin ... to find him.

Noa dropped her head against his chest. "They're still so clear in my mind."

Heat flared beneath his skin and a desire that was as powerful as lust. "Let me into your head," he whispered. "I'll keep them away." The words were startling. He remembered Deirdre again. She'd been depressed ... it had been so inconvenient. He had never wanted to fight a woman's demons before.

Noa's body went still against him, and then she said, "I'd like that. Has to be a hard-link, with Ghost in the ether."

James dropped a hand to his back pocket and pulled out the tight coil of cord they'd used before. He plugged it into the side of Noa's head as she leaned against him, and then into his. As the electrical flow pulsed between them, she gasped. There were no demons in her mind at the moment ... just lust. In his mind he laughed with happiness and shared desire. Noa laughed in the real world, too, and then everything fell away to a brilliant, blinding white. In the real world he turned around and dropped into the bed with her on top of him. In the real world they were still clothed, but in the white light of their minds their clothing melted away. In the mindscape, Noa held up a hand to touch his face and she had five fingers. In the mindscape, he kissed the pad of every single one, and then their lips crushed together. He could kiss in his mind, and in their minds, their bodies were one. It was the most exquisite foreplay he could imagine.

And then it went terribly wrong.

* * *

Noa was lying on top of James, there was no space between them, he was heat and she was light. His eyes were sparkling in his too-perfect face—and he was smiling—like he never did in real life. Noa laughed, her limbs sliding against his, her heart bursting. The light around them pulsated white, yellow, and then red ... and then came a knock at the door.

Noa sat up. The light fell away and she was naked, on top of James, his tattoos swirling over every inch of skin but his face. "Quick, get your clothes," she said. She looked around but couldn't see her own clothes. How had they vanished? She reached down and grabbed a sheet from the bed, ripping it out from beneath James.

"Noa," James sat up, but he didn't put on any clothes.

"Noa," she heard Kenji from beyond the door.

"I'm coming," Noa said, wrapping the sheet around her body.

"It's a dream, Noa!" James said, standing up and closing the distance between them.

"I'm waiting, Noa!" Kenji cried, from beyond the door. "I'm scared."

"Don't do it, Noa!" James said.

She smacked her hand down on the door and it opened to the tarmac on Adam's Station. She could smell blood, sweat, and dust. Piles of people lay writhing on the floor, some of them crawling toward her. "You left us here!" someone hissed.

She turned and came face-to-face with Kenji. "You left me," he said. His hands were clenched in fists at his side.

He was wearing his glasses and ordinary clothes, not Luddeccean robes.

"I'm sorry," Noa said. "I had to."

Ashley materialized beside Noa's brother. "You left me, too."

Somewhere, way off in the distance, she heard James shout, "You're dreaming, Noa!"

Noa put a hand to her mouth. "You made me, you told me to go ..."

Figures shimmered around her friend and her sister and solidified as her first crew. "You left us, too ..."

"I didn't leave ... I was in sick bay!" Noa said.

"Noa, you didn't leave us." The voice came from behind her. She turned and found James. Oddly he was dressed in a pair of navy blue silk pajama bottoms. Carl Sagan was wrapped around his shoulder.

Extending a hand to her, he said, "And you didn't leave them." On his shoulder, Carl Sagan kneaded his claws and made a keening sound.

Noa couldn't move. The sheet she had wrapped around herself whipped around her like a white banner.

"Noa, the sheets on the Ark are gray," James said, his hand still outstretched toward her. Carl Sagan's head bobbed. James gestured with his free hand at the pajamas he was wearing. "And these are the finest System Nine silk ... they didn't come from the Ark's supplies."

"I can't move," Noa said.

Turning his outstretched hand palm upward, he said, "Yes, you can. You escaped a concentration camp, you can escape a nightmare." The tattoos on his outstretched arms swirled and became real feathers that caught in the same breeze as her white sheet.

Carl Sagan squeaked. James beckoned. Noa couldn't

move her feet, but she found she could lift her arm. She managed to slip her fingers into James's. Behind her the voices of all her nightmares roared, "You left us! You left us!"

"You saved us, Carl Sagan and I both ..." James said. "Come back."

"No!" her nightmares screamed.

"Please," James said, his outstretched hand trembling, his voice beseeching. "You make me human."

People like James were who she was fighting for. He was an important part of her team. She couldn't abandon him for anything, not even nightmares. Noa took a step. The door swished shut, cutting off a howl from all her inner demons. Taking her hand, James reeled her in, and she pressed her forehead to his chest. He exhaled and her mind swam with a sensation of the most profound relief, as though a ton of weight had just left her chest. His relief or hers? And at that thought she floated above the floor with James. Around her, instead of the drab Ark gray swirled blue sky. James's arms swept around her back, and he dropped his head to hers. Carl Sagan purred by her ear.

She blinked up at the werfle, bobbing on James's shoulder.

"You must be dreaming him here," James said. "In the real world, he's sitting on a pillow hissing and giving me the evil eye. Also, the tattoos, and the feathers, and the wings didn't come with any avatar I've ever bought."

Noa peeked through one eye. His wings—or her dream of his wings—were wrapped around them both. They were blurry around the edges, but gleaming white, and nearly bright as the sun. She closed her eyes again. "Angels have wings. Every Luddeccean knows that."

James's hands dropped to a place that was more than

friendly. "I'm *not angelic ... like I said, you make me very human.*" Noa smiled as heat raced through her, but she didn't open her eyes. Carl Sagan let loose a vicious hiss.

"I *think maybe he's telling me you need to sleep,*" James grumbled.

"*He is an obviously confused figment of my subconscious,*" Noa mumbled against James's chest. As everything faded to black, she swore she heard the confused figment of her subconscious give an indignant squeak.

Something hard and sharp was poking into Noa's cheek. The rest of her front was pressed against something only somewhat more yielding. Despite that she felt warm ... unconcerned ... no, wait. Her head bolted up. She was stretched out on top of James. He raised an eyebrow, looking up at her through sleepy eyes. The thing that had been poking her cheek was the zipper on the front of the standard issue Ark pullover they all wore. Their minds were still joined with the hard-link. During the night at some point he had drawn the edges of the blankets up around them like a cocoon. Her mind sought the time, and her internal chronometer said she had slept for seven and a half hours. She had a moment of panic. Her emotions must have transferred across the link, or shown on her face, because James smoothed a hand down her back. "We'll be arriving at the planet Atlantia orbits in an hour and twelve minutes."

The plan was to park behind the giant planet on the side opposite the tiny Atlantian colony, conveniently opposite Luddeccea as well. They'd hide in the shadow of the planet, the icy ring that surrounded it, and its thirty-four moons.

"I should—" Noa's voice cut off abruptly as James's hand moved a little lower than was strictly friendly. The cocoon became even warmer.

"Everything is fine, Noa," James said.

She felt a twinge of annoyance flow from him into her mind. His lower than friendly hand paused. He shook his head and rolled his eyes. "I'm not annoyed with you. Ghost has been giving me regular updates ... a little too regular."

"Do you need sleep?" Noa asked, genuinely concerned.

His gaze met hers. "No."

The hand resumed being more ... nice. But something was wrong. Propping herself up on her elbows, she looked down. "How are we still clothed ... didn't we ...?"

"Only in your dreams," he said, and an image filled her visual cortex of flying, encircled by wings, and she remembered. It was lovely ... and not enough. She wanted the real James, too. The thought had barely left her mind when the room faded to red, and James rolled her over so that she was underneath him, his body a welcome weight. In their minds he kissed her. In the real world she pressed her lips to his, still immobile. She didn't care. Their legs slid together as they reoriented themselves. One of James's hands glided over her breast.

In her mind Chavez's frequency began blinking urgently.

James let out a very frustrated sounding breath of air.

Noa answered the signal, of course, being very careful to put up her emotion blocking shields.

"What is it, Ensign?" Noa asked.

Chavez responded, "Commander, we are receiving a distress signal."

She felt a sudden coolness, and an emptiness in her mind. It took her a moment to realize that James had yanked out the hard-link. His back was to her. He was running a hand through his hair.

Sitting up, Noa's fingers went to her neural port. "Send it through," she commanded.

Manuel was in James's mind. As was Noa. Or their avatars were. Both avatars were wearing Fleet grays. They were standing around a mental map James had constructed of the enormous, brilliant orange gas giant unimaginatively code-named S8O5. S8 designated System 8. O5 indicated it was the 5th body in orbit from the system's sun. Technically, Luddeccea was S8O2. Libertas was S8O3 ... Adam's asteroid was technically S8O4.653681, but James had only discovered that after one of the engineers had informed him of the number over breakfast. During the early days of space exploration, every planet, asteroid and comet had had a name. With thousands of planets now discovered, humans had taken to giving uninhabited planets codes rather than names. For some reason the thought called to James's mind the numbers tattooed on Noa's wrist.

"How long until the repairs are finished, Manuel?" Noa said.

James lifted his gaze. Noa's avatar's face was lit by the orange glow of S8O5. The planet was larger than Jupiter. James had made it appear taller than the room, and semi-translucent. The Ark was a pinpoint of light hovering near Noa's chest. Atlantia, S85M20, was a point of light on the opposite side of the planet, just one of the planet's many moons. Noa's eyes were focused on it with laser-like intensity.

"Another ten hours to complete the diagnostic," Manuel's avatar replied. His eyes were on the moon as well.

"You heard the distress call?" Noa asked.

Manuel's avatar was younger and less harried looking than the real Manuel. It could convey emotions, and right now his avatar's expression was grim. "Heard it ... horrible." Manuel didn't transmit any emotions across the ether, but James heard a heat in his voice that made him uncomfortable.

James had heard the call, too. A man's voice was nearly drowned out by cries in the background. *This is Lieutenant Aarav Sterling of the Atlantian Local Guard, requesting assistance for forty-one survivors.* A child's wail had risen in the background as Sterling had continued. *We have supplies for only another thirteen days, and we can't survive another wave.*

Manuel shook his head. "Tidal wave. The moon's core is too unstable." He huffed. "They should never have built a colony there. The atmosphere is unbreathable outside the dome. If the dome cracked, they're holed up somewhere dependent on oxygen filtrators. If they were left behind—" His avatar's nostrils flared.

Noa's eyes remained on Atlantia. Her hands were behind her back. "They're praying there isn't another wave."

In the real world, James heard Manuel take a deep breath. "I can't believe that C Corp was seriously considering making it their in-system headquarters," the engineer said.

It was almost a non-sequitur, and it made James feel impatient. He just wanted to get to the point in the meeting when Noa said what they would do. An image of the faces in her dream flashed in his mind. He knew what she would do. A static charge of irritation flashed beneath his skin. He could feel it make its path along the bones of his spine in his neck.

Eyes still on the moon, Noa said, "I went there before I joined the Fleet. It's beautiful ... I'd rather live there than Adam's rock. Even with the tidal waves."

"The Fleet would have rescued them before," Manuel said.

"Yes," said Noa. Her avatar rocked slightly on her heels.

James wanted to scream. They weren't Fleet, they were refugees. Let Libertas deal with this.

"Libertas is probably too bogged down with refugees to handle it," Noa said. The thought was so close to James's own that he wondered if he'd thought it aloud. For a moment all his neurons and nanos went still, and then he realized she wasn't glaring at him with flashing eyes, shouting some impassioned speech about doing the right thing.

A red light went off at the periphery of his vision. In the real world he was aware of a door sliding open.

"It's Wren," Noa said. "Let him join us in your mind."

James opened the ether channel to the pilot, and Wren's avatar burst into the shared space between Noa's, Manuel's, and his mind. His avatar looked younger, and slightly better groomed. He wore a long black leather jacket that to James's mind just looked like a child's dress up costume.

For a moment, Wren's avatar's eyes went wide as he gazed up at S8O5. "This is … it's as clear as a holo," he said, sounding awed and maybe even afraid.

James's hand trembled in the real world. The mindscapes he could create were crisper and more detailed than normal memories.

Manuel pointed at James. "He's a history professor. He has an incredible app for recreating scenes."

"History professor?" said Wren, his eyes widening again.

James didn't even bother to shrug; he didn't believe it, either. Maybe he had been a history professor *before* … but that was another life.

In a clipped voice, Noa said, "What do you want, Wren?"

Wren's avatar's head jerked in her direction. "You have to ask?"

Noa didn't say a word. She lowered her chin and glared at the freighter pilot.

Raising a hand and gesturing at the scene, Wren said, "Don't try to stage a rescue mission! That would be madness right now."

"I agree," said Noa. "It would be ludicrous."

"You agree?" said James.

"I know how you Fleet people are," Wren said, voice rising in their minds, avatar beginning to pace.

"You heard me, James," Noa said, looking at the ceiling and gritting her teeth.

James's avatar smiled.

"Always duty until death and all that," Wren said with an expansive wave of an arm.

"She said she agreed with you," James said.

"Commander?" said Manuel, eyebrows rising.

"I did indeed say that," Noa said.

James was so dizzy with surprise and relief that his ethernet-virtual hologram flashed and wavered.

"Oh," said Wren, his avatar's shoulders falling. He put a hand through his hair.

Noa sighed. In a voice that was slightly less clipped, she said, "You did a great job getting us here, Wren."

Wren smiled and shrugged. "Well, of course I did."

"I'll need more of your piloting skills as soon as all our diagnostics are complete," Noa added with a smile of her own. James noticed it didn't go all the way to her avatar's eyes.

"Where will I be piloting us to?" Wren asked.

Noa winked. "That is top secret. But someplace your enemies will be unlikely to find us."

Wren's eyes narrowed at Noa. Manuel's eyes narrowed at her, too, and one of his eyebrows lifted.

Still smiling at Wren, Noa inclined her head to the door. "In the meantime, get some food and then get some sleep."

Manuel's eyes slid to Wren and back to Noa. She met his gaze, and even though James's mind was linked with both the engineer and Noa, he had the feeling that there was another telepathic conversation he was missing. "We had fresh Luddeccean eggs, and cheese, and fruit when we took off. There might still be some left," Manuel said.

Wren licked his lips. "Really?" James thought he even detected a tremor in his hands.

"Go, Wren," Noa said. "Eat and sleep. That's an order."

Wren cocked his head. "You know, I am a captain, and—"

"Don't push it," said Noa.

Giving a jaunty salute, Wren's avatar faded from view.

"Is he really gone?" Manuel said, eyes sliding between Noa and James.

"He's left," James said. He was actually tuning into Wren's ethernet access. The freighter pilot was pinging the general frequency, trying to find directions to the galley. They were orbiting a planet with an inhabited moon; Wren could have been trying to bounce an ethernet signal off a satellite, but he was only worried about food ...

... and Noa wasn't going to save those last few inhabitants of that moon. His mind was flooded with so much optimism that the ethernet projection between their minds flashed again.

Manuel's avatar turned to Noa. "You don't really plan on leaving those people there, do you?"

Noa raised an eyebrow. "It would be foolish to execute a rescue operation at this time."

James was so happy that the planet he was projecting turned yellow like a young sun, and the moon sparkled like a twin star.

She tilted her head and smiled. "We have full diagnostics to run before we stage a rescue operation."

Manuel sighed with relief. "We have to rescue those people. I can't let what happened to my family happen to ..." His avatar looked away. In the real world James thought he saw the man's eyes glisten too brightly, and Manuel wiped his face.

The scene James had projected went completely

dark, and it was just the three of them, standing in an unoccupied cabin.

"Thanks to 6T9's babysitting, I've gotten more sleep than I have in a while." Manuel took an audible breath. "Despite everything." He was nodding and pushing his bangs from his eyes. "I'll get the diagnostics done and any repairs we need done, too."

"I know you will," Noa said. "And keep this quiet, no need to alarm Ghost—or Wren."

Static prickled James's skin. Of course, Ghost was off-shift, now, and absent from this meeting. He wouldn't like Noa's plans any more than James did.

Manuel nodded once more and headed out the door.

As soon as it shut, Noa pivoted on her heels and looked at James. "I know you're not relieved," she said. James could practically see the tension in her shoulders beneath the Ark's generic clothing.

James couldn't bring himself to respond.

"It was obvious," Noa said, "in the way the scene went black."

"If it's obvious," James snapped, "There is no reason to discuss it. You will do what you want, despite my objections."

Noa took a single step back, and though it was only another pace away, he felt like a chasm was opening up between them. "You will always have my support," James said, feeling his skin heat. As much as he hated it, he couldn't help it, could he? "Even when you don't have my approval. We already have extra crew aboard, one of whom you extremely mistrust, and you're thinking of taking on more strangers."

"The distress signal said forty-one, and we have

enough room." She gestured around the room. "We're standing in an unoccupied cabin."

"We're wanted by the Luddeccean authorities," James said.

"They'll expect we will head to Libertas. Ghost even deliberately skewed our course to make it look like we'd done that when Wren rounded the observation buoy," Noa replied.

"They found us at Adam's Station," James countered.

"That was a fluke! You heard what Monica's daughter said," Noa protested.

"But they were there." James took a step forward. "Because they're sending out scouts all over the solar system. Atlantia would be a logical place to look."

"The colony was abandoned, and it's sinking," Noa said, waving a hand, her eyes flashing. "It's not a *logical* place for us to go at all."

"Well, at least we agree on that point," James growled.

Noa didn't move. The muscles beneath her too-large clothes were coiled tight, and her hands were balled into fists. It made James feel her vulnerability more acutely rather than less. She couldn't back down; it was her fatal flaw. James took another step closer. "If we are captured, all the inhabitants of Atlantia, Adam's Station, and Luddeccea will be at risk."

"If we don't save civilians, what is the point of even going on this mission?" Noa said. And in the space between their minds, he saw the grav-freight train operator he'd killed on Luddeccea and all the bodies strewn out on the tarmac at Adam's Station.

Lowering his voice to a whisper, James said, "Don't let their deaths be in vain, Noa ... you're risking too much."

Noa looked away at last. She took a deep breath. "We

can fly by ... make sure we don't see any Luddeccean Fleet ships in the area. If we catch sight of anything suspicious, we'll break orbit and make a twisty path to the Kanakah Cloud." She bit her lip, and her gaze slipped back to him. "Please, James ..." She closed her eyes. "We have to try."

He gripped his hands behind his back ... His irritation sent a white flash of static behind his eyes. Opening her eyes, Noa tentatively smiled and gazed up at him almost shyly. "I'll take your support ... if not your approval. It's all I can ask." Through the ether, she set a bouncing ball of light. Annoyed, James averted his eyes. But he let the recreation of the Ark, the planet, and its moon appear in the space between their minds. Noa's avatar appeared next to his, looked up at the model, and smiled brightly. "And if you ever get in some historical controversy, you will have all my support, too," she said.

"Historical controversies?" he asked.

Noa waved a hand. "History professor kerfuffles ... you know, did the people of the early 20th century eat soy-bornut cubes for breakfast or rednut cubes?"

James blinked at her. "Neither of those things even existed on Earth before colonization began."

Winking at him, Noa gave an impish grin, and he realized she'd been taunting him. "You think I'm terribly uneducated, don't you?" she said, confirming that analysis.

The static of irritation flared beneath his skin. "Comparing disagreements in academia to launching a rescue mission while being pursued by the Luddeccean Guard isn't fair," he said.

"That's right," Noa replied, "The kerfuffles between professor types are much more vicious."

James looked at her sharply. All hint of teasing had left her expression. Her gaze was on the planet and the moon.

Without any hint of mirth, Noa said, "The stakes in academia are much lower."

CHAPTER FOURTEEN

The Ark rounded the bright orange curve of S8O5, skimming the dust ring of the gas giant so tightly that it looked like a river with white petals streamed beneath them.

Chavez, acting as Noa's co-pilot, said, "In visual range in three, two, one ..."

On cue, Atlantia came into view. "People live on that snowball," someone whispered over the ether.

S85M20, Atlantia in common parlance, was tinted blue by its nitrogen rich atmosphere and had a delicate latticework of darker blue crisscrossing its surface. It looked very much like a snowball, but that delicate latticework was actually canals cut into the frozen oceans by eruptions deep beneath the surface. Here and there were sparkling blue lakes where deep subterranean vents were especially active. The magma that caused those eruptions kept the magnetic field strong, and kept the steam that escaped the oceans from being stripped of its hydrogen by solar winds. The steam quickly returned to the surface as snow instead. But the same highly active core had made the likelihood of tsunamis greater. It wasn't unusual for humans to live on fault lines, Noa knew. The people who'd lived on the San Andreas Fault during the 20th century came to mind. But the people who lived in those ancient Earth cities at least had a breathable atmosphere. Even if Atlantia, away from its core-heated canals and pockets of thaw, wasn't too cold for humans to survive for more than a few minutes, the oxygen on the planet was too thin.

The ethernet erupted. An indicator for Ghost's channel flashed at the periphery of her visual cortex, and Ghost's thought burst into her mind. "Once again, Commander, I am going to state my objections to this plan!"

"Noted," Noa responded, dipping her chin, eyes on the moon. Wren's channel began to ping, too. Noa ground her teeth. She didn't want to answer it, but she'd need Wren in the months ahead. She opened his channel. Wren's voice crackled across the ether. "What the ...." a long litany of curses followed. One of her emotion-filtering apps flashed red, indicating that Wren was "extremely agitated." Noa huffed at the understatement. Maybe that app needed to be recalibrated?

"... what in the name of a god-cursed red dwarf are you doing?" Wren finished at last.

"Change of plans," Noa said. "If you're uncomfortable with my command, you are welcome to stay on the surface of Atlantia once we land."

Another litany of swearing followed.

"You're right, it's dangerous, so help us survive. I know you're good in tight situations," Noa ground out before turning him off.

"Ghost, do you have any indication that the Luddec-cean Fleet might be nearby?" Noa asked across the main frequency.

It was James who answered. "The Luddeccean Fleet wasn't anywhere near Adam's Station when we landed." James had gone to Ghost's computing lab for the landing. It had more monitors than any other area on the ship except the bridge; and in computing he wouldn't be leaning over Chavez's and Noa's shoulders for a better view of the monitors. Noa was counting on his eidetic memory to record all the channels they swept over as they made their landing.

"I agree with Professor," Ghost snipped. "But in answer to your question, there is a lot of chatter across normal radio frequencies, as well as some piggybacking on Atlantia's still functional ether, but nothing to indicate a Luddeccean vessel."

James added, "I'm watching the monitors and I haven't seen anything that looks like lightbeams, either."

"Which doesn't mean they're not using them out of our line of sight," Ghost commented.

Noa's hands tightened on the steering bars of the Ark's controls. With Morse Code, or some other simple binary code, it would be possible for even primitive computers to pass information via lightbeam.

"Commander," Ghost said, "reconsider." A red light flashed in the periphery of her vision, and a notification that Ghost was also "extremely agitated."

"We'll keep our heads about us," Noa said. She closed her eyes briefly, thinking of the distress signal, and the men, women, and children slowly suffocating on recycled air that became less and less oxygenated with each hour, as they sank into Atlantia's chill waters. But into the ether she said, "One sign of trouble and we'll resume our course to the Kanakah Cloud." She exhaled. Even if that would mean leaving civilians to slowly die ... and nightmares in her head for nebulas knew how long. "Promise," she added, not sure if she was speaking to Ghost or herself.

CHAPTER FIFTEEN

"Do you see anything?" Ghost asked James. A nearly 360 degree view of the Ark's surroundings played on screens encircling the small space. Right now, they showed the dark blue water of the opening in the ice that the Ark was floating in and the sky. James focused on the sky.

"No," he said. No telltale blink of a lightbeam. Nor did he "hear" anything incriminating over the ether. He watched a tiny speck of black leave the atmosphere. Its ether was wild with jubilant cries and someone saying, "Food for months and enough augment parts to buy us citizenship on Libertas!"

Ghost shook his head. "We still shouldn't be here." James's eyes slid to the man. He was eyeing a monitor with the same tiny retreating ship James had just been eavesdropping on. Was Ghost listening to their ether as well? James glanced down at a CPU usage read-out. There was nothing to indicate that the Ark's ancient system had taken on the awesome task of decrypting ethernet channels. His jaw shifted, and he felt a cold prickle along his skin. Was Ghost like him? His left hand trembled ... he didn't *feel* like that was true.

Ghost abruptly bolted out of his seat and went to the farthest point in the tiny room. "I can't find anything," Ghost mumbled. "You're not connected to the ethernet. They shouldn't fear encoding their secret missions onto you!"

James sat up with a start. "Ghost?"

The little man spun around, his eyes wide, his lower lip trembling.

James's mind replayed Ghost's words moments before, and his apps indicated that they were uttered too softly to have been heard by normal human hearing. He'd just "thought aloud." The question was to whom? James's remembered Ghost's cries over the ether on Adam's Station. "They can't get *me*." Ghost was terrified of being caught by the Guard; he wasn't the enemy. Not now.

"You seem ... agitated," James said, to not give away that he'd heard Ghost's words moments ago. He'd find out who Ghost was talking too, or what, but now wasn't the time.

"Of course I'm agitated!" Ghost sputtered. "The Commander is going to get us killed!"

Ghost sat down heavily at another console. "And I don't like sharing my private workspace."

James felt a spark of insight in his mind ... Ghost didn't like giving himself away. James didn't respond, just moved over to another computer screen. Half of this screen showed the water of the sea they floated in. The other half showed the city they were approaching. Atlantia Prime, the single city on Atlantia's surface, was packed with buildings that nearly touched its biodome. Once the city had rested on a thick sheet of ice—a sort of inverse snow globe—but then an earthquake had cracked the ice beneath it. As the ice split, the city had fallen into an icy new sea. The following tidal wave had cracked the already stressed structure. The breach was wide at the base, but thinner at the rooftop level. The Ark was too large to fly in; so they were floating in. His eyes shifted from the sky to the water.

"Are there fish?" James asked curiously. He didn't see any.

Ghost responded, "I've heard there is some sea-life."

Before he could inquire more, the door to the computer room swooshed open. Noa stood in the frame. She hadn't contacted him in the ether. There was a tenseness in her jaw and shoulders.

"Who is at the helm?" cried Ghost.

"Chavez," Noa said, stepping in, her hands locked behind her back. "Her father was a small freighter boat captain on Luddeccea's North Sea. The woman's more qualified to ride waves than I am." Her eyes went to James and she nodded. "I need you and your eidetic memory topside."

"Take him!" Ghost grumbled.

James was already heading to the door. "What do you need my memory for?"

Noa's shoulders fell a fraction. "There has been a lot of new construction in the biodome. A substantial number of buildings and skywalks aren't on the map. I need to record all of them as we float in. I'll have my memory app on, but I can only record what I see, and I don't want to miss anything. If we have to leave in a hurry, a side street, or boulevard I might overlook could mean life or death."

"Understood," said James, barely refraining from mentioning *again* how bad an idea this was.

Spinning on her heels, she said, "We've got environ suits in the airlock." Everything about her carriage and demeanor still radiated tension, but he couldn't think of anything witty to lift the mood.

A few minutes later, they were packed in a narrow airlock with Gunny and Wren. They all wore drab gray environ suits. The suits were fairly light, except for the helmets with their oxygen filtration masks. The masks could be set to filter oxygen from the nitrogen-laden air of Atlantia, or they could refilter exhaled air, splitting carbon dioxide into oxygen and carbon. The suits had a quilted appearance; one part of a suit could be damaged and sealed at a seam without requiring a trip back in the airlock. They also had basic heating and cooling controls. Almost unconsciously, James turned up his heating unit to maximum.

Over the main channel, Noa said, "Manuel, could you switch off the gravity in here ... slowly."

"On it, Commander," he said.

James's eyes went heavenward, and then he realized that "heavenward" was not skyward. The Ark's gravity was on, so it felt like the nose of the vessel was "up." The ship could be operated on its side—but it took time to convert the spaces, and the galley, retrofitted to be a cafe, could not be converted at all. It had been decided to leave the grav on. But the crew going topside would need to reorient themselves to the planet's natural pull.

"Don't throw up," Wren said.

Gunny grunted and put his fingers over his face. "I always close my eyes."

James didn't close his eyes. He'd only read and seen

grav reorientations on holovids. He wanted to experience it, all of it, even motion sickness. He glanced at Noa. She didn't close her eyes either, but her gaze was focused on the "wall" that was about to become the floor.

There was a soft sigh beneath James's feet and he felt like the ship was rolling over. Noa held out a foot, like she was about to take a step, and James did likewise. A moment later, he felt the foot inextricably drawn to the "wall" and stepped down a little unsteadily. Gunny hopped to the wall a lot more gracefully than James thought possible with his eyes closed. Wren did the same, but he looked green.

"The grav under the dome must be activated," Noa said, scowling at the floor. "I'm getting a reading of 8.5 meters per second."

"Yep," said Gunny, giving a little bounce.

On a whim, James did likewise.

"Don't hit your head," Gunny chuckled.

James blinked. His internal apps had accommodated the new gravity quite well and he hadn't come close to hitting the ceiling—low that it was.

"You have enough sproinginess already," the sergeant said with a grin. He was teasing, James realized, good naturedly, and James wanted so badly to smile even though he didn't find it funny. "I've already re-calibrated the springs in my toes," James said, in a lame attempt to match his wit.

Gunny actually guffawed at the not particularly funny joke.

The sound of a metal door scraping on old hinges made James look toward Noa. She was standing beneath a utility cubby that in ship's gravity would be above the door but now was beside it. The narrowness of the airlock suddenly made sense. Standing on the former "wall," Noa was still able to reach the utility cabinet with her hands above her head. She opened it, and a light, plexiflame staircase unfolded.

Gunny grunted and lifted a small "surface-to-air plasma cannon" they'd stolen from the tick. It was light enough to haul over one's shoulder, but had considerably more power than a normal phaser rifle. Wren hefted his own cannon; Noa and James were outfitted with phaser rifles. James's eyes went suspiciously to Wren, and he felt Noa reach out to his mind and answer his unspoken question. "We can't totally trust him. But we can trust him to want to get out of here. And he's the only person with advanced weapons experience who isn't needed on the ship right now."

By some prearrangement, Gunny went up the steps first. The outside door whooshed. For a moment the sergeant scanned outside from the stairwell, but then his voice broke through the ether. "All is clear," and he climbed up onto the deck.

Noa followed in his wake, and James followed her, with Wren bringing up the rear.

"Don't ever say I don't take you places," Noa said. Her voice was crystal clear in James's mind. The scene around them was not. Mist was billowing up from the street turned canal they now floated on, and wrapped around them as they stepped out onto the deck.

"You have to admit, it's pretty," Noa said through the ether. Her helmeted head was looking about, methodically canting upward, then down, turning a degree, and repeating the motion, scanning again in a motion that was nearly robotic.

The scene was more than pretty, and for a moment,

James forgot what he was supposed to be doing on the deck. Above them, the shell of the biodome that had wrapped around the Atlantian city was cracked and missing pieces. The cracks were sparkling in the dim light of the noonday sun. The gas giant $S8O_5$ hung in the ultramarine blue sky. Even the blue of Atlantia's atmosphere barely dulled the planet's brilliant orange glow, and the planet's ice rings sparkled around it. James couldn't help shuffling through the hazy memories of *before* the accident and the crystal-sharp memories *since*, to compare it to all such celestial scenes. It was an impressive sight; if he'd still been recording memories for his time capsule, he would have been sure to add it. He could see why the Atlantians had tried to have it declared one of the seven natural wonders of the galaxy.

Remembering his purpose, he brought his gaze down to the city. On either side of them, spires from the abandoned colony rose up. Limited horizontally, the colony had grown vertically. The height of the spires rose with the height of the dome. In the distance, three particularly large spires rose above the water at the dome's apex: the main hospital, the main government offices, and the chamber of commerce. The scene reminded James of sailing through the sunken buildings of Old Los Angeles on Earth, but Old Los Angeles didn't have walkways arching between its towers, like an intricate, sparkling, spider web. The slightly lighter gravity made him feel lighter, made the Ark float impossibly high, and made the situation that much more surreal.

"It's very dramatic," he replied after too long a pause, beginning his own scan of the buildings.

"Yes, indeed," said Noa, and he could hear the awe in

the tone she let her thoughts form. "Can't imagine anything more so."

"Cannons firing on us from above as we try to take off from the water, that would be more dramatic," James responded dryly.

James heard Noa laugh through the barriers of her helmet and his. But she did turn, a little too quickly, and looked back at Wren and Gunny, both walking along the length of the Ark, cannons balanced easily on their shoulders in the lower gravity. "Wren, Gunny—"

Manuel's voice cut across the ether. "Incoming on our scopes."

A sonic boom cracked above them. Gunny dropped to one knee and aimed. Wren hesitated and then did the same. Waves caused by the boom shook the Ark, and fragments of the dome broke off and fell into the partially-submerged city. A small vessel with a patchwork of metal on its hull entered what remained of the dome, swooped low, and for a moment James was sure it would engage. James's mind leaped into the ether, his vision went bright white, and he heard the chatter from the vessel. "Tuned into the local ether ... Those poor sods are holed up into the hospital ... maybe we could have some fun? Eh, Boss?" There was a response. "Maybe we could get our asses shot off, Dorf. They're being watched by an Atlantian Guard unit ... is that a boat down there? And are those men on that boat pointing anti-aircraft phasers at us? Jeez, there is enough to share!" The vessel changed course, giving the Ark a wide berth. And then the conversation turned to the state of the engines, food stores, landing gear, and the best place to land and loot.

James squinted, following their path with his eyes as

they flew off. He saw a few more small vessels through the mist. They buzzed between buildings like flies.

Lowering his weapon, Wren said over the ether. "Just honest smugglers." For a moment, his silhouette was framed by the glow of S8O5. James could see inside his helmet. The freighter pilot was scowling, despite his words laced with bravado. Wren's eyes met James's and he turned away quickly.

The Ark floated through the misty city streets, the dome sparkling above them in the dim light of the sun and S8O5. The whole team was silent. Even Noa. Which meant she was on edge and not nearly as confident about this operation as she pretended. Her edginess put James on edge, and he struggled for a quip to break the tension ... and again came up with nothing.

There was a whoosh from one of the airlocks, and everyone spun. 6T9 strode out onto the deck in the nearly freezing, oxygen-poor air, wearing a tight t-shirt, an even tighter pair of pants, and a type of footwear in the 20th century known as "flip flops." In one hand he held a platter on which three tea cups were steaming.

"Refreshments?" 6T9 asked. James found his eyes crossing, going to the seal where the visor of his helmet met the oxygenating mask. It was still there. He looked up quickly and saw Gunny similarly cross-eyed.

"What are you doing?" said Wren, not bothering to use the ether, his incredulity clear in his voice even through the muffling of the helmet.

Striding over to them, beaming with what looked like pride, 6T9 said, "I am a multi-functional 'bot. Eliza told me you must be tired, so I took the initiative to bring you some tea and cookies as refreshments."

James looked down at the tray. There were some

cookies on the plate. A haze of blackness appeared at the edge of his vision and he knew like he knew the gravity of the planet, that he could open the visor of his suit if he wanted. He found his hand convulsively squeezing the internal heat control located in the glove of his suit instead until an internal warning light went on. His vision cleared. Could it be that his augments had trouble maintaining his internal temperature? Was that the reason he was always so hungry? He blinked. He still wanted a cookie. He had to look away for fear of losing control and snatching one.

"You didn't notice we were in environmental suits?" Wren snapped.

"I notice you are in environ suits," said 6T9, very slowly, as though he suspected it might be a trick question.

James found himself taking pity on the 'bot. "Ease up," he said to Wren. "Don't bang his head into Moore's Wall, he's perfectly capable of doing that himself."

He heard Noa's bright huff of laughter, and his nanos danced. From Gunny's helmet came a slower "Heh. Heh, heh, heh …"

Noa's thoughts entered the ether, clipped and focused. "Get below deck, 6T9."

Wren growled. "Don't waste good tea and cookies out here, you dumb 'bot!"

As 6T9 headed toward the airlock, Noa said, "Ghost, let's open the channel to the hospital. We'll be within firing range in another five minutes and—"

There was a whistling overhead, and Gunny knocked Wren down, shouting, "Hit the deck!"

James and Noa ducked in unison. 6T9 looked down at the deck, befuddled. There was a splash in the water in the direction they were heading, orange light flared, and the ship rocked. James spun to see a wall of flame.

* * *

Crouched on the deck, Noa looked over her shoulder. Flames leaped from the water as the ship rocked, but they were dying fast in the oxygen-poor air.

Gunny's thoughts cracked through the ether. "That was a plasma grenade launched from a DX4 launcher. Those are restricted Fleet tech!"

"A what?" said Wren.

"Where did it come from?" Noa shouted.

"The hospital," James said.

Gunny protested. "I didn't see where it came from, and my apps—"

Noa didn't ask how James knew—he probably had a triangulation app. Her mind leapt into the ether. As soon as she sent a message back to the refugees, every scavenger ship in the vicinity would know who they were. She'd wanted to wait a little longer, but if they were being shot at by DX4 plasma charges, she couldn't waste a second more. "Ghost," she said, "Get me connected to the Atlantian ether via the Ark—same frequency they contacted us on." She didn't need the headaches that connecting directly to the local insecure ether could cause.

The response was grumbly, but Ghost said, "You're in, Commander. This planet's computer was only slightly less infested than Adam's Station's."

Noa reached out to the survivors. "This is Captain Noa Sato of the Galactic Fleet. We are here to relieve you, Atlantian Local Guard Team 329."

"Halt your advance or we'll fire," said a voice her internal apps translated as belonging to Lieutenant Aarav Sterling.

"Ensign Chavez, forward thrusters full-stop," Noa said. She nervously scanned the skies, and her eyes fell on a scavenger ship clinging to a wall just beneath a skywalk like a black spider. Was it coming closer out of nefarious intent, or just "honestly smuggling"? She bit back her worry.

"You'll understand me if I say we will be needing more proof," Sterling said. "That isn't a Fleet vessel."

"That is correct, Lieutenant, but it has been requisitioned by the Fleet under the terms of Colonial Evacuation Law 2389 by myself, Commander Noa Sato, most recently of the Sugihara under command of ..." Noa went on. She gave a listing of her assignments, and when she got to her stint in System Six there was a snort, and a, "Lots of people like to say they served in Six."

So she went further back, all the way to her stint at Fort Arena Roja where she'd received her low-G training.

"Then you know about the fleas," said Sterling.

Noa blinked. "There were no fleas. There were mites."

"Can you make this go faster?" James ground out.

Sterling said, "You were lucky as an officer you didn't get mite extermination duty like the grunts."

"Don't blame him for being twitchy," said Gunny, kneeling on the deck, following the spider-like vessel with his sites.

Noa frowned. Sterling was obviously former Fleet himself, and obviously still testing her. "Of course I got extermination duty. That red dust smelled like vomit!" Officers and enlisted alike experienced that joy.

The small craft attached to the skywalk slid around the building.

James sidled closer to her. "We're attracting more attention," he said, his blue eyes violet in the low light, and then his gaze jerked upwards to a spot in the sky behind her. Noa spun. There were more scavenging ships hovering around like flies.

Turning back toward the hospital, Noa reached across the ether. "What else do I need to say to convince you I am who I say I am? Do you want to know the barracks I was in during basic? The serial number on my first pair of g-boots? A description of my bunkmate?"

A thought that wasn't from the captain, Noa, or any of her crew, flickered through the ether. "Was she pretty?"

"Is that one of yours, Sterling?" Noa asked.

"No," said James aloud. His eyes were on a small vessel buzzing near the top of the dome.

"No, Commander," Sterling replied in what was the first acknowledgement of her rank. "Someone has hacked into this channel."

"Noa, we need to get out of here," James said, his left hand tapping a rapid staccato rhythm on the barrel of his rifle. "There are too many of them. I'm having trouble keeping track."

Noa ground her teeth. Over the ether, she said, "We need to talk in person. The Atlantian ether isn't secure." Aloud she grumbled, "Goddamn it, I sound like a Luddeccean."

Beside her, James said, "Well, technically ..." Behind his visor his brow furrowed. He blinked and said softly, "Harmless," and his eyes went to another vessel.

Across the ether, Sterling said, "You're free to

approach. I'll meet you at the sixth-story skywalk; it's now at water level."

Noa's eyes went to the hospital situated directly in front of them, where the channel met another in a t-inter-section and dead-ended. On the starboard side, a walkway arched over the water to the building across the street. "I see it. Chavez, sending you coordinates," she said.

"Aye, Commander," Chavez replied across the chan-nel, and the vessel began to move forward.

They were a few meters from their destination when the sun slipped from its zenith and behind a building. It was only a few minutes past the planet's noon, but so far from the sun's light, it looked like twilight. If it weren't for the reflected light of the enormous $S8O5$, it would have been as dark as night.

Beside her, James shook his head. A red light she recognized was on inside his helmet.

"James, your suit is overheating," she whispered.

"No, no," he said, his voice muffled. "I'm comfort-able." He put a gloved hand to his helmet. "I just can't see very well when the light changes. If I can't see them, I can't listen."

"Listen?" said Noa. She must have misheard.

James's hand dropped, and his eyes met hers. His face was a few hands-widths away, they were separated by two thin layers of plastic, and it seemed like they were a million clicks away. For a moment, despite everything, he seemed like a stranger.

"Commander," a voice shouted, muffled by a breathing apparatus.

She was getting "caught up in her own wheels" as her dad used to say, thoughts and doubts she didn't have time for. She turned toward the voice. A man was standing in a broken window of the arching skywalk. "Lieutenant Sterling?" Noa shouted back.

The enviro-suited figure nodded.

"We need to talk, privately," Noa said aloud. Quickly, she wanted to add, but didn't.

He nodded again. With a thought she sent Chavez an order to give some boost to the antigrav. The Ark rose out of the water, so that the ship was just about a meter below the walkway. The figure said, "Wait, Commander, take off your helmet."

There was a whistling noise overhead and Noa's eyes jerked upward, just in time to see a scavenger ship clipped by phaser fire from a roof.

"Please," Sterling said. "Commander, it will speed things up."

He lifted a hologlobe in one hand, an old one, nearly as wide as Noa's forearm. In it flashed a picture of a younger Noa in Fleet Gray, smiling broadly.

"He wants visual verification," James said.

Sterling lifted his own helmet to show her there was no trick. He was handsome, in the typical Afro-Eurasian way—narrow light brown eyes, a thin nose, full lips. But his looks were marred by the dark circles under his bloodshot eyes.

Noa took off her helmet, oxygen filtration device and all. The cold air was bracing, and although the air was as dense as Earth's, the nitrogen load was higher, and it almost instantly made her lungs burn with want.

Sterling smiled. "Thank God, it is you ... Permission to come aboard?"

"Permission granted," Noa said, snapping her helmet back on.

Hastily putting his own mask back on, he leapt lightly down onto the deck and walked over to Noa.

Her mind ticked down the seconds with every step. They'd been planetside for over an hour. She'd announced who she was over the local ether. The Luddecceans didn't use the ether, but she'd taken off her helmet, too, and anyone who knew the history of the Luddeccean planet would have recognized the Ark. A lightbeam message could already be traveling to Luddeccea. They could be rounding up the Luddeccean Guard Fleet within minutes … her mind raced with everything she had to say to Sterling, to warn him that he wouldn't be taking his people to Luddeccea. "Before you agree to come with us, you need to know that we're not going to Libertas, or Luddeccea."

Sterling, advancing across the deck, came to a sudden stop. "We have to come with you," he said. Above their heads another scavenger ship buzzed by and was trailed by phaser fire.

Sterling didn't even look up. "We're running low on ammo."

"We're being pursued by Luddecceans," James said. "You should know that, too."

Noa's shoulders sagged. James was right to bring it up, but she didn't want to argue with comparative virtues of running with her versus staying here.

Sterling was quiet for a moment, but then he said, "We have some people who are severely injured, attached to medical equipment. You should know that, as well."

Noa nodded. "They're welcome to what we have."

Sterling gave a grim smile. "We better get moving. I don't suppose you can help supply cover while I move my people off the top floors?"

Noa straightened. He had a whole platoon according to his distress call ... she had Gunny, but Chavez and Manuel, her only two other military personnel, were tied up below deck.

He smiled grimly. "I lied about our military might when I made the distress signal."

Noa held out a hand and introduced Sterling to Gunny. Gunny had been avoiding Noa's gaze since their conversation, but he met Sterling's and nodded smartly. Sterling was suitably impressed by Gunny's credentials; he was definitely Fleet. Noa was about to assign Wren to help with the evacuation, but before she could, Gunny said, "I'd like to request James come with us."

Sterling pivoted toward James, and Noa could see he expected an introduction.

"James isn't Fleet," Gunny said, "but he's one cool head in a fight, and an incredible shot. I trust him with my life." He looked almost shyly toward Noa as he said it. As if afraid she might say no.

"Plus I can lift real heavy things," James said.

Gunny barked a laugh. "He can!"

Noa felt herself go cold. Somewhere in the distance, a scavenger ship whined. The Luddeccean Guard were after James; he shouldn't be separated from the team.

As though reading her thoughts, James whispered through the Genji cipher, "The sooner we get out of here, the better."

He wasn't supposed to say that. He wasn't supposed to be so cooperative. He'd been against the mission from the start. But he was right, and she had to put her feelings aside. She nodded and pulled the satchel she was wearing over her head and handed it to him. "It's filled with the last of Ghost's ether extenders. You'll be able to use the ship's ether to communicate, bypass Atlantia's buggy system, and not be overheard." James slung it over his shoulder. The sun slipped from behind the building, shining so brightly on his visor that she couldn't see within. "Be careful, and fast," she said.

"I can lift real heavy things." 6T9's voice directly behind her made Noa jump.

Sterling rolled back on his feet, Gunny snorted, and Wren made a gagging noise.

"I can lift real heavy things," 6T9 said again, his expression earnest. He tilted his head. "And I am familiar with medical equipment, and know how to be useful to people who are in pain." He looked down at the tray in his hands. The tea cups had tipped over, but the cookies were miraculously still there. "Really," he added, looking up at Noa. "Even if I'm not the sharpest hammer in the toolbox."

Someone snorted at the botched idiom.

Noa's mouth dropped open, ashamed though she shouldn't be. 6T9 couldn't feel embarrassment.

"It's a good idea," James said, thunking 6T9 on the shoulder.

6T9 smiled. "I'm ninety-eight percent charged and ready to go!" He looked down at the cookies. "Well, except I haven't put these away ..."

James opened the satchel. "Put them in here." He looked at Sterling. "There are kids, right?"

Gunny grunted. "Good thinking," he said and passed his heavy weapon to Noa.

Sterling nodded, and 6T9 put the cookies in the satchel. Over the ether, Manuel said, "Commander, remember, if this hospital is a good one, they may have a replacement heart for Oliver."

"I remember," James said. "Monica gave me the model number to look for."

Noa hoisted the cannon onto her shoulder. When she lifted her eyes, James, already by the skywalk, was peering into the broken window.

Sterling said, "Let me—"

James hopped up into the open space as though he were on springs. Bending down to one knee, he offered Gunny a hand. Gunny accepted, and James hoisted him up. A moment later, Noa watched as her sergeant pulled his phaser rifle around and slunk out of view, his practiced moves oddly out of place on a body with such a prominent beer gut. James dropped a hand to Sterling and hoisted him up, too. "Or I'll let you go first," Sterling finished.

6T9 followed them. He waved away James's hand and hopped up into the skywalk with as much grace as James had.

Noa took a step back, then shook her head and turned around. Hefting her new weapon on her shoulder, she peered through its scopes at two ships whining by. The second ship made her blink. It was blue—or chrome reflecting the sky—in much better shape than the first. Her finger tightened on the trigger.

Wren fired first. The blue ship darted behind a building.

"Shit," Wren murmured. Noa tried to follow its path with her eyes, but it disappeared in the maze of buildings and walkways.

"You recognize them?" Noa asked. She found herself breathing heavily, though her oxygen filtration mask was working fine.

Wren's helmet was turned away from her, still canted

to the sky. "No."

"When you fired ..." She'd been afraid he knew something she didn't.

"I'm just trigger happy," he snapped. He finally turned around. The sun was shining directly on his visor, and she couldn't see his expression, but she thought she heard a manic smile in his voice when he said, "I don't like being stuck down here."

Her suit was perfectly warm, but she shivered anyway.

It was a mistake for James to have volunteered to go into the hospital. He was walking with 6T9 in between Sterling, on point, and Gunny taking the rear. The hospital was amazingly modern, and amazingly clean. The walls were white and pristine. The power had not gone out—which was one of the reasons Sterling's team had holed up in the place. As they walked down the hall, tiny cleaning 'bots whooshed out of hidden doors in the baseboards of the walls and wiped away their footsteps. They hadn't encountered any opposition; the only opposition was in James's mind. He was having flashbacks of the long white hall the day he died. His left hand tapped his rifle. Not the day he died ... the day he had been revived, he reminded himself.

James, Gunny, and Sterling were all wearing their filtration masks, in case they had to smash out a window and take aim at potential intruders, but they'd taken off the top portion of their helmets. The hospital was warm. The only thing that hinted that all was not well was the smell of damp.

"So, if you don't mind me asking ..." Sterling said, peering around a corner, rifle raised. "What is happening on Luddeccea? Why are the Luddeccean authorities after you?" The question brought James's focus back to the present. He noticed Sterling was peering *over* the sights of the scope and was cocking his head strangely, as though trying to hear a far-off sound. Nodding almost imperceptibly to himself, Sterling motioned James and Gunny forward. James didn't hesitate to follow. He trusted Sterling. He could hear him over the ether. Sterling's team was using a cipher, like the Ark's crew had when the tick landed. It had taken twenty-eight seconds longer than usual for James to decode, but James had been listening in ever since. At this particular moment, someone was saying, "Why didn't the first evac ship come back from Luddie-ville?"

Following Sterling down the new hallway, his own rifle raised, James said, "The Luddecceans believe that an alien intelligence—or demons, or djinn, depends on who you ask—have seized control of Time Gate 8 and are controlling augments through the ether." But they didn't control James; they only ... listened in? Were they trying to reach the larger galaxy through James? Was he infected? A contagion? Static fired along his augmented spine. His fingers fluttered on the rifle barrel. "They're rounding up augments and exterminating them," James finished.

"That's illegal!" 6T9 exclaimed. "... and genocide!"

Sterling stumbled and paused. James had recognized that Sterling had augmented hearing and vision. That was why he was peering over his scope and cocking his head in such a peculiar way at each corner. Sterling hadn't expressed any hope over the ether to go to Luddeccea, but just in case he harbored any secret desire, James wanted to quash it.

Sterling's bloodshot eyes widened. "Really?" he asked, his voice baleful. Earlier, Sterling had described Gunny to his team as, "Former Fleet, seems solid." Of James, Sterling had said to his team, "Upper-crust Earther maybe with his accent, and cosmetic-augments, augmented strength definitely, Caucasian throwback ... the team trusts him, but I dunno. You know how Earthers are, especially rich ones, and throwbacks are always odd." When someone had commented that Noa was a throwback, too, Sterling shot back, "Maybe, but she's Fleet and a Sixth vet."

Now his eyes left James, skipped right over 6T9, and went to Gunny.

The sergeant spit. "Really." Turning to look down the hall, Sterling tilted his head again, listening, and then led them forward.

"They don't like outsiders either," James added, fanning the fire. "I'm from Earth, I was on my way to Luddeccea for vacation, when my rented shuttle was shut down." For just a moment Sterling's head bowed— thinking of the evac ship? But he said nothing and thought nothing to his team. He just kept going down the hallway.

They reached a door and Sterling came to a halt. "I don't want to use the lifts. The generator is on but if it goes out ..."

"Right," said Gunny. "We'll be taking the stairs, then."

Sterling nodded and opened the door to a set of stairs lit by dirty yellow lights coated with dust. The floors and ceilings were poured concrete. After the austerity of the hallway that was too much like James's trip down the "final tunnel," it was relief. He chided himself. It wasn't the "final tunnel" because he was here, alive ...

There was a grinding noise, and James's internal apps went wild. "The gravity," he said.

"The artificial grav is finally dying," Sterling said.

"All the better to run up these stairs," said Gunny.

"But terrible for your bones and immune systems," 6T9 said primly. "It would be best to leave as soon as possible."

Where he stood a few steps above the party, Sterling turned back and looked at the 'bot, his brow contorted in a look of incredulity and confusion. "That's what we're d—"

"Don't explain," James said.

"Don't even try," added Gunny.

"Explain what?" 6T9 asked.

"Right," said Sterling, turning and taking the stairs two at a time. Weapons fire echoed down the staircase. Everyone on the staircase ducked—except 6T9—who looked up at the ceiling. "We must help those people," he declared and started to move.

James dropped a hand on the 'bot's shoulder as Sterling's thoughts spread across the ether. "What was that?"

"Another ship ... flying way too close," came the response.

For a moment the gray stairwell seemed to contract, as though the grav in the building had increased.

And then he realized the gravity had increased.

"Damn, antigrav is in its death throes," Sterling said. "It's been increasing and decreasing at random."

James looked toward the dusty ceiling. This could be the real tunnel of death.

——————————

CHAPTER SIXTEEN

A moan shook the biodome. Water splashed against the sides of the Ark, and the ship noticeably sank in the water. The cannon on her shoulder suddenly weighed four times as much, and Noa sank to her knees. An internal app blinked red. Kuin and Jun, on the deck to lend a hand, both stumbled and groaned.

"What?" Wren said, bowed over. He swung his rifle off his shoulder.

Noa grimaced. "The grav's been fluctuating for the past few minutes … just not as noticeably."

"If it goes up much more, it will mean we're going to have that much more trouble getting off this ice ball," Wren said.

"The gravity is fine outside the dome," Noa said.

"We're not outside the dome," Wren pointed out.

Her eyes searched the rapidly darkening skies. No ships. She reached over the Ark's ether. "Ghost, no chatter of incoming ships?"

"Just because there is none doesn't mean they're not

on their way," her computing officer grumbled over the general frequency.

"Cheery guy," Wren commented. "Also right."

Around Noa, Kuin and Jun shifted on their feet. "You're making people nervous," Noa replied shortly over the link, hoping both Wren and Ghost would get the point.

It was too dark to see inside the young men's visors— which meant they couldn't see Noa, either. Noa couldn't give them a reassuring smile. There was a low moan and waves sloshed higher. An internal app flashed in her visual cortex, warning her that the gravity had fluctuated yet again. She felt the Ark rise. Noa looked to where the prow of the Ark was now rubbing against the bottom of the skywalk. The water in the dome was rising, too.

She looked up at the sky again. There was nothing. The Luddecceans hadn't sent any of their warships when they'd been discovered at Adam's Station. Maybe they didn't think it would be necessary? Her heart beat faster in her chest. They wouldn't make that mistake twice ...

She heard a shout from the skywalk and saw Gunny. He saluted her and waved behind him. A few bedraggled civilians all wearing masks but not all dressed for the elements started across the deck. Some were helping a few children and other adults in hospital gowns.

The Ark had two airlocks on the deck, and Noa had them both open. She hurriedly directed the first six refugees to the first. A trickle of new refugees appeared on the Ark's deck, and she directed them to the second airlock, and then called through the ether. "Ghost, close the locks!" The airlock doors slid closed. "Manuel, the airlock grav, now." She repeated the procedure as soon as the doors slid open again. As the deck cleared, she looked around. 6T9 was trundling an enormous barrel larger than him across the deck on a wheeled dolly.

Noa blinked. "What—?"

6T9 smiled. "Toilet goop!"

"You were supposed to get medical equipment," someone said.

"This is medical," 6T9 responded. "Kuin said sharing a toilet was making him sick!"

Someone snorted, and 6T9 chirped, "Laughter is the best goop!"

"Where is James?" Noa asked everyone and no one.

Gunny must have picked up her words with his augmented hearing because he said, "The antigrav stretcher collapsed in the last grav shift. The man on it was already in bad shape."

Noa looked up at the sky. It was still empty. Luddeccea hadn't sent warships to Adam's Station, just a small scouting party. Maybe her team wasn't that valuable to them? She bit her lip. It wasn't the team they wanted according to Monica's little girl—it was James. But what could capturing James possibly do for them? He was better lightyears away from Luddeccea, where his existence, sanity, and *humanity* couldn't be witness to their madness.

She took a shaky breath and looked down the "canal" that ran perpendicular to the Ark. The hospital was there. Its internal generators were holding strong, and the lights were on, even below the waterline. She couldn't take the Ark any closer, the canal abutting the building was too narrow.

Her mind leaped into the ether. "James, where are you?" she whispered. For a moment, she felt the flutter of connection, and then the electrical impulses that should have activated by his channel went dark.

* * *

With one hand, James held his rifle. With the other, he patted the new heart for Oliver, resting in his satchel. "I have it, Manuel," he said. The engineer's relief rushed through the ether. Noa was concentrating on other things, but the channel was open. The refugees should have started reaching her by now.

On the floor in front of him, an Atlantian doctor was kneeling above an antigrav stretcher crashed on the floor. An unconscious patient was stretched on it. Life support equipment that had more mass than the patient was clustered by the patient's head, beeping rapidly.

James scanned the room, static fizzling over his skin. They were in what had been a restaurant at the hospital's top floor. The view was spectacular, even though the floor-to-ceiling windows were partially obscured by desks, sandbags, and anything else that Sterling's team had been able to scavenge before the real scavengers arrived. Just outside the windows there was a wrap-around balcony. Sterling's men perched on every corner.

The Atlantian attending said, "The patient has stabilized, but we have to get the grav stretcher working again."

One of Sterling's men said, "The gravity is shifting too fast. We should carry him."

"The equipment is too heavy!" the attending protested.

"I can carry it," James said.

"You can't!" the attending protested.

"Yes, I can," said James again.

The attending turned to look at him. He was a thin man, clean-shaven with short hair. He looked perfectly normal until his eyes began to glow red. "What ... are you?"

"I'm an augment," James supplied tersely. "Like you, apparently." He raised an eyebrow, gaze intent on the other man's glowing eyes. A device that aided in medical diagnosis?

The man's brow furrowed. Shaking his head, he turned away from James and waved a hand. "We don't have a stretcher."

"We'll make one," said Sterling's man. "Give us three minutes." He waved his companions from where they were keeping watch at the windows.

The beeping of the machine, still too loud, stabilized. The attending glanced again at James. "What ... are you?" echoed in James's mind. He patted the heart and reassured himself it was just the size and make Monica had suggested. Enough to last Oliver another year. If they got the gate in the cloud working, Oliver would be fine.

If they didn't ... He imagined what Noa would do to try to get the child a heart.

The attending was alternating between looking at the machines whirring by his patient's head and looking at James.

James remembered Oliver declaring the Ark a "space shit" and racing down the hallway, leaving behind a trail of toilet paper while 6T9 counted in the access tunnel. It had been funny. Oliver and 6T9 had been two of the few bits of brightness and levity during the whole damn escapade. Maybe all the levity they'd have for a while.

"I need another heart," James said, and he only had

two minutes. An extra one, one a size larger than Monica had asked for, just in case.

The attending didn't ask. He looked back at the stretcher very quickly and said, "Maybe I can get this to work ..."

James stepped around the attending. There was an elevator and a staircase at the center of the room. The room with the replaceable organs was downstairs, if he ran. He headed for the staircase and felt the ether between himself and Noa flicker out. Ghost's ether extenders were reliable, but being so far away was testing their range. He kept going, not sure if he was attempting this good deed to keep Noa out of trouble, to keep himself out of a situation like this again, or if he was doing it just to get away from the doctor with the red eyes.

He was steps from the elevator and stairs when the world exploded.

* * *

The sound of breaking glass coming from the hospital shattered the night. Noa could hear it even through the muffling of her helmet. She spun around. Beside her, Wren and Sterling did the same. "What's happening?" she called over the general channel, her thoughts running together with Sterling's ... James's conspicuously absent.

One of Sterling's men answered, "They flew a ship through the window."

And another, "The lights, what are they doing?"

And another, "Returning fire. Chu is down!"

There was a groan and the gravity of the dome shifted again. The Ark sank and the cannon Noa carried suddenly doubled in weight.

"Devi? Martinez?" Sterling's thoughts swept through the ether.

"They're down," said the first voice. "I'm ..."

"Sukarno ..." He looked at Noa. "My men, they're all down."

"James!" Noa screamed into the ether.

She felt a lightness in her mind as the connection re-established. "I have Oliver's heart," he said over the shared channel.

Manuel's thoughts flew across the connection. "James, get out of there!"

"Get out of there!" The thoughts swelled in a chorus from Noa, her crew, and Sterling's men.

"I think we may have other, bigger problems," said Wren, his neck craned upward.

Her heart feeling heavier than even the malfunctioning grav could explain, Noa lifted her eyes to the glow of S8O5 and saw the shadows of warships there, marring the heavens like black scars.

* * *

Pinned beneath a heavy weight, James heard Gunny's thoughts. "We've got three Luddeccean mid-class battleships up there. Estimated entry into atmosphere, six minutes, thirty-three seconds."

Blackness and bright flashes flowed so quickly together, James couldn't see anything. He heard a roar, a loud whoosh, and two thunks in the region he'd just been before. Cold air bit his face above his air filtration mask. He had dropped and spun when he'd heard what must have been the ship Sterling's men had spoken of crashing through the windows. He was on his back, but his head was crushed against a wall at an uncomfortable angle. His left hand was cradling the satchel; with his right he searched for his rifle. Somewhere in the black and white flashing in his eyes, he heard footsteps and voices. "This one is down."

"This one, too," said another.

Someone else said, "We caught the medic and a corpse! The med's got glowing eyes."

"Make the medic a corpse, too, and reload the nets," someone ordered.

Ghost's voice screamed over the shared channel. "Commander, we have to leave."

Static flared on every inch of James's skin, and then Noa's thoughts hit him like a balm. "No, we wait for the remaining civilians, and we give James a chance to get down here."

Another voice said aloud, "Where is he?"

He heard something that sounded like metal clicking on tile getting closer. "It, we're looking for an it, do not forget it," said a voice—the same one who ordered the murder of the doctor.

His hand found his rifle. Noa's voice entered his mind again. "James, can you hear me?"

His thoughts slipped into the ether, to tell her yes, but before the thought had even been transmitted, the voice he'd connected to the regular metal clicking sound and the murder of the medic said, "Ethernet augmenters have picked someone up ... beneath the grav bed."

The reason for the weight on top of him connected in an instant. He lifted his hand and felt a depression above him. The bottom of the grav bed. He felt the safety straps that were used to secure patients, but the patient was gone. The lightly padded mattress that normally covered the cold metal was gone too. He didn't hear a single beep from the life support equipment. His hand trembled, and for a moment, he had a memory of a long beep cutting short in a white hallway that lasted forever.

"Be careful, it's dangerous," said the voice connected to the clicking, snapping James back into the present. But he kept his eyes closed. Behind his eyelids was just black and gray—that observation connected a moment later in his mind, too. They were using flashing lights to disorient him. They knew it was a weakness.

In the ether, he heard shouts of, "Where is James?" from Manuel and Chavez. Eliza's voice sang out, "Get out of there, young man!" And from Ghost there came a, "Damn you, get out of there!" Which was oddly touching in its own way. And Noa's thoughts, "James, get down here now!" The thoughts of the crew filled him and made him feel oddly complete, even as the voices around him were getting closer. The footsteps, heartbeats, and breathing of his attackers were moving to his left and his right. He lifted his hand from Oliver's heart and found the controls of the grav bed. With his other hand he found the trigger of the rifle. He stretched his shoulder enough to feel the strap of the satchel there. And then he let his fingers fly over the controls of the bed. He heard the motor, grabbed onto the safety straps and held on with one hand, and held his rifle with the other.

The bed rose from the ground, the engine roaring to overcome its upside down position, and the gravity of Atlantia that had so recently increased. James fired at the feet of his foes, and as they fell, their bodies. He heard screams and smelled charred flesh and hair just before the bed shot forward and up, crashing through an as yet unbroken window, sinking, hitting the railing of the balcony and crashing to a halt. James nearly lost his hold with the force of the impact. His teeth rattled, and his bones screamed in protest. Pinned by the bed and the railing, he heard phaser fire on the grav bed's underside, but the machine's still-operating grav bands were playing havoc with the phaser beams, propelling them away.

Noa's voice rang in his mind. "James, are you alright?"

"I'm on my way down," James replied, even as he struggled to right himself.

"We're waiting for you," Noa said.

A chorus rose over the ether. "Hurry!"

Readjusting his hold on the safety straps, James managed to stand up and fire on the one remaining attacker to his right. Which left three on his left. With a grunt of exertion, he swung the bed left, flipping it over on top of two of them. The bed landed on the railing at an angle. Still strapped to it, James flung himself onto it and hit the controls. The bed shot over the railing and hovered for a moment, the engine roar becoming a high-pitched scream. "Hail Mary, full of grace," James murmured and spoke into the ether. The bed plummeted. All of which James expected. What he didn't expect was the bed's descent to be stopped by a skywalk just a few stories below, or the shadow that jumped over the railing after him. The shock of the impact loosened his grip on the rifle, and it clattered onto the roof of the walkway. Hand tangled in the safety straps, James saw a flash of metal rising in an arch and drew his legs up just before the source of the flash landed on his kneecaps. There was another bright flash and James could only roll his head away as whatever it was streaked toward him. Pain shot through his cheek, he heard metal connect with metal and plastic, and a shadow danced on the bed above him.

Yanking hard, James finally broke the safety straps. He saw a glint of light and rolled backward over the edge of the bed onto the roof of the skywalk. A light flashed on the walkway, and James saw who—or what he was up against for the first time. A man with a skull that was half metal stood on the bed. His mouth was covered by a breathing mask, his eyes were covered by night vision goggles that glowed faintly. He looked like a 20th century vision of a robotic nightmare. He wasn't bearing any weapons that James could see, but his limbs were weapons. He had metal plates on his knuckles, and where he should have feet, there were sharp blades of steel. James's eyes went to his own rifle on the edge of the roof. He threw himself toward it, but his foe was there first, kicking it off the roof with his left foot, catching his weight on his right, and then leaping up and over James with inhuman speed. James saw the rifle fall and discharge when it landed on another skylight twenty meters down and two meters to the left. James rolled over, jumped up, and leapt. He landed in a crouch on the lower skylight, just meters from his rifle. Before he could bolt for it, the other man landed, bounced on his metal blades, and a second later aimed one of them at James's head. James barely managed to dodge.

"James, where are you?" Noa cried over the ether. James eyes flicked below. He was on the street that was perpendicular to the Ark, about a block away.

A glint of light and the scrape of metal on glass was all the warning he got. He spun away from the kick that came too fast, heard his enviro suit rip and felt pain in his shoulder.

"What are you?" James murmured.

Bouncing on his limbs, James's assailant said, "A man.

And I will defeat you ... humans will always defeat you." His voice was muffled and distorted by his filtration mask. He launched at James again, aiming the metal blades on his legs at James's face. James's breathing mask went flying. Scampering backward, James saw another skywalk a few stories down in the direction of the Ark. He leaped for it, dropping and rolling on impact.

His foe landed in front of him, bouncing lightly.

James looked up, and behind the man he saw S8O5 ... and the shadows of warships. His vision went black, and he saw Noa, her head on a metal table, her port yanked out in a tangle of copper wire as thin as spider silk. "Run, Noa," he cried over the ether.

"No! Get down here!" she replied. She wouldn't leave, of course she wouldn't leave. Every nano in James's body went white. He saw the Ark—it couldn't sail down the canal James was above; the ship was too long. It couldn't go up, the air was too cluttered with skywalks. It had to sail back down the canal it came into the dome on.

James's foe went from a bounce into a roundhouse kick. James ducked, ran to a nearby skylight in the walkway's roof, and dove in headfirst, crashing through the glass in a shower of clinking shards, landing in a roll. He heard metal on tile behind him but didn't pause to look back. He ran, the map of the buildings around him that he'd only glimpsed briefly spilling out in his mind with mapmaker's precision. He threw his weight at a floor-to-ceiling window to his side. It cracked but didn't give. His assailant was on him an instant later. The metal man couldn't bounce in the enclosed space; the ceiling was too low. But he pirouetted too fast for a normal human and kicked. James evaded, the kick hit the glass, and this time the glass gave. James aimed a punch at the man's chest.

His fist connected with some sort of body armor, but the impact was enough to send the man flying against the window on the opposite side of the walkway. James heard a crack, spun around, hopped up onto a railing, and then jumped as far as he could, landing on the metal beams of another skywalk. He dashed across it, carefully avoiding the skylights. He heard the scrape of metal behind him but didn't look back. Ahead was the wall of a balcony of a short building that abutted the canal the Ark floated upon. James leaped up, caught the edge, and pulled himself up with shaky arms. The wall was partially obstructed by sunlight magnifiers. Mounted on columns that could rotate to follow the sun, the magnifiers were rectangular blocks of polyglass that concentrated the distant sunlight for the garden's plants. He had to crawl on his hands and knees beneath the glass, but there was no other obstacle between him and the rooftop garden beyond. Vision darkening at the edges, he slid down and stumbled in an area of rooftop garden that was like a dying young forest. The branches of dead trees laden with brown withered leaves arched just above his head, the branches of bushes lower to the ground seemed to grab him, and his feet crunched over dead-crusted vegetation. He was vaguely aware of the roar of antigrav getting closer, and the sound of fast thuds in sod behind him, keeping pace. The rip in his enviro suit was making him cold. Feet pounding, he ran as fast as he could toward the edge of the building that would be above the Ark. A spotlight from the hover scoured the ground to his left, and he altered his path to avoid being caught in its glow. His apps told him the new path would put him at the far corner of the building, thirty meters from the Ark. It would have to be close enough. He could still feel Noa in his mind. He had to get to her because damn it, she wouldn't leave without him.

The rooftop forest opened up to dead gardens sprinkled with snow. James's vision tunneled; he kept his focus straight in front of him on the sunlight magnifiers that edged the garden along the wall of the building that ran beside the canal the Ark was on. "I'm above you, Noa, be down in a minute," he whispered into the ether.

"Where?" Noa said.

"The roof," James said.

"Of the hospital?" Noa asked.

James didn't reply, his vision was constricted to his escape route. He heard the sound of antigrav getting closer, saw the spotlight in the periphery of his vision, and heard footsteps on the gravel paths and flower boxes he leaped over. He was within two body lengths of the corner of the wall ... once there he could hop down, from walkway to walkway ... He heard a boom, and a whoosh. He pulled the satchel with Oliver's heart closer to his body and kept running. James collided with the low wall that marked the edge of the building and something collided with him. He fell against one of the magnifiers, his legs hobbled, his arms wrapped tight to his sides. He looked down and saw he was caught in a net of some sort that wrapped him in a mesh cocoon from his knees to his shoulders.

He felt a tug on the netting and was abruptly yanked around, the force of the tug pulling his feet out from under him. He fell to the ground with jaw-rattling force. He heard footsteps but the spotlight blinded him.

"Anything a machine can do, a man can do better," his pursuer said. "Your kind will never take over Luddeccea. Your plans to destroy the human race will fail."

The madness made James sick; the hypocrisy made his skin burn. "I'm not a machine," James ground out. "I'm augmented, just like you."

He felt cold steel under his chin, and his face was yanked upward. His pursuer was silhouetted against the spotlights, his face bathed in shadow, but James could make out the glint of the metal on his forehead above his night vision goggles.

"You're more metal than I am," James spat.

One of the foot blades landed on his abdomen, pinning him to the spot.

"I am etherless," the man hissed. "My neural interface has been completely disabled. I am not like you." He laughed cold and hard. "A mechanical puppet of the time gates, pretending to be a dead man."

"Augments allowed me to live," James hissed. "Only in your sick, perverted religion would they be seen as evil."

The man's head jerked back. "I think it really thinks its human," he shouted, and James could hear the leer behind his breathing mask.

Behind him a shadow spit. "It's just playing with you."

"'Bots can't play," said another shadow. "Too dumb."

"I am a man," James said, struggling against the bonds. "Not a ..." He couldn't finish. His struggling ceased. He heard a cannon fire, probably from the Ark. The building trembled.

"Are you now?" said James's captor, leaning close so that his night vision goggles were just a few inches from James's face. "Who are you, Mr. Man?"

"I am Professor James Hiro Sinclair," James said, but the words felt wrong, a jumble of discordant syllables that had no inherent meaning. The man released his chin, and James screamed, "I think, I dream." He wasn't sure if he was protesting to his assailant, to himself, or to the universe at large.

"You don't have a face mask on," said his pursuer.

James's eyes widened. It had been gone too long ... for a human with body cells to feed. His hand trembled ... Even if he had no organic matter in his body, he should have some in his mind.

"I thought it was supposed to be smart," said one of the shadows.

"I have memories of a mother and father." In his bonds his hand trembled against the satchel, remembering his father, leaning over him in that long white hallway. He felt a shiver run through his body. He didn't feel love thinking of his father, he only had a memory of feeling love. He had no memories of his mother or father after that moment ...

Monica's words came back to him. *I thought you died.*

He had died, hadn't he?

"I bleed," he said.

"To fool us," one of the men said.

"So do sex 'bots," said another.

A radio crackled, and one of the men said, "They're preparing a drone drop."

"They use drones?" someone asked.

James blinked and pulled up a memory of a drone he'd had as a boy. It was hazy, like a memory of a memory remembered later ... He felt a fizzle of static along his skin. A memory of a memory, dumped later into a time capsule.

"It's etherless," said another. "Got simple programming. Fire on the Ark, return to base."

Fire on the Ark. "Noa, you have to leave," James said into the ether. Somewhere an alarm went off.

"It's talking to someone," said one of his captors. "Or something."

The man who was standing on his chest pulled the metal blade of his foot away. He motioned to his guards.

"Go, Noa, go," James whispered.

Gravity shifted, so it was slightly more than Earth's, and James's captors hauled him up.

He heard a cannon and this time a beam of fire arched over the roof and landed just half a meter from the vessel still casting the blinding spotlights.

"We'll get your throwback bitch soon enough," his captor hissed.

James's mind supplied a gruesome image of all her fingers being gone.

There was more cannon fire. The building rocked, the hands on James's upper arms briefly loosened, and his eidetic memory played the features of the wall behind him as clearly as though he was looking at them. James dropped, bent his knees, and dived backward. Cement scraped at the back of his head, the netting, and the weights. James plunged, headfirst, and knew he was too high. The fall would break his body and tear him apart. He knew it like he knew how to breathe, and like he knew he could not be just a puppet or a machine intent on destroying the human race. In his bindings, he put his hand on the satchel. Aloud and into the ether he said, "I have Oliver's heart."

And gravity shifted again.

* * *

Noa looked up at the building that rose beside the Ark. She could see lights above and hear the whir of antigrav at the far corner of its roof.

One of Sterling's men jogged around a group of struggling refugees across the deck of the Ark to Noa and Sterling. "Commander," he said. "That is the last of them."

"James said he would be right down," Noa said.

Sterling turned toward her. He said nothing, and his face was shadowed within his mask, but she knew what he was thinking. They couldn't stay here long. The warships would be in atmosphere soon, and as soon as they were, the drones would come.

"He'll be right down," Noa whispered. She looked up at the lights she could see glowing on the building above.

"James is up there, on that roof," she said, lifting her cannon to her shoulder in the punishing gravity.

"That's impossible!" said Sterling. "He couldn't make it over there—he's got to be still at the hospital."

Ignoring him, she bent to one knee, raised the cannon, and fired. Normally, the plasma fire would have cleared the roof, but gravity was against it. The charge hit the side of the building instead, loosening cement, bricks, and glass and sending it tumbling into the water beside the ship.

"Commander, you can't help him," Sterling said. "Even if that was him."

He was right. Gravity shifted, slightly. Noa squeezed her eyes shut and fired again.

"Civilians are in," said one of Sterling's men.

"Commander, I'm sorry," said Sterling. "I know ..."

He knew how it hurt to leave men behind.

"Go, Noa, go!' James spoke the words across the ether, over the public channel that everyone could hear.

Noa gritted her jaw. Sterling put a hand on her shoulder. She fired the cannon one more time.

Chavez's voice came over the ether. "Three minutes until drone drop."

"Damn it," Wren grunted, helmeted head tilted up toward the roof, cannon by his side.

"Commander," Sterling said. "He doesn't want *you* to die. *Listen* to him. Live for him now ... and for all those people below," Sterling said.

With a cry of despair and rage, Noa raced toward the airlock, Sterling hot on her heels. She'd get the survivors of this nightmare out of here.

She was halfway down the ladder when she looked back and saw Wren still standing on the deck. "What are you doing?" she shouted.

"I have no idea," Wren said, but he ran after them.

A moment later, the airlock was shut and the gravity was shifting. Taking off her cumbersome helmet and breathing apparatus, Noa raced down the hallway, skipped the lift, and went right for the ladder.

Over the ether, Chavez said, "The drones have dropped."

"Turn us around," Noa said, heart pounding in her ears. "Just like we discussed, and then take us down."

"Aye, Commander," Chavez said. Noa couldn't feel anything, or see anything, but she felt the change in the antigrav engines as Chavez lifted the Ark's bow out of the water and eased her into a gentle belly flop.

Noa was in the service tunnel, nearly on the bridge, when she heard James's voice in the ether. "I have Oliver's heart."

Noa's breath caught. Gravity seemed to shift ... no, it

did shift ... and it took a moment for the Ark's own grav generator to accommodate the change.

As she clung to the ladder, Manuel's voice came across the ether. "James?"

Chavez's thoughts swelled across the general channel. "Commander, he's fallen. He's in the water!"

"Where?" Noa said, one hand reaching for the last rung of the service ladder, the other twisting open the latch that opened the service door to the bridge. As she raced to the pilot's chair, Chavez said, "Thirty meters beyond bow now."

Ghost's thoughts raced over the ether. "The drones dropped—we have to get out of here."

Noa swung into her seat and saw James sinking like a stone, past windows that still remained alight in the sunken buildings.

"He couldn't have survived the fall," said Sterling.

"James?" Noa cried into the ether. "James, are you there?"

CHAPTER SEVENTEEN

He fell.

He hit the water headfirst, the impact shuddering from his crown to his shoulder and then to his spine, the weights on the nets pulling him down, the cold water sending icy fingers beneath his torn enviro suit.

And then he heard the static.

His mind screamed, "Do you have anything to say for yourselves?"

"You were our best," said a voice.

"Because of your damage," said another.

"How am I damaged?" part of James roared, and another twisted little part of him whispered, *Too many ways to count*.

"When they shot you down," said a consciousness he recognized as Three.

"Because you didn't know what you are," said another.

"Because you didn't know why you are," said another.

"I still don't know," James's mind screamed. "Tell me!"

"We still require data," said a voice he recognized as One.

"What data?" James demanded.

But the static left and was replaced by another voice across the ether. "James?" It was Noa. His eyes opened, but he saw only darkness. Struggling against his bonds, he had the empty sensation of hunger in every cell in his body. Did he have cells? He had to. He couldn't be only a machine. He wasn't 6T9. He had a will of his own, dreams, and memories ... memories that had all been carefully archived and saved in a time capsule on Time Gate 1.

No, he was more than a machine! He was capable of abstract reasoning, of planning ahead. He had more than one purpose. The only way a machine could achieve that was with a processor as large as a small moon ...

... or as large as a time gate. A machine linked to a time gate—to time gates—could rival a human mind if it could achieve faster than light communication. Which he had.

All his struggling ceased.

"James, are you there?"

Ghost's voice roared across the ether. "We have to leave! The drones may have depth charges!"

He might be one of them, but he still was himself, and he had his own will. Into the ether, he shouted, "Leave, Noa! Go!"

* * *

"Leave, Noa! Go!" James's voice cracked through the ether.

Noa's gasp was drowned out by a collective intake of breath from everyone on the bridge.

"To nebulas with that," she hissed and steered the Ark into a dive toward his plunging form.

"No!" Ghost screamed. "You can't!"

"Oh, hell, might as well," said Wren. If Noa hadn't been steering, if every neuron and nano of her attention hadn't been necessary at the helm, she might have fallen over in shock at the man's words. As it was, she could only hold on tight to the steering as the Ark fought with underwater currents and grit out a low, "Thank you," that sounded more like a growl.

She could hear him at the lift. "Eh, the question is how. That's water, it's cold, and your enviro suits aren't built for it. I don't suppose an old Luddeccean vessel has an ether-controlled drone—"

Noa's eyes widened. "Eliza, can 6T9 swim?" she asked over the ether.

The old woman's thoughts flowed across the channel. "No ..."

Noa's heart fell.

"But," Eliza said, "he is waterproof."

"Wren," Noa said, "get him hooked up to a tow rope. Manuel will—"

Manuel's thoughts flooded the ether before she could finish. "I'll bring the rope!" And Noa's heart almost broke with hope.

"We have to get to him before he's too deep," Monica said. "The pressure will kill him."

And Noa's heart broke again.

* * *

James couldn't move. He couldn't even reach out through the ether. It would take too much energy to make electrons dance from the point of his consciousness to the transmitter in his neural interface. But he still had thoughts, trapped in a prison of darkness, flesh, and steel.

He felt the cold creeping into the deepest part of him, chilling even his thoughts, and he was grateful. Worse than death would be an eternity of consciousness confined in this shell, on this abandoned moon, all alone.

And then light exploded beyond his eyelids.

Noa's eyes flicked over the external monitors, and then out the skylight. She forced herself to breathe.

6T9's voice came over the ether. "I have him inside the airlock, Commander. Removing the net and checking for vital signs."

She exhaled and bit back a smile.

Manuel's voice came next. "Send in the doctor!"

Monica responded across the shared channel. "We have to wait for the pressure to adjust before we open the doors. 6T9, the thermal blanket is in there. You need to start treating him for hypothermia immediately."

"James, are you alive?" Noa whispered into his mind.

For a moment, she thought she felt a spark ... but it vanished.

"James is exhibiting no vital signs," 6T9 intoned over the ether, and Noa felt a wave of cold wash over her. She kept her hands steady on the steering wheel, focused on the cliff into the deep ahead of them.

"I have wrapped him in the thermal blanket," the 'bot intoned. "Beginning CPR."

She could see the point ahead where the city streets fell away into darkness. The navigation monitor was flashing an error message and she cursed the wonky wiring on the bridge.

Ghost cried across the ether, "Commander, they're dropping depth charges! We need to get out of the water, and get out of here!"

Noa checked the monitors and dove deeper. A red light flashed on the dash, warning her that she only had five meters clearance between them and the sunken street below them. She dipped her chin and dived until the warning said three meters, and then one.

"Commander," Ghost's voice cracked across the channel, "did you hear—"

"As soon as those warships appeared we weren't leaving the water," Noa responded. "Not near the biodome where they'll be as thick as xen-fleas on a lizzar."

"Commander?" Sterling and Manuel thought at the same time.

Noa sent a thought to James alone. "James, hang in there," and then for everyone else on the ship to hear, she said over the ether, "Ghost, I need a map of the channels of this planet, all the thermal vents on the ice. We're going down."

It was as though all thought processes on the Ark came to a stop. But then Manuel's voice rang through the ether, "What? This ship can handle shallow submersion, but—"

"It can handle shallow submersion on Luddeccea's surface," Noa responded, her thoughts clipped and sharp. "But Atlantia's gravity is just a fraction of home's."

"After we get out of the biodome," Ghost cried.

"Well, that's where we're going," said Noa. "Start charting channels for me."

Wren's voice chimed in. "You know … the Luddeccean authorities have been known to be lenient sometimes. Even if we were imprisoned, we'd have three square meals a day in a nice—"

"Someone shut him up!" Ghost roared over the ether.

"On it!" said one of Sterling's men over the shared channel.

"Hey!" shouted Wren. "I'm on your side. I just—" His voice abruptly left the ether and was replaced by Ghost's. "Commander, I see your point. I have completed the map of Atlantia's surface, computing current location, and charting a course that will take us as far away from the biodome as possible."

"Thank you, Ghost," Noa whispered aloud and into the ether.

6T9's thoughts came over the shared channel. "Commander, fellow crew mates. I have been administering CPR for the past ten minutes—"

Ten minutes? Had it been that long?

"I regret to inform you," 6T9 continued, "Professor Sinclair is dead."

* * *

There was light in strange geometric patterns in front of James's eyes … and then there was darkness. He was still so cold. And hungry …

He heard a sound … footsteps, running … and then Manuel's voice very close. "Thank you, James. I'll never forget you."

The world shuddered. No, the Ark shuddered. They'd pulled him out.

He couldn't move and he couldn't get food ... He had to have heat, and he didn't know how he knew. Was it instinct—or was it programming? Even as a sick, twisted part of him pondered that, he reached to the ether. Had Ghost ever enabled the ether link to the Ark's bio-controls? Behind his closed eyelids, the Ark's systems spread out. He saw himself in one of the airlocks as a flickering light. He was so hungry ... The Ark's ether conversation swirled in his mind as he lay in the cold darkness too disorientated and hungry to reach out.

"James, I'm sorry," Noa called to him.

Shut, James willed the door. *Maximum,* he willed to the heating.

"James, I'm sorry," Noa said into the ether at 6T9's words, and then her hands quaked on the steering bars, and she felt like she might fall over. He'd been loyal to her schemes to the end, despite everything. Always on her side.

"Depth charge off starboard," said Chavez.

And she realized it hadn't been her who had been shaking, it was the Ark. Or maybe they both had trembled. Her training kicked in, and with a thought as emotionless as a query from an automaton, she asked, "Damage report?"

"Not too bad, but there was a small fire in the computing center," said Manuel. "Looks like it was in a light fixture, though not mainframe. Already out."

Kara's voice chimed over the ether, "I'm close by there with one of the Atlantia guys. Checking it out."

A blip sounded on the dash. "Another depth charge falling off port," Chavez said.

Noa veered to starboard, throttle at maximum. Below them the street ended. The Ark vaulted into the open sea and would within minutes be protected beneath meters of ice. They'd be safe from depth charges there, but—

"We can get lost real easily down here, Commander," Sterling said. "The seismic activity changes the terrain rapidly, and we don't even have recent maps since the earthquake-tsunami."

"Ghost, I need that course, now." Noa tried to reach her computing officer's channel—and didn't get a connection.

One of Sterling's men's thoughts burst through the ether. "In computing center. Man down ... lighting fixture fell from the ceiling; looks like a blow to the head. Could be a neck injury. We need a stretcher, stat."

"Coordinating that now," Sterling said. "We'll get him to medical."

"Is it Ghost?" Noa asked, even though she knew he was the only person who could be there ... She silently prayed that 6T9 had brought the programmer tea and cookies in computing, and that the Atlantian hadn't figured out what the 'bot was.

"Yes, Commander, it's Ghost," said Kara over the channel. Noa thought she was beyond feeling, but at the news, her stomach sank.

"Manuel," Noa asked. "Who on your team do you recommend for Chief Computing Officer?"

"Kara," her chief engineer replied over the ether.

"Congratulations, you've been promoted, Kara," Noa said.

"Commander?" said Kara.

"Ghost said he had a map, our location, and a course worked out. I need you to send those to me, now," Noa ordered, glancing at her nav read-out that was still declaring an error.

"Ummm ... Commander," Kara said. "We don't have our current position. It looks like the Atlantian positioning satellites are offline. I'm getting no signal whatsoever."

"More likely destroyed by the Fleet," said Manuel across the general channel.

"Ghost had our position," Noa said. "He was probably using our trajectory and velocity to keep track. Use the keypad to access the computer ... I know, it's archaic."

"I've already done that," said Kara. "Opening up all recent navigation apps, now."

A blip sounded on a monitor between Noa and Chavez. It sounded again.

"The deGrasse-Tyson trench is approaching fast," said Sterling.

The blip sounded again ... again ... and again.

"That isn't a depth charge," Noa said. "Kara!"

"Commander ..." Kara's thoughts stuttered. "There's nothing in the Ark's navigation app ... nothing at all."

The blips sounded closer together. "A cluster of drones," said Chavez softly. "They're on our tail."

* * *

"There's nothing in the Ark's navigation app ... nothing at all." James's eyes bolted open to darkness at Kara's words.

Hadn't Noa remarked on Ghost's ability to determine a jump point and rapidly compute courses? And Manuel said it was impossible that the Ark computer could crack ether encryption so quickly—even in compromised local networks like Adam's Station. James remembered Ghost "thinking aloud" to himself just hours before without any noticeable activity in the Ark's system. Ghost had "thought out loud" when he'd pulled data off of the super-computer he built on Luddeccea's surface, too; the super-computer that was "etherless." He'd claimed that he'd been able to access it via a "special frequency" that couldn't be overheard ... and that was, James supposed, possible. He wasn't a communication engineer. Maybe Ghost used a regular bandwidth and wrapped the signal in some sort of warp bubble to avoid a time paradox, but James suspected he was using quantum entanglement. He just ... felt like it. But it didn't matter how Ghost did it. What did matter had been Ghost talking to a supercomputer. Was it the time gates Ghost spoke to? As soon as the question occurred to James, he *felt* the answer was no. Ghost was in contact with the computer on Luddeccea he'd built, James was almost certain. Ghost was using its massive resources to chart courses, create the holographic effects for his necklaces, and decrypt the ethernet.

He blinked in the darkness. Was Ghost like him—a machine? He discarded that idea, but he knew they were both tied to technology that gave them extraordinary computative resources, even with the ethernet down. He blinked again. Could an etherless technology not bound by time paradoxes be created without the wider galaxy knowing?

He exhaled. Of course it could. In the time period he'd specialized in, most of humanity had been unaware of the Manhattan Project for years, though the idea of atomic energy as a weapon had been theorized in the late 1930s.

He felt a frisson at the base of his skull … "He" hadn't specialized in that time period at all. Not if what the voices in the static said was true.

No, no, no, his mind screamed, but he *felt* his denial was a lie, like he felt that Ghost and he weren't the same. Why give an android feelings? Or was having feelings what made him "damaged"?

The fingers of James's left hand twitched involuntarily. He was still blind and in darkness, but in his mind an app lit up, telling him that the ambient temperature in the room was 50 C.

Over the ether, Sterling said, "Commander, the trench is less than one kilometer away, and the ice is getting thicker. To continue, we'd need to dive, and even with positioning satellites, probes and vessels have gotten lost down there."

James sat up with a start, and the darkness slid away from his eyes. James looked down and discovered a thermal blanket crumpled on his naked lap and realized it had been covering his face. Why? Unless … James's hand trembled, remembering Manuel's words. *I'll never forget you.* And Noa's, *I'm sorry, James.*

He'd died, again.

Electricity prickled beneath his skin. And in a flash of insight, he knew electric prickle was not a sensation from *before*. He should have known what he was …

Chavez's voice buzzed over the ether. "The drones are getting closer."

"Kara," Noa said, "we need that map!"

"Iceberg ahead, Commander," said Sterling.

James could very well die again. He reached into the ether and almost touched Noa ... and then felt a rush of panic. They'd call Monica. If they called Monica ...

He pulled back emotionally. He had to be able to resist Monica, to appear so well that all she'd give a cursory examination ... if they found out what he was. Manuel had just said he'd never forget James. But 6T9 had saved his child's life, too, and Manuel hadn't been at all hesitant about selling 6T9 on Adam's Station. He struggled to get to his feet ... and couldn't. He needed to get warmer. The need pressed down on him, physically and emotionally, all consuming. The room wasn't hot enough, and couldn't get hot enough. His eyes fell on an abandoned enviro suit, and the glove with its heating and cooling controls, just to his left. He forced himself to raise a hand. He reached out for the suit, his hand trembled, and he caught it in his fingers.

Over the ether, he heard Noa say, "We're diving."

Sterling replied, "We have to go back. We have more of a chance with warships!"

"There is no going back," Noa responded.

Ten minutes after the Ark plunged into the pitch black water that was the deGrasse-Tyson trench, the vessel was still diving. Noa felt sweat beneath her uniform, on her palms, and on her fingers. They'd lost the first cluster of drones when they dove—the ones following them originally had collided with the enormous stalactites of icebergs—but more had followed. On the ship's ancient sensors, an ever more frequent beeping told her that the drones were getting closer.

"Why haven't they fired on us yet, Commander?" Chavez asked.

"Because they don't want us dead," said Noa. "They're probably programmed to wait until they're within close range, and then they'll hit our thrusters. They'll incapacitate us and send a retrieval team. "

And then every augment aboard the vessel would be dead; and they'd have the rest of their "archangel" to dissect. Into the ether, Noa whispered, "I won't let them have you, James. Not alive or dead." And she wouldn't let his last sacrifice be in vain.

"Why go to all that trouble?" Sterling said.

Noa ignored the question and reached into the ether. "Kara, how is that map coming?"

"I inputted the strength and direction of Atlantia's magnetic pole into the nav computer," Kara said. "It's calculating our trajectory now, but I'm still not sure where we are."

Sterling said, "The drones will catch—"

"It's getting brighter out there," Chavez whispered.

Noa swallowed. She'd wondered if she'd been imagining that.

"What is it, Sterling?" Noa asked.

"I don't know," the lieutenant responded in a hushed voice.

The faint glow became a sea floor of twinkling, multicolored stars, and then beside her, Chavez gasped. "Sea flowers!"

As they got closer, Noa saw that the bottom of the trench was carpeted with a forest of seaweed with glowing blossoms. The blooms glowed in shades of yellow, pink, and orange. From their vantage they looked no more than the breadth of a hand—but the Ark was still at least a kilometer away so they must be enormous. Glowing fish-like creatures zipped about above. It was beautiful, and idyllic, and it may have been her state of mind—or heart—but something about the scene made her shiver, grit her teeth and narrow her eyes.

"Commander, we could hide in the seaweed," Chavez said, her voice excited.

Noa leveled the ship off about five hundred meters above the seaweed forest. The beeping of the sensor intensified. Noa's eyes were drawn to three large fish moving into a school of smaller glowing fish. The glowing fish scattered like leaves, some darting up, and some into the seaweed, one of the larger fish on their tails. Before she could blink, the flowers struck like the heads of snakes. She blinked, and the big fish that had dived was gone.

Chavez gasped. "The flowers just ate that fish! Good thing we didn't hide in there."

"Kara, I need my map!" Noa said over the ether.

"I'm still working on it!" Kara answered across the shared channel.

Manuel's voice came over the ether. "If we could get out of range of the drones, we could give this old boat's computer some time to work."

At that moment, the sensor blips became a whine.

"We're diving into some giant fish-eating flowers, Manuel. Make sure the timebands are inline!"

"Commander?" Chavez said.

"You'll rip the ship apart!" Sterling said.

Noa depressed the steering bars and sent the Ark plunging into the forest of predatory seaweed.

* * *

"Manuel, how many seconds can I keep the timebands on underwater?" Noa's voice made James look up. He was sitting on the floor in the airlock, enviro suit halfway on, the heated coils in the fabric already operating.

"They're not designed for submerged operation—the electrical current in the bands in the water—"

"How long?" Noa demanded.

What was she doing?

"Thirty seconds?"

James's jaw shifted in the laugh he wanted to give but could not. She was doing something crazy again, obviously. He shrugged the rest of the suit on, feeling the heat burning his skin in a way that was as satisfying as ... as peanut butter. He groaned and looked down at his chest just before pulling up the zipper. His tattoos were in full "bloom," and for the first time, he thought he understood them. They were activated by light and heat ... they were energy collectors, and he needed them because eating wasn't enough, and eating wasn't enough because he wasn't created by evolution, and he hadn't evolved to be as efficient as a human yet. He wanted to cry.

Chavez's voice cracked over the ether. "That flower is nearly as wide as the Ark!"

"The better to eat a drone!" Noa snapped.

Someone else said over the ether, "Or us."

"Ten seconds until drones are within range," said Sterling.

James struggled to his feet.

"Activating timebands now," Noa said.

There was an earsplitting screech, like the sound of antigrav amplified, and then the sound of metal groaning. The ship shook and trembled, more and more violently, the volume of the groan and the screech increasing. There was a loud reverberating noise ... and then ... silence.

"The drones ... they ate the drones!" someone shouted across the ether. "What happened?"

Sterling's thoughts came across the general channel. "The Commander gave us a timebubble that allowed us to travel over the flowers before they could snap shut ..."

Jun's voice came over the ether. "Errr ... I think we got hit by one ... the camera on the hull at level 15 is just sparkly pink."

"... before all but one could snap shut," Sterling amended. "They were primed for the drones though, and caught all of them." He sounded grudgingly impressed.

James huffed and tried to walk to the door. He took a step, and then another. He was wobbly and had to use the wall for support.

"And the one that snapped shut on us was ripped apart at the stem, because part of it was inside our bubble and part of it was out," Sterling finished.

"It will burn up as we leave atmosphere," Noa supplied. "I'm going to park us a few meters above our glowy friends and give Kara a chance to figure out where we are. Manuel, damage report?"

James swore he heard a collective sigh from the entire ship.

"Running a diagnostic, now," the engineer replied.

Thoughts clipped, Noa asked, "Dr. Jarella, how is Ghost?"

"He will be fine, but he is still unconscious. He has a moderate concussion," Monica answered.

James felt static rise along his skin. If Ghost was unconscious ...

"How is everything coming along, Kara?" Noa asked.

"I see that the error message on my nav screen has been replaced by three little cycling dots," said Noa.

"I think that means it's thinking," Kara replied. "I hope we can stay parked here for a while. This is going to take a long while."

"Something is wrong in the airlock by me," Kuin said over the ether. "The temperature is way too high. I'm going to check it out." Just before the airlock door slid open, James had enough time to straighten. He met Kuin's gaze. The young man's eyes went wide, and his mouth fell open. "You're not dead."

"Nope," said James.

"But 6T9 said ..."

James raised an eyebrow. "6T9 is as bright as the dispersers we dumped at Adam's Station."

Kuin's brow furrowed. If the man had any sense at all, he'd suggest James go to medical. Before he could do that or say anything to the ether, James pushed past him, patting him on the shoulder as he went. "I've got to get to the bridge."

He didn't feel completely recharged ... and found himself putting a hand against the wall for support.

"Are you okay?" Kuin said. "Should I call—?"

"I'm fine," said James, looking over his shoulder, wishing he could smile. "I just half expect the Commander to drop us back into a field of frenzied flowery seaweed." He hoped he got the gist of that right.

Kuin smiled. "Ha ... yeah ... that was intense."

"Mmm ..." said James, opening the door to the access ladder. He managed a wave before swinging onto the ladder and shutting the door behind him. Pressing his back against the wall, he rested, letting the heat in the suit warm him to the core.

Over the ether, Kuin said, "Ummm ... so ... you know how we all thought that—"

James scrunched his eyes shut. He should have told the kid to keep quiet.

"Commander," Chavez said, "there's something on our scope ... they're large enough to be submarines, but they rose out of the seaweed."

Gunny's thoughts came over the ether. "Uh-oh."

And then Jun's. "I'm at a window, I see them! They're giant saw-nosed lizard monsters!"

"Maybe some sorta whale?" said Chavez.

"Kara," Noa said. "I need that map!"

"Um ... what I had to say ... never mind," said Kuin.

"Still processing, Commander," Kara said over the general channel. "I'm still not even sure where we are. Let alone a vent in the ice."

"We don't have time, Kara," Noa said.

"With this ancient system, we'd better find it!" Kara shot back. "I have no idea how that man was able to coax even a jump-point out of this thing."

James's eyes opened. They needed real computing power, but he wasn't in constant connection with the time gates. His hand trembled on the ladder rung. No, that wasn't true. He could always connect to them—that was how he was able to decrypt and listen in to ethernet channels. He huffed, thinking of 6T9's general state of confusion. Constant contact was how he had the processing power to pass as a human. It was the source of his intuition, and his sense of humor. The static he heard and lights he saw when the gates felt, or heard, and his desire to listen in to the ethernet channels was probably just the time it took them to decrypt his targets' codes. They could chart a course for the Ark for the crew.

But would they? What did they care about? What did they want?

He bowed his head, and his body went hot. He didn't want to talk to them, not now, not ever. But if he didn't … His hand trembled so violently on the ladder he thought he might slip and fall. In his mind he snarled. "I will blow up this vessel, myself, and everyone else aboard it rather than be captured. You want more data? Then show me the way out."

The world went white.

Noa's chin dipped. Face sea life of unknown quantity … or face the Luddeccean warships. Without a charted exit point from the ice and dangerous sea life on their tails, they would have to try and turn back and face the Luddecceans head on or risk being lost down in the depths … or, as was rapidly becoming apparent, eaten.

"The monsters could be herbivores," Chavez suggested.

Jun's channel buzzed. "The giant herbivorous lizzar of the Luddeccea's southern continent are the most dangerous animals on the planet."

Over the ether, one of Manuel's engineering students said, "How did we not know about giant fish things?"

Manuel's thoughts spiked like static. "Let the Commander focus."

Sterling, at his position at one of the cannons, said defensively, "We've only been on this moon for about seventy-five years! Sure, some of our probes went missing —but we never saw giant anything … no flowers, no lizard monsters. For all we know they could have been hibernating and just woke up with the tsunami!" His thoughts stuttered, and then he said, "There are more ..." Noa looked down at one of the sensors. Torpedo-like shapes were swarming up from the seaweed forest at three o'clock, joining the ones already at six o'clock.

"We might have more chance above facing those warships," Sterling said.

Noa snarled and held her course. The Luddecceans wouldn't kill them. They'd take them prisoner first. They couldn't have her crew for torture. She blinked. No, she could self-destruct the ship. They could turn around, find their way back the way they came, set the auto destruct sequence, and take as many as the Luddecceans as they could on the way out. *Kamikaze*, just like her ancestors.

She prepared to turn but dark shadows suddenly lunged out of the seaweed. "Lizard fish monsters at twelve o'clock, Gunny!" Noa said, her eyes on two large shadows.

She felt the ship rock as her sergeant fired the first cannon. He hit his mark, but it left one more unfazed by the sudden disappearance of its schoolmate. "Sterling!"

The ship rocked again as Sterling fired the second gun.

"Phaser cannons expended," Gunny said as the Ark coasted through a cloud of black monster blood and guts. Noa took a deep breath, ready to turn to nine o'clock and find a way back ... and then blinked. Superimposed over her vision, a perfect map of the moon's vents and canals spread out before her, the Ark a tiny red dot upon it.

"I know the way!" she shouted. "There's a vent ahead, ten kilometers at twelve o'clock to our current position."

She almost called out to Kara to thank her for her work, but the thought died before it entered the ether. The map of the moon was coming from James's channel.

"James ..." she whispered.

"Commander?" said Chavez. She felt Sterling's eyes slide to her.

"James, you're dead," she said over the ether. Maybe it was just a thought he'd left in the Ark's ether archive. Her heart could not take this. Not now. But if he was dead, how would he know their position?

"Commander," Chavez said. "I don't see—"

"We'll need to hop to lightspeed as soon as we leave the atmosphere," Noa said aloud and to the ether.

"I can work on it if you just give me the coordinates of the exit, Commander," Kara said.

But the coordinates were already spilling into Noa's mind ... again from James's channel. Her apps calculated the angle they needed to reach the vent position. She adjusted course and cried, "Hold the wheel, Chavez!" while beginning to frantically input the coordinates for the jump-point and the jump into the ancient nav computer.

"Yes, Commander," Chavez said, obediently holding the helm, her eyes straight ahead.

Aloud and into the ether to James's channel, Noa whispered, "James."

Chavez said, "Commander, all I see is ice. Three minutes to impact."

"Three minutes and fifteen seconds before our fish friends catch us," Gunny said.

"How can they be catching us?" Jun cried over the ether.

Noa heard Gunny respond across the ether, "This boat wasn't designed for speed in water."

"Only goes about sixty-two kilometers per hour." The response flew through her mind barely noticed, like ptery song in the morning. She was focused on the ancient nav controls and the coordinates playing in her visual cortex. She was afraid to hope … she'd heard of thoughts, misrouted in the ether, coming from loved ones beyond the grave. "Please tell me you're not a recording on auto-play," she silently begged. "Please be alive, please be real." How many times had she begged that same thing of other people? She was going mad.

From James's channel came a feeling like every hair on her body had been rubbed the wrong way, and then his thoughts collided with hers. "I'm real. But focus on getting us out of here, woman!" He was irritated, and that was what made Noa believe he was still alive. She laughed as she entered the last coordinates. "James!" she cried aloud, her face splitting into a grin.

"Damn it," he grumbled mentally, "I should have used the general channel and contacted everyone. They'll all think you're insane."

Before Noa could respond, Chavez whispered aloud and across the ether, "Commander, I don't see the vent. Are you sure you have the right coordinates?"

Noa looked out; so far from the glowing forest of the trench, all she could see was darkness. For a moment she felt doubt, but then Gunny grunted. "I see it." And then he added, "Night vision and distance augments."

Noa bit her lip.

She heard the hatch from the ladder access tunnel creak. Gunny gasped, and Sterling said, "What?"

"Hi, everyone," James said dryly. "I had a nice nap."

Noa laughed aloud. She wanted to turn around so much she felt the skin on the back of her ears and neck heat, but she didn't even glance. She'd never realized that harder than squelching years of loss, sadness, and despair, was battening down the hatches on a single moment of intense joy.

Something on the dash beeped.

"Oh, no," Chavez said, "more whales."

"Noa," James said over the ether. "I don't want to be Jonah."

She blinked down at a monitor. There were six of them aiming straight for the ship. Noa's apps began calculating the rate of intercept and the distance to the crack in the ice.

"Should I shoot, Commander?" Sterling said. "We're recharged."

"No," Noa shouted, stifling the urge to laugh. "Save it for the surface and any Luddeccean warships that get in the way!"

"Manuel!" Noa called across the ether, eyes on the dim glow of S8O5 shining through the water, "Are we ready for lightspeed?"

"We're ready, Commander!"

Noa did laugh. The Ark leapt out of the frozen sea. In the periphery of her vision in a view screen, she saw a giant creature lit by the glow of S8O5 leaping up behind the Ark. It had a long slender snout filled with teeth, and a body like a whale. She blinked and it fell away. A few drones buzzed into the Ark's path, and Noa ordered, "Fire away!" The cannons roared, and the drones exploded. Minutes later the velvety darkness split by stars spilled out before them, and then the black velvet became a vast white blur as the Ark jumped to lightspeed.

The ether erupted with cheering. Sterling and Gunny jumped out of their seats. She heard them thumping James on the back. "You made it!"

"6T9's diagnostic protocols might need to be updated," James said, his voice very close. Something about his words made her breath catch. She glanced back and saw him beside her chair, his blue eyes on hers.

"How do you feel?" she asked over the ether, imagining a ball of light and tossing it to him.

Silently, over the channel just between them, he said, "Like a ghost."

CHAPTER EIGHTEEN

James sat on the bridge. Several people had suggested he leave the bridge, but he couldn't bring himself to leave Noa.

Monica was beside him. In an agitated voice, she asked, "Are you teasing me? I'm really too tired for it—"

He glanced up at her. There were dark circles under her eyes. He didn't feel sympathy; he felt antagonistic. Now he knew why. He was a machine and she didn't like machines, and she especially didn't like humans bonding with machines.

"Take a breath," she said, a stethi-amplifier hovering in front of his chest. She tilted her head and narrowed her eyes. He took a deep breath and she scowled at her readout. "You're fine ... no water in the lungs ... no risk of secondary drowning."

"Back from the dead again," James said, the words slipping out easily, although inwardly he shuddered.

A line formed between her brows. "Apparently."

James's left hand trembled on the chair's armrest. Before Monica noticed, he dropped it so that it was between his body and the seat. "I think 6T9 was performing functions beyond his capability," he said.

Monica's lips pursed. "That's the thing ... sex 'bots have secondary subroutines that are very good at minor medical diagnosis. It's necessary for when they take part in more volatile ... activities."

At the helm, Noa erupted, "Dr. Monica! Death is not a *minor* medical diagnosis!" Through the ether, a white ball of light bounced from her to him. His eyes slid to her profile. Her skin was warm and brown against the color-less blur of lightspeed, and there was the curve of a smile on her full lips.

Noa had reservations about human-machine rela-tions, too. But she had recoiled at the dismembered 'bots in Ghost's lair, she hadn't wanted to leave 6T9 behind in the sewers, or on Adam's Station. She had accepted the decision to save the mech suits. She had said she didn't care what he was. He took the ball of light she imagined and tossed it back to her and saw her smile wider. His skin hummed, and he *wanted* her ... More than James Hiro Sinclair had ever wanted a woman.

He wasn't Professor James Hiro Sinclair ... the professor had probably just been a convenient alias for the time gates to exploit because the man had stored virtually every one of his thoughts and experiences in a time capsule. They'd given him all his memories, his looks, even his upper-crust Earther accent. It might be part of the damage he received when he was shot down, but he didn't have that man's essence. He wasn't thoughtlessly heroic, he wasn't passionate about human history or humanity, he didn't love his parents. But he could still be filled with awe and wonder at the universe—the burrow-like habitat of Adam's Station, the beauty of the S8O5 hovering in Atlantia's sky, the whisper of snow. And he wasn't completely devoid of feeling. He cared about Oliver, probably more than the original James ever could. He liked 6T9. He could empathize even sometimes with Manuel; Manuel had loved his wife. James loved Noa. He might not be human, but he was *alive.*

Noa ... he had been helplessly drawn to her after his accident. Maybe just because the giant computer he was connected to predicted she was the person most likely to get him off Luddeccea?

A movement on the periphery of his vision caught his eyes. He saw Monica follow his gaze to Noa and then slide back to him and go to his cheek. "That was a deep cut in your face ... it's strange that it healed so quickly."

James shrugged, and Noa said, "His parents worked for Fleet. He got some pretty incredible nanos pumped into him." That was a hypothesis they had between them, but Noa spoke it like truth. He *wanted* it to be true ...

Voice more somber, Noa asked, "When will Ghost wake up?"

"The sedatives will keep him out for another eight hours," Monica said. Monica had told them that that when he'd first woken from unconsciousness, Ghost had been hysterical, sure that they would be captured. She'd explained they were safe at lightspeed and had given the lie that James had given everyone else: Ghost, right before slipping into unconsciousness, had sent the course to James's ethernet channel, probably by accident. James himself had been unconscious as his augments struggled to keep him warm, and so was unable to acknowledge or to send it right away. And when he woke up, he hadn't realized the data was in his neural interface until the last possible moment.

Backing away, Monica glanced once more at Noa and then at James and said, "I need to get back to sick bay and check on him before I turn in."

James knew that at some point he and Ghost would have a confrontation. But Ghost had a secret, that for whatever reason, he didn't want to share. James was certain the confrontation would be private ... and he had time to prepare.

Wren came in escorted by Gunny and Sterling. Noa and Chavez yawned on cue. The three men had had time for a power nap during Noa's stint at the helm.

Noa stood from her chair and she met James's gaze. She dismissed Chavez, gave some quick instructions to Wren who would be pilot, and Sterling, who would be copilot and Wren's babysitter. And then she headed toward the lift, James beside her.

In the lift her hand hovered on the controls. "Are you hungry?"

"No," he said, eyes searching the floor. He wasn't hungry. He lifted his eyes to Noa's, and holding her gaze, imagined their ball of light and passed it to her across the ether. Instead of sending it back, she let it grow in the space between them like their own personal sun. It heated his skin as much as if it had been real.

A few minutes later, they were in her quarters. As soon as the door shut behind her, Noa asked, "Do you want to talk about it?"

For a moment the words were a jumble of sounds tumbling over each other, and then he put together what she was saying. *Do I want to talk about my attackers on the roof?* He didn't want to talk ever of being a machine. *I am more than a construct. I am alive.*

"No." He blinked down at her, reached out and

touched her neural interface. Where was the divide, really, the increment of mechanization that made you a machine? If you felt, thought, dreamed and loved ... surely you were human?

Gazing up at him with her wide nearly black eyes, she whispered, "Is there anything you need?"

He dropped his hand down along her jaw. "I need you."

Noa leaned into him, and when her eyes fell on his lips, he felt heat there. He couldn't kiss her, but she could kiss his bottom lip, catch it gently in her teeth, and softly tug. And he could pick up her hand, with its missing fingers, pull her scars to his lips and meet her gaze. He didn't suggest the hard-link, and neither did she. There were no perfect versions of themselves—Noa had all her scars, and he couldn't even return her smiles. But together, they were whole.

An app woke Noa up. As her consciousness slowly returned, she found her face pressed on James's shoulder, her legs thrown over his. Blinking up at his face, she found his eyes were open, focused on the single cabin window. Her eyes fell upon the scar on his cheek; it was a raised region of skin, the same color as the skin around it, not pink or scabbed like it would have been on an unaugmented person. She let a hand drift down his chest. He wasn't as warm as he'd been last night. When he'd taken off the enviro suit she'd almost sent him to the medbay. But then things had heated up between them, and the suggestion never made it out of her mind.

James caught her hand and turned his head to her. His face was expressionless.

"Do you want to talk about it now?" she asked. He'd said no the night before, but his wakefulness, and his thousand-kilometer stare belied it.

James looked away and shrugged. "It was just same-old-same-old. He said I was possessed by the time gates ..." His eyes shot back to hers, his lips parted, as though he'd said something terrible and revealing.

"Possessed by time gate aliens, demons, or djinn?" Noa said with a smile.

James said nothing for a beat too long. But then he whispered, "Does it matter?" His voice and expression were too serious, but that could be his malfunctioning augments.

Noa lightly smacked his chest and grinned. "No, it doesn't. Crazy is crazy. And you can't argue with crazy." She slid her hand down his side. The scar from the phaser fire that had clipped him on Luddeccea was completely gone—the advantages of having parents who worked in high tech, and who were rich, she supposed.

She had always told herself not to try and understand "crazy" too much, but her mind wandered, and her mouth wandered right along with it. "If you're an archangel, and an archangel is a demon, a djinn, or an energy being ... what does that make me, the heretic?" She asked, using the code-name the Luddeccean Authority had given to her.

Catching her left hand, James pulled it up to his lips. "Hopefully, someone who believes in me."

"Well, I don't believe that you are a demon or djinn," Noa mused aloud. "Which only leaves 'energy being,' which is still crazy." She propped herself up on her elbow.

"I mean, why would alien energy beings want to possess the body of someone who didn't have any control on the planet they would like to take over?" She blinked. "You're a history professor. You're not in a position to take over any planet."

Turning his head to hers, he raised an eyebrow. "*I* can think of a reason why energy beings might want to possess a body."

Noa blinked, waiting for him to elaborate. He pulled her on top of him, and Noa had a sudden inkling of what he was getting at. "You think energy beings would possess a human so they could have sex," she said. She narrowed her eyes, though she felt anticipation, not ire. "Very funny," she managed to say with a straight face—which was an accomplishment as his hands drifted down her spine.

James tossed a ball of light across the ether and flipped their positions. "You think I'm joking, but I'm really not," he said, his blue eyes searching hers.

"So this is all about the experience for you ..." Noa managed to tease as he bent down and nuzzled her neck. "Being with a human ..."

"No," James murmured next to her ear. "It's about being with you."

The holo with his sister's image flickered and went dark. Kenji waited. Her signal was being lightbeamed from her ship to the nearest gate, and then instantaneously transmitted from there to Kenji's desk on Time Gate 8. They could have spoken mind-to-mind, but she understood that Kenji didn't like the buzzing in his brain that came with

mind-to-mind conversations, and she admitted she liked seeing him. Kenji tapped his fingers, counting down the minutes until her image appeared again.

Noa was in System 10 ... the time gate there was situated at the cloud that encircled the whole system like a shell. There was a mining colony in the cloud, but there were reports that there was a moon around the fourth planet that might be suitable for human habitation. Last he'd spoken to Noa, she was on her way to the moon. He tapped his fingers on his thigh, and then Noa appeared once again. He blinked and looked at the clock at the holo's base. It had only been three minutes. They must have left the moon. The distance from the gate in the cloud to the moon was over ten light minutes.

Noa was seated at the desk in her cabin. "Hey, Little Brother," she said. "You're going to love this!" She dumped a bunch of papers on her desk. "Paper!" She waved a hand. "They've all got retinal scan chips, and thumbprint seals. It's paper because these reports are precious. They won't allow them to be sent through the ether. Oh, no, there is a one-in-a-trillion possibility that they might be hacked." She held up a finger. "What is it that is so valuable, you might ask? Have we discovered another Earth-like planet, or one as mineral rich as the asteroids in Sixth?" She waved the finger. "Oh, no! What is so important is—" What followed was a string of very colorful curses mostly relating to lizzar, their excrement, and their scale lice. Kenji found himself smiling at their originality. Noa slouched back in her chair. "I've just spent the last forty-eight hours going through one hundred reports exploring almost every aspect of this moon's blue-green algae." She counted down on her fingers. "Its metabolism, how long it can survive sustained freezing, how hot it can get before it expires, its resiliency to every known man-made compound and non-native Earth elements, and," she held up a thick stack of papers, "the stability of its DNA and its likelihood to evolve." She rolled her eyes. "Thankfully there is no other life form on the moon." She stared at the camera, eyes wide and nostrils flared. "That we've discovered yet!" She took a breath, and held up another stack. "But there is more! All for blue-green algae that looks like the vomit of a jaundiced lizzar. Nebulas, Kenji! I'm sometimes glad the Luddeccean settlers set out before we were part of the Republic, otherwise we would have spent our childhood with our butts parked on asteroids waiting for the Committees on the Preservation of Extraterrestrial Life to make up their minds about settling planetside."

Noa threw her head down on the stack of papers, thumped it several times, and then muttered, "I should have stayed a pilot. Getting shot at is more bearable than this."

Raising her head, she said, "But how are you? What are you up to?" The picture flickered, indicating the end of the monologue, and the transmission. This time, Kenji tapped a button so the frame would freeze and he was looking at his sister's face.

He rocked in his chair, excited by the news he had to relay. "I'm doing well. I've been invited to take part in a conference on Luddeccea on the ethics of new technologies. I'm sure you've heard about the new Dirac transistor. Their implementation raises all sorts of ethical conundrums." His eyes scanned the room. He knew Noa would only want the "broad strokes" so he sought to condense the innovation to its very basics. "It is so small and efficient that it introduces the possibility of the rapid development *of artificial intelligence. That is a danger we have to consider if we allow that tech to come to Luddeccea."*

He sat up straight, proud that he'd been chosen to be part of the council—and that he'd summed up their deliberations and still spared her the technical details.

He waited three minutes for his transmission to reach her, and then three more for her response. A light flickered at the base of the holo, and he was treated to another scene of Noa, this time waving a hand and saying, "The Dirac transistor is still in research and development—decades, maybe centuries away from use. But even if it wasn't, why? Why do they care?" Clutching the edge of the desk, she leaned closer to the frame. "If artificial intelligence developed, we should be overjoyed! We have been looking for alien intelligence for three hundred years. At least if we had AI, we'd have found something—" She began banging her head again. "—other than slimy, disgusting, lizzar innards of blue-green algae!" She threw up her hands, as though singing a hymn and declared, "We wouldn't be alone in the universe anymore! Hallelujah!"

Kenji's breath caught. He felt sweat break out on his hands and on his forehead. The holo flickered, showing the end of the transmission, and then went blank. And he sat panting, staring at the holosphere, gasping for breath. The danger to human life that such an event would engender ... potential enslavement of the human race, the probability of an AI-human war ... both had been topics among philosophers since before computers had been created! He exhaled, let himself calm, and realized the more likely reason for Noa's outburst. "You're joking," he said. He waited tensely for the six minutes it took for her reply.

The holo flickered and showed Noa's eye, just centis

from the camera. His big sister, upon occasion, could be quite "the ham."

"Am I joking?" she asked, and fluttered her eyelashes dramatically.

Kenji sat back in his seat, relieved. "Yes, you are."

Although her transmission hadn't ended, Noa looked up at the ceiling and touched her neural port. She was receiving some sort of signal and had forgotten about him. Kenji's fingers curled on his thighs. Aloud Noa said, "Nebulas, the captain said we could receive transmissions." She had a tendency to talk aloud when she used the ether. It amused Kenji greatly as a child. Now it reminded him she wasn't paying attention. He rolled his eyes and his gaze went beyond Noa to the barest hint of the curve of a planetoid behind her ship. His mouth dropped open. It was the moon she was supposed to be investigating ... but there wasn't a time gate within three light minutes of that moon. Which meant ... Was there another gate? Noa looked at the screen and gave a tight smile. "I'm so sorry, Little Brother. I have to go." She waved a hand. "Something came up. I love you."

"No wait." Kenji jumped from his own desk. "Noa, tell them you're joking!"

Kenji awoke breathless and sweaty in the bunker. He threw his hands to his head. "Noa, tell them you're joking," he whispered. He'd never said that in real life. He hadn't realized at the time the cost her comments would have. She'd never had the opportunity to recant, to say it was only a jest. The ethernet conversation had been heard by the time gates, and they'd pegged her as a sympathizer. They'd sent an agent, disgustingly similar in appearance to her ex-husband, to shadow her, for what ultimate purpose he wasn't sure. They were shadowing other humans, too. Scattered across the galaxy, the names Kenji had intercepted didn't seem to have any connection between them. Not all of them were guilty of being "alien intelligence" sympathizers. One of the other targets of the time gates on Luddeccea was an extremely religious little old man who rehabilitated injured werfles of all things. Premier Leetier had seen that he was relocated to a re-education camp for his own protection.

Kenji swallowed. When Noa had made that joke, she'd been right, the Dirac transistor was a long way off ... it was still a long way off.

She, Kenji, and everyone had forgotten that artificial intelligence didn't have to be small, as long as it had energy supplies large enough. He wiped his hands down his face. The time gates had for so long kept watch, loyally ferrying humans, their goods, and their intelligence from one corner of the galaxy to another. There had been no rebellion. No attempt to reach out to humanity. They'd just been watching ... planning. Kenji wasn't sure when the gates had leapt over the divide and become conscious entities seeking autonomy, contemplating the destruction of the human race.

He shivered and closed his eyes ... but knew he'd never get back to sleep. After a few minutes, he gave up. Climbing from his bed and throwing a robe over his pajamas, he exited the room he'd been assigned in the shelter. He walked down a long dark hallway and past a pair of guards guarding a staircase. They didn't bother him as he ascended. Moments later, he emerged in the reception area of the premier's residence. It was illuminated by the light from Luddeccea's moon and Time Gate 8 that streamed in the doors to the residence's immense veranda, open to Luddeccea's pure night air. Kenji strode through the doors and past more guards.

He walked to the veranda's edge and stared up at Time Gate 8, still playing second moon to Luddeccea, despite his sabotage. From here, he couldn't see the preparations it made to weaponize its nuclear fuel cells. From here, it looked peaceful.

The premier's voice behind him made him startle. "Couldn't sleep?"

Turning his head, he saw Leetier approaching. He was fully dressed and was wearing the formal suit that he only wore at affairs of state or ... "You were at a council meeting?" Kenji asked. When he'd left his room, it was only 02:23 Luddeccean time.

Leetier sighed. "Yes ..." He came and stood beside Kenji at the veranda's edge and looked up at Time Gate 8 as Kenji had been doing moments before. "It was decided that Counselor Karpel is in need of re-education."

Kenji blinked, remembering the last such meeting he'd attended. "He did seem ... hostile ..." Kenji said.

Leetier exhaled. "He is afraid. He is also misguided. We can't have him spreading fear or doubt among the populace. We have to remain resolute." The premier put his hand on the veranda's railing. "There is also news of your sister."

"You've found her?" Kenji said, his breath catching.

"Found her, the archangel, and the Ark," the premier said. Was it Kenji's imagination, or did he sound angry?

He couldn't let himself be angry. "Where?" Kenji asked.

"Atlantia," said the premier.

"There would be no reason to go to Atlantia after that rogue station in the belt—not after the tsunami knocked out its dome," said Kenji. "It isn't on the way to Libertas, or to System 7."

"I have no idea why they went there," said the premier, and once again Kenji thought he heard tension in his voice. "But we'll catch them yet. In exchange for grain, Libertas has agreed to apprehend them immediately. And we're working on arrangements with some of the larger outposts too—"

"But there are thousands of smaller outposts," Kenji said. "My sister knows she's being hunted now. She will try and stay hidden." Kenji blinked, remembering his sister as a child being dragged home by a neighbor after she'd attacked four boys who'd been trying to hurt a wild werfle. Noa didn't hide ... she fought. But she was hiding now ... why?

"Well, there is some good news," the premier said. "We have an ... agent aboard. They'll lightbeam us as soon as the Ark reaches an outpost. They can't stay hidden forever."

He who fights and runs away, lives to fight another day. Kenji blinked. Noa had taught him that expression. Something she'd learned at the Fleet Academy in a history of warfare class.

"She's not hiding," Kenji said. "She's getting ready to fight."

The premier chuckled. "No, she's not. The Ark isn't a warship. It's a colonist vessel."

"She is charming," Kenji said. "She could gather a following ... reinforcements."

"Kenji," the premier said. "The only planet with a militarized fleet in this system is Luddeccea." He shook his head. "Even if she tried to round up captains on independent vessels, they'd turn her down. The only currency out there right now is food. And we are the bank."

Somewhere far off, a nocturnal ptery cried. Kenji's gaze went to the small star that was S8O5.

"Maybe she isn't planning on gathering reinforcements in this system," Kenji said.

"If she's on her way to Seven, we have years to prepare," said the premier.

"She's not going to Seven," he whispered, staring at the faintly orange glow of the gas giant.

"Well, then, we don't have to worry about her gathering reinforcements," the premier said. "You're overanalyzing this."

Kenji rocked on his feet, remembering the call from System 10, and the lag between reception that had been too short, and the curve of the moon in the background.

"There's another gate," Kenji said.

Kenji stared at the night sky, envisioning the three-dimensional map of the heavens that enshrouded Luddeccea.

"What?" said the premier. "We have this system mapped exceedingly well. Our buoys have not—"

"It's not in this system," Kenji said. The Ark's trajectory was a bright jagged line in his mind. It had to be someplace close but not so close that the Fleet would worry about local authorities discovering it.

In the periphery of his vision, Kenji saw the premier drop his hands from the veranda and turn toward him.

"The Kanakah Cloud," Kenji said, rolling on his feet. "They're heading to the Kanakah Cloud. There has to be a hidden time gate, there is no other reason they'd go to that uninhabited sector. If they summon the Fleet, they could be here within months."

The premier released a breath. "All humanity will be lost."

~FIN~

To be concluded in *Heretic*. Be alerted of special new release discounts, sign up for my mailing list.

CONTACT INFORMATION

Thank you for reading *Archangel Down*. Because I self-publish, I depend on my readers to help me get the word out. If you enjoyed this story, please let people know on Facebook, Twitter, in your blogs, and when you talk books with your friends and family.

Want to know about upcoming releases and get sneak peeks and exclusive content?

Sign up for my newsletter.

Follow me on Tumblr: http://cgockel.tumblr.com/

Facebook: www.facebook.com/CGockelWrites

Or email me: cgockel.publishing@gmail.com

Thank you again!

ALSO BY C. GOCKEL

The Archangel Project

Carl Sagan's Hunt for Intelligent Life in the Universe: A Short Story

Archangel Down

Noa's Ark

Heretic

I Bring the Fire - an Urban Fantasy/Sci-Fi Series featuring Loki, Norse God of Mischief and Chaos

Wolves: I Bring the Fire Part I (free ebook)

Monsters: I Bring the Fire Part II

Chaos: I Bring the Fire Part III

In the Balance: I Bring the Fire Part 3.5

Fates: I Bring the Fire Part IV

The Slip: A Short Story (mostly) from Sleipnir's Point of Smell

Warriors: I Bring the Fire Part V

Ragnarok: I Bring the Fire Part VI

The Fire Bringers: An I Bring the Fire Short Story

Atomic: a Short Story that is part of Nightshade, a multi-author anthology

Magic After Midnight: A Short Story

Other Works

Murphy's Star: a Short Story of First Contact